The Bones of the Earth

Scott Hale

THE BONES OF THE EARTH

Copyright © 2015 Scott Hale
Cover art by Natasha MacKenzie
Edited by Eve Marie

First Edition: June 2015

ISBN-13: 978-0-9964489-0-1

BOOKS BY SCOTT HALE

The Bones of the Earth series

The Bones of the Earth (Book 1)

The Three Heretics (Book 2)

The Blood of Before (Book .1)

The Cults of the Worm (Book 3)

The Agony of After (Book .2)

The Eight Apostates (Book 4)

Novels

In Sheep's Skin

The Body Is a Cruel Mistress (Coming Soon)

KEY

1. CALDERA
2. ALLUVIA
3. TRAESK
4. RIME
5. ELD
6. LACUNA
7. GEHARRA
8. NORA
9. ELDRUS
10. NYXIS
11. ISLAOS
12. HROTHAS
13. BEDLAM
14. GALLOWS
15. CATHEDRA
16. PENANCE
17. CADENCE

18. NACHTLA
19. LYNN
20. TRIST
21. MARWAIDD
22. RHYFEL
23. ANGHEUAWL
24. COMMUNION
25. SKYGGE
26. FORMUE
27. BRANN
28. HVLAV
29. KRES
30. THE DISMAL STICKS
31. GARDEN OF SLEEP
32. DEN OF UNKINDNESS
33. SKELETON'S KEEP
34. SCAVENGER'S TOWER

 CORRUPTED   NIGHT TERROR

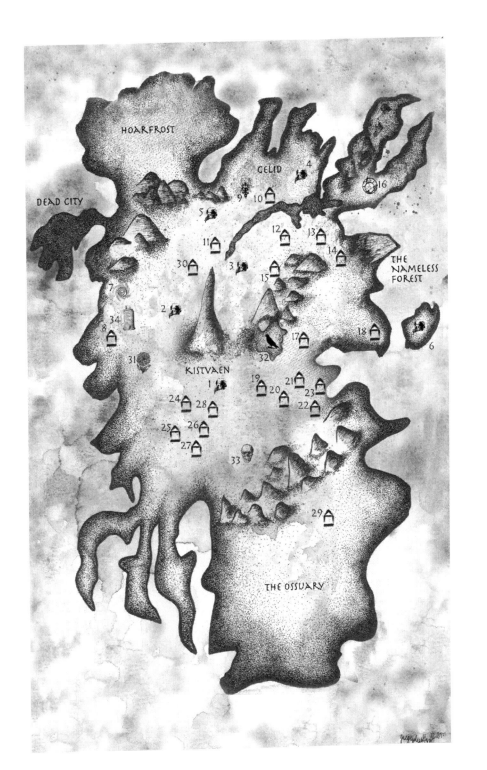

CHAPTER I

The smell of blood was quickly becoming one of Vrana's least favorite smells, and the inside of her mask reeked of it. She could feel the insects at her feet and on her legs, a congregation of pincers and carapaces called by the scent of decay. To swat them away would undo the hours she'd spent sitting stationary in the field, so she left them to their hungry wanderings, knowing that their disappointment would come soon enough when they realized the only part of her that was dead was the part she had stolen.

Vrana's grip tightened on the ax across her lap as the sounds of movement passed through the forest in front of her. The trees here were much fuller, much healthier than those found in the Den of the Unkindness she'd attacked a few days ago. Even now, she could still hear the beating of the ravens' wings and the caws and cackles that had risen around her as she buried the ax into their Cruel Mother's neck and took its head for her mask. She wondered if the birds were better off because of the murder and if the same could be said for what was about to happen here.

Vrana's body tensed as the sweat from the midday sun seeped into the wounds along her back. Carefully, she moved one hand behind her and felt for the bandages that covered the lacerations. She winced as her fingers grazed the tender flesh. The Cruel Mother's talons had been sharper and dug deeper than Vrana anticipated. She'd meant to cut them off and bring them back to Caldera, to fashion them into a pair of daggers, but between doing that and being shredded by the remaining ravens, surviving seemed the smarter choice.

"Oh well," Vrana mumbled, her voice hoarse. She hadn't used it in over a day. She centered her mask, the Cruel Mother's severed head, and tightened the strap that kept it over her own. "Just don't fuck this up and—"

A cloud of dirt exploded beside her as an arrow impaled the ground. Vrana sprang to her feet and tore through the field. A second arrow soared overhead to the place where she'd been sitting. She could see the archer at the tree line—a shirtless, sinewy man with a bow in hand and a quiver slung over his shoulder. He raised his weapon, nocked another arrow with his crimson-colored arm, and fired.

Vrana ducked, the missile whizzing past the beak of her mask, and chased her victim into the forest. Branches whipped her head as she ran, her eyes trained on the fleeing fool. The man looked back, his age-worn face stricken with fear. He loaded another arrow and let it loose carelessly; it grazed her leg. Vrana cringed and pressed on harder, blood leaping from the wound onto the dew-laden grass. She readied her ax as the man stumbled over rocks and upturned roots. He whipped around and fired his last arrow, inadvertently sending it into the canopy. Scrambling on all fours, he made for the nearest tree and hoisted himself onto the lowest bough, determined to find safety in the mottled sky.

But the man was too slow and the bark too slick. Vrana swung her ax and caught him in the spine.

She wrenched him from his perch, and his body hit the ground with a satisfying smack. She worked the ax from the man's back and turned him over, to see him unobscured by distance for the first time. He looked to be at least sixty years old and definitely in no condition to attack her. Several faint tattoos ran the length of his chest, the markings too worn to be read. His complexion suggested he wasn't from the South, but he was dead now, so it didn't really matter.

Vrana lifted the man's right arm, scrutinized the crimson pigmentation that was characteristic of all Corrupted, and set it back down. It was by this genetic defect inherent to all humans that her people's killings were justified. Or at least that's what they told themselves. She fell back on her heels, adjusted her mask, removed a knife from her belt, and dug into the man's chest, hacking through flesh and muscle, until she saw with wide eyes white bone.

A few minutes later, Vrana dropped the man's heart into one of the preservative-lined pouches at her waist. She took one last look at the Corrupted, the first human she'd ever killed. She didn't feel remorse, just unfulfilled. The elders had insisted she return to Caldera as soon as the second trial was completed, and yet she found herself drifting eastwards, looking for something else to murder.

A family of deer was drinking from a stream when she came upon it. Startled at first, they eventually calmed as Vrana kept her distance. She dipped her hands into the water and washed off the man's blood, recalling a member of her tribe as she picked at the gore beneath her fingernails. He, too, was of the deer, a Stag, and it never failed to amaze Vrana how much he was like the animal, in both behavior and temperament. Her mother and the elders promised the same would be said of her in regards to the raven, but Vrana found that she bore little resemblance to the bird, and liked the notion of abandoning herself to fulfill an ideal even less.

"But you're not," her mother had said, the memory of the encounter overtaking her. "You have always been the raven, in one way or another. Vrana, you got to accept who you are so that you may live a fuller life..."

Blah. Blah. Blah.

Vrana's head snapped up. Somewhere, a child was crying. And then: across the stream and through the trees sat the outline of a small, stone house. There would be no reason short of barbarism for Vrana to investigate, but much to her own surprise she couldn't help but feel sick with the thought of leaving a child to fend for itself, Corrupted or not. Vrana quickly cleaned off the head of the ax and trudged through the crystalline waters, disappearing into the overgrowth on the other side.

The boy was already waiting for her in the doorway of a small house by the banks. Tears ran down face and body to his clenched fists. She sized him up. His clothes fit too well and his teeth were too clean to suggest he actually lived in the South. Vrana went to him because she saw no sense in delaying what was to come, for it was obvious he'd figured it all out. The boy radiated hate. When he was close enough to hit her, he did, fists feebly pounding her stomach and chest.

When he'd finished, Vrana pushed the boy away, taking note of the strange marking on his shoulder—a circle inside which strange, tentacle-like symbols were held. As he dried his eyes, Vrana scrutinized the boy's right arm, which was pink in coloration, not red, presumably because of his age. She gripped the top of the satchel, which now held what was most certainly his father's heart, and let herself into their home.

The house was sparsely decorated, like they had just been passing through; but what little they did have looked comfortable enough. A large pile of old pillows, worn blankets, and tattered clothes sat in the corner, as though it had been a makeshift bed for the boy and his father. Food didn't seem to have been an issue for the family, as the woven baskets and cracked jars across the floor were overflowing with fruit, honey, and meat. Even their defenses seemed to have been in order, with two swords and a shield in fairly good condition resting against the uneven wall.

Clearly, they were doing alright, Vrana thought, *so why'd his dad attack? When he stopped and decided I needed to die, what did he see? Another stupid Night Terror? Some big ass bird?* She laughed.

Vrana turned her attention back to the little boy as he stepped across the threshold. Perhaps she had hoped that by coming here she would've found a community of Corrupted to care for the orphaned boy in the house or somewhere nearby. She gritted her teeth, ran her fingers through the oily feathers of her mask, and commanded with an outstretched hand for the boy to begin gathering necessities.

In its descent, the tired sun cast the sky ablaze with streaks of red and bands of orange. Soon, night would come, and so, too, would the creatures whose livelihood depended on it. Vrana picked up the pace to make the boy, who could hardly see over the pile of clothes he held, do the same. The forest was dense and vast, but as long as they continued eastward, they would be clear of the Den of the Unkindness and nearer to the closest Corrupted settlement. Or so Vrana hoped. The map back in her village, Caldera, wasn't exactly known for its accuracy.

An hour later, they found a lake within a quiet clearing and dropped onto its shore. They set their provisions down and sat in silence, watching as bugs skidded across the lake's glassy surface, like tiny messiahs of unseen kingdoms. With the boy in her shadow, Vrana's pouch felt heavier. While she didn't regret what she'd done, because it'd needed to be done, it did make her wonder about the "balance" as a whole. Didn't seem the right word for something so one-sided. "The Bullshit" didn't quite have the same ring to it, though, did it?

Vrana watched the boy as he took a stick from the dirt and drew shapes in the sand. She figured he'd be handsome if he survived into adulthood, but there was a kindness in his face that worried her. How easy it would be, she thought, to deliver him to Death with a broken neck or a bashed-in head so that he may not suffer life alone. The ax would hit him quicker than the sting of betrayal, certainly, and would he not be better for it? Wouldn't they all? Vrana shook her head and went to take a piss in the bushes.

When Vrana came back, the boy was gone. The clothes, blankets, and food they had been carrying were scattered along the water's edge, with tracks of struggle dug into the earth beside them. Here stood a chance to turn back, to do away with the burden she was never to bear, and return to Caldera, her character unsullied by sympathy.

"Fuck." She looked around. "Fuck, fuck, fuck."

Vrana unfastened the satchel from her waist, placed the ax on the ground. Wielding the knife she'd used to cut the father's heart out, she made for the panicked ripples that'd started spreading outwards from the center of the lake. She took one last gulp of air, and then she plunged into the inky, warning waters.

Violent shivers coursed through Vrana's body as the cold lake engulfed her. Schools of fish and solitary frogs scattered at her approach, darting in and out of the shafts of twilight that cut through the dark. Her feet fumbled for purchase on the softening slope, until it tapered off and she was left with no choice but to swim. Lungs itching for oxygen, Vrana swam quickly to the heart of the lake where a small shape floated, one tiny hand clutching a clump of weeds. Vrana pushed toward the boy, or the trap waiting to be sprung.

Hundreds of bubbles burst out of Vrana's mouth as a great weight slammed into her from behind. She tumbled to the lakebed, her long, black hair wrapping around her mask and obscuring her vision. She swung the knife back and forth as she bounced off the trash that'd collected at the bottom of the lake. Aluminum cans, plastic bottles, and cellphones—Twenty-First Century corpses—spun past her as she searched its depths for her vanished attacker.

There. Vrana twisted around and saw the creature that meant to kill her. It was a man, or at least it had been at one point in its life, and wrapped around its heavily scarred skin were coils of thorns and barbed wire. The Horror of the Lake lumbered through the water, spasms of pain sending its body into grotesque convulsions. Vrana glanced up at the boy, who still showed no signs of life, and with burning lungs, met the Horror midway in its death charge.

The creature's claw clamped down on Vrana's shoulder and dug in deep. She shoved the knife into the Horror's chest, immediately regretting her decision as the thorns that covered it bit at her skin. She pulled away, kicked the Horror back; cried out as the creature's nails slid down her arm. With warm blood pouring from her wet wounds, she grabbed the Horror of the Lake by the hand and sawed at its wrist, the knife cutting through its flesh as though it were paper.

As the Horror wailed and gripped its spewing stump, Vrana looked at the boy floating like a fetus in this amniotic-like hell. She threw herself at the Horror, took the blows it threw at her. Its jaw dropped open. She shoved the knife in, stabbing the back of its throat and cutting open the top of its mouth. She shoved the Horror of the Lake back, and as its blood swirled around her, she took the boy under her wing and soared frantically toward the sky.

Vrana dragged the boy back to shore. Immediately, he came to, coughing up water as she smacked his back, because that seemed like she ought to do. Sighing, Vrana collapsed against a rock on the lake's edge. She gave herself a once-over: the wounds from the Horror of the Lake were getting darker and darker. *What the hell was that thing?* She rubbed at the punctures in her skin, a black liquid oozing out with every pass. *Fuck me.*

The boy looked at her looking at her wounds, got up, left for the forest. Vrana couldn't bring herself to chase after him. A few minutes later, he came back with a bundle of blue flowers. At first, Vrana punished him when he tried to touch her, but the mounting pain and creeping paralysis broke her will. Her little doctor chewed the flowers into a paste and rubbed it over her arms and the deeper lacerations on her chest and stomach. The boy had soft hands, unspoiled by hard labor, and they worked Vrana's wounds she wouldn't expect from a kid. There was no way he was some run-of-the-mill scamp from the South.

She couldn't believe it, but the run-of-the-mill scamp had done it: In a matter of seconds, the poison was out of her system. She didn't feel like herself, but she didn't feel like dying, either.

Though every impulse told her to do otherwise, she gathered herself, the boy, and their belongings, and together, kept going by moonlight through this hostile land. Maybe it was because they looked like death warmed-over, but apparently no predator they passed was interested in seeing Vrana and the boy beneath their claws. Even the moon cats, who were notorious for their brutality, turned a blind eye to their stumbling, apparently finding no satisfaction in spoiled meat.

Vrana had lost all sense of time and direction when they finally spotted a village and bonfire on the distant horizon. Shadows of shapes stretched across the landscape as figures danced around the crackling inferno. The ground shook from their primal vibrations. She looked at the boy, who was nodding off beside her, and decided this was as good a place as any to leave the Corrupted. There was no great city to take him in; because of the Trauma and her people, the Corrupted were only allowed small villages and towns. She took a quarter of the remaining food for her return to Caldera and set the rest atop the clothes and pillows the boy held.

Together they made their exhausted march toward the village. Vrana kept close to the darkness, too weary to risk another encounter. When they reached the first building, a slanted house crumbling beneath its own weight, Vrana looked down at the child, the beak of her mask nearly touching the top of his head, and told herself she'd said goodbye. The boy started to cry, and as Vrana went to comfort him, she heard something rustle behind them.

Vrana spun around, rending the air with her ax. The boy grabbed the pouch holding his father's heart, and she stopped, her own heart dropping into her stomach. An old woman with white braids stood before them, wearing the wild shadows of the blaze like a cloak. She seemed indifferent to Vrana, and smiled toothlessly as she held out her arms to embrace the boy.

"Thank you," he said as Vrana walked away.

She understood him well enough and could have turned around to carry on the conversation, but she didn't trust herself to have the strength to end it. Vrana was to be feared by her enemies, to be seen as a harbinger of death, an agent of entropy—not a giver of compassion or life. And yet here she was, a confused girl wearing a stinking mask and wounds that wouldn't even look cool when they scarred over, aiding her foes in the final hours of her eighteenth birthday.

CHAPTER II

Vrana knew she wasn't going to make it back to Caldera before the Black Hour started. On top of that, and al she was almost certain it was days away, she was lost, and the last thing she needed was to stumble into the Nameless Forest. She tried to retrace her steps to the lake, but the darkness that covered the land was thick, and she had no way aside from her fevered memory by which to measure her progress.

The farther Vrana delved into the forest west of the Corrupted village, the more obvious it became that something was wrong. The trees took on an ancient and harsh texture, like that of petrified corpses. The light of the moon faded, replaced by a glowing mist that rolled over the damp soil. Vrana strained her ears for the sounds of nightlife but found no sounds save for her own.

She should've listened to the elders. She should've gone home.

Lightning split across the midnight sky. Vrana jumped, the peal of thunder rattling her bones. Her skin prickled as fat drops of rain fell from above, their weight pulling loose leaves from the branches. Alarmed, Vrana scanned the area for refuge. As the temperature plummeted, her teeth started to chatter. *There's nothing,* she thought as she went, upturned roots tugging at her feet. The rain began to fall in sheets. *I'm an idiot. Why do I do these things to myself?*

A strong wind funneled through the forest. It flattened Vrana, driving her into the muddy. She started to sink into the oversaturated soil. She struggled to get free, but every twist of limb and strain of muscle only made her sink faster. Vrana panicked; she imagined the soil sliding over her, the mud filling her throat. And then, as though her mind had cleared, she found something calming about the entire experience, something unexpectedly enjoyable about being completely vulnerable and at the mercy of a force greater than herself.

She shook the idiocy out of her head, spat the dirt out of her mouth. Her eyes shone with hatred and determination. She formed her hands into claws and pushed forward like a bird taking flight, dislodging herself from the widening pit.

And, coming to, that's when she saw it: a ravaged keep like a crumbling crown sitting on the dreary horizon, its walls broken bones jutting from the earth's waterlogged carcass. Vrana stumbled toward it, her feet sinking into puddles and pools as the glowing mist climbed around her, its vapory tendrils like the legs of a formless spider. The mask kept her head dry enough, but the rest of her body was quickly becoming a breeding ground for sickness. She wrapped her arms around herself and made a desperate sprint for the keep.

Vrana clambered over the piles of rubble on the outskirts that'd once served the building so well, keeping watch as she climbed for other stragglers caught in the storm. With the front doors being too obvious an entrance, and now close enough to spot it, she found a hole in the keep's walls and pushed through, bits of foundation cascading around her as she went.

A great hall filled with debris and detritus awaited her as she shimmied out of the hole. In the center of the hall, where the floor had buckled, a small pond sat, stone and wood from the ceiling clogging its surface. The banners, massive curtains, and gold-framed portraits that lined the walls appeared as though they were melting beneath the streams of water that poured down them. Not finding a place to warm her bones or lay her head, Vrana kept going, following a hallway half-hidden by an upright table.

After passing through various ransacked rooms, a kitchen covered in charred bones, and a library where most of the book covers and spines were stained with dried blood, Vrana happened upon a small study untouched by water and thievery. Much like the Corrupteds' home, clothing and blankets were piled high upon one another; without consideration, she fell into them, her shivering body begging for heat. It was there she lay for a moment, too exhausted to beat herself up for helping the kid.

"I'll wait until morning," she slurred, pangs of hunger guiding her hands to the pouch that held food. She slid the ax close to her beak, and then she pushed a piece of bread through her lips. "I'll wait it out."

The teeth of winter sank into her neck. Vrana's eyes snapped open. Terror tore through her gut as she found herself on the edge of an icy chasm. *I'm dreaming*, she thought, looking between the snow-capped peaks of the surrounding mountains. She came to her feet, shuddering as pellets of hail pelted the area, and scanned the frozen expanse for an escape. *The hell is that?*

On a withered bluff smothered in fog, her first victim stood, snow gathering in the old Corrupted's heartless hole. At the man's feet, the little boy sat, fingers clinging to the fabric of his father's pants. At first, they didn't see Vrana, but when they did, they began to speak to one another. Sweat poured down her face as an impossible heat washed over her.

"Wake up," she commanded, the ground beneath her trembling, the crag before her filling with the sounds of clapping hooves. "Wake up, wake up," she begged as black fire poured in melting waves over the mountain range. "Wake…"

She rolled over, short of breath and full of pain, but awake and alive. The cuts and lacerations along her arms and chest were seething, and she had more bruises than she could count. She slowly peeled the bandages from her back, the cloth sticky from clotting, and sighed. At this rate, she would be in pieces by the night's end.

Vrana stood up, stumbled. Using her ax for support, she hobbled toward the doorway, the stone floor far less comfortable than it'd been a few minutes ago. *This place is big enough*, she thought. *There has to be more…*

The sound of laughter echoed through the hall. Her heart seized in her chest. It was an insane laughter, hearty and deep, thickened by madness and a lust for blood. The remnants of sleep slid off her body as she lifted her ax and leaned into the corridor. Screaming came next, a guttural, spit-choked cry for release born from gnawing agony. Vrana crouched low and followed the terrible chorus through the winding passage.

The keep shook at the sky's thunderous bellows, rain spewing through its cracked façade as Vrana stalked the lightning-lit halls. She slipped through narrow paths and under fallen support beams, stepped over dried corpses in rusted suits of armor, and crept through beds of shattered glass, until the floor fell away to a pit from which the grotesque sounds emerged. Vrana stood there for a moment, listening to the sharpening of blades, and then she descended the rope ladder that led into the butcher's den, not entirely sure what she expected to find or why she wanted to find it at all. But she had to do this. She didn't know why, but she had to.

Her feet landed softly on the floor of the pit. Using the gasps and moans to mask her movement, she went towards the winking lights at the back of the cavity. It took her eyes a moment to adjust to the darkness, but Vrana found the source of the sorrow soon enough: an altar of wood and rock upon which a nude man lay, his arms and legs splayed and bound to the pillars on each side of the rickety dais. Over him a robed figure loomed, tugging on tendons and veins and prodding the man's exposed organs with unflinching indifference.

Vrana winced as the figure lifted its head to greet her. It was faceless, featureless—all bone and no flesh—the skull atop its spine a house for the hardened eyes that stared at her, unblinking. A black tongue like a fat salamander flicked at the inside of its jaw bone. Its chest heaved as though it were breathing, but through the gaps in its armor, Vrana could see the half-missing ribcage was without a set of lungs.

At last, it spoke. "Well, what is it?"

Vrana studied the Skeleton as it continued to work on the dying man, extracting bits of flesh and muscle with a childlike but scientific sense of curiosity.

Offended by her silence, the Skeleton stopped mid-peeling, put down its tools loudly, and stared at the girl with the raven's head. "I expect you want to know what it is exactly that I am doing. Yes?"

The Skeleton didn't give Vrana a chance to respond.

"Is it not clear? I am looking for the essence of life. Yes, I know of blood and breath and organs and all the biological processes, but there is something more, something primal, much like the soul, but without all the religious annoyances and contrivances. Past endeavors …"

On cue, a red candle came to life behind the Skeleton, revealing a wall of bodies in various states of dismemberment and rot.

"…Have not been fruitful. But my eyes grow keener with every experiment, my mind more creative, more mature with every passing day. The sick man seeks cures for his ailment, the dying man cries out to a god for salvation. Why, then, should the undead not seek out life to reverse this most horrible condition of death?"

"Let him die," Vrana said.

"He already has," the Skeleton replied, gesturing to the body gone silent.

The Skeleton bent down, producing from beneath the altar a white sheet and placing it over the man; blood bled through and spread outward in thick petals. To Vrana, the act seemed unnecessary, but then again, so did the maniac's entire wayward philosophy. She clutched her ax, waiting and hoping for the creature to give her the slightest reason to use it.

"Like me," the Skeleton said, eying Vrana's weapon, "you are something of an oddity, are you not? You are neither human nor bird, yet you present yourself as both. In fact, there is something curious about your arrival here tonight. I am not shocked by it, as though I knew it was going to happen all along. Tell me, do you feel the same, girl? Tell me, what is the nature of your feeling? You stand before a grisly scene unmoved by what you see. Tell me of what you feel, for this interests me more so than the life you hold deep in your chest."

"He's Corrupted," Vrana muttered as her excuse for being unaffected.

The Skeleton looked at her, surprised by her remark. In an attempt to strengthen her statement, she pulled back the sheet and pointed to the dead man's right hand, which was covered in blood but lacked the distinct crimson defect. By this the Skeleton was even more perplexed, but soon its confusion gave way to amusement. Vrana let the sheet fall back over the corpse as her mind tried to cope with the situation.

Outside, the storm worsened: Thunder boomed like a cannon in the swollen sky; lightning snapped like a whip, felling trees where they stood; streams turned to rivers, and the rivers formed a flood. Vrana knew that she had to escape this place. It would fall soon, and now she could hear what sounded like the fevered howls of a mob tearing through the night, complete with clanging tools and makeshift weaponry.

"They come for me, if it wasn't obvious enough from the theatrics of this entire event. I expect fate would have this be my final hour," the Skeleton said, watching as Vrana moved towards a trapdoor she'd found in the pit's floor. "They'll join my pile, too, once I've seen what I need to see. Oh do stop. I have the key."

The Skeleton removed a long key from the pockets of its robe and tossed it at Vrana's feet. She ignored it, left the door, and mounted the rope ladder.

"You're too interesting to kill, girl. I should hope we meet again, preferably with your tongue waggling some." The Skeleton suddenly had a twangy accent. "You're not much for conversation, are you? Wait, where are you going?"

And then another voice, young and female and somewhere nearby, shouted, "You have to bring her back! I've been trying to find…"

Vrana's stomach turned as the rope faded from her fingers and the walls of the keep dissolved. Halfway up the ladder, she fell, her head smacking against damp earth. Vision doubled, she closed her eyes, waiting for the pain and disorientation to subside.

When she opened them once more, it was still night, and she was still in the forest, and except for some scattered stones and bits of foundation, the keep was gone. She scurried backward until she bumped up against an embankment, and using it to help steady her trembling legs, she rose to her feet.

Vrana was at the bottom of two sloping hills that were marked with protruding rocks like jagged teeth. Before her, the end of a long, rusted key glinted in the moonlight, the soil that surrounded it ruddy and soft. She pushed her hands under her mask and rubbed at her eyes and face, wiping away the sweat that had formed there. She moved forward to take the key.

She knew she was safe now, for the Black Hour stays true to its name in regards to length. *The Black Hour*, she thought to herself, hiding the key in the pouch beside the satchel which held the old man's heart. *Just my fucking luck.*

Vrana pressed on, too numbed by her brush with madness to do much else but think on madness itself. She'd heard about it before, the Black Hour, and she felt like something of a scholar on the subject given how often it'd come up in her life. The Black Hour, that infernal slice of time that overlays midnight for an hour in some unpredictable manner, at some unknowable location. Details of the phenomenon were often handed down through giddy whispers from

SCOTT HALE

older siblings or in-the-know peers. Depending upon who was speaking, the Black Hour became sixty minutes of terror for those towns built upon the subterranean tunnels of the now extinct flesh fiends. Or it became a ghastly recollection of a village whose waters had turned toxic, reducing all who drank from it to bones. For those of a more romantic inclination, the Black Hour marked a time when ephemeral men and women would emerge from the ground, causing those who came upon them to fall in love with them. For those whose worldviews sat upon a political slant, they spoke of the Old World cities made richer in the hour by uncharacteristically kind dictators and monarchs, who tossed their wealth from their high towers to the masses they lorded over below.

Of course, Vrana had never heard of any story mentioning a keep or a Skeleton, but that didn't matter. There was no truth to be had from the Black Hour, nor lies; during its passage, anything was possible, and for those who were not there, nothing was provable. Sixty minutes, and then it was over. Those killed by flesh fiends remained killed by flesh fiends. Those who drank the toxic waters remained ruined by toxic waters. Those who had fallen in love fell out and were left with nothing, for they had given everything. And those who had nothing and were given everything were beaten down, with each coin confiscated from their person by the royalty who had thrown it to them one minute prior.

But what was most feared about the Black Hour was Death, which was said to roam the land in disguise during the temporal aberration, taking the lives of those It passed as It saw fit. Vrana's people were said to possess the ability to see through Death's disguises, regardless of whether It was in the form of a man, beast, or inanimate object. And although its behavior and appearance would suggest otherwise, she knew the Skeleton had not been Death, even if the two did seem to share some of the same amusements.

Vrana was on the outskirts of Caldera when the sun overthrew the moon from the sky. The village sat inside a forest whose center had been cleared for fields and homes. The village had been built against a large mountain, Kistvaen. She had been told numerous times never to expect to rely on the mountain as a landmark for navigation, and it wasn't until she'd departed for her first trial that she truly understood why. Kistvaen, despite its massiveness, seemed to shrink into the land the farther one traveled from Caldera, disappearing entirely once one cleared the forest that surrounded the village. Somehow, her people, the Night Terrors, had used some sort of trickery to make the mountain vanish a mile out.

"Well, isn't that something," Vrana said to herself as she pushed through Caldera's forest, the mountain's peak growing out of the land, as promised.

It was the field workers who saw Vrana first on the edge of town, and they watched her silently from behind their masks of roots as she went. They nodded at the girl with the raven's head and then returned to the reaping.

Vrana was sore, and sharp pains bit at her legs with every plodding step, but she kept her composure. A green snake with white speckles crossed her path, stopped, and seemed to study her before slipping into a small hole in the sunbaked earth.

Vrana's mother, Adelyn, met her at the village gates. She threw herself so hard at Vrana to hug that the both of them nearly toppled over. The bones of her mother's mask, which was also a raven's skull, shone through where feathers had been removed to celebrate her accomplishments as a warrior and a healer. Vrana envied this, and after what she had experienced, she felt she was at least entitled to have a handful of her own feathers plucked away.

"Vrana," Adelyn said softly, releasing her daughter, "I tried not to worry. Thought about what my trials were like, but I couldn't help it. You know me. I wanted to send a party after you, to bring you back, but the elders wouldn't listen." She smiled as she noticed the fullness of the satchel at Vrana's side. "Is that it?"

Vrana nodded, loosening the trophy bag from her waist and holding it up to let the light pass through, revealing the outline of the heart. "A Corrupted's heart," she said. Her words fell on deaf ears as her mother became more concerned with the cuts and scratches on Vrana's arms and chest from the Horror of the Lake. "I'm not sure what it was, but it's dead now," she said. "I made a paste from blue flowers to—"

"Blue flowers?" Adelyn snorted. "After all that I've taught you, girl, that's the best description you can come up with?" She ran her fingers down Vrana's arm. "These don't look good."

"It had to be done," Vrana said, her voice pained as she thought about the boy.

"We need to disinfect these, like, yesterday," her mother said, caressing Vrana's shoulder. "Come on, the elders are waiting for you."

Vrana nodded and followed along. It was all she could do after everything she'd been through in the last day. She'd went seventeen years leading a more or less eventful life. In one day, she'd made up for that, and then some. She thought back to the Skeleton: *What the hell was that even about?*

CHAPTER III

Vrana sat in silence at the center of Caldera, the heated earth burning the backs of her legs. She looked to the elders beside and before her—Anguis of the snake, Faolan of the wolf, and Nuctea of the owl—and wondered if they would catch her should she pass out. Her mother had done the best she could for her wounds given the short amount of time they had between the gates and the village circle, but it hadn't been enough. Her mind remained unsettled, overwhelmed.

Anguis held the Corrupted heart in one hand as the speckled snake from the field passed between the fingers of the other. "You've done well," he said, handing the organ to Faolan. "Did the human suffer?"

Vrana shook her head.

"Did you enjoy the hunt?"

Vrana hesitated to answer; then nodded.

"Good. You cannot do well that which you do not enjoy. But you found it difficult taking the life, did you not?"

Vrana nodded: a half-lie.

"That is also good. Those who enjoy killing lose sight of why they are doing so in the first place. Remember these words, for many have forgotten them."

Faolan spoke next. "Why do we hunt the Corrupted, Vrana? And what did you learn of the human you killed?"

Vrana turned to Faolan and recited stiffly, "Because of what they have done and will do if permitted. Their right arms and hands are colored by their cruelty and destruction. It has become a part of their genetic code, and therefore, it has become a part of their culture and way of being. We are to keep the balance between the natural and supernatural, to establish harmony through acts of disharmony. None are exempt, not even our own."

The elders appeared pleased by her answer, so she continued. "The man lived…" She paused for a moment. "The man lived alone. He attacked me. I think he felt threatened and knew why I was there. I cut him down. I don't know if he deserved it, but he really didn't give me a choice."

Faolan handed the heart to Vrana, which felt dry and turned her stomach, who then gave it to Nuctea.

"You've always a choice, Vrana," Nuctea said. "You must weigh the importance of appeasing others when their requests diverge from your own beliefs."

"How can—" Vrana swallowed her words, but it was too late: She knew the elders would force her to continue. "How can I be myself when I am hiding behind this mask? Every day I feel like I'm losing myself to it."

"We are not human, though physically it would seem otherwise," Nuctea said as she set the heart on the ground before her. "You took the head from that wretched raven because it was yours to take. This heart, too, was meant to be here today. All of these things you've done of your own volition, with pride and respect. You wonder of your identity, and it is through these trials, whether you choose to complete them and how you complete them, that who you are, not who you wish to be, will become clear. One trial remains."

Vrana ripped off the raven's head, dropped it to the floor, and collapsed on her bed. She buried her face into the blankets and inhaled the perfect, immutable smell of home. She was no longer an idea, a harbinger, a murderer; just an eighteen-year-old girl too tired to speak and in desperate need of a bath.

"I'm proud of you," her mother said as she entered the room with a spoon and wooden bowl.

"No, please, just let me be," Vrana said, her voice muffled by the bedding.

Adelyn laughed and took a seat beside her daughter. "Shut it, tough girl." She dipped the spoon into the bowl of soup and pressed it to Vrana's lips. "Rest when you're full."

She was asleep before she knew it.

Vrana opened her eyes to a dream of a place that appeared to have no beginning or end. Great, thick, blood-spattered curtains billowed around her, offering startling glimpses of the vague shapes moving through the milling fog beyond. The air here weighed heavily in her lungs and soured her mouth.

Is this really a dream? Vrana's toes tingled as the slate-colored ground liquefied, plunging her knee-deep into dark waters. She spun around in place, looking for an escape from the seamless gray Void. *This isn't a dream,* she thought, pinching and scratching and willing herself to wake, *this is happening right now.*

A faint sound entered the Void like wind creeping through a small crack. Where there had been nothing now stood a woman dressed in flowing rags, the rigid husk of a hollowed-out infant in her clawed hands. Her skin was pale, semi-translucent, and her hair long, thick, and oily. Her face had hints of a beauty lost, of a beauty stolen, and the wicked, chapped-lipped smile she wore suggested she'd given up trying to find it some time ago.

The woman cocked her head, stared at Vrana with mild intrigue, and moved her lips without speaking. Immediately, the paralyzing pain of Vrana's scars from the Horror of the Lake resurfaced. Blood flooded her mouth as she gnawed uncontrollably at her tongue. The woman, the Witch, levitated forward as the Void contracted around them.

Vrana closed her eyes and waited for Death. This time she would know It when she saw It.

But Death didn't come. Instead her pet crow, Blix, was the one to wake her, with a tapping on her forehead that any other day would have sent Vrana into a rage. Now, however, she threw her arms around the bird as it cawed and beat its wings against her perspiring body and thanked him.

She'd found Blix when she was three, at the bottom of a tree, fallen from a nest that'd been snuffed out by disease. Vrana thought the crow was a raven and brought it with blushing cheeks to her mother, to please her. Adelyn laughed sweetly at the gesture, and together the two had nursed the malnourished chick back to health. And he had been annoying her ever since.

"You can tell me now, or you can tell me later, but the longer you wait, the more irritating I'll get," Vrana's mother said from the doorway, looking like she'd been there the whole time. "You think you don't need my help anymore, but at the end of the day, girl, you're only eighteen."

Vrana released Blix, who nibbled her ear before flying off into another room. "I didn't even say anything."

Her mother grinned and disappeared into the darkness of the house. "You didn't have to."

Vrana sat on her bed for some time afterwards, trying to make sense of what had happened to her. Dreams were supposed to be images cobbled together from fragments of memories, fears, and expectations. The gray Void had been none of those things, and the very real pain she felt from the wounds of the Horror of the Lake suggested they were to blame for what she'd seen there. Maybe there was still some poison in her system.

At nightfall, Vrana headed into the basement where she knew Adelyn would be, diligently tending to the nocturnal plant life that grew there. Black sprites with purple luminescence circled the vegetation and minerals protruding from the walls and floor, their origin just as much as a mystery as their intentions. Apparently, Vrana's father had taken an interest in the creatures and took what he had learned of them to his grave.

"I didn't sleep well after the second trial either," Adelyn said from the back of the basement, "but I think that's the point." She moved forward, becoming clearer with every passing second, as Vrana's eyes adjusted to the dark. "That's not what you're worried about, is it? At least, not entirely, right?"

Vrana shook her head. There was no use in feigning a smile or telling a lie: Her mother's vision in the dark was impeccable, and her ears knew all too well her daughter's voice when it twisted the truth. But with one trial remaining, she couldn't tell Adelyn about the boy—her words carried far too much weight with the elders, and Vrana had no intention of being labeled a traitor, even if that wasn't her mother's intentions—so she told her mother everything else instead.

"The Black Hour?" Adelyn ripped a handful of roots from a stone and slipped them into a bowl. She cleared her throat and looked the other way. "Are you sure?"

Vrana nodded, stepped aside as several sprites rushed past her and crammed themselves into the hole where the roots had been.

"Yeah," she said, her hand instinctively reaching for the key, which was now on her bedroom floor. "I didn't realize it'd even happened until it was over."

A sprite hummed about her mother's head, tugging on her hair. "Your father wasn't enough?"

"Mom," Vrana started, stopping before she uttered something that she didn't even believe herself. Her father had been researching the Black Hour when he disappeared years ago. She didn't need a corpse to figure out what'd happened to him.

"I'm sorry." Adelyn slacked her shoulders as she made a conscious effort to relax. "Is that what you were dreaming about? The Skeleton? I could hear you from the kitchen, calling out in your sleep. It wasn't real, Vrana. You won't see him again."

"I know," Vrana said, nodding, accepting that she would get no more out of her mother on the matter of the Black Hour. "It's these," she continued, pointing to the grotesque marks all over her body, "from that thing in the lake. I dreamt…"

When Vrana finished describing the details of her nightmare, Adelyn said, "I'll ask the watchers if they've ever seen such a creature," and began to busy herself at the workbench. "Let's not get too far ahead of ourselves," she added, doing the opposite as her voice deepened with concern. "The dream may have been caused by toxins still in your bloodstream."

Vrana ran her hand over the tender cuts and darkening bruises. "I don't know. It felt like something else. I'm just…" She shrugged. "I'm just tired; seeing things that probably aren't there. I need a day to myself. It's been nonstop since graduation."

Adelyn sighed, twisted a Night Eye's stem until it snapped, and poured its white blood into a vial. To the extract she added shavings of Snare and Solace and watched as the vial glowed vibrantly, like fresh snow catching midday sun. The sight never failed to stir Vrana's heart with wonderment. She approached her mother to take the vial and instead received a hug, which comforted her more than any potion ever could.

"This will help you sleep." Adelyn handed Vrana the vial. "You won't dream, won't feel much better in the morning, but at least you'll sleep." She paused for a moment and held her daughter's face. "I'm proud of you. Others would've fallen apart." She stroked her cheeks, softly wiping away a tear there. "I know your father…" She swallowed hard. "I'm proud of you."

CHAPTER IV

And sleep Vrana did. It was late in the afternoon when her body showed signs of life, and this was only because Blix had been treading across her face out of boredom. She didn't dream, nor did she feel fully recovered, but it would be enough to see her through the day.

The raven's head waited for Vrana on the opposite side of the room, with her ax beside it. As her eyes ran down the blood-encrusted blade, she found it remarkable how quickly her mind had adjusted to the killing of the man. Even her feelings toward the boy felt diminished—a slight sense of discomfort where once a nagging pang had been. Was there an immune system just for murder? She shook her head as though the act would physically rid her of the memories, donned her guise and gear, and left the house.

A side effect of her mother's potion was an increased sensitivity to the sun. Vrana had forgotten this, hadn't noticed this in the darkened den that was her room, but was soon reminded when she pulled open the front door. Searing light flooded her mask; her eyes begged for the comforts of blindness.

"Fucking mother fuck!" she yelled. She fell against the doorway, clawing at her eyes like a holy man who'd seen the face of god. "Son of a bitch," she hissed, groaning as she heard the laughter of children erupt around her.

When her vision returned, she sought out the blacksmith, Bjørn; and even if she'd been blinded for good, she still could have found him by the sound of his hammer striking the anvil. He was a man of muscle and scarred flesh, hands hardened from his work, body browned from the sun. A large bear's head sat atop his shoulders, and it was through its gaping mouth that he watched the world quietly, contemplatively. It was said that Death met Bjørn on a forest road once, nodded at his moonlit silhouette, and stepped out of the way.

Then again, Death had never been around to tell Its side of the tale.

"I sharpen blades, girl, not clean them," he said, eying the filth on her ax as she approached.

"Why haven't you let your mask go to bone?" Vrana prodded.

Bjørn grumbled, ripped the ax from her hand, and doused it in the barrel of water beside him. "I'll take warmth and protection over that any day. Don't goad me, girl. Yours is looking a little too big for your body."

"I'm growing into it," Vrana said through her teeth.

Bjørn grunted. "Come back later. I don't like the look of this ax anymore."

Vrana cocked her head. "You're the one who made it. What if I need it?"

"You won't. Go accept your third trial and leave me alone."

Vrana's head became dizzied, and her stomach fell into a pit of nervousness. "From who? When was this decided?"

"While you were away chasing Corrupted and fighting with thorn bushes," Bjørn said, amused with himself. "He's waiting for you in the Archive."

Vrana sighed, shook her head. "Isn't he always?"

The Archive was a circular building with a dome-shaped roof that had been built at the foot of Kistvaen. Inside, information from various cultures and time periods was collected and catalogued by genre, subject, and author. Inside, the learned and the patient could find philosophical treatises, scientific journals, religious dogmas, various lexicons, media and fashion trends, pieces of art, musical compositions, and governmental laws and statutes from the Old World. If one were trusted and had good cause, one was then granted access to one of the three collapsible tunnels hidden in the Archive that led underground, under the mountain, to a safeguarded chamber. There, the original documents and works of art were held, as well as blueprints for advanced technology and weaponry, containers of viral bodies, and any other horror that had been imagined by man and brought forth into the world.

It was these remnants of ancient civilizations that Vrana's village, Vrana's species as a whole, was built upon, with each past discovery and revelation measured and integrated depending upon its usefulness, as well as its destructiveness. If the Trauma had been good for anything, it'd been for this: to force the world to regress, so that they could decide what was truly worth remembering.

After leaving the Bear, Vrana entered this place, the Archive, greeted the librarians Lyre and Gul, who did the same from behind their masks of cat and hawk, and let the cool air of the building wash over her. The place smelled of knowledge, a scent not unlike the dusty odor found in the faded pages of ancient novels. Vrana marched toward the back of the building to a shelf from which she took a small book on grave digging. She brought the book to the center of the Archive and placed it in an empty spot on a shelf dedicated to Psychology. Small, imperceptible grooves locked the book into place. Requirements satisfied, she left the Archive, but not before taking a torn piece of paper from Gul's outstretched hand.

Outside, the village teemed with life: Tired harvesters shuffled in from the fields as stoic watchers converged in the center, carcasses and artifacts slung across their shoulders. Even the children joined the homeward march, kicking up dirt and swinging their wooden swords while they boasted their bravery. Vrana ignored them, and when they'd gone, she snuck behind the Archive and followed the path there, to the four nondescript five-foot statues that stood at the path's end and the mountain's beginning.

She unclenched her fist and read the symbol on the paper: an "A" from the English alphabet. On the first statue, she pushed in a rectangular plate on its side. She moved to the second statue, analyzed the shape of the paper itself, which was also a hint, and pressed another plate at the statue's base. The third statue she skipped, and the fourth she activated with the twist of a key wedged into a crack along its exterior. A soil-covered plate slid back. Vrana descended the ladder beneath it into the earthy darkness.

She didn't know the location of the other tunnels, and the effort she had put into learning the mechanics of entering this one killed all further curiosities. She hopped off the ladder. Glowing stones filled the tunnel with pulsating waves of soft amber light. Vrana didn't know if their placement was natural, but she was thankful for them all the same, as the tunnel often crossed vast chasms of black space towards its end point at Kistvaen's base.

It wasn't a long walk, no more than half a mile, but occasionally Vrana heard voices in the dark, whispery and wet, making the trek seem as though it were ten miles. She minded her footing as she came across and crossed the thin slice of stone that acted as a bridge over unseen waters below it. She had long since lost track of the amount of times she'd traversed this hazard, and yet she always felt an unease when she came to it, for this is where she most often heard the sinister sounds.

Nothing yet, she thought to herself, pausing to press her hand against one of the glowing rocks and stealing its warmth. *Maybe I ought to try one of the other tunnels*, she mused with a smile. Vrana pulled her hand away, and while she rubbed its heat against her neck, she felt her arm begin to tighten. Her wounds from the Horror of the Lake throbbed and pushed outward as though they meant to be free of her skin. Tempting whispers told in a vicious tongue filled her mask with sordid promises, each utterance a blow to her skull. She broke into a sprint and ran the rest of the way, the voices fading along with the bridge behind her.

"Out for an evening jog?" The shape ahead spoke, his words echoing from his silhouette farther up.

Vrana stopped to catch her breath. She picked up the closest rock and hurled it at Aeson.

He ducked; the rock soared over his head and through the doorway he stood in front of. "What was that for?"

Vrana glanced at Aeson and the Corrupted skull that he wore as his mask and then passed beside him, into the Inner Sanctum. Another wall, one created by her people, split the Sanctum in two and housed behind it the delicate and dangerous treasures of the past.

Vrana fell onto a bed of pillows and stared hard at Aeson from behind her mask. He stood unmoving at the entrance, his skull drenched in candlelight. Sometimes she forgot he was from their tribe, and sometimes she wondered if he felt the same. The first cramped partition, where they were staring at each other like mortal enemies, was his home. She was likely his first visitor this week, because Aeson had no family—only Vrana, the elders, and the familial tradition that saw him confined here—imprisoned here—among the bones of the earth.

"What happened?" he asked as she absently ran her hands over the wounds.

"Where do I begin?"

"Well..." He sat down beside her. "Now you have the scars you've always wanted. They do look tough, I'll give you that."

"They're not quite what I had in mind," Vrana said, adjusting the weight of her mask. "How goes things down here? Are the elders remembering to feed you?"

Aeson spoke through his teeth. "Are they remembering to loosen your chain when they let you out?"

Vrana cocked her head. "At least mine isn't wrapped around my neck like a noose."

He laughed and shook his head. "Who told you?" he asked.

"About the third trial? Bjørn," Vrana said, flicking Aeson's arm.

"How'd he find out?"

"Don't let his manly exterior fool you. He can be a gossipy bitch when he wants to be." Vrana stopped for a moment, her eyes fixed on Aeson's. "What do you want me to do?" She took his hand and squeezed it.

"I need something from Ødegaard's..." He trailed off, already feeling Vrana's gaze tighten on him. "I didn't know they'd make it your third trial, Vrana, I really didn't." He stammered through his words. "But—but I'm glad it's you. I know you'll do it right! I'm sorry."

Vrana imagined her fist colliding with Aeson's mouth. For someone who rarely interacted with others, he was especially skilled at turning the tide of a fight in his favor with just the right amount of sincerity. She looked at his face, or what little could be seen beyond the skull, and wondered if he ever roamed the village under a different guise, a different name, observing that which the old documents lacked and practicing it to a mastery for moments such as these. Like Death might, in Its own way.

She released his hand. "I thought we were friends. I know things have changed, but last time I checked—and maybe I need to check again—but last time I checked, friends usually do their best not to have the other one killed. I mean, I probably need to check again. Who knows what's happened since I last checked. You might say my understanding on these things is hazy, checkered, even..."

"God, stop." Aeson stood up and stepped toward the avalanche of books and parchments against the partition. "It's not what you think, Vrana," he said as he cleared away the mess to reveal a desk. From a drawer he pulled a frosted glass bauble and a dagger bound in linen, both of which he discarded to the floor. "Here!" he exclaimed, shoulder-deep into the drawer. He rose up and began unfolding a square piece of paper, a map. "You can't leave with this, but it's better than going in blind."

Vrana stood up and took the map, a blueprint of Ødegaard's Hospital, and winced as her wounds began to ache once more. "If it's not what I think, then why are you showing me this? I'm not supposed to see this."

Vrana looked at the map intensely and committed every room, hallway, and staircase to memory, despite knowing that most of them would have now fallen to decay. On the fourth floor, the laboratory had been circled, the ink still wet on the paper. "What's in there?"

"Research, a cylinder from a sealed room I'm pretty sure hasn't been opened in a very long time. At least, that's what the watcher said." He paused and cleared his throat. "I told the elders I needed it—there was a journal a few years ago that mentioned what was inside—but I didn't know they'd send you. I'm grateful, because I know you can do it, but..." Aeson rambled incoherently for a moment, shrinking under the burning gaze of the Raven. "You know, I've never heard of anyone proving the stories to be true."

Vrana interrupted and said, "Aeson, you're trying to convince yourself, not me." She gave him the map and took one final look at the Inner Sanctum and the wall guarding the room beyond, where death slumbered in vials and metal shells. "Don't you ever worry about those things going off down here? The bombs and shit."

"Better down here than up there."

"I don't think so." Vrana sighed. "I don't blame you for this, but I definitely like you less. You owe me."

He followed her as she left the Inner Sanctum. "Of course, anything you want."

"Good, because it'll be something you don't," she said. The darkness of the tunnel swallowed her whole as she walked the hidden corridor back to Caldera.

CHAPTER V

Vrana was exhausted when she returned home from the Archive, so much so that she forgot to ask her mother for another mixture of Dreameater to hold the nightmares at bay. Blix followed Vrana into her room with the intention of being a pain in the ass, but she was out after a minute.

While it had been fatigue that brought Vrana's head to her pillow, her dream kept it there. She stood in a rubble-filled field, the blades of grass that came up to her chest infused with the light of the head-stone-gray sky above. Ghostly tendrils of smoke curled around her, like the fingers of phantasms beckoning her forward to unhallowed plots. Vrana shivered and wrapped her arms around herself to soften the bite of the wailing wind. She leaned forward on the tips of her toes to have a better look at her surroundings. Before she knew it, the ground began to move away from her, the shackles of gravity no longer keeping her down.

Vrana floated with trepidation through the gray Void, over black mounds and rattling woods. The fog was too thick to see much more than a few feet in front of her. Picking up speed, she tried to slow herself down, but she found her body unresponsive, indifferent to the damnation towards which it glided. The Void contracted, pulled her inward, and pushed her downward. Through the air and the fog she tumbled, stomach in her throat, to the wasteland below.

Vrana's eyes watered as she plummeted through a noxious cloud of gas. Bracing for impact, she threw her hands out, only to pull them back as her body jerked upwards. Thorn-choked valleys and boiling craters passed beneath her as she hurtled towards a hill on the somber horizon. There, she saw a small house grown out of the hill's crest, candles burning against the soot-covered windows.

"Oh no," Vrana said softly as the front door creaked open. The young boy she'd saved was standing behind it, his father's bloody heart in his tiny hand.

She forced herself to turn away from the house, doubling over as she did so from terrible cramps in her side. Behind her, the Witch waited, one finger outstretched in cruel judgment. Vrana strained herself to speak, but before she could find the words, she was falling once more, flailing wildly as she plunged into a yawning pit wreathed in millions of black flies.

All the air blew out of her lungs as she slammed into the bottom of the pit, and all the flies that waited there flooded her mouth and filled them up again. She wheezed and wept, and as she beat her chest, she saw through the swelling death an Ashen Man standing nearby. He looked upon her with contempt, raised his arms over his head, and willed his minions onto her, into her, and by their master's decree, they ate at her mind and at her dream, until her mind went dark and the dream was no more.

Vrana told her mother everything, and her mother said nothing in response. Adelyn had spoken with the watchers, and neither she nor they could account for what was happening to her daughter.

Desperate for an explanation, Vrana went to Aeson for help, and with a look of consternation, he told her he would consult the records of the Inner Sanctum for clarification.

"Maybe you should put off the third trial," Aeson suggested as Vrana took one last look at the blueprints of the hospital. "You're going to have to sleep on your way there. No one will be around."

"I know I should," Vrana interjected, dropping her head against his shoulder, "but you know I can't."

On the commencement of her third trial, Bjørn stopped Vrana at the outskirts of Caldera and returned the ax, which looked untouched ("You should bring a bow, girl," he mumbled). She brought the Skeleton's key with her, although she didn't hold out much hope that she would find a use for it. The people of the village laid out food for the journey, and Vrana took what she could carry in the four satchels at her side.

Adelyn saw Vrana off with a kiss and a hug and slipped two potions, one green, another yellow, into her pocket. She told her daughter she would see her soon, and though Adelyn's mask hid her face, it was obvious she was crying.

It would take four days traveling northwest from Caldera to reach the hospital. A horse could shorten the journey, but it would draw unwanted attention, and after everything she went through these last few days, Vrana was over unnecessary delays. The other trials had been different, for they were frequently discussed and hardly varied between the participants involved. The third trial, however, was unique, and it most often served an immediate need of the tribe, making its requirements impossible to predict. It was shame the Night Terrors hadn't done away with humans tendency to make the youth do their dirty work.

Toward the end of the first day, after over ten hours of travel, Vrana was near the continent-spanning highway, the Spine, when she spied a crimson glint from a hollowed-out tree. Inside, she found the leathery corpse of a man whose throat had been slit, the chain of the necklace he wore wedged into his wound. Vrana bit her lip as she worked the piece of jewelry from the man's neck. Holding it up against the sun, she saw that the red gem it bore was held within a silver tangle of worms. It felt heavier than it appeared and irritated the palm of her hand, as though she were allergic to the metal.

"You've no use for it now," Vrana said, dropping the necklace into a satchel, "and it probably wasn't yours to begin with." She smiled at the hypocrisy of her own statement.

Feeling exposed and hearing footsteps, Vrana retreated away from the Spine, back into the forest, behind the curtain of vines that hung from the trees like loose strands of hair. The entire area looked like an oil painting, deceptively coherent from a distance but, up close, chaotic and alive with points of color. Grumblers grumbled as they passed beside her; three inches from the ground, their black eyes were always fixed on their feet, making sure that they never stepped on their long coats. Above her, birds called to one another in a hundred different languages, their feathery shapes dark fangs against the sky. Vrana dipped her hands into the stream that cut through the trees and splashed the water under her mask, against her face, startling the starving leeches waiting idly in the shallows.

On the second day, she woke to a gray-sky morning, well-rested and clearheaded. She ate some of the food she had with her, caught a rabbit by chance and ate that, too. In the afternoon, she came to a small pond where a naked man sat, fishing its sparkling waters. The Corrupted was gaunt but proud, and seemingly indifferent to the observable fact that he would be dead in the next few days if he didn't get a bite to eat. Vrana was uncertain as to whether she should kill the man, and the man appeared uncertain as to whether he should run or wait it out. Later, after she left the Corrupted, Vrana decided it had been unwise to have let him see her and live to tell others of her kindness. But when she returned to the pond, he was gone, with a dead fish as an offering where he had once sat.

On the fiery dusk of the third day, Vrana descended into a ragged ravine and made camp in an alcove behind a wall of roots. The journey was beginning to take its toll on her. She hadn't slept well since leaving Caldera, afraid that if she slept too deeply, the Witch would drag her back into the Void. Vrana sighed, tried to convince herself the nightmares were just the result of the toxins her mother had talked about, and set out her supper for the evening.

By nightfall, she felt a little better; her stomach was a little fuller and her mind a little calmer from the yellow potion given to her by Adelyn. The ravine howled and hissed as she worked her body into a smoothed groove. With no fear of being found by the clashing wildlife, she let her heavy eyes close.

And then the screaming started.

Vrana jolted awake and pushed herself harder into the groove. Her hand found the ax before her mind willed it. An endless scream poured through the opening of the alcove and scraped at her fortitude. The shadows outside massed and moved with malevolence, spilling across rock and boulder like ink. Laughter filled the alcove, and somewhere in the ravine, an infant wailed and wept.

Vrana didn't need to hear anymore to know it was time to leave.

She came to her feet and gathered her belongings. With both eyes fixed on the space before her and her resources in her periphery, she didn't expect what came next: teeth, pointed and long, biting down hard on her calf. As she twisted her head toward the source of the pain, light flooded the ravine, and what little was left of the night was burned away by the day. She held herself tightly, gritting her teeth; the wounds from the Horror of the Lake ached as though they'd been reopened. *Something's wrong*, she thought, her joints stiff, her stomach empty; the hair on her legs and underarms was more than just stubble. She looked down at her calf, where the faint outline of teeth could be seen on her skin. *Wait? How long have I been here? Where did the day go?*

On the fifth day, disoriented from the time loss and certain the Witch had something to do with it, Vrana found the hospital. It looked as though it had burst through the ground, a cancerous protrusion of cement, wood, wiring, and glass. When the wind passed through it, a groan escaped its blown-out doorways and windows. She recalled the map Aeson had shown her in the Inner Sanctum, walked around the property once, and found the former irreconcilable with the latter. A blanket of glass shards crunched beneath her feet as she returned to the entrance. Broken medical beds sat sunken into the ground, covered in ivy and bird nests. Dirty bed sheets tied to one another dangled from the fourth floor window to the first. Strung across the front doorway were a series of blood bags, drained and dried out. Vrana passed below them with caution, into the hospital, ready to kill.

The reception area was bathed in flypaper light, and the air that circulated it was filled with particles of dust and loose bits of floating debris. Benches sat askew, their seats caved in and covered with dirt. Busted computer monitors lay face up on the linoleum floor, water-stained papers clinging to their plastic shells. At the far end of the reception area, an elevator shaft sat open, its doors retracted and its cables snapped. Vrana had seen most of these things before in books from the Archive, but even in their state of decay, they made her feel dizzy with excitement.

"I'll take what I can get," she mumbled to herself as she proceeded forward, lifting a patient's gown from a chair with the tip of her ax.

If Aeson's map was correct, and if it hadn't fallen through to the floors below, the laboratory was on the fourth. She climbed over a toppled vending machine, knocking aside the perforated aluminum cans that surrounded it, and pushed through a door into an unlit stairwell. She scrambled over trash, boxes, and medical equipment, using the blood-covered wall for support as she went.

She found the door to the fourth floor held open by a gnawed leg bone. Somewhere higher on the stairwell, she heard running, heavy footfalls going up and down the fifth and sixth levels. Quietly, she moved the leg bone aside, went through the door, and then placed it back where it belonged, so that the creature above, whatever it was, wouldn't know she'd been there.

A single halogen light burned brightly at the end of the hall, buzzing like a wasp nest. It looked new, and even though Vrana understood little of electricity, she was sure that there was no reason for any to be coursing through the hospital's copper veins. Rooms lined the hallway, and photographs of happy children, animals, and picturesque landscapes lined the walls. A portrait in an ornate, golden frame caught Vrana's attention. It was of an older woman, with bright blue eyes and gray-streaked hair. A stethoscope hung from her neck, and she wore a white coat. An inscription below it read "Ødegaard" but the rest that followed was too faded to make out.

Vrana followed her memory of the blueprints as she went around wide corners and even wider doorways. She walked down the middle of the floor, keeping equal distance between the right and left side, for each open room held a potential threat. A strong wind stole into an office ahead and tossed a few papers into the hall, where they landed in a puddle of black liquid oozing from the ceiling.

Vrana passed a sign that read "Genetic Counseling" and stopped. She blinked, her heart pounding ahead of her thoughts. Her knuckles turned white as she gripped the handle of the ax. Something was standing in the room behind her. She swallowed hard and turned around.

It had seen her, Vrana was certain of this, and that meant she had to face it. She could hear it breathing—a raspy kind of breathing, one reserved for the sick and dying. From the corner of her eye, she could still see it, pale and scrawny, with flesh too loose for its jutting bones; human perhaps, she thought, though she couldn't be sure.

She stepped in front of the doorway where it stood, ax held high. On the other side, her victim was thoroughly unmoved. It was human, or at least it appeared to be: The curvature of its body and face suggested it was female, but it was hairless, without clothes, and otherwise ambiguous in regards to sex. When Vrana stepped closer, its downturned eyes focused harder on the broken tiles at its feet. It had no fingernails, navel, or crimson Corruption along its arm. And when it opened its mouth, Vrana saw that it had very few teeth and no tongue.

Despite its deformity, it said, "I will not stop you."

Vrana's eyes widened. She stumbled, refusing to accept what she had just heard.

Again, it addressed Vrana, its voice soft and slightly feminine. "I will not hurt you, I do not think."

A cold shiver scaled Vrana's spine and froze into a tightness around her neck. "How are you… how are you doing…"

It continued to stare at the tiles. "Without a tongue, one can speak freely, I imagine." It rubbed its arm, sending flakes of dust into the air. "Why have you come here?"

"I need something. I need something from the lab," Vrana admitted, worried about the repercussions of being dishonest with the creature.

It nodded, raised its thin arm to its stomach, and pulled back the skin there, which was not skin at all but a spongy material. Inside, its organs glinted artificially as though they were plastic, and there was no blood. It reached up into its ribcage, removed a plastic keycard, and held it out for Vrana.

"This will let you into the laboratory," it said as Vrana took the card cautiously. "I've had it for so long that I've forgotten why it was so important in the first place. You are strange, for a human."

Vrana gritted her teeth. "I'm not human."

"Then neither am I," it said, sarcastically, as Vrana backed out of the room. "The others will let you through, but after that I cannot promise safe passage."

"Others?" She stopped and looked around to find the fourth floor still empty. "How many are you?"

"We are one hundred now."

Black liquid began to leak from the hole in its stomach, dripping down its legs and forming an oily puddle across the tile. For the first time, it looked up at Vrana and then all at once fell apart into a cloud of dust.

CHAPTER VI

Keycard in hand, Vrana passed through the series of steel doors that would lead her to the laboratory. The first was severely dented and covered in blood, but the three that followed it were pristine, as though whatever had tried to breach the entryway had died before reaching them. Each door closed behind the other, sealing off the area until the next was opened. Glass tubes, like arteries, lined the entryway as well; and with every step she took, the liquids inside the tubes bubbled and popped, creating a golden light for Vrana to find her way.

The laboratory itself was untouched, awash in the same golden light that drenched the entryway. It smelled metallic, like blood, and of antiseptics. It was smaller than she imagined; it contained five computers, two large freezers, and various microscopes and mixing devices. Reports unreadable to Vrana were kept in large binders, some of which had had their pages torn out. Large ventilators looked down from the ceiling, the shafts behind them appearing to have been welded shut. She riffled through the room for Aeson's cylinder, digging in the semi-translucent bins stacked in the corner and the cabinet with the electronic locks that had failed.

For a moment, out of impatience and dread, Vrana considered leaving, but this was her third trial, her final trial, and nothing short death could justify forsaking the long held ritual.

And as is often the case in times of frustration, the answer was in front of her, disguised by its obviousness: an outline, rectangular and raised, painted over, perhaps to appear as a part of the wall. She pressed the keycard against the wall and then watched as the wall shuddered and slid back.

On the other side, a second laboratory waited, swathed in violet light and plastic sheets. More workstations lined the walls, their computers covered in bags like cadavers. At the center of the room, several large glass pods protruded out of the ground, acting as hosts to the swirling black liquids inside. From their glistening base, heavy tangles of cords and wires fed into the floor. Going to her knees, Vrana saw through the grating the machine to which they were connected: an orb, larger than herself, which coughed out an orange mist at three-second intervals.

Using the little light she had, Vrana came to her feet and moved from chart to chart, diagram to diagram, in search of anything that would help her locate the cylinder. For her, most of the scientific jargon was indecipherable, but among the blocks of text between every readout and poster, one word was repeated—"homunculus." Vrana found an illustration swinging from a tack, and when she unrolled it, she saw a mirrored image of the creature from before. Beneath the illustration, she noticed a notebook, its pages heavy with faded ink from a perfectionist's scrawl. Though she didn't understand the language it was written in, the sketching of the homunculi inside was enough to convince Vrana that it was important, and that she should take it, so Aeson could uncover its meaning.

She turned around and passed beside the pods, minding the blade of her ax so as to not rupture them. She bent over and looked into the black liquid that churned beyond the glass. *Everything in this room could be harvested,* Vrana thought. It didn't make sense that she should be one of the few to enter the hospital and then return with only a simple cylinder. If she told the elders of what she'd seen, of what she'd found, would they send others? Why hadn't they already? She stood up and, like with the keycard reader, noticed the cylinder in question, across the room on a desk, in plain sight. *Maybe I shouldn't tell them what I've found,* she thought, *maybe that's part of the trial.*

"Anyways," Vrana said, releasing the breath she'd been holding, the thoughts she'd been considering, "time to go."

She scooped up the cylinder, and after recognizing the various warning symbols that lined it (biohazard), she gently lowered it into her satchel beside the journal, the necklace, and the Skeleton's key. She exited the laboratory, ensuring all the doors were shut behind her, leaving everything as it was, except for what she had taken, unwilling to give the homunculi a reason to attack. She hurried across the fourth floor, not toward the stairwell but toward the room she'd seen earlier from the outside, with the rope made of bed sheets dangling from its window. She ignored the feces smeared across the floor, went to the window, dropped the cylinder into a patch of grass, and started her descent.

But the descent was much shorter than she expected. By the second floor, when her hands were sufficiently greased with whatever suffering stained the sheets, the rope uncurled. Vrana screamed, and before she could grab onto anything else, she hit the ground hard, her head smacking against the earth. Consciousness and blood spilled out of her scalp, and when consciousness returned, it brought back all the pain she could've done without.

"God damn it," she said, sitting up and kicking the knot of sheets. She rubbed her head, collected the cylinder from the grass, and hobbled toward the front of the hospital.

As she rounded the corner, it was not a homunculus that greeted her but three humans; two male, one female, in a motley of tired clothes and beaten armor.

"Took quite a fall," said the man in a dented iron helmet, his rapier dangling at his side.

Vrana said nothing as she studied the Corrupted. The man in the iron helmet was the largest and probably the strongest; though when he spoke, he held his side as if injured. The woman was the tallest of the group, her thick, matted braids held in place by small, chipped bones; in each hand she held a dagger, gripping them as though they were an extension of herself. The last man was sinewy, sunburned, starving; he clung to his battered bow the same way a child would a blanket and kept looking over his shoulder at the nearly empty quiver there.

"You have something of ours, Night Terror. A necklace," the archer said. "Thought we'd leave you to the shadows, to this place, and collect when they'd finished with you." He stared at the cylinder in Vrana's hands. "We'll take that, too."

Vrana ignored them. She set the cylinder down and stepped forward, holding her ax outward. The woman with the daggers tensed as the Raven approached. The man in the iron helmet drew his rapier. The archer nocked an arrow and looked nervously at his companions.

Vrana felt lightheaded, from the fall and the sheer number of enemies before her. *I can't do this*, she thought, focusing on the bow, which would be enough to end her before she even started. *Can I do this?* She remembered Bjørn and his insistence that she bring a bow and hated that, for the first time in a long time, he'd been right.

"One on one, Gregory?" the bandit woman said, looking at the man with the rapier.

All three laughed, shaking their heads.

In a flash, the archer's arrow whizzed past Vrana's mask, just above her shoulders. She sprinted toward the three of them, for they left her no other option. The archer fumbled to load another arrow, so his companions picked up his slack. Gregory rushed Vrana, swinging his rapier like a bastard sword. She sidestepped his attack, hopping back as the woman closed in from the side, swiping with her daggers as though they were claws. The archer broke away from the group and then, with steadied hands, launched a volley of arrows at the skirmishers. Vrana, Gregory, and the woman ducked and dodged the missiles as they rained down haphazardly around them.

"You fucking idiot!" the woman shouted to the archer.

"I'm sorry, Nel, I'm sorry."

"Put that thing away, and go do something else. We'll take care of the bird." She stood upright and nodded at Gregory, and together, they ran at Vrana.

The archer was a novice, a distraction, so she took her eyes off him and met the others screaming. She swung her ax, catching the rapier and ripping it from Gregory's hands. As he struggled to reclaim it, Nel stepped in front of him and slashed in a frenzy. Vrana gasped, dipped, and dodged, and tripped the woman when she'd extended herself too far. Nel slid across the grass, staining her hands. When she looked up, Vrana kicked her in the face, knocking a tooth down her throat.

Gregory was panting loudly now, so Vrana heard him when he tried to stab her in the back. She whipped around and punched him in the side, her fist crashing into a wet patch of tender flesh. Gregory wailed in agony and retreated back toward the hospital steps, dropping his rapier along the way.

As Vrana decided who to kill first, someone else made the decision for her. A dull thud and then choking: Vrana looked over her shoulder and saw the archer gripping an arrow shaft protruding from his neck. Something moved through the trees a few meters away, but before Vrana could get a good look at it, Nel was on top of her, spitting hot blood into the holes of her mask. Vrana yelped and then kicked her away, but not before Nel drove part of a dagger into Vrana's thigh.

"Cunt," Nel said, looking at Gregory, who was lying across the hospital steps, dabbing at his side with trembling fingers. "You don't even know what you have."

The necklace? Vrana wondered what Nel was talking about and then decided she didn't care enough to find out. She ran forward, and as the woman crossed her arms and sliced outward, Vrana slid beneath the attack and rammed the ax head into her gut. While she was stunned, Vrana came to her feet, grabbed both of Nel's arms, and pulled; with a sharp snap, they broke. As she screamed and flailed in agony, Vrana bashed her head against Nel's, goring her eye with the beak of her mask.

Nel pulled away and collapsed into the grass, weeping bloody tears from the hole in her face. Vrana kicked the woman's weapons away. Determined to deal with Gregory, she picked up the ax and turned toward the hospital. But Gregory was gone; a severed arm where his body had been. Vrana approached the stairs slowly and saw running up the front steps a long trail of blood that disappeared into the darkness of the hospital.

"Oh my…" Vrana stopped. The darkness was not darkness at all but bodies, hundreds of them, packed together, staring with glinting eyes and gnashing their teeth at her, the intruder, the thief, the murderer. She moved back from the hospital and found the cylinder; with it secured in her pouch, she walked into the forest, shaken and empty, like a stranger who'd seen something she knew she shouldn't have. She held her ax tightly as she walked between the trees and, cringing, waited for the homunculi to swarm her and give her the deathblow.

But it never came.

When she was certain that she was not being followed, Vrana collapsed beneath a large tree and gorged herself on provisions. When a fourth of what she had in meat and bread remained, she stopped and started on the water. The extra day in the ravine, the one she couldn't account for, had taken its toll, and it seemed it was finally catching up with her.

She found some soft bark to rest against and took off her mask to clean the woman's eye from its beak. Four Corrupted. She had killed four Corrupted—five if the young boy had perished at the hands of the townsfolk. Each death had been easier than the last, and each seemed no different than slaughtering an animal out of a need for defense or sustenance. For a culture that was built upon the history of its enemy, so much so that it nearly lacked an identity of its own, Vrana found it surprising how little sympathy, let alone respect, her people—including herself—possessed for the Corrupted. There was little doubt in her mind that the thieves, her attackers, had earned their fate, just as the villains of history had deserved theirs, but could the same be said for the whole of humanity? Seventeen years of nothing, and now… Everything.

It was on the seventh day of Vrana's return that she realized something was amiss. The surroundings were similar—there would be no delays into the Black Hour this time—yet something was missing, something which Vrana could not place.

A snapping of branches stole her attention from the thought to the shape lurking behind a crop of trees, watching her as she watched it. The shape stepped into the light, revealing a man of average build with what appeared to be a large, discolored bat's skull over his head. Bow in hand, the man nodded at Vrana, then vanished into the forest.

She stood in place for a moment, eyebrows furrowed, and considered the man. She had little doubt that he wasn't a Night Terror given the mask and lack of Corruption. Vrana searched her memories of Caldera for his image, wondering if the elders had ordered him to follow her to ensure the trial's completion.

"I'm not that important," she said to herself, turning her gaze from the forest to the sky, where snow-covered spires rose out of the sharp slopes of the mountain in the distance. "Hold on," she said, spinning around. "Oh shit."

Vrana tore through the forest, stopping only to kill and take what didn't need to be cooked. Two days. She had two days before she would reach Caldera, and yet Kistvaen stood before her. *Something's wrong*, she told herself as the forest gave way to a swamp, *I shouldn't be able to see it from here. It's not possible to see it from here. Don't use it as a marker. You won't find your way home that way.*

Day gave way to night, and the forest to swamp. She plunged into the waters, giving little consideration to what may be beneath them. She made no attempt to mask her presence to the things that called the swamp home, for care would cost her time she didn't have to spare. Brightly colored wisps darted about her head as she went, their spherical bodies blooming and wilting like flower petals. They whispered to her in a language she couldn't comprehend, though she knew well enough what they wanted by the way they salivated when they spoke.

"Get out of my way," she told them. "I have to get home."

Two days, three sprains, and sixteen thorns later, Vrana reached Caldera. Her lungs clamored for oxygen; her legs begged for a chair, a bed, or a new body entirely. The sky over the village was caught between day and night, a soft pink fading into frosted gray through which the lights of a hundred dead stars shone. Vrana drank the green potion, the last of what her mother had given her, to dull the pain and heighten her senses. She made sure the cylinder was secure before she crossed the fields. There were no harvesters behind the rows of crops to be seen, and save for the rustling of branches from the forest, there were no sounds to be heard either.

Vrana proceeded on shaking legs into the sweltering heat of Caldera. A wave of embers slid over her body as the wind blew through the blackened buildings before her. *Oh no.* She peered through open doors and windows, searching for friends and finding only smoke. *Please let her be all right.* She followed large gouges in the earth to Bjørn's anvil, where the Bear was missing from his station. She trembled at the thought of finding her mother strewn across the basement, a handful of tonics by her side. She made for home.

Vrana pushed farther into Caldera, coughing as she went, and found her house and those around it untouched by the fire. She hurried to the front door, reached for the handle. She jumped as something collided against her neck. She spun around, rending the air with her ax, just missing Blix as he dove out of harm's way.

"Take me to them, Blix."

The small crow, full of renewed energy and purpose, led Vrana to the Archive, where small fires burned atop boiling pools of blood. Vrana ascended the steps, pushed open the double doors, and then put her hands to her mouth when she saw what suffered beyond. The large tables that once held books were now cleared and covered in the contorted bodies of men, women, and children; their twisted hands calling for or clinging to their teary loved ones nearby. Vrana chased after Blix as he darted through the Archive, ducking under the gory sheets that hung between the aisles.

"Where is she, Blix?" Vrana pleaded. Her feet slipped on a strip of flesh that was laid out across the soiled floor. She nodded at a family huddled around a small boy whose chest was charred, a poor form of apology. "Where is she?"

Ahead, at the center of it all, Vrana's mother stood in a blood-stained apron, tending to the writhing with potions that had once been held in reserve. A dim light surrounded her as she moved from body to body with knife, rag, and vial.

Blix stole Adelyn's attention away from a small child with streaks of rot down her neck. "Vrana," she said, placing her hand on the child's sweating forehead. "Vrana, I'm so glad you're okay."

Knowing that her mother would never leave the child's side, Vrana stepped closer and produced the cylinder for her to see. "What's happened?"

Adelyn looked down and stepped away from the girl, who had fallen unconscious. She dipped her hands in a bowl of murky water, her own mixture of a mild anesthetic and an antibacterial, and then dried them.

"It was the Witch of your nightmares, Vrana. She came for you."

CHAPTER VII

When the moment presented itself, Adelyn pulled her daughter aside, down onto a chair, and told her everything.

"The morning after you left, Mara returned from the east. It's been so many years since I've seen her. You've never met her, no, but I knew if anyone could tell us anything about your nightmares, it would be her. And I was right. She'd heard stories of men and women who had been twisted and disfigured and left to die in the wilds. Like that creature you saw in the lake. She even found one once, on a bridge: two twin boys stitched together at the chest, black eyes, no arms, their mouths stretched all the way down, down to the ground.

"Mara killed the twins. She's always had sympathy for the Corrupted. Later, Mara found out those same boys had been haunting that bridge for months." Adelyn paused for a moment, shaking her head. "Why did this have to happen to you? I..."

Vrana reached out and held her mother's hand.

"Mara couldn't let what she'd seen go. She's not like that. The uglier the issue, the more she wants to know about it, so she did what she does best—investigated. But she didn't find much at first, only a few anecdotes about a woman, a Witch, who lived in the sea, in a field— a Void.

"Very good at pretending to be human, Mara is. For a while, we all thought she'd pack her bags and live with the Corrupted. She's spent more time with them than our own people. I found it strange then, we all did, but I'm thankful now, for you, because she did find something: two books in a barn outside the town where the twins were from.

"Aeson has the books with him now. He filed them away years ago when Mara lost interest. He said he must have been busy, but I suspect he was distracted more than anything else." She tilted her head at her daughter.

Vrana's face went red. "What about here? What did she do? I don't care about all that right now. Whatever else there is can wait."

One of her mother's patients began to cough up chunks of phlegm, causing the entire table they were lying on to shake.

"I'm sorry, Vrana. My mind is a mess. I... just if I don't tell it as it happened, I'll forget something." She sighed. "You've got your father's eyes, intelligence. His stubborn determination. I cherish those qualities in the both of you, I truly do, but I'll be damned if I don't wish you hadn't inherited his bad luck, too."

"Mom," Vrana said, redirecting her.

"Everything was the same, and then it wasn't. I couldn't tell you when it started, but it had to have only been a few days after you left. People reported feeling ill, the wind carried a foul odor and warmth. Bjørn..."

Vrana moved to interrupt, to ask where he was and if he was okay, but she remained silent.

"Bjørn said he saw flickering images on our doorstep of a woman in a dress with long, matted hair. The children started having nightmares; they kept complaining about a deafening drone that none of us adults could hear. From these problems alone, my supplies dwindled fast. After a while, even I felt her strange effects, a horrible unease like when your father... The elders thought it was an infection, so we treated it like one, but then the Witch appeared, and we knew.

"She was awful, Vrana. Looked like a rotted corpse pulled out of water, yet somehow, there was a heat about her, the kind of heat that makes you dizzy and sick. She was so... angry—slashing and burning anything, everything. She had no... I don't know. It was just killing for the sake of killing. One of the spellweavers tried to paralyze the Witch—" Adelyn paused, realizing what she had said and that it was far too late to take it back. "—but she gutted him."

"I hurried home because I saw Kistvaen days out," Vrana said. "I thought they'd all died out, the spellweavers. No one said they were still alive. I don't understand... that's how the mountain..."

"Yes. Without the third spellweaver, the other two cannot make the mountain disappear. Until help comes from Eld or Alluvia, it'll stay that way; the humans will get curious, and eventually their curiosity will bring them here, again."

Vrana looked at her mother with a feeling of emptiness in her stomach. Suddenly, she was very aware of how close to death the ones she cared for had come because of her meddling with the young boy. She was afraid to ask the next question, but before she could stop herself, the words spilled out. "How many?"

"Twenty-two. I can heal those you see here and those farther back, but I couldn't save the others. She had done things to their bodies. Melted them from the inside. At least Bjørn gave her a good punch—a small victory, if nothing else." Adelyn laughed weakly and looked away. "Your mom wasn't always this soft, Vrana, but it's been a long time since I've seen such…"

"I'm so sorry," Vrana said, throwing her arms around her mother. "I'm sorry I brought this to our village. I didn't know."

Adelyn pushed Vrana back and gripped her shoulders. "You are not to blame. Self-pity is for the Corrupted, not for us, okay?"

Vrana nodded.

"This is one of the most important days in your life." She stared through the raven mask, into her daughter's watering eyes. "In my life, despite the circumstances. Go to Aeson and finish your trial. We endured the Trauma. We can endure this."

Vrana considered her mother for a moment and then turned away.

"Vrana," her mother added, "words fail to express just how proud I am of you."

In the Archive's doorway, Vrana and Adelyn hugged once more. Then the clouds of confusion cleared, and Vrana's mind opened itself to her. "If she knew where the village was, then she had to have known I would be gone; otherwise, why not attack it sooner? There is an entire day I can't account for, when I made camp in a ravine just west of the hospital. I don't think the Witch meant to kill me by coming here."

Vrana turned to look at the village, the burned buildings and scarred earth. "I think it was revenge for killing her creature, for seeing her in my dreams and knowing she exists."

Adelyn shuddered as the cries of one of the children echoed through the Archive. "You may be right, Vrana. She's an ancient power, a ghost from the Old World. I can't imagine the connection between you two was on purpose… unless she wanted to be found, wanted to be known."

"Did Mara give any suggestions? Where is she?"

"No. She left the very same day she arrived, back east. Aeson's locked away in the Inner Sanctum. I'm sure he's found something by now." Another child joined the weeping chorus. "I'm sorry. I have to go." She touched her daughter's mask. "I love you."

There were no archivists to provide Vrana with the daily hint to enter the tunnels, and when she reached the three statues, she found there was no need for one, for the plate had already been pulled back. As she descended into darkness, she heard heavy footfalls from above, many in number, and remained very still against the ladder. Vrana imagined it was an army of the Witch's conjurations, returning to lay waste to those who had survived.

But it was something far worse.

Climbing the ladder, Vrana saw that it was the people of her village returning from their Witch hunt. Their presence alone told of their misery: effortless movements punctuated by moments of pain; a vow of silence for fear that their words would give way to screams. Hawks, Bears, and Goats; Foxes, Deer, and Toads; Spiders, Swans, and Owls; Alligators and a Beetle, and many others all passed over Vrana, disappearing into their homes to be greeted by loved ones or no one at all.

Vrana swallowed her guilt and continued down the ladder.

Aeson was already waiting for her in the tunnel, at the location where Vrana most often heard whispers and chanting, where the walls fell away to an underground lake that seemed to stretch on forever. He was sitting on the edge of the tunnel, legs dangling over the side, lost in thought. The glowing stones cast his skull mask in an eerie light. He had dirt on his arms and legs, or was it blood? It was too dim to tell.

"Hey," Vrana said quietly.

Aeson lowered his head and removed his mask. His dark hair fell to his neck. "Hey," he said, setting the skull aside.

Vrana reached for her raven mask, faltered, and then lifted it off her head. She took a seat beside Aeson, their masks on opposite sides of one another, and briefly forgot about everything that had happened. They smiled at one another awkwardly.

Vrana swung her legs over the glassy pit and reached for the cylinder. "Here," she said, handing it to Aeson. "What's in it?"

"You didn't look?"

Vrana shook her head, gesturing towards the warning labels written on the cylinder's side.

"Fair enough," he said, laughing. "It's a preserved form of a virus from the Old World. AIDS. It's spread through sex, bodily fluids, what have you. It killed a lot of humans by shutting down their immune system. They eventually developed a cure; we've had that in the Sanctum for years."

"Oh." Vrana looked at the cylinder and remembered the multiple times she had dropped it. "And you knew it was in the hospital because of a journal you read?"

"I didn't know for certain." Aeson set the silver canister on his lap. "But it seemed that way, yes. I'm really sorry about that. The world as it is right now can't afford to have a virus like this spreading through it again, and we've been searching so long for it. I'm avoiding the subject, I know. I'm sorry, Vrana. I'm still not sure what happened."

Vrana shook her head, knowing Aeson was referring to the events that had occurred only hours ago with the Witch. "My mother filled me in," she said, "in her own comprehensive way."

Vrana proceeded to tell Aeson about the third trial, producing the notes on the homunculi to verify her story. His eyes darted back and forth across the page. Vrana took out the Skeleton's key and the silver necklace and told their stories, too. Her travels with the young boy, however, remained unspoken.

"Things are never easy for you, are they?" Aeson held the silver necklace up against one of the glowing rocks. The light refracted through the gem onto the wall.

"That's not true," Vrana said, pointing to the raven's head. "I took that easily enough. School was more or less uneventful. You and my mother are setting me up for some sort of self-fulfilling prophecy."

Aeson traded the necklace for the Skeleton's key. "Do you remember that time your mother was showing you how to make a potion to help with memory recall?"

"No."

"Well, that's because some of the ingredients had fallen into the wrong vial, and you ended up getting a face full of Forgetfulness. You sure this is from the Black Hour? You might still be feeling the residual effects of—"

Vrana punched Aeson's leg hard, and Aeson almost dropped the key into the waters below. As he rubbed the spreading redness, Vrana took the Skeleton's key and the cylinder and secured them in her bag.

"I feel guilty," she said, unable to ignore the issue any longer. "I know I shouldn't, but I do. I fucking do. And I realized it's not because of what happened, because horrible things do happen. Just—I couldn't at least be here to face the Witch, like the rest of you."

Aeson scratched at his arms and legs, breaking up the dried dirt along them. "So what you're telling me is that you don't necessarily feel responsible for those who died; rather, you feel guilty because you weren't here to have the chance to die alongside them? You know, you don't have to be cold and callous like the elders. No one is going to blame you for this. No one else besides me, your mom, Mara, and a few watchers even know about your dreams. Why should you feel guilty for the choices someone else made? Don't turn Corrupted on me now." He took a breath. "You really stabbed someone in the eye with your beak?"

Aeson helped Vrana to her feet. They put their masks back on. They said little to one another as they traveled the length of the tunnel. Vrana asked if he knew more about the homunculi, and he said that he did, but thought it was more important she receive and read the two books on the Witch instead.

"I have an idea," he told her as they entered the Inner Sanctum, which looked as though it had been ransacked, "on how to find the Witch. I need a few days to think it over, so don't ask until then. I don't want to get anyone's hopes up." He walked over to his bed, which was swamped with books, and picked up two coverless, hardbound novels. "Here," he said, holding them out for Vrana to take.

"Did you see her?" Vrana asked, stuffing the books into her leather bag.

"I did. I knew something was wrong, even down here. It took me awhile, too long, to convince myself to leave the Sanctum." He sighed. "There wasn't much I could do. No one could do anything. I don't even know why I left.

"When I saw her, she was standing at the village center, wrapping that spellweaver's intestines around his neck. I couldn't stop shivering, even though I was covered in sweat. I'd never seen Caldera like that—torn apart and red... red like Corruption." He laughed and shook his head. "What would I know about how the village looks anyways?"

Aeson took off his mask again, this time dropping it onto the bed; signs of trauma were etched into his face. "She laughed at me when she saw me, said something I couldn't understand, then floated away, like a wisp, into the woods. Half the village went after her, while the other half stayed behind to do what they could for everyone else. The strange thing is—" he looked toward Vrana but was really looking inward at the terrible memory eating away his mind, "—it felt like it had happened so quickly, but it had to have been going on for hours. Days, maybe? I don't know where we go from here."

There was little left of the night when Vrana decided to make her way home. She considered staying with Aeson as she had done many times in the past; however, the warmth of her bed and the quiet of her room held an allure too great to ignore. To say she was tired would be an understatement so severe that Vrana would deem it punishable by death. The mere act of having a thought alone threatened to collapse her entire system. Now more than ever, she hoped for the Witch to invade her dreams, or for her to invade the Witch's, but what she would do to the woman was something she had yet to decide.

There would be a lot of blood, though. Of that she could be certain.

Vrana could hear the grumblers grumbling in the fields as she walked through the rows of battered houses, but it was possible that it may have been her stomach begging for a well-cooked meal. An eerie blue mist swirled around her feet and washed against the foundations of the buildings like ethereal waves. They would recover, she knew, for her people seldom dwelled on the past, lest something could be learned from it. There had always been attacks prior to the Witch's, from desperate and deranged humans, to starving animals and sadistic specters. The worst had been a charge led by a band of zealots under the impression Vrana's kind were not only servants of death but evil incarnate—the former being true, the latter more a matter of opinion.

But this was different. This concerned her and the ones she loved, and she didn't have the benefit of history to make of the tragedy a rousing tale. Of course she was to blame, and blamed she would be, because she had opened the door, and the Witch had walked through.

"Why did I think they were dead?" Vrana muttered to herself as she looked upon the mountain. "It only makes sense…"

"I would not worry over the spellweavers," said a gentle voice.

Vrana stiffened as a shape appeared before her. She had her ax but hadn't the strength to swing it. The shape took a step forward and then another, until the blue mist parted at its approach. The light of the moon left nothing to uncertainty: it was the man from outside the hospital, with the bat skull and bow. He was neither large nor small in stature, nor did he present an air of hostility, and but for the white markings on his body, he was utterly average in every respect.

"Why did you rush the bandits?" he asked. "There is nothing dishonorable in knowing your limits."

Vrana remembered the archer and the flood of blood pouring out his neck. "It was you," she said, moving her eyes from the man's mask to his bow. "I… I don't know if I would have survived if you hadn't…"

The Bat stepped closer; not only was his mask discolored, but it was also covered in hundreds of hairline cracks. "It's hard to say. He was a poor shot."

"T-Thank you," Vrana stuttered. "Really, thank you."

She caught herself staring as a child would in fearful admiration of the oddity of bone that sat upon his head. Sensing the man's gaze, she laughed and said, "I don't know what my limits are."

The man ignored Vrana and decided to feed her curiosity. "I have no family. I cannot remember where I am from, and I do not care enough to find out. Your elders took me in when I was very young and very nearly dead."

He cleared his throat. His gentle tone became unenthused, as though the story he was about to tell was one he had told many times before. "For my first trial, I decided I would take the head of a bat. I found no bats large enough to take a head from, but there were bats in the area no larger than small children, which had, coincidentally, developed a taste for small children. I found their cave and killed them all. I crushed their skulls and, from the fragments, made my own. Where there is white on my body, there is no feeling, only a reminder of the diseases they carried. And now that you know my tale, and nothing is left to mystery, we can talk."

CHAPTER VIII

The man's name was Deimos, a name he had given to himself as a child. He roamed the midland beyond the mountain belt, keeping watch over the human settlements and, occasionally, taking on the role of messenger between the villages in the area. His reasons for being near the hospital and at Caldera that night, he told her, had to do with a Corrupted city she'd never heard about. Until now.

"Geharra is a vast city divided by great walls. It sits between two rivers that empty into the sea," he told Vrana as he walked her home. "Its population is no less than ten thousand. Yes, ten thousand. They are fairly self-sufficient and have waged no wars on us or others."

Suddenly, Vrana felt very cold, and her hand began to shake. She tried to remember her schooling, what she may have misinterpreted or missed altogether. It seemed even the Archive's map, which she had studied so carefully in her youth, had been misleading, for it had said nothing about Geharra. "How is that possible? Why did no one stop the Corrupted from building it?"

Deimos shook his head. "Because they did not build it. It had survived through the changes of the world, and they made what was left of it a home. The presence of our people in the north was little then, and the humans reproduce quickly. They are very fond of that, reproducing. It is not the only Corrupted city, Vrana. There are two more, Penance and Eldrus, farther North. They are even larger."

He stopped as bewilderment spread across Vrana's face: her eyes down and to the right; her brow wrinkled; her mouth quivering. She felt naïve for thinking the Corrupted had lived in groups no larger than a few hundred at a time. She felt betrayed for having been led by the elders and adults of the village to believe that their efforts maintained the balance. She wanted to ask Deimos how many remained of their people, because she doubted that number as well.

"The North is not like the South, Vrana," he said, stopping as they reached her house. "The humans are not interested in the South. It is known as the Cradle of Death to them because of the beasts who call it home. They have these great cities in the North, but they are isolated from one another, because of us. Or so we tell ourselves. I am telling you nothing more than what you'll learn in the next few days."

Vrana felt naïve once more, not for her ignorance of the lands beyond, but for so hastily assuming the elders were nothing more than well-respected deceivers. "Then why did you tell me?"

"Because our people in the midland are missing: Alluvia, our village, is empty. And the city of ten thousand is ten thousand no more. I scaled Geharra's walls and followed its streets. There is nothing, no one. Geharra and Alluvia have vanished.

"That is how I happened upon the hospital and you, on my return to tell the elders. They will send me back to learn more, though with a smaller party than I had hoped…" He gestured to the destruction around them. "I followed you closely after the hospital. I was impressed with what I saw."

It took Vrana a moment to realize what was being asked of her, and when she did, Deimos said nothing more. He looked down on her from behind the patchwork of bones, nodded, and walked away into the mist, which closed around him like a hundred ghostly arms.

She knew he wanted her to think on what had been said tonight, for he could have waited until the ceremony to tell her, but that would be impossible in her state. She entered her house, saw that Adelyn had not yet returned from the Archive, ripped the raven's head from her body, and threw herself into bed.

Vrana slept away an entire day, and not because the Witch had somehow willed it. When she awoke at dawn, she remembered all that had been told to her by Adelyn, Aeson, and Deimos, and almost convinced herself that it had been a fabrication of the Black Hour. The elders would be expecting her, Vrana thought as she forced herself out of bed, but she had no intention of seeing them and completing the rite today. After the second trial, she had told her mother she needed time alone, and now that she felt too guilty to be among her people—she might've told on herself just to let the secret out—it seemed that time had come.

Bjørn was passed out over his anvil, his knuckles raw from where he'd punched the Witch. Twice he stirred as Vrana skirted around him, looking through his creations for a bow and quiver of arrows. He had a tendency to overproduce weapons and armor, which had the unintended effect of increasing the likelihood that the youth would destroy them in training. He didn't mind, he'd told Vrana once, but she didn't believe him, as she remembered more instances than she could count in which Bjørn had threatened strangulation and dismemberment after being presented with a cracked breastplate or shattered spear. She felt confident that he wouldn't mind her, of all people, borrowing his wares without permission; however, seeing no reason to test this theory, she took the first bow she found, grabbed a handful of arrows and an empty quiver, and stole away into the forest.

Droplets of dew leapt from the grass as she walked between the trees. An ocelot stared at her from atop a boulder and scampered off, puzzled by the imposter raven. Hundreds of birds called to one another from the canopy above, while spider monkeys scaled and swung from the branches below. Vrana nocked an arrow and loosed it at one of the primates, but it came nowhere close to hitting it. And to make matters worse, one of the monkeys returned, ripped the arrow from the tree, howled hysterically, and threw it back at her.

Archery had never been her strong suit, so she decided to clear her thoughts before being embarrassed by the animals of the forest again. There was a stream to the southwest that Vrana visited on occasions such as these, and this is where she sat now, not on the edge of the water but in it, straight-faced, if one could see her face, and completely relaxed. The stream had been one of the last few places she and Aeson had played as children, before the Inner Sanctum had taken him away from her. She had also kissed him here, but that was another matter entirely.

Too much has happened too quickly. Vrana pulled her mask off, pulled her knees to her chest. A fish nibbled at her back; a bug buzzed in her ear. *The boy, the Skeleton, the homunculi… the Witch… Geharra.* She wrapped her arms around her knees and buried her face against them.

Twenty-two. Who had they been? I don't even know. Somewhere, something made a splash in the water. *I should be helping them, not giving them a reason to suspect me.* She looked up at nothing in particular. These trials were supposed to give something back to Caldera, but all she'd given them was death. Sure, they would move on, but they wouldn't, not really, no one ever does, not from something like this. Maybe she should've told them. They'd have found out anyway. A secret is never a secret here.

Vrana studied her mask, the dead thing she wore that kept her alive. Twenty-two. Why did that seem so much worse than ten thousand? She leaned over and lifted the mask. It felt much lighter than it had been weeks ago, before she'd cut and cleaned the life out of it. *I've always wanted to leave, and here's the perfect opportunity. But they'll find out, and they'll say I ran away.* She set the mask down on the embankment once more. *I don't run away. I'm not running away. I fucked up. I'll fix this. If the Witch wants anything, it's to do this to me, to make me suffer. Of course she wants this. That's why I'm still alive. Bitch. Fucking bitch. I'm not Corrupted. I'm not falling for it.*

Craning her neck, Vrana looked back at Kistvaen, which no longer inspired a small smile and a faint curiosity, but dread. She was confident that the spellweavers were only mentioned in discussions of the past, while conversations of the disappearing mountain never moved far from the realm of speculation. *Why then,* Vrana wondered as she turned away, *would a task so important go without acknowledgement?* She understood the need to ensure the spellweavers' safety, but there was something amiss about one of the privileged and the protected suddenly taking it upon himself to attack an enemy about which nothing was known. She could not help but feel their situation bore some similarity to Aeson's, who swore to her he separated himself from society out of need and heritage. *They lied to us about the northern cities. They lied to us about the spellweavers.* Adelyn was always the first to tell her daughter she came to conclusions too quickly, but in this case, no others seemed to exist: The elders could not be trusted, because they'd become the revisionists they swore they despised.

The fingerlike rays of the rising sun crept over the horizon. The heat of summer washed over the land and seeped into the stream where Vrana sat. She could stay here, she thought, and she would be happy, undoubtedly happy and contented, and like her mother, she would regret every day spent not doing what she'd wanted to do all her life. The little boy didn't matter—she was certain others would've done the same—and the Skeleton mattered even less. He probably never even existed outside that fleeting hour. The homunculi, well, how were they any different from any other unexplainable monstrosity that roamed the land? No, the Witch and Geharra, that's what mattered. Vrana would be running, yes, but only so that the woman of her nightmares would follow.

She wrung out what she could of the water in her clothes, took up the bow and quiver, and started back towards the village. Along the way, she fired seven arrows, only one of which managed to meet its target, and that had been a frog so bloated escape was physically impossible. The kill was a mixture of both triumph and mild depression, but that didn't change the fact the frog would taste good for dinner.

At the midpoint of her journey home, Vrana thought about the Den of the Unkindness and decided to see how they had fared without their Cruel Mother. It was easy enough finding the way: All one needed to do was follow the dying trees, until one could look in any direction and see nothing but the color of ash. When Vrana asked Aeson why the land had never healed here, he'd scoffed and scolded her on the importance of knowing history and then proceeded to tell her the tale of how zealots had drained the land of life during their makeshift siege on Caldera. She found it curious that the elders never made an effort to reconcile that part of the forest, but apparently Aeson didn't.

The ground shifted and sloped beneath her feet, becoming a bed of all things dead. Clouds of dust coughed into the air from wheezing vents, while broken bones rolled lazily on their sides. When she'd first approached the Den weeks ago, the ravens' sounds were overpowering, so much so that she considered turning back out of fear the noise itself would leave her deaf. Now, however, there was nothing to be heard but the sounds of dried leaves crumbling underfoot and the thirsty moans of the twisting trees from which they'd fallen.

Has the Unkindness left? She squinted, trying to pierce the dim darkness that surrounded the Den. She moved closer and saw that it had not. At the center of the hollowed-out tree, amid a flurry of feathers, an engorged raven of at least three hundred pounds sat, mouth agape, its beak stained by its gluttony. Overhead, birds flew through the gaps in the branches of the massive tree, bearing bloody gifts of squirming animals. One by one, they dropped their tributes into the wretched maw. The fat raven's eyes rolled in its sockets, and its tongue licked the air uncontrollably. For those whose gifts were not sufficient, the bloated beast extended its neck, snapped down on them, and forced their twitching bodies down its gullet, to settle the balance owed.

The feeding stopped as soon as the Greedy Father saw Vrana. *I fucked up*, she thought as she went for the ax she'd left in her room. She had five arrows left, barely enough to kill the beast, and that was only if she managed to hit its vital organs. The Unkindness had seemed so thankful to be rid of the Cruel Mother. How had a successor so much worse risen to power so quickly?

She considered running, but feared that by doing so, she would provoke the Unkindness and be torn to shreds and hauled off to be fed to the Greedy Father in partially digested chunks. She gazed at the Unkindness, as though appealing to them for sanctuary, and saw that they gazed back not with hate but with a kind of reluctant reverence. It was the mask, her trophy from the first trial, she realized, that kept the birds' talons clutched to the branches and boughs.

"I haven't found my limits yet," Vrana whispered as she stepped farther into the Den, ignoring Deimos' words, which were repeating over and over in her head. "And if I don't know them, Bat, neither do they."

The Greedy Father went into a spasm of rage, belching into the air its noxious breath. It screamed and shrieked and snapped at the ravens, spraying chunks of rotted flesh and bone against the sides of the Den. Eventually, the ravens returned to their duty; they took their eyes off Vrana and continued to drop carrion into their Father's gore-stained mouth. Like a hungry infant begging for the breast, it ate hungrily, sloppily, and then fell into slumber.

Vrana covered her nose; the Den smelled of shit and decay. She looked at the bloated Father with an even greater disgust than before. *How many do I have to kill until they get it right?* The fat raven shivered in its sleep, causing the blood that had dried on its feathers to crack off in scabby sheets. The Unkindness watched as Vrana trained the bow on the fat raven's neck. "You're not going to stop me," she said, speaking to the ravens. She laughed and lowered her bow. "You don't care anymore."

Few took notice of Vrana as she passed through Caldera's gates.

All attentions and efforts were focused on restoring what the Witch had undone. Vrana took a seat at Bjørn's anvil and returned what she had taken. From there, she watched as builders and their apprentices, some hardly heavier than the tools they carried, repaired the buildings touched by fire. Those harvesters that the fields could spare mended the earth where the Witch had turned it black, cutting away the blight as a doctor would a tumor. Farther on, cooks danced beside their fires, pirouetting around one another, handing off ingredients to be chopped, ground, stuffed, and made edible for the workers. Much to Vrana's surprise, even the elders were helping, taking the bloody sheets from Adelyn's hospital in the Archive and washing them in the purifying waters of their garden.

I should be with them, Vrana thought. *They're cleaning up my mess.*

It was amazing how much progress Vrana's people had made in such a short period of time. Another day or two and none would be the wiser that anything had happened here. But no hand could lift the unease that blanketed the village or heal the scars its people would have throughout the years to come. In comparison to Alluvia and Geharra, Caldera had gotten off lightly from its brush with Death. But that may not be the case the next time, Vrana thought, and if a village of hundreds and a city of thousands can go missing without anyone realizing it, what's to stop the same thing from happening here? And if she had the chance to change this outcome, shouldn't she take it?

CHAPTER IX

It is the darkest corners of the world that she calls home. It is from the deepest depths of the mind that she is inspired. None shall gaze upon her and think her fair or kind, for she is neither, and has never known these words to be said of her. They are foreign to her, painful to conceive. There is no place for her in our world or the worlds beyond; she exists in the space between, where she pledges allegiance to neither God nor Satan but only herself. Her acts of cruelty are beyond measure, for it is seldom realized that it was her hand that guided the knife to the back, the child to the cliff, the lover to the liar, the poison to the well. Of her sculptures of flesh, which merge life and death into one torturous state of being, little can be said by the pen which could rival the sight seen by the eyes. She is horror if horror should ever take upon a form. She is death and despair. She is the Maiden of Pain.

The Maiden's origins vary from culture to culture, from storyteller to storyteller. In Africa, they speak of a child who was taken by evil spirits to Hell, only to be dropped accidentally along the way, lost forever in the endless forever of the beyond. In the East, she was a little girl led to the river by her mother, who saw the Maiden as she was and tried to drown her for it. The townsfolk intervened, however, saving the girl. Bedridden, the girl waited until the day came when she was able enough to kill them all. The West tells a story of an older Maiden, one in late adolescence, who travels the land with her twin sister, living off the hospitality of others and forcing them to murder one another out of lust and jealousy. Even the artic regions of the world have their tales, which speak of a pale woman in rags who walks upon the snow, kidnapping the sleeping and forcing them to endure cruel experiments on their bodies.

Of late, there is little said of the Maiden; the air is heavy with sounds of machinery, of progress, and humanity's cry for help; few have time to concern themselves with the supernatural. If there is a reward to be reaped for actions taken against her, it is overshadowed by the nightmares and bouts of insanity one receives should they survive the encounter. Ignorance has no effect on her, nor will it make the final moments of pain any easier should she darken one's doorstep. No, it is from awareness the Maiden recoils. As the collective conscious becomes increasingly aware and anticipates her violent arrival, she is left with no choice but to wait in the Void until she is again forgotten, so that she may carry on once more, cloaked in secrecy and panic. Let this passage be the first blow against her, a sign that her reign of terror has reached its end.

Should one wish to seek out the Maiden, they need only consult the newspaper or the local tavern. Become invisible, hidden in the shadows, and listen to the trembling rumors told in sharp whispers. Scour the written word for evidence of the macabre and follow its sordid trail, however illogical or impossible the case may seem. Deformities are her signature and irrational behavior her entertainment. Make known your cause, so that when you find the hole the Maiden has curled up in, you are not alone, nor are you compromised by fear. In our world, she is vulnerable. There are no other options.

Dagmar

Vrana took a breath, set the book aside, and picked up the other, turning to the page bookmarked by Aeson.

189X

Day One

I've arrived at—, a small town in the foothills of the — mountains. There seem to be no less than one hundred lakes and ponds in the surrounding area, which I find bewildering, as it does not appear this part of the world has seen rain in quite some time. The ground is hard and dusty, and faint streaks of purple and green can be seen on the soil when the brittle grass bends back. I've no complaints about the air, however—these city lungs have never breathed so freely.

The driver could tell me little of this place along the way, and he turned his back to the town as soon as we arrived. If I should die here, I hope it weighs heavily on that rude man's conscience. I had no intention of mocking the driver's beliefs; I only wished to be prepared for them should they come my way.

The people seem nice enough, but so did the people of the marsh before they tried to cut my heart out. Still, I'll give them the benefit of the doubt (sorry, Herbert, I won't let my heart, in peril though it was, turn to ice like yours). For the duration of my stay the local inn shall be home, and if it were not for the lingering dampness, I'd dare say I prefer it to my own.

There is much more to be written, but the hand grows heavy with exhaustion. Before bed, I think I shall go pester the lovely lady next door, whom I caught staring at me as I carried my bags down the hall. When she's had her fill of my humor and charm, which I'm told does not take long, and chases me off like some sort of persistent animal too sad to realize its own feebleness, I will return to my room, tail tucked between my legs, and sleep the sleep of defeat.

Day Two

The lady next door was very lovely indeed; however, the alcohol she poured for me was anything but. I will thank her for the migraine and bad dreams the next time we meet, which, if my memory is correct, should be tonight at nine fifteen. You thought you had me, Herbert, when you agreed to Europe, but I expect you're doing anything but meeting lovely women as you mosey about that frozen cemetery, minding the body parts as you go.

I began with my patrons at the inn, who expressed a wish to be referred to and shall be known henceforth as Eva and Vaughn. They started the interview by asking me about my familiarity with the Witch, to which I responded with wide eyes and a dash of ignorance. The wife, Eva, looked at her husband, Vaughn, and together held a conversation between each other without saying a word; then, they turned to me and spoke, the words they said like razors to their throats.

Two weeks ago, in the dense fog for which the foothills are known, one by one, the children of the town awoke, not in their beds but at the many lakes and ponds. It was not until the children began to cry, sounding their sorrow all across the landscape, did their parents realize something was amiss. A desperate search and rescue ensued, and all of the children were recovered. When asked what had happened, most of the children could present no explanation, only tears; but of the few who could recall the details of the episode, the story was always the same: A woman had come into their rooms, sat on the edge of their beds, told them their mother and father had died, and if they wanted to be taken care of, they would have to follow her without complaint.

Eva and Vaughn refused to continue at that point, and seeing as I was their guest, it was not in my best interest to harass them any further. Of course, I already knew the story and all its permutations from colleagues and crumpled magazines. Word of the tucked away town and its sleepwalking children had spread like wildfire (almost too fast, if you ask me).

I tried to leave Eva and Vaughn in a better state than they had been following the telling of the tale. Once I saw the warmth return to their faces, I smiled and tipped my hat and left with a skip in my step, a skip put there not by me or them but by the thought of the lovely lady in the room next door.

I followed the old streets for quite some time, ducking into alleyways occasionally, hoping to catch some supernatural entity off guard (looking foolish and insane, as I often do to those who don't know me). I saw four children as I perused the stores. Never had I seen such solemn children. I could not blame them—I, too, would court sadness after such a trauma—but the issue did not appear entirely affective; rather, from looking at their hollow faces, it appeared as though something were missing, taken from them, or replaced with something that had not been there before. Does that make sense, readers?

A knock at my door.

Until tomorrow, then.

Day Three

A little old woman who I will call Misha was standing outside my room when I opened the door to leave today. She had a scarf around her mouth and above her eyes, a dress down to her feet, and gloves covering her hands. She looked like a mummy wrapped in hand-me-downs. I asked if she had leprosy, to break the ice. She shook her head, sneezed without moving an inch, and told me she was ready to talk. I said "sure" and followed her down the hall to a couch beside a lamp and a large window that overlooked the courtyard.

My head hurt. It still does.

After the little old woman finished telling me some irrelevant story concerning her daughter's eye patch, I lifted myself from the couch and told her she was very helpful, instrumental, to my work. I vacated the hotel, and once outside, I found an overcast sky and the overly anxious eyes that awaited me, my presence now known to all. I made harmless queries and petted passing kitties to show I was no beast, but it did little to open their closed minds. I announced loudly, to no one in particular, that I'd be willing to exchange coin for information; then took a stroll down the hillside, into the trees, and finally to one of the many lakes.

On the rocky shore, a fisherman stood, securing a line and bait to his makeshift pole. The mountains in the distance looked like ghosts, floating ever so slightly above the mist. The man heard my approach but not the offer I made earlier, so when we were through, I was all the wiser and none the poorer.

I think I'll have a nap. My writing suffers when my head does.

Day Three—continued

The man was a bleak sort; one who had seen the world and retired from it, for the pain of living in it was too great to endure any longer. Dennis, as I shall call him, said he lost a son two months ago.

"He drowned," Dennis said, eyes puffing. His boy had been the strongest swimmer in the entire town. "But I know who did it," he continued, launching a worm into the placid waters.

"Who?" I hooted like an owl.

"The woman at the inn."

I bit my tongue, and the taste of blood overwhelmed me.

Day Seven

Letting the townsfolk know I'd compensate them for their time was a mistake for two reasons: People are liars, and I had no money. It was a terribly amateurish act on my part, but truth be told, this entire operation has felt unprofessional; it was thrown together at the last minute because of cockiness. The lovely lady next door is of no help either, and now that I know the town thinks her to be the culprit behind the crimes, I understand why they toy with me and cast looks of disdain. I have not slept well (damn you, dampness), nor have I had much of an appetite.

All in all, it would be a fairly typical investigation, if not for the niggling feeling that I am in no way prepared for what's to come, should it come. I will go at it for a few more days, and then I shall bid these strange folk farewell forever.

Day Eight

Annabel: "I can't be long."

Me: "No, I expect not. When you're ready, child."

Annabel: "I was playing hide and seek on the old mountain trail with my brother, Jack. We go up there a lot. We like to watch the birds. Don't know where they come from or what they're called, but what colors. Sorry."

Me: "No, it's quite all right. Please, continue."

Annabel: "Well, Jack always ends up hiding in the cave up there. Every time. He thinks it's funny, because it scares me, but I always tell him he'll be sorry the next time he goes in there and finds a hungry bear waiting for him."

Me: "What happened when Jack went in the cave this time?"

Annabel: "He, uh, screamed and came running out white as a sheet. Said I had to see It, and I saw It, and It was awful, mister."

Me: "What did you see, Annabel?"

Annabel: "Bodies, strung across the pool like a net, all skinny and... like a spider had got to them. But that wasn't the worst of it. I don't know if I can keep on. My mother is expecting me."

Me: "We're almost done. You've done so well. Just tell me what else you saw in that cave."

Annabel: "A woman. I saw a woman. She was naked, I think, and was sitting on top of the bodies. She... she had... I thought it was a stick, but now I'm certain it had to have been a bone. She was banging it on the backs of the bodies, and the water was splashing up through the gaps between them, and I think she was laughing, but there was nothing coming out of her mouth... I can't..."

Me: "It's okay, Annabel. You did so well. Take this, for your troubles."

Day Nine

A pattern is emerging: water.

Day Eleven

We discussed literature and our previous partners—what

went wrong, what made it difficult to say goodbye, and so on. She's a scientist, conducting a research assignment on hysteria. I'm not supposed to know this as it may weaken her results, but I can be very persuasive should the need arise. She's leaving in a few days, and I lied and told her that I was leaving, too. I am certain she knows this is not true, but if she's maddened by it, her lips tell me otherwise.

I couldn't write a decent sentence to save a life right now, let alone my own, which is what will truly be at stake if this investigation goes nowhere. This is serious. I need to be serious.

Nightmare One

Flailing wildly, I tumble through the biting air like a circus performer, reaching for the sky as an infant would its blanket. Black, buzzing clouds meander above me. I hear a piercing wail, followed by a deafening drone that persists throughout the entirety of my stay. I soil myself and feel the hairs fall from my head.

I crash into a field, unharmed, and see that it stretches onward in every direction, unimpeded but for the broken stone walls here and there. The air tastes like pus; sweet and foul, it turns the stomach, until the stomach, my stomach, is on the ground before me.

While I'm sitting on the ground, I can feel water seep through the soil and dampen my skin. I start to think of the lovely lady next door and become dizzy with lust. I hate myself for it, for thinking of her in such a place and state, and start hitting myself. I do not stop until my arm is too heavy to lift.

Day Twenty

Why have I come here? And why can't I...

Day Fifty-Six

Black flies follow me wherever I go. No one else can see

them, and that may be true. I have not felt myself lately. The stories are really coming in now, readers. Can you believe the last two? The Maiden of Pain. What a horrible name. No wonder she's vengeful. Water is the key, but if I should turn it, what doors will be opened?

Day Seventy

The lovely lady let me in to her room when Eva and Vaughn ejected me from mine. I want to ask her why she's still here, but I'm afraid that she'll leave. Forgive me, readers, I cannot....

She still blushes from time to time when we speak. I like that.

Day—

It took me awhile to clear the flies from my lungs this morning. They are worse in her room than they were in mine. She's leaving today. I ask if I can follow her, and she says "yes." She got on top of me, tied me down, and I fell asleep. I'm packing now. With no more crimes to report on, there is no need for me to stay. She said we're going to the country. I said okay.

I wear the flies like a robe, and yet she doesn't mind. A thousand tiny deaths between us every time we touch.

Note: This is all that has been recovered from Seth Barker's journal. There are still many pages missing. If you should believe you are in possession of said pages, please contact us for verification and payment.

Thank you,
Connor Prendergast, Editor-in-chief of *Black Occult Macabre*

The segments were only parts of a much larger whole detailing all sorts of horrors, but Vrana was done. Her eyes felt too large for their sockets, and her head was spinning. It was a completely inappropriate response to what should have been a poor attempt at frightening a gullible audience, but she knew better. She ran her fingers over the ruined books, imagining what they might have looked like when they were first printed, who might have bought them and what they thought of their contents. *If only they had known how right they were*, she thought as she set the books aside.

"Hey," her mother said softly, leaning into the room.

Vrana bit down on the side of her mouth, startled. A cold sweat overcame her. She started to laugh. "You're home."

"I have been for awhile. You've just been asleep. The elders are ready for you." Her mother sounded tired, liable to collapse at any moment.

"Is this really the right time?"

Blix burst past her mother and landed atop Vrana's matted hair.

"Yes, it really is. A celebration is just what we need. Some of us might want something a little stronger than the usual offerings to get us through the night, but I don't think you'll find anyone complaining about that."

Vrana smiled. She stood, picked up a comb, and ran it through her hair, wincing at every knot. "What do I say to them? The elders, I mean."

"You say what you mean and nothing more. Honesty is important to them, and let's face it, my girl, you're a terrible liar."

Blix cawed happily, hopping back and forth over the comb as it went. She looked at her mother differently now, aware that, in a few days, she may be leaving with Deimos. "I'm going to kill this bird," she said, choking back the tears.

After every third trial, a feast always followed to celebrate the accomplishments of the individual and to induct them fully as a member of the tribe. For this occasion, the elders open their garden and their house and invite the entire village to enjoy the great dinner with the new initiates. Food and drink of all varieties and rarities line the massive tables at the garden's center and are refilled from a seemingly infinite stock. For the children, but mostly for their inebriated parents, games are made that have them searching the deepest parts of the garden for hidden rewards. The feast has been known to go on for days, and in some cases, one feast has followed right after the other, leading to a week of uninterrupted revelry that required a second week just to recover.

"I understand why it's important," Vrana said from the kitchen table as her mother ran between the rooms. "I don't understand why it can't wait. Sure, they may not know I know about the Witch—" She stole her mother's cup and finished the wine inside. "But hell, they may as well. I'm going to look like a selfish, spoiled little girl."

"You're going to look like someone who just finished her third trial and wants to celebrate," Adelyn shouted. She bumped into something and cursed. "Listen, this isn't just for you. It's for everyone. We've been over this"

"Two days!" Vrana knocked the cup off the table and groaned. "It's been two days since she killed twenty-two. I don't even know who the fuck to apologize to."

"Pick up that cup, you selfish, spoiled little girl."

Vrana sighed and slouched in her chair. "This doesn't feel right."

Without saying a word, Adelyn returned to the kitchen, but this time she was holding something across her chest. It was an iridescent dress fashioned from black feathers that had been stitched together over dyed leather. The plumes that ran across its asymmetrical edges were especially luminous, as though careful hands had coaxed the colors from the feathers' black grip. Tiny bones ran down the center of the bodice from neckline to waist, like grommets, like precious gems long overlooked by the privileged and pure. The shoulders were short, jagged pieces of raised feathers, their tips colored with streaks of teal. Highlighting the low neckline were ancient symbols in astral thread; visible only in moonlight, the intricate weavings related the story of the Raven's three trials.

"It's beautiful," Vrana said. She laughed, felt the dress, and laughed again. "Did you make this?"

Adelyn nodded. "Anything look familiar?"

Vrana shook her head. She ran her fingers along the shoulders, touched the smoothed bone embellishments.

"When you left for your second trial, Bjørn and I went to the Den."

Vrana looked up at her mother, one eyebrow raised high. "This is from the Cruel Mother?"

"We couldn't let that bitch go to waste." Adelyn handed Vrana the dress, kissing her on the forehead as she did so. "Feel better about tonight?"

Vrana nodded. "Very much so."

As was customary, Vrana was the last to arrive to the elders' garden, and as soon as she passed between the lattices, an outpouring of congratulations closed in on her. She greeted the blur of animals and insects calling from the smoky torchlight. In that dress, under that mask, Vrana could be anything the night required, so with that confidence, she went to the head of the main table and waited until everyone was seated.

Vrana raised her hand, and Caldera stood. "I'm very sorry to put you through this," she started, her voice shaking slightly, "but the elders won't let us eat until I embarrass myself with a speech."

The village laughed and encouraged her with nods and claps to continue.

"I thank you all for coming tonight, but this night is not for me. This is for you, for the ones we've lost, and for those who lost them." She scanned the crowd, taking note of who lowered their heads, who looked away; for it was to them, the grieving, that she spoke. "I can't stand up here and pretend as though I've done something great, something remarkable. This isn't the first feast, nor will it be the last. But here we are, in the lingering twilight of tragedy, and look how far we've come, how close we've remained. That's what's great, that's what's remarkable.

"This night is not for me. This night is for you, for the ones we've lost, and for those who lost them. This night is for the Witch, a last moment of reprieve, because tomorrow, she will be hunted mercilessly until we drag her back here in bloody fetters and take her apart, twenty-two pieces a person, until nothing remains but her skull. And we'll take it and raise it high, because it is ours, and not even in Death will she find mercy, because not even Death will expect us to give it, for we are Its faithful servants."

Vrana lifted the mask from her head and set it down on the table. One by one, each villager did the same, as a demonstration of their approval for her initiation. She smiled at her graduated classmates— Korr, Gul, Galan, Verda, Aka, Cressida, and Vit—and they smiled back, silently shouting words of praise. When the final mask met the table, the elders stepped away from their seats, moved to where Vrana was standing, and went to their knees, bowing before her as though they were her subjects. She helped Anguis, Faolan, and Nuctea to their feet, and with their feeble arms, they lifted her up against the starlit sky and then released her. As though made of nothing at all, Vrana floated down to the ground, and when her feet finally met the grassy earth, the gathering erupted into applause and welcomed her as a full member of the tribe.

"I can count on one hand the amount of times I've seen you in a dress," Aeson said, flanking her from the darkness as the village members settled into their seats.

Vrana threw her arms around him and hugged him longer than most friends would hug. She pressed her fist into his side and said, "And I only need one to make sure you never forget."

Aeson took off his mask and grinned. His eyes traveled the length of the dress, lingering on the places most friends' would not. "You look badass."

Vrana shook her head, wiped the tears of joy from her eyes. "You just like to say that word any chance you get."

"It's my favorite Old World word, and is there not a more appropriate moment?" He sat in the empty chair beside her own, which Vrana hadn't noticed until now. "How do you feel?"

Vrana looked at her mother, who was busy picking at the surplus of food from Bjørn's plate. "Like I'm still floating up there."

Aeson's eyes never left hers as she sat beside him. "You earned this. Did you practice that speech?"

She shook her head. "Just the first part. I don't know where the second half came from."

Aeson nodded. "You must be starving. Let's eat, before you float away for good."

An hour later, when the night was noticeably darker and bellies noticeably larger, the dishes were cleared away by the ever-diligent harvesters and relegated to a second, smaller table as leftovers. Vrana finished her wine, and then her mother's wine, as the village turned its attention toward her once more. The speech had been given, the initiate accepted; all that remained were drunken admissions and endless questions from those who had been close to Vrana throughout her life.

"I'm going home," Vrana said, leaning into her mother. "Tell everyone I said thank you."

Bjørn slammed his fist against the table, scaring away an ambitious vine that had tried to carry away his underworld rice. "I've been waiting for this moment a long time, girl."

Vrana squinted as though to burn a hole through the Bear's head with her gaze. "You don't have anything on me, old man."

Bjørn shrugged, grinned the smallest of grins, and tore into a haunch of meat with his teeth. Chewing with his mouth open, he added, "I've got a drawing that says 'Vrana loves Bjørn' that begs to differ."

Vrana's jaw dropped; she fell back in her chair, arms locked cross her chest. "I was five."

"Little hearts, little flowers. Wasn't there a poem?" He looked to Adelyn, who nodded, her face frozen to hold back the laughter. "Bears and Ravens don't go together, but me and you, we're two of a feather!"

Vrana closed her eyes. "I'm going to kill you, Bjørn. I really am."

The first question posed to Vrana asked her to relate to the village the details of each of her three trials, so she did just that, while omitting anything that concerned the young boy and the Witch.

"The Black Hour? You don't say!" Helga of the Frog exclaimed. "That Skeleton sounds an awful lot like an old boyfriend of mine! Always wondered what happened to him. Hell of a lover. You know, now that I..."

The second question, which, to the village's relief, interrupted Helga's ramblings, came from the Beetle, a watcher by the name of Lucan. Vrana seldom saw the man, and as a child, she had been grateful for his absence, as his mask, a pale carapace with two large, imposing pincers, had terrified her.

"Where will you go next?" he asked, his face wrapped in shadows, his wife beside him gripping his arm, studying him. "You're an explorer, like your mother. Where will you go, eh?"

"I'm... not... sure," Vrana said. *Why does he care?* "Perhaps North," she said, "where the Corrupted live." Glances were exchanged between several of the older adults at the table. *Do they know what's happened in Geharra?* "I'd like to see everything for myself, as it really is."

Lucan nodded as he rubbed the top of his wife's hands. "I hope that you do."

The third and fourth questions were trite and trivial recollections about Vrana in her youth—"I remember the day you brought your bird home!" and "She was always a pleasure to have in class."—and the fifth and sixth not really questions at all but the Wasp and the Boar presenting political dilemmas they'd hoped to force on Vrana, so that they could have one more person, other than themselves, to rely on to validate their well-known opinions.

"We call the Corrupted human, but is it not possible they are of another origin entirely?" the Boar insisted.

"What does it matter, you fool?" the Wasp stung. "Corruption is contagious. We've seen it in every species, except our own. Our purity is what gives us the right…"

Aeson glanced at Vrana, who pretended to listen while watching and wishing she could be with the children, who were dancing around a pond with the black sprites from her basement.

"That's not true. Corruption is not contagious," Aeson whispered. "Did you know these idiots—" he stopped and smiled at the Cat who had overheard him, "—tried to be Archivists?"

"I can see why they were denied the job," Vrana said, taking another sip of wine. "But I'll put in a good word for them if it means they'll let you come out in the sun more often."

Eventually the Boar and the Wasp were silenced by groans and thrown bits of food, and Bjørn, helping himself from the leftovers on the second table, took advantage of the lull to speak on Vrana's training over the years.

"She was a chubby thing, wasn't she?" Bjørn fell into his chair, tried to nudge Adelyn with his elbow but missed, instead dipping it into grumbler sauce. "Very round." He belched and made the shape of a sphere with his hands. "Used to roll all over the yard. That's how she dodged attacks. She'd hit the ground and roll away. It did a number, psychologically, on the other kids. Do you still do that?"

"Practice three times a day."

Bjørn cocked his head: He didn't like it when Vrana played along. "Truthfully, I've never met a more competent woman. With that ax of hers, she could outfight the lot of you. If anyone can bring that Witch back to us, it's her." He raised his cup to the Raven, the glint in his eyes telling her he knew more than she thought. "Now, about that poem!"

Under the cover of night and the pulsating rhythm of drums, Nuctea snuck up on Vrana and touched her shoulder. The Raven excused herself and followed the Owl into the house of the elders. Flickering candles lit the way, their flames an impossibly bright black. The wood floor creaked beneath Vrana's feet; purple sprites, not unlike those found in her basement, passed through the cracks between each panel. Nuctea kept her hand on the small of Vrana's back, gently guiding her through the labyrinth of narrow halls that seemed far longer than the house itself.

Before Vrana realized what had happened, they were standing in a small room lit by a single gray-flamed candle. Around the light sat Anguis, Faolan, and Deimos.

"Have a seat," Nuctea said, leading by example and sitting beside the Wolf.

Vrana sat opposite Deimos, who, unlike her and the elders, still wore his mask. She nodded at him and then started to nod off, the wine and the warmth of the room, which smelled of fire, overpowering her.

"Your contribution to the village has been great, Vrana," Anguis said as an albino deathrattle wrapped itself around his arm. "Greater than you may realize. We are indebted to you."

"You are young, with so much potential, but there is no denying you've become a part of something ancient and terrible," Faolan added as a wolf pup trotted over and laid its head on her lap.

"There are questions for us." Nuctea shifted and rested her chin upon her palm. "And you should have them answered."

Vrana looked to Deimos for guidance, but he didn't stir, and if he was breathing, he didn't show it.

"What…" Vrana began, her thoughts racing, each overcoming the other, begging to be articulated. "Why didn't you tell us about the North?"

"We had done so in the past, but we found it instilled fear in the young, discouraged them, because it is difficult to imagine and accept. We wanted to see if it were best to wait. If not for Deimos, you would have been told tonight," Faolan said, petting the purring pup. "Our people are excavators and executioners. There is much for us to find and many for us to kill. We mustn't become overwhelmed."

"Are we outnumbered?" Vrana asked.

Anguis leaned forward. "Very much so. We have always been, and yet we persist. Our knowledge is beyond theirs, and they fear us. It keeps the balance." The albino deathrattle uncoiled from his arm and began to climb his chest. "Their leaders depend upon our actions as well. It is, no doubt, a parasitic relationship, but should the time come, we will emerge the stronger."

The gray flame whipped back and forth as a gust of wind blew through the room. Vrana spoke again, feeling more confident. "Why are the spellweavers kept in secret?"

Nuctea straightened up and responded quickly. "The spellweavers are not like you or I, nor will they ever be. They are kept hidden to protect them, so that they may protect us."

"'Not like you or I.' I don't understand."

"Vrana," Anguis interjected, "I'm sorry, but not all questions can be answered."

Vrana tilted her head. "Then tell me why he tried to fight the Witch."

"That, we do not know and wish that we did," Nuctea said. "We've spoken with the other two spellweavers, and they informed us they felt the Witch's presence when she arrived."

"Fine," Vrana conceded. She asked about the Witch, to which they said that they had no solution.

"Her existence was known to us, yes," Faolan said as the wolf pup started to snore, "but only as rumor, myth. You have seen her, Vrana, and the Void; it is you to whom we look for guidance. Mara spoke of her and her horrors and warned us long ago, but we had and have no means of reaching her, this Witch. There are many terrors in this world. We cannot attend to them all."

"And so we must be selfish and ask of you to learn more of her on your northward journey," Anguis added. "It is the humans she enjoys the most, and beyond Kistvaen, they do not want for Corrupted."

"I…" Vrana stuttered, images of Aeson and her mother flashing through her mind. "I haven't decided yet."

"Vrana." Nuctea touched her again on the shoulder. "We know you better than you may think. Fight it if you like, but you know that you want this, even if it hurts."

Vrana sighed, nodded. "I guess there is no sense in asking how long I will be gone, so who's coming?"

"There are two more. You will meet them soon," Anguis said, the light of the candle glinting off the scales of the deathrattle. "If the task cannot be done with you four, that is worrisome. Deimos and the others are unmatched. And if what Deimos tells us is true, you, too, are fearsome."

"Oh," Vrana muttered, feeling heat rise to her cheeks. "What…" She considered revealing her ordeal with the Black Hour, then decided against it. "If Alluvia is really gone, how many of us are left?"

"Three villages, not including our own, so no more than twelve hundred," Anguis said, pained. "But we are not convinced all is lost. Our brothers and sisters in the North have been trying to repopulate, though they've little to show for it."

"Why is that? I've never fully understood why so few of our own are born each year." Vrana thought back to her classmates. "You don't want to overwhelm us, because there's so few of us."

"It is our fault," Nuctea said as an owl descended upon her from above. "Like the Corrupted, who are weak to temptation and violence, we are unfit to reproduce." She removed a piece of parchment tied around the owl's leg; the owl flew off into the smoky darkness. "They know Alluvia is empty and are heading east now for a spellweaver."

"Good," Anguis said, not lifting his eyes from Vrana.

"Then what did we do in the past? The Corrupted are that way because of what they have done. What did we do?" Vrana moved her hands to her stomach, suddenly feeling very estranged from her body.

"It has always been like this." Faolan stood up, the sleeping cub sliding off of her lap onto the floor, undisturbed. "We are not perfect; that belief alone has been the demise of many of our brethren."

Anguis, too, stood up, and so did Nuctea. Vrana knew that her moment with the elders was over, and she felt she had wasted it. "Wait," she said, pushing herself off the ground. "What happened? What did the humans do to make the world this way?"

"It is a culmination of their downfalls," Deimos said, drawing the gaze of not only Vrana, but the elders, too. "With their gods they made of this world a wasteland, time and time again, and we can only assume the Trauma was the same. But they do not deserve to be destroyed. Where would we be without them? We are their images reflected through broken glass. No." Deimos stepped forward until he was looking down on Vrana, his horrible mask like the face of Death. "They must be maintained, just as we must be maintained."

Vrana opened her mouth to speak, but before she could do so, the gray flame of the candle was extinguished, and the darkness of the room became the darkness of her eyelids; and when she opened her eyes, Vrana found she was still sitting at the head of the long table, surrounded by her people, the music and the garden swelling around her, with Aeson's hand around hers.

CHAPTER X

Vrana had two days to say goodbye. Her mother was more than supportive of the proposed journey ("Are you really?" Vrana asked her), having already been informed by the elders prior to the feast. Aeson, however, didn't share the same enthusiasm as Adelyn. This worried Vrana most of all, because in her absence, she knew that it would be all too easy for Aeson to seal himself in the Inner Sanctum and never emerge until word of her return reached him.

"I'm fine, Vrana," Aeson said as he paced about the Inner Sanctum, appearing anything but. "I will manage."

"I suppose you will, seeing as you let me go to that hospital and all," Vrana said as she attempted to juggle the bauble that had been on Aeson's desk. "What is this, anyways?"

Aeson snatched the bauble from the air and put it back in its place. "It's a prophecy stone, or a paperweight, and I didn't let you go to the hospital. You know, trying to make me feel bad is an odd way of trying to make me feel good about you leaving."

"So you're not fine with it!"

Aeson rubbed his face red. "Of course I'm not, Vrana, and you wouldn't be if it were me. How could I be?"

"Promise me you will not stay down here the entire time while I'm away." Aeson moved to interrupt, but Vrana held up her hand and continued. "You owe me. When I left for the third trial, you promised me that you would do whatever I asked, and this is what I'm asking of you."

Aeson sighed and slumped down onto a chair. "I don't think

those were your exact words." His eyes darkened as he retreated inwards for a moment. "I don't hate them. I'm not scared of them. It's just my parents…"

"I know," Vrana said softly. She stepped towards him and went around the chair, placing her hands on his shoulders and rubbing them gently. "Don't go back on your word." She wrapped her hands around his neck and squeezed. "Or else."

"Water," Aeson rasped. Vrana released her grip, and he turned around to face her. "Water: That's how the Witch enters our world."

"I picked up on that, too," Vrana said as Aeson stood up, massaging his neck. "Sorry. You're so fragile."

He waved off her apology. "Water can represent life, as well as death. What better an example of those two concepts than something which has been living and killing for longer than anyone can remember?" His voice increased in pitch as it often did when he became excited over a topic. "And there is water in nearly every story told about her. Whatever tale is true, it began in water, so water is how she enters this world."

"Well, good thing about seventy percent of it is covered in the stuff." Vrana pulled back her hair to braid it. "What's stopping her then? Why not leave the Void permanently? She clearly takes pride in her work, the cunt."

"Fear, I think," Aeson said, walking toward the large wall of stone that divided the Inner Sanctum. "It's what gives her power over us, but too much, and we've power over her, like it said in one of those books. She's had ages to learn how to keep the scales balanced, like us. The Void is her home, her hideout. The one place she can be safe when people start asking questions and saying enough is enough."

"How do we kill her?"

Aeson laughed and bit his lip. "You find a way into the Void and drag her out of it. I wouldn't be surprised if the Void exists simply to sustain her. I've never heard of it in any other writings."

"Point me in the right direction, and I'll cut the bitch's throat."

A look of solemnity fell across his face, the excitement in his voice gone. "Vrana, I don't want that. I… I know more about death than anybody else. I know the effect it has on people. I know the necessity of it and all the awful ways to induce it. I know more than I should and need to about countless subjects, yet here I am, underground, only as useful as the person forced to do what I say needs to be done.

What I'm trying to say is… it doesn't have to be you. Besides, I don't know how to reach her."

"You're lying," Vrana said. "You at least have ideas. Tell me them." She put her hands together in front of her and made a choking gesture. "We're not children. We can't just talk and expect nothing to happen. She came to Caldera and killed our people. If we have a solution, we can't sit on it, twiddling our thumbs, hoping she dies of—what—old age? Come on, please."

"A spell maybe," Aeson said through his teeth.

Vrana stepped forward.

"I meant to ask the spellweavers, but I took too long. Maybe the Witch knew that I'd found a way and that's why she came."

Vrana took another step.

"When his replacement arrives, I'll try to convince him to tell me, but I doubt that'll happen; the elders won't even let me talk to the ones that are left."

Vrana continued, halfway to Aeson.

"Also, there are artifacts—black bangles with red Death engravings, bone goblets scorched in hellfire—kept in the northern cities, used for religious purposes. I don't know how they work, but some say they can be used as portals to the Exuvia lands. There's the Black Hour…"

Vrana stopped an arm's length away from Aeson.

"But we can't control the Black Hour, or predict it, so that's out of the question." He coughed. "It may be possible to reach her if one could convince Death to ferry them to the Void. There's that old Nature Preserve near…" He closed his eyes and shook his head at the ridiculousness of the statement. "This isn't worth discussing. I'm sure this is what the Witch wants, for us to kill ourselves trying to find a way to kill her."

Vrana took a small step nearer to Aeson and placed her hands on his shoulders once more.

"What the hell are you doing? I thought you wanted to know these things."

Vrana leaned in and kissed Aeson on the lips.

"I'll… that's… I mean, that's better than choking me, I—what?" He smirked, trying to make light of the situation.

Vrana ignored Aeson and kissed him again. She felt different, aware of the finality of things. She needed him to stop speaking, for she realized that, with every suggestion he gave, he drove her father away, into the North, into death; because if she knew how to stop the Witch, she'd have to try. She kissed him again, and he met her half-way. This wasn't the first kiss they'd shared, but the thought of it never happening again was too painful to imagine. He pulled her closer, and where she had once pulled away, she now stayed. She was tired of talk about the Witch and no longer felt the need to inquire about spellweavers. She kissed him on the neck, and he did the same to her.

"This didn't quite work out before," Aeson said, pulling away, flushed. "Would you be doing this if you weren't leaving?"

She threw her arms around him, catching a glimpse of her raven mask on the other side of the room. "No, probably not." She put her forehead to his. "But I needed to be leaving to know what I'd miss."

Aeson nodded, twisted his mouth. "This feels forced, Vrana."

"I know," she said.

Aeson dipped down and kissed her on the side of the mouth. "Don't get me wrong, I'm not saying it doesn't feel right, either." He laughed and held her tightly. "At this point, I think we can endure just about anything. But I can't take losing you, whether you're my friend or my lover. You have to come back. You're the only light I have down here."

"No pressure, right?" she said, sniffling, hating the tears she felt weighing down her lashes.

He smiled and wiped her eyes. "Not for a badass like you."

Vrana woke early on her last day in Caldera. Outside, she could hear the weeping of those sleepless bodies that had lost all to the Witch. Her mother, who was tending to the garden in the basement, shrieked when she saw her daughter descend the stairs, spilling a cup's worth of tea all over her feet. Thankfully, the sprites were more than eager to clean up the mess, hovering over the spill and drinking it until nothing was left.

"That was the last of the tea," her mother said, cleaning her hands in a small pool of water "You've really screwed up now, child."

"I'm sorry," Vrana said, trying not to laugh.

"You will be, girl," Adelyn said, pointing with one dripping finger. "The sun is still rising, and you're awake. Did Blix leave a surprise for you on your forehead again?"

"Nerves, I think," she said, using all her strength not to say something she would regret. "That's never happened again."

"When you're gone, I'm not going to have anybody to talk to, and Aeson is not going to have anybody to talk to so…"

"If you—"

"I'm just teasing." Adelyn walked over to Vrana and hugged her. "I won't get to do it for a while. Are you ready?"

"I am." She was not. "Should I see Bjørn before I go?"

"I'd recommend against it, because it would make him feel important, but he may have some things for you." She ran her fingers through Vrana's hair, putting her immediately at ease. "Listen to Deimos. There are few I trust more than him in this village."

"Who is he? I've never heard you talk about him before."

"He wouldn't like it if I talked about him. You'll see." She reached toward one of the sprites. "I'm sure the elders have asked you to do all sorts of things for them while you're gone, but your mother has a request that takes precedence: ingredients. I need them. I'm not going to tell you what I need, that's up to you to decide. So don't forget about your dear old mother, otherwise the Witch won't be the only thing haunting you at night."

Vrana stared at her mother, and her mother stared back; all at once they began to laugh hysterically. There was little reason for the outburst, or the tears that leapt from their eyes, but it made the pain of leaving a little easier.

The cup Adelyn had been drinking out of was a gift from Vrana's father, and she only drank from it when she could think of nothing else but him. Vrana slid the cup into the small pool of water while her mother was looking away.

Bjørn was fastening straps to the sides of a leather chest piece when Vrana happened upon him. From his sluggish movements and the sheer black cloth draped over the mouth of his mask, she could see he had yet to recover from the festivities. Grunting, he set the armor aside for a pair of dusky daggers made out of a material she'd never seen before. In one pained motion, he reached for a jar of oil, freed its lid with a struggling hand, and with the other dipped the daggers into the swirling liquid. The substance was a rare and highly valued coating extracted from the glands of nethers, which left whatever it touched nearly impervious to wear.

"What have you got there, buddy?" Vrana chirped.

Bjørn sat upright so fast the black cloth flew from his head and landed behind him. He gasped as the sunlight flooded his mask. "I've got one fist to be followed by the other should you shriek once more into my ear!" He moaned and bent over where he sat. "How long have you been standing there? I can hear Anguis whispering sweet nothings to his snakes, but where did you come from? Ah hell, girl, you're not supposed to see this."

Vrana looked at the daggers and then the chest piece, neither of which she had requested. "How much did you drink the other night?"

Bjørn shook his head. "Only what was left. I've no mind for waste. Well, here you are." He held out the daggers and pointed to the full set of leather armor behind him. "They are yours to have, and you best have them. There's nothing I hate more than working with a headache."

"You've been at this all morning?"

"All morning? No, I've been at this all your life."

The armor appeared as though it was a sister to the dress her mother had created for the feast. On each piece of dark leather were intricate engravings of feathers that, upon closer inspection, were comprised of tiny runes of protection and power. The breastplate had splashes of crimson along its sides, as though stained with the radiant blood of Vrana's enemies. A charcoal-colored cloak flowed down from the shoulders to the tassets; when Vrana went to touch it, the material slithered through her fingers, refusing to be grasped, like it had a will of its own.

"Faerie silk," Vrana realized. "How?"

"Running around nearly naked is all well and good, but it is only a brief distraction at best in battle. Truth be told, I thought my work had been for naught when you started putting on the pounds like you were going into hibernation, but thankfully, that passed. You can't roll in it, I'm sorry to say."

Vrana was too ecstatic and overwhelmed by Bjørn's display of affection to make a witty retort. Instead, she lifted her raven's head and planted a kiss on the cheek of his mask.

"Thank you," she said, letting him glimpse her smile before she pulled the mask over her face. "Where did you get the daggers? I've never seen anything like them."

"Yes, you have," Bjørn said, dipping them back into the nether oil. "Taken from the same bird whose head you now wear. When you came back and told me you'd forgotten the talons, I left with your mother to fetch them. Cut myself plenty on these things. You're lucky that beast didn't flay you. They're not ready yet, so you will wait until Bjørn is satisfied."

Vrana cleared her throat. "Not that I don't appreciate this, but does Bjørn have a spare bow?"

At dusk, Vrana's companions were revealed to her, one which she had seen occasionally, the other a stranger to all but the elders and Deimos. The former was the watcher, Lucan the Beetle, the last of his name and aspect; the man who had asked her during the feast what she intended to do next with her life. *He was testing me*, she thought, looking for the seam between his mask and his neck and failing to find it. *He disagrees. He doesn't think I should be here.*

The stranger's name was Serra, of Traesk, and he wore the head of a piranha, which shone an infectious yellow and green when light passed through it.

Lucan's appearance was frightening, but was made less so by his oafish voice. Serra, unfortunately, didn't have this luxury, because he had no tongue with which to speak. Like Bjørn, Serra saw the world through his mask's tooth-lined mouth, but unlike the Bear's mask, the darkness inside Serra's was unrelenting. Vrana couldn't see his face even if she were standing right in front of him.

Vrana ate her last meal with Adelyn very slowly. They talked about her father, because they hadn't done so in quite some time, and at dinner's end, they were thankful that they had.

"What did he look like?" Vrana asked, feeling the fullness of her stomach with her hands. "I don't think I was old enough to remember, really."

"Looked like you, mostly," Adelyn said. "People used to tease us, because they didn't see any of me in you." She bit her lip. "He was average height, average build. His hands had a certain look to them that I liked. It's hard to explain." Her mother laughed. "He was a quiet man; not terribly adventurous, but he could be persuaded if needed."

"His mask—what was it?" Vrana cringed. "I see it, but not really.

I know he wore one, but every time I imagine him, he's wearing something different."

"Iguana," Vrana's mother said, her voice heavy with dreamy reminiscence.

"Really?"

"Yup. Not a common aspect."

"Can't say I've ever seen one." Vrana thought for a moment. "I don't think he's dead."

Adelyn smiled, reached across, and took her daughter's hand.

"But I don't think we'll see him again." Vrana felt her mother squeeze her hand as she said this.

"Probably not, love."

"Have you… have you ever considered—?"

"Another man?" Adelyn laughed, smacked the top of Vrana's hand playfully. "Every day. But I'm picky."

"What about Bjørn?"

"Get out."

Vrana told her mother about Bjørn's gift as they cleared away the food, and Adelyn told her that it had been the only thing that made the man bearable over the years (pun fully intended).

While Vrana was getting ready, which was taking longer than usual—she could count on one hand the amount of times she'd worn a full set of armor—Aeson let himself into her room. They finished what they had started two years ago in the Inner Sanctum, and then, after the sex was over in record time, he helped her into her armor once more. She asked him if she should bring the books on the Witch, the Skeleton's key, and the silver necklace, and he could offer up no reason as to why she shouldn't pack them. He told her that he remembered the necklace was a symbol of a dead faith indigenous to the North, and Vrana told him it probably fetched quite a price up there, which was why the bandits wanted it so. They kissed, and then kissed again; they regretted their timing; and then set another world record.

At nightfall, the village gathered at the gates, where Deimos, Lucan, Serra, and Vrana waited beside the elders. Together, Anguis, Faolan, and Nuctea spoke in unison, and a portion of the field began to sink inwards, sucking in nearby crops, scavenging animals, and the wind itself. The ground eddied as the contents of a cauldron would, and from it ghastly shapes formed, building upon one another with earth, rock, and root, blood, bone, and flesh, until the forms were not one shapeless mass but four horses, horrible and beautiful to behold.

"They will see you to Nora," Faolan said as the riders mounted the beasts. "And then they will return to nothingness."

Vrana swallowed her trepidation as roots grew out of the sides of her horse and wrapped around her trembling legs and hips, forming a harness. Bjørn approached and handed her the daggers, a bow, and a quiver filled with arrows, and he gave her a hard slap on the back. Her mother followed, held her hand tightly, and told her that she loved her above all else. Aeson, much to the village's surprise, but not Vrana's, bid her farewell, too. His voice was heavy with hurt, and he peered up at her from behind the human skull, with eyes that begged her to stay. Vrana tried to speak, but it was too difficult, so she turned her horse and followed the others into the night.

CHAPTER XI

Vrana pushed one dagger into the priest's chest and another into his stomach. Warm blood sputtered and seeped from the wounds, soaking her hands. The man bit at her mask as he pulled her down to the ground, desperate to inflict one last ounce of suffering before departing for Death. She shoved the daggers in deeper and twisted; the man writhed, wept, and wailed, and as he writhed, wept, and wailed, she took a moment and looked at her surroundings. Deimos had finished with his Corrupted and was sitting beside his kill, catching his breath; Serra was at the tree line, looking over his priest as though wondering what to do with him; and Lucan, with one foot on his attacker's crotch, was twisting the man's neck, tearing flesh and breaking bone, as though he aimed to rip his head from his shoulders.

"He has returned to us," the man said, struggling to speak. "Your sins will go unanswered no longer." He opened his mouth to say something else, but Vrana dug the daggers deeper, until the light left his eyes.

"Vrana," Deimos said as he approached. He helped her to her feet. "Are you all right?"

She nodded, wiping the blood from her hands onto the leaves of a nearby bush. "Did he escape?"

The "he" to which Vrana referred appeared to have been the leader of the group of Penance missionaries, and as Serra traded one body for another in the woods, she noticed that "he" had not made it very far at all. It was Lucan who could be thanked for that, having launched a well-aimed rock that shattered the leader's knee. As with the Cruel Mother and Greedy Father, and even the elders, this leader didn't appear worthy of his station. He had attacked Vrana and her companions carelessly, without any strategic considerations.

There was one part of him that Vrana found commendable, however: He didn't scream, not even as Serra dragged him by his bleeding, broken leg across the clearing.

"You could have passed unnoticed," Lucan said as he joined Vrana and Deimos, wiping blood from his pincers.

Serra released the man at their feet, and the man let out a stifled groan.

"On what god's behalf do you murder today?" Lucan added.

The missionary spat at Lucan. "There is only one, as there has always been. Kill me, so that I may sit at his side. I do not fear death as you do, godless beasts of the South."

Deimos grunted and sheathed his sword. "What are you doing in the South?"

The missionary's face contorted. He tightened his throat so as to not vomit from the agony. "Spreading word of his return."

"God's?" Vrana asked, afraid that if she didn't, she may never know.

Again, the man spat. He reached for his leg with his Corrupted arm and then retracted, tears forming in his eyes. "You will not find him. He will not be killed by you, like so many others who have fallen to your hate. I do not fear death! Mother Abbess hear me."

Serra stepped away, only to return shortly thereafter with a large rock that Vrana estimated to weigh at least forty pounds. He stood above the missionaries' leader, looked at Deimos for approval, and then released the rock, dropping it onto the man's other leg. The leader shrieked as his bones snapped and broke through his flesh.

Deimos stepped back. "You may not fear Death, but you will fear what comes before It. Call it what you like, but suicide and martyrdom are one and the same." He touched Vrana on the arm. "Come."

They returned to their site in the woods. Vrana smothered the last embers crawling along the charred logs, trying to no avail to ignore the missionary's pathetic pleas from the field. Serra nodded at her as he moved about the area, covering their tracks. Lucan tore chunks out of the sides of their conjured horses to stow their blankets and earthenware and then went about his business as root and soil moved across the beasts' bodies to patch the wounds.

Vrana picked up her ax, which had been forgotten in the confusion, and turned around to find Deimos before her, one hand behind his back. "You should have killed him," she blurted out, surprised by her audacity.

"Lucan heard them this morning, before we woke. They were laughing, boasting how they'd kill us, take you—take you with them, a prisoner, to pleasure them as they spread the word of god. Our masks are worth money to some, but the young, like you, are worth even more. While you slept, we pretended to, and when they thought they had the advantage, they moved in. If you believe that man to deserve mercy, I assure you he is still waiting for it."

Vrana didn't say anything.

At that moment, Deimos revealed what was hidden in his hand behind his back. "Your mother said you may need to be reminded." It was a bundle of blue flowers with green markings that spiraled outward on the petals. "A snap of Delirium; she said you may need to be reminded of the names, too."

Vrana took the flowers from him, simultaneously moved by his thoughtfulness and revolted by the intentions of the Corrupted. She mounted her horse rigidly, still adjusting to the armor Bjørn had given her. Deimos took the lead, followed by Lucan, with Serra holding up the end of their formation. Body chilled by the strain of battle and biting wind, she pulled the faerie silk cloak close.

They were following the Spine, the highway which she had only seen at a distance during her third trial. They called it the Spine because it had once been part of a network that connected the northern lands to the southern, as well as all of the human settlements along the way. Vrana's people, however, made a habit of destroying it to prevent expansion and flirtations with war. The highway would take them to Nora, a small town by the sea. Afterward, it would eventually fall into disrepair.

Soon, they would reach the place where she had found the corpse and its silver necklace. She'd asked about the necklace the night prior, but her companions only shook their heads, said that it looked familiar, but that they could not place it.

"They do what they can with the Spine, fixing it when they can," Lucan told her, "but for no reason other than to show us that they can."

When Vrana asked how they had managed to dismantle a highway with so few, Lucan responded, "Our numbers were greater then. Now we must supplement our ranks with misinformation to keep them none-the-wiser."

This made Serra laugh, though Vrana was unsure as to why.

Cement pipes had burst through the embankment to their left, drooling fetid water down the hillside. The Spine had all but vanished as they passed valleys and crags. Vrana was glad for the midday sun, for in it no shadows could harass her as they had in the ravine during the third trial. She wanted to stop when she thought she saw Ødegaard's Hospital through the windswept forest, but Deimos didn't give her the impression he was a man who would allow delays. And when she heard Serra relieving himself while on horseback, she knew she'd no find support from the others.

Vrana looked down at her horse's stone hooves as they clapped against the uneven ground; mud sloughed from the beast's legs, while sticks and branches twisted free. Like most things, the conjured horses' time was limited.

"Deimos," she called out, "will these…?"

Her words became lodged in her throat as something collided against the back of her mask. She turned herself around, ripping free from the restraining roots, expecting to find Serra with a rock in hand and a smug grin somewhere inside the maw of his mask.

But he was empty-handed, pointing at something above her head. When she looked up, that something slammed into her once more. Heat rose to her face as she spun around, daggers out, trying to find what was hitting her. She could hear Lucan laughing, now privy to the situation, and when she turned after another collision, she found the culprit hovering before her.

Blix.

Fucking Blix.

She sheathed her daggers and snatched the crow from the air, ignoring his beak as it pecked at her hands. She searched him for a message, and when she couldn't find one, she held the bird at arm's length and began speaking to it as a parent would to a troublesome child.

"What are you doing? What's happened? How did you find us?" she said, unable to decide if she should be happy or sad by his sudden arrival.

She realized she was speaking to a crow, and while some could expect an answer back—and she most certainly did—the fact of the matter was Vrana did not possess such an ability. "I'm sorry," she said, smoothing Blix's feathers. "You followed me this entire way?"

The bird cawed and perched itself atop her head. Deimos, without stopping his horse, yelled from the front that Blix could stay so long as he was willing to let the group make use of his wings and eyes. Vrana doubted the bird's likelihood of coming through on such an expectation, for his greatest achievement in life was not shitting on her belongings every day, but only every other day.

"At the very least, Blix, you'll make a decent snack." She reached up and tapped the bird. "You'd do the same to me."

After dinner, they came to a halt and dismounted from their horses, abandoning the Spine as it bent eastward into the Dires, where the land was arid and cruel. The ground beneath their feet was a hard bed of shale that covered their armor in dust when broken. They made camp in the sparse patch of woods a mile from the highway, moving without words as they each completed their assigned duties. Beyond the woods, numerous torches sputtered in the dark, revealing brief glimpses of the buildings and figures upon the midnight horizon.

Through the withering trees, where the land fell away, Vrana saw, for the first time, the sea and watched breathlessly as its black waves crashed against the shore. She wanted nothing more than to stand among them, to feel their force against her body, to hear their secret words from faraway places. She found herself vexed by the shifting surface and how it seemed to stretch on forever, so much so that Serra had to nudge her back to reality on more than one occasion.

"Should we be this close to Nora?" Vrana asked as she took a heat rock from Deimos, who had decided against another fire.

"Well, any farther and it will be quite a walk," Lucan said, tearing off a piece of dried meat and handing it to Vrana.

"What do you mean?" she asked, lifting her mask to eat the meat, while Serra slurped something down beside her. "Are we going into Nora?"

Lucan and Serra finished their meals and stood up, brushing the crumbs off their hands. "We are," Lucan said, patting Serra on the back. "You're welcome, too, if you can keep your voice down and head low."

Deimos fashioned a robe from a brown blanket and threw it over himself. "You may stay at the camp with me if you like, but Nora has a library that sees little use from all but its mayor. You may find something on the Witch if you look hard enough." He cleared his throat. "And don't forget about your mother's request. I'll see to Blix if you go."

"I could do without seeing her again, that Witch," Lucan grumbled as he fastened two knives to each leg.

Serra grunted in agreement.

"I hope you'll fill us in about that sometime," Lucan said.

"Alright," she said.

They took off without another word. Vrana braced herself against the stinging wind as she followed her companions through the woods, pushing back the branches that clawed at her armor as she passed. Heavy, gray clouds limped across the black firmament, a warning of the rains to come. Twice, Lucan stopped Vrana, listening for things she had not heard, looking for things she had not seen. They ignored her when she asked quietly what was happening— information which she felt entitled to, given the circumstances.

She gripped her ax tightly as strange shapes flailed on the beach before them, telling herself Deimos would not have entrusted her to these men if they were not more than capable of defending her. *I don't need their help*, she thought. *I wouldn't be here if I did.*

They kept to the shadows as they crossed over a small stone wall and into Nora. The torches Vrana saw earlier were now nothing more than smoldering remnants coughing ashes into the night. A lone sentry tower, battered and vacated, stood watch over the empty streets. Vrana felt her heart beat fast as they walked between the stone houses.

Every footfall was deliberate, slowed to the point of near silence. Yet, despite her caution, Vrana could not help but indulge her curiosity: She peered into a nearby window and found an older couple in bed, the wife's head resting comfortably atop her husband's chest. She thought of Aeson and then thought about something else.

Lucan grunted to Vrana for her attention. He pointed left to a domed building on the edge of town that overlooked the coast. Serra was already gone when she turned to find him, and when she turned once more to ask Lucan what they were doing, he had gone, too. With no choice but to press on, Vrana did just that, abandoning her view of the shadow-swarmed beach for the shadow-drenched innards of the library.

CHAPTER XII

While Nora's library could not be compared to the Archive, the amount of effort put into its maintenance was more than enough for one to overlook its lack of scale and volume. The floor was made up of millions of pieces of stone that appeared as though they had never known a speck of dust, dirt, or sand. The walls were spotless and held portraits and paintings of people and places long since dead or destroyed. Every row of every shelf, eight in all, was filled. Even the air was clean, unlike outside, where it stung the eyes and tasted of salt.

Vrana tried to imagine who would have the time in a town such as this to make use of all of the knowledge here, but before she could formulate an answer, the scent of perfume swirled around her, and a woman's voice, low and gravelly, called out. "Can I help you with something?" the woman said, her words echoing around Vrana. "It's not that easy to get turned around in these parts."

Vrana's eyes searched the dark for signs of life, stopping on the candle in the distance and the open book beside it, the pages of which turned as though by a phantom reader. She listened for sounds of scurrying between the rows, for heavy breaths taken after being held for too long. She cast her gaze to the domed ceiling, following the sparse scaffolding, which suggested the dream of a second floor not yet realized. She thought back to the rocks in the tunnel leading to the Inner Sanctum and wished for their warm glow, wanting nothing more than to throw a handful of them at the shadows and reveal the coy woman lurking within.

"Who's there?" Vrana called.

"The bird speaks," the woman responded, her voice followed by what sounded like the loading of a mechanism. "Have you a song to sing, little bird?"

"I'm looking for something," Vrana said, trying to determine how much information to divulge.

"Aren't we all?" the woman replied, taking a step forward, her location still unknown. "But I expect your something is someone and that that someone is not one but two, and so I must ask you to leave, as you will not find them here."

Vrana didn't understand what she was trying to tell her, but she saw no reason for the woman to know this. "I want books."

The woman cleared her throat and deliberated. Finally, she stepped into the light, revealing herself to be of average height, dark of skin and hair, and graced with a worn face found only through hard labor. She held a crossbow at her side, and it was loaded.

Vrana shifted her weight, ready to dive behind one of the shelves as soon as the woman brought the weapon to her chest.

"There's no sense in moving," the woman said, tapping her fingers against the stave. "I'm a good shot. I don't miss my mark unless I've reason to."

"You're arm isn't... Corrupted." The words seemed to hang in the air as Vrana searched the woman for any indication of the crimson defect.

"Neither is yours."

"I'm not human," Vrana said defensively.

"Maybe I'm not either," the woman said, a smirk on her face. She lifted the crossbow. "Tell me..." Then, she lowered it as a scream pierced the veil of sleep that had fallen on the coastal town. "My apologies, little bird. You're looking for books?"

Could that have been Lucan or Serra? Vrana considered how they had slipped through the town with such ease; whereas she had once found it convenient, she now found it disconcerting. The woman leered at her as she weighed her options for escape, none of which seemed to guarantee anything but a slow, painful death from the loaded bolt.

Vrana's teachers had told her that conflict resolution came in many forms; that words could penetrate that which a sword could not. Sighing, she relaxed her arm and set aside thoughts of dismembering the woman. "Who are you?"

The woman laughed, caught off guard by the question. "Allinora, though none may call me that but my mother. Nora will suffice, and no, I did not name the town after myself," she said. "I am the mayor," she added, realizing Vrana had failed to make the connection. Nora cocked her head and continued. "I know better than to ask your name, little bird, but I do know that you're new to this world. You're the Caldera kind, aren't you?"

"I am," Vrana admitted, feeling increasingly uncomfortable with the situation. "I'm looking for books, old stories, about a woman, a Witch." She paused, swallowed. "She lives in a Void. She comes out of the water to twist and torture Corrupted."

Nora shook her head. She stepped away from Vrana, setting the crossbow down onto the table beside the candle. She stretched her arms outward, upward, and cried with delight. "Sorry," she said, "I've no books on that. There was a woman, though—and I suppose Witch would be the most appropriate name for her, now that I think about it—who came to our little town when the sea refused to do anything but spit back empty nets and lures. The men took to her, of course, like the bottles they took to at night to drown their feelings of inadequacy. Stupid, dumb, weak men.

"Their wives came to me, asked me to send the woman on her way. I'd been planning on it before they asked, but a lot needs fixing around here. That Witch, she was very pretty and charming; I couldn't fault the men for their lapse in logic, but I couldn't let them keep at it. There was something foul about her.

"What little money these families had left was thrown at the woman's feet, and I'm sure she'd no need for it. She took it, but I found it months later, hidden in the walls in the house she'd been staying in. Eventually, I grew tired of her giggling and the morons she had made of my workers and decided to be rid of her. The next morning I stepped outside and found her at sea, on the sea, standing, yes, on the waves, and I watched as my people walked one by one into the waves, choking on the water as they called out to her. Men, women, and children were all lined up on the shore, ready to make the plunge. They weren't afraid of dying, and that's just what they did on that shore. You see those shadows out there on your way in? That's them, their ghosts. Every night, for all nights since.

"I went back inside, found my crossbow, and when I opened my door there she stood, drenched and rotted. She laughed, touched me on the cheek with her hand, and walked off, disappearing in that mess of trees on the outskirts. Seems she was content enough to go on her own. Does that sound like your Witch?"

Vrana nodded, making a mental note of the similarities between Nora's story and those she had read and discussed with Aeson. "Did she ever return?"

Nora laughed, leaning back against the table. "No, she did not. You make for good company, little bird, unlike some of your kind. There are traders who pass through on occasion. I'll see what I can find on this Witch, now that you've piqued my interest. But don't hold me to it. I was expecting only three, but we've the horses to spare. Strange tidings in the North, I hear. For once, I think I knew something before the Bat did. Well done with the mountain, by the way; set the town ablaze with rumors, you all did. Rumors are welcome here. Anything to keep the worry away."

Vrana realized something about Nora as she rambled on, something which she suspected the woman would only admit to in the late hours of the night, when even humans take off their masks. She was lonely, incredibly lonely, much like the boy who roamed below Vrana's village, searching for solace in the words of the dead.

"What do you mean by 'strange tidings'?" Vrana asked, redirecting Nora.

"I heard the water has turned bitter near Geharra, and your people were on the move. Holy men came all the way from Penance with gifts and never left after Geharra's gates were opened to them. Some even passed through here a few days ago, spewing nonsense as they often do."

Nora yawned as she stepped toward Vrana. "I did not see the Bat for two months. I'm lucky if I do not see him for two weeks. Whatever you intend to do in the North, I fear it will be too little too late. But I do have two children from two mothers who would each like to see their fathers, traders, come home; so if you find them, please send them my way. Jakob and Richard are their names. It's a long shot, but you'd be surprised how small the world can be."

Sensing that their conversation had come to an end, Vrana nodded at the mayor of Nora and reached for the door handle. She contemplated and then her tongue loosened with curiosity. "What is it that the Bat does for you?"

Nora produced a flask from her pocket and drank it dry. "It is hard to live on these stony shores when there is so much life farther off. I maintain the flowers that bloom here. He cuts the weeds that try to smother them."

Lucan and Serra were waiting for Vrana at the foot of the library's steps, the four horses' reins in hand. Lucan asked Vrana if she found anything of use in the books, and she told him that she had not. They funneled the beasts through town as quietly as they could, but there was little that could be done to silence the clap of the horses' hooves on the hard earth.

Whereas their entry into Nora had been exciting, their departure was something entirely different: a mixture of alarm and trepidation as the air around them seemed to fold from the tension. Vrana sensed the eyes of the awoken following them through windows and doorways as they marched back to camp. She bent over as they passed through a breach in the town's stone wall and plucked an aquamarine Whisper that had grown there.

Vrana could feel her teeth chattering as the wind buffeted her from the west, where the shadows were dispersing into the sea. Her horse brushed its head against her mask affectionately, and she imagined it leaving behind a large patch of saliva for her companions to gawk at. Nora, both the town and the person, were not what she had expected, which, in some way, was exactly what she expected given the elders' penchant for withholding information. She would need to ask Deimos about the mayor's lack of Corruption, as well as his own reported disappearance, though she expected the latter to be brushed away or met with cold silence.

"Look," Lucan said pointing toward the forest. "Do you see it?"

At first, Vrana didn't, but slowly the moonlit darkness took on a shape, and then it became many shapes, all moving independently of one another, their colors fluctuating between a somber gray and dull white. Immediately, her thoughts turned to the Black Hour, and her hands scrambled for the pouch where the Skeleton's key rested, as though, by holding it, the item would keep her anchored to reality. Lucan and Serra displayed no signs of worry, however, and when Vrana realized the period for that infernal hour had already passed, her heart steadied.

"What is it?" she asked as the shapes became visibly human,

watching as they interacted with one another, oblivious to their surroundings.

"Echoes," she suddenly remembered. "They are Echoes."

Serra grunted in confirmation. The elders told Vrana and her peers in their youth that no actions were without consequences, that all choices would be remembered and felt throughout time, for time itself was alive. Others said that when the earth slept it sometimes dreamt of what had been but no longer was.

Vrana subscribed to neither theory and instead found enjoyment in watching the ethereal men and women before her pass over cobblestone streets and into surging crowds, the towers that loomed over them spewing flickering smoke into their future sky.

And then her enjoyment faded as the scene dissolved, quickly replaced by another comprised of tall buildings, speeding automobiles, and an act of violence in the foreground: a child bludgeoned in a small square of a room, his skull breaking off at the spine and rolling into the corner. More shapes entered as others faded away—airplanes, carriages, and fields of dying men—until the Echoes coalesced into one massive and terrible shape that was there for a moment, and then it was gone.

"They never fail to impress," Lucan said, with Serra grunting in agreement. "Some places are better for it than others, you'll see. Or maybe you won't." Lucan laughed, slowing his pace as they entered the thicket where their encampment awaited. "It's only fair that I take first watch. After all, it was my Corrupted who screamed."

CHAPTER XIII

The first had been a charming man, a lecherous man; a pauper who had happened upon Nora by chance and charmed its citizens, until he found himself abed with a grieving widow. He took all of the widow's love, even when it was not his to take, and then took her money, too. When he tired of the widow, he left, flicking his silver tongue at the first man or woman to cross his path. Those who called Nora home were not known for invading the privacy of others, but when the man's appetites became such that none but the children could satisfy them, a decision was made in secret by the townsfolk.

He had been waiting for Serra in a spare bedroom, dressed in rags that befitted his person, weeping as he clutched a lock of stolen hair.

The second had been a kind man, a generous man; a husband and father of three who had lived in Nora since before the building of the stone wall, when the trees were nearer and the sea crueler. He never took what was not earned, and went without so that those he loved wouldn't have to. He had a child in the Heartland with a successful business and a plot picked out near the Elys, where he could build a house and grow old in it.

He had screamed as Lucan pushed the blade into his heart, not because of the pain, but because in the man's dying moments, his sleeping wife had reached for his hand and smiled.

"Why kill him?" Vrana asked from within her cocoon of blankets and cloak, Blix nestled against her neck.

"It's not the first time this has happened, Vrana," Lucan said, stretching out his legs. "If we only killed those who we felt deserved it, then the Corrupted would be quick to realize this, and we would be passing judgment. Did your second trial deserve his death?"

"It must seem random," Deimos added, his voice barely rising above the howling wind. "The Corrupted thrive when they are united by purpose. So long as we remain a threat, so long as stories are told and nightmares of us are had, they remain in their lands—their lives, and the lives of others better for it."

Vrana shook her head. She looked at the horses tethered to the trees, their coats streaked with white moonlight. "But you didn't kill them because you felt they deserved it. She asked you to do it." Vrana had told them of her meeting with the mayor.

"Yes," Deimos said, "as she has done in the past. I told Nora of our need as I made for Caldera, and she told me of hers. Did the elders not send you into that forest to kill a Corrupted?" Deimos pulled a heat rock closer to his body. "This was the only way to make up for lost time. The elders approved."

Vrana remembered what Nora had told her about Deimos' disappearance. "How much time was lost?"

"Too much," he said, lying down on his side. "Go to sleep."

Vrana looked at Serra, who sat beside her, unmoving. She assumed he had fallen asleep an hour ago, but when she saw his eyes glint from the mouth of his mask, she knew that he hadn't. She stared at him for a while, trying to envision what it would be like to live without a voice. In her studies of the Old World, she found there were professions dedicated to the art of listening. She imagined Serra would be very good at this kind of work, should it ever exist again.

"Nobody expects you to do as we have done here tonight," Lucan said quietly. "But don't expect it to stop because you refuse to take part."

Blix pressed himself closer to Vrana's neck, his claws clamping down painfully on her skin. "I know," she said, moving the bird to her lap. "Killing doesn't bother me. I just need a good reason to do it." She bit her lip. "Do you think it works?"

Lucan laughed and lay down. "It has for the past two hundred years." He sat back up, as though he had remembered he was to keep watch over the encampment.

"I should know these things," Vrana said to herself, again bewildered by the decisions of the elders. She looked over at the tangled, bubbling mass on the edge of the camp that had been the conjured horses from Caldera. "So much time wasted on things that don't even matter. Old World politics? Old World religions? Fucking Old World subway stations?"

"Not all villages are the same, girl," Lucan said, shivering as he spoke. "You'll learn, you'll see. You may be thankful for all that fucking Old World nonsense one day. Go to sleep. You're distracting me."

Vrana knew that she was dreaming, because her father was alive. She was young, no taller than his waist, and the village was still a vast expanse begging to be explored. She liked the way she had to look up at him and the way that he looked down at her, and how his arms seemed to lift her from the ground so effortlessly. Never had she found a place more comforting than by his side or against his chest. He wore no mask when they were alone together, and she liked that, too. They were playing hide-and-seek in animal corpses when the dream came to an end.

"Vrana!" she heard Lucan hiss. "Get up. They've found us."

To whom he was referring Vrana didn't know, but the worry in his voice was enough to wake her up and send her hands scrambling for her mask and weapons. The thicket glowed with the light of countless torches, their hungry, orange flames flailing at the skeletal trees. Talk of revenge, injustice, and insurrection fell upon her and her companions from all sides, like one wall closing in upon the other. She came to her feet, hastily scanning the distance for signs of the Skeleton's keep, its absence another confirmation that the Black Hour had passed.

"Murderers. They are nothing more than murderers. Look, they sleep as men do!"

"I told you those were only masks."

"Christopher was a decent man. He didn't deserve to die in his sleep like a dog."

And then a voice familiar to Vrana cut through the rabble. "There, at the center," Nora said in a tone that suggested she was enjoying the fury. "Mind yourselves. They do not fear pain as we do."

At once, the crowd emerged through the trees, a closely packed chain of countless hateful, heaving bodies clamoring for warmth and bloodshed. Held in each Corrupted hand were shovels, pickaxes, knives, hoes, sharp rocks, and heavy branches—makeshift weaponry for a makeshift assault. Though he wasn't alone, it was Deimos to whom they spoke and spat, for the people of Nora knew and feared him most. They recited names like sins—Joseph, Alex, Liza, Howard, Christina, little Peter—and the ways in which they'd died—stabbing, strangulation, stabbing, suffocation, stabbing, strangulation—and demanded bloody expiation for the Bat's crimes.

At the behest of his drooling father, a boy no older than twelve threw a stone at Vrana and her companions, but it sailed off course, overhead, into the leaves. The horses snorted loudly, tugging to be free of their tethers, frightened of their owners, who had once treated them so well. More stones flew through the air, cracking against Vrana's armor, Serra's mask, followed by handfuls of wet feces.

"Someone must have followed us back," Vrana said as she leaned toward Lucan. She felt her stomach turn when she caught a glimpse of Nora with her crossbow. "She betrayed us."

"No," Lucan said, ducking to avoid a rock. "She did the only thing that she could."

Serra grunted and then pushed Vrana away. A townswoman came at him, sickened with the madness of the group. Nora's people watched and cheered as her hand scythe danced with Serra's sword. Vrana twitched at every deflected blow, stepping aside to avoid the townswoman's frenzied swipes. Beads of sweat leapt from Serra's body as he moved. The townswoman's scythe found his flesh and tore a chunk of it away. He didn't cry out in agony as his blood ran down the townswoman's skirts, but she did, as her blood ran down his blade, when he ran it through her gut.

In groups of two and three, the townspeople flooded the encampment, swinging their torches and their tools with abandon. Most were not skilled fighters, but with their numbers, it didn't matter. Vrana backed away, batted away those who were hesitant to engage. If they were to prevail here, how many would be left, and would it be enough to sustain the town? Hearing footsteps, she turned around to find a woman bearing down on her with a pitchfork. She went sideways, the prongs scraping against her armor, and took the woman's leg off with her ax.

A wiry, bare-chested man followed, armed with nothing but his massive hands. Vrana pushed a dagger through each one, and then screamed as she felt a torch being rammed into her back. Deimos wrenched the torch away and pierced the bearer's lung with his sword.

"Watch out!" Lucan said through his teeth as a bolt from Nora's crossbow ripped through air, catching one of her own in the thigh.

"Here!" someone cried out in the night. "They're here. They have them!"

As his father urged him onto her, Vrana pushed away the little boy who'd thrown the first stone. Again, he put his son before him, sending the child to Vrana with nothing but tears upon his cheeks. She swallowed her pride and knocked the boy unconscious with the handle of her ax. The father, outraged and somehow offended, launched himself at Vrana, driving his torch into her chest. Silently, she thanked Bjørn for the armor, and then took off the father's head. His blood sprayed into the holes of her mask; it burned hotter than the fire he carried.

For a moment, the mob was stilled, exhausted. Vrana reached into her mask and wiped away the sweat that had formed there. Lucan put his hands to his hips and struggled to catch his breath. Serra and Deimos stood stoically by one another, covered in blood and burn marks. A murmur spread through the crowd; those who had initially stayed back in Nora now emerged and bolstered the nearly beaten ranks.

A man with braided blond hair stepped forward. "It starts here!" he bellowed. "Too many have suffered at your hands. We will be haunted by your kind no longer!"

The crowd surged forward. Embers swirled around the thicket, catching falling leaves and loose kindling aflame. Vrana braced herself for the impact, trying not to think of her mother, of her father, of Aeson, and of all those she'd left behind. The ground shook beneath her feet. She thought she heard Lucan say something to her, but it was drowned out, not by the voices but by something else, something...

Vrana and her companions fell to the ground as a powerful gale swept through the area. It drank fire from the torches and places where it had dared to spread. The sweat and blood froze on Vrana's skin as the temperature plummeted. All sound ceased, smothered beneath a blanket of noise, a droning song of buzzing and clicking. Hate had united the horde, but now it was terror, as a black cloud descended from the sky.

The cloud slammed into the ground, covering Vrana, Deimos, Lucan, and Serra, and then it spread outward. Vrana could hardly lift her head, but when she did, she watched as thousands of black flies filled screaming mouths, as bare flesh wept bright blood from a million bites. Bodies of those who had fallen in the skirmish bloated around her, the insects funneling through each orifice, searching for innards to eat and a cavity in which to nest. Vrana reached for the young boy she had knocked out, but there was little left to hold on to. Serra put his arm around her and held her down, and as she lay there, breathing dirt, these words from the Old World journal repeated through her head: "*I wear the flies like a robe, and yet she doesn't mind. A thousand tiny deaths between us every time we touch.*"

The black cloud dispersed seconds later, leaving Vrana, Blix, her companions, and the horses untouched. They lay there for a moment, too overwhelmed, mentally and physically, to do much of anything else. Corpses exploded around them, sending maggot-covered chunks of fat and muscle around the thicket, the flies escaping under the cover of the gore. Vrana pushed herself up from the ground and looked at Lucan, who kept repeating to himself, "What the hell was that?" She knew well enough what the hell had happened: The Witch had saved them.

Her companions were not shaken or hysterical as others may have been, but there was a stiffness in their movements, a poverty in their words that told Vrana they were frightened. She was the first to begin packing, and by her example, they stopped their pacing, uncrossed their arms, and lifted their gazes from the ground to do the same.

The fires burned brightly in Nora that night and would continue to burn brightly for all days and nights to come.

"What happened back there, Deimos?" Lucan asked the next day as they entered the Dires of the North.

"Another gift from the elders, perhaps," Deimos replied, sounding thoroughly unconvinced by his own words.

A gift from the Witch, Vrana almost considered saying aloud. "What's that?" she said instead, pointing to a tall building in the distance.

Blix appeared to consider investigating it but chose to fall asleep instead.

"That is where the weak-minded go to die," Lucan said with disdain.

Deimos steered the horses away from the Spine to what Vrana could now see was a tower. In its shadow makeshift homes had been erected from wood and stone and animal hides. At its base, twenty-five or so Corrupted worked the soil with pickaxes and shovels. They dug with an intensity that made them indifferent to the blisters and boils on their hands, faces, and feet. The tower was constructed from a metallic material, but its smooth, achromatic surface gave off no reflections. A small boy brushed against it as he handed water to his mother and yelped as the tower's heat seared his skin.

"Do you see?" Deimos turned to Vrana. "There are no doors, no windows. There is no way in."

Vrana took her horse by its reins and led it around the tower, searching every inch of it for any evidence of an opening. Deimos had been right: There was none. On the other side of the squalid dwellings, she found even more Corrupted, some asleep on their beds of grass, others awake, nursing drinks from stone cups or bared breasts. They paid Vrana no mind. She was not a threat.

"I don't understand," Vrana said as she rejoined the group. "What are they doing?"

"The land was higher here, but they dug it out," Deimos said, scratching his neck. "They believe their god is inside. They toil in the day, searching for the entrance to heaven. At night, they say the tower speaks to them in whispers. There are many bones beneath us: They bury the dead and useless here as tribute."

Vrana looked at Lucan, who only shook his head. He tapped Serra on the back, and together they headed toward the Spine.

"Are they part of the same religion as the missionaries?"

"Same god, different practices," Deimos said, his horse trotting up beside Vrana's and nuzzling it. "They, the Scavengers, would sooner kill each other before working with Penance."

"They don't fear us?" Vrana watched an old woman in a dirty white dress cut into the carcass of a dead squirrel and suck on what fell out.

"They are in the presence of their god and are doing his work. They have no reason to be afraid."

"And the elders don't find them to be a problem?" Vrana asked incredulously.

Deimos laughed and the two of them joined the others at the

road. "I've asked the same question. They are more of a threat to themselves than we could ever be, or so the elders have said. But when supplies are low, they raid Geharra and the Heartland, for they've no coin to spend. Isn't it funny how the holy make the best rapists and murderers? If the elders would only say the words…"

Lucan cleared his throat. "I think the elders are just waiting to see if they do find an entrance, so that they themselves can take what's inside."

Serra grunted in agreement, his toothy maw stained with blood from the battle. He seemed to linger on the tower for a moment, and then he grunted again and took the lead, putting some distance between himself and the others.

"What's wrong with him?" Vrana asked Deimos.

But it was Lucan who spoke, his words hardened by hatred. "This is where we found him, where they cut out his tongue so he couldn't say no."

Vrana felt a chill radiate through her body as she watched Serra disappear over a hill wreathed in golden grass. "He's not human, is he?"

"No, but he told me once he had been born in one of their hospitals," Deimos said, kicking his horse to quicken its pace. "I think you're familiar with it."

CHAPTER XIV

Vrana let out a groan of pleasure as her bare feet sank into sand. Her skin became a story for the blind as the icy water filled in the place where she stood. She watched with excitement as the ocean tumbled over itself, each wave fighting the other to be the first to the shore. She couldn't blame the sailors of ages past for thinking the sea infinite, for even now she found herself entertaining the notion.

It pained her to have this experience without her mother and Aeson nearby. In the Old World, the humans had telephones to communicate with each other. Vrana wished she had one at this very moment, to call her mother in her basement and Aeson in his, to hear their voices once more before she entered the empire of the likely dead. To mark the bittersweet occasion, she searched the coast for components, found Wormwood roots winding out of a pitted rock—"What a strange place to grow."—and turned back the way she'd came, toward the cliff she'd descended to be here.

Vrana climbed the starved bluff slowly, muscles still exhausted from the battle outside Nora. The fog over the Elys was thick, obscuring all that didn't fall directly within arm's reach, and it seemed even thicker along the cliff. She'd asked Deimos if this was normal, and he'd said that it would soon pass. It had been Deimos' idea for Vrana to see the ocean, and given the weather, the idea appeared to be more of a quick test than an act of kindness.

"It's not that interesting," she heard Lucan shout through the murky, white air. "Deimos is starting to get antsy, and you know how he is. Up with you. Strange things live here in the Elys' fog."

Vrana grinned, stopping for a moment on a sturdy foothold. She cursed the beak of her mask; it kept scraping against the rocks. Blix tore through the air, his vision apparently unhampered by the fog, and in an unusual display of helpfulness, he began to leap between ledges, aiding Vrana in her ascent.

"You're only doing this because Deimos told you to," she said to the bird, her hands grasping the slick stones. "Mom would have a heart—"

A hand reached through the pale miasma and closed around Vrana's. Her stomach lurched, and her foot slipped loose from the bluff. She called out to her companions, but there was no response. Her mind immediately went to the daggers, which were fastened tightly at her side. With one shaking arm, she held onto the cliff, while the other felt for the Cruel Mother's talons. She yelled again, and then her body went limp as the hand weakened its grip. Her limbs scrambled for stable footing as another hand descended upon her.

"Deimos!" she cried.

Someone grunted. Serra peered over the edge. He shook his head at Vrana as he hoisted her up to solid ground. She brushed the dirt from her armor and kicked off the sand that had dried on her feet. Blix scampered over, taking up residence on her shoulder with a fat, wriggling worm in his mouth. She tried to look into Serra's mask to see his face, but even in the daylight, there was only darkness.

"I'm sorry," Vrana said, feeling foolish. "I thought... I don't know what I was thinking. Thanks Serra."

Hours away, miles ahead, the fog cleared with the midday sun, and what it left behind was perhaps more awe-inspiring than the ocean itself: Geharra. Even at a distance, the city's expanse was breathtaking. It was built upon a gradual slope, tilting upwards as it followed the landscape, until it was checked by a haggard mountain range. A massive wall encircled the entirety of the sprawl, with smaller walls sectioning off portions of the city from the inside. Domed towers and threatening spires rose out of the miles of stonework, while great golden and azure buildings with intricate flying buttresses demanded one's attention. Along each side of the ancient city, two green rivers flowed, the western pouring into the foamy sea, the eastern into the southern cradle.

"I had no idea," Vrana said, shouting over the turbulent waters ahead. "They should not have kept this from us. What are the others like?"

Lucan slowed his horse, falling back beside Vrana. "Just as impressive, if not more so, I think. Eldrus is greater in size, the architecture unlike any I've ever seen: black stone, precisely cut, with an air of sterility about it. I've only ever seen Penance from a distance, from the mountains it hides behind; the buildings were ghostly, nearly indistinguishable from the falling snow." Lucan slipped some food into his horse's mouth.

Vrana nodded. "And our village, Alluvia, that's east of here."

"Yes," Deimos said with a hint of despair. "If we'd the time, I would take you there. What did Nora tell you that night in the library?"

"She heard the waters had turned bitter in Geharra. She sent people to the city, but they never returned. Nora seemed to think this has been going on for a while."

Deimos contemplated for a moment. "Each city is different from the other," he said, changing the topic entirely. "Geharra is not unlike our own village, choosing representatives to make decisions for its people. Eldrus is a monarchy; though, this may change: All but one of the royal family of Eldrus was murdered two years ago. People suspect the survivor, King Edgar, may have had something to do with it."

Deimos paused, slipping into his thoughts, the muscles in his forearms flexing. "The leaders of Penance are chosen by their god, as well as those who were chosen before them. They scheme from their self-inflicted isolation." He began to breathe heavily through his nose. "The missionaries were not the first I've seen; there were others, before the disappearances, and after as well. Penance wants to become a part of the world again."

"When he gets like this, we could push him off his horse, and he wouldn't notice," Lucan mumbled, leaning into Vrana.

"No, I would notice," Deimos said flatly. "I am saying this because she needs to know and because the leaders of Penance have always looked upon Geharra with disdain."

Lucan cantered forward and planted his horse before Deimos, stopping the procession. Vrana looked to Serra, who only shrugged. All at once, with a snort of gratitude, the horses dipped their heads to the ground to feast on the grass.

Lucan ran his fingers across his pincers as a wise man would through his beard. "I've no love for Penance, but this is your land, Deimos. You know all of its secrets. Yes, they scheme, but they are also on the other side of the world. I don't know any incantations that would cause what's happened here. Not even the spellweavers are that talented."

"Lucan," Deimos said quietly, "I have not seen these parts in three months."

Vrana felt her throat constrict, her heart flutter: Nora had told the truth.

Lucan laughed, cocked his head, and then slumped in his saddle, taken aback. "Where have you been, brother?"

"Mourning at the edge of the world."

They rode to the gates of Geharra in silence, though Vrana felt that she was the only one who didn't understand why. A weakly muttered "Oh" from Lucan's lips told her that Deimos' inaction was not only excusable but, in some ways, expected. A short embrace between Serra and the Bat told the fledgling Vrana there had been a tragedy. But just as Deimos himself was a mystery to Vrana, so, too, was his plight; for no attempt was made, not in passing nor broken whispers, to bring it to light. A stronger woman who was confident in her abilities may have demanded an answer, but Vrana, despite the blood on her hands, was not that woman. Not yet.

"Vrana," Deimos said finally as they crossed an elevated bridge over the verdant marshes, "look to your left."

He'll tell you when he wants you to know, she thought to herself, and then did as he asked.

At first, she didn't see what he had expected her to—the foliage was thick, teeming with life—but then, there they were, in the shallows and the western river, fifteen in all: reptilian creatures covered in green and blue scales, with elongated heads beset by the black jewels that were their many eyes. Their bodies had a hint of humanity in shape and were covered in a sinewy substance not unlike a spider's web. Some plaited this mucous material across the surface of the standing waters; while others ignored it, choosing to crush the bones of unfortunate fish with their unhinged jaws. If not for how calm the others seemed, Vrana would have thought she had stumbled upon perhaps the cruelest of the Witch's creations.

"What are they?" she asked, watching with fascination as the creatures ambled out of the pools, arms heavy with soft, glassy orbs.

"The Merfolk; they are new to this world," Deimos said over the clap of the horses' hooves on the groaning bridge. "In the Old World, these creatures called the sea their home. More creatures, like them, will return should science remain stifled."

"The life of a sailor must be a lonely one," Lucan mused. "Beautiful is not the word I would use to describe them." He nudged a snickering Serra. "There," he said, suddenly sounding quite concerned, "on the ramparts."

Vrana squinted, spotting what appeared to be a white dog with a black face atop the daunting wall. "That worries you?"

"That's a cursed wolf," Lucan said, straining his neck as the animal padded out of sight. "An ill omen, if you believe that sort of thing."

"My mother said they had died out," Vrana reminisced, her voice fading under the surging rivers.

"Death does not die," Deimos said solemnly, "nor does It need the Black Hour to make Itself known. Come. We may already be out of time."

CHAPTER XV

The massive front gate was a lattice of corroded metal, raised high enough to allow a body to move under its jagged teeth. Beyond, Geharra stood silent and imposing, with no signs of life or any indication of what had taken it. Vrana volunteered to cross into the city first, all too aware of the fate that befalls those who go last in the horror stories of old.

"The air is so clear," she said, pressing her hand against the light breeze.

"The calm before the storm," Lucan groaned as he joined her.

Serra and Deimos followed, swords clanging against the ground as they went under. Inside Geharra, the light of the sun seemed weakened, leaving the buildings in an otherworldly glow. Vrana's heart trembled and stomach turned—a mixture of awe and unease. Dried leaves chattered as they skipped down the empty cobblestone streets, into wilted gardens choked with weeds. Battle-scarred cats and foaming dogs leapt and padded about their newfound kingdom, eying Vrana and her companions with hungry intent. Doors swung back and forth on their hinges, giving glimpses of dinner tables still set with food and belongings yet to be pilfered. Never had she felt such a terrifying loneliness before. Even the buildings buckled under its weight, backs bent like the old men and women who hold daily vigil at the graves of those whom they had loved and lost forever.

Deimos led Vrana up the stairs of the gigantic wall that protected Geharra, stopping a quarter of the way to orient her to the city. They had entered through the Southern Gate, where most lived. The

Western Gate was smaller, meant for access to the dockyard; and the Eastern Gate, when it was not being repaired, led outside travelers directly to the center of the city, where the market stood. Despite its name, the Northern Gate was not one but many, and it divided most of Geharra from the opulent edifices beyond it: the mansions built for two that could house twenty; the striking statues of dead royalty carved from rare rocks; the ancient churches on every corner, abandoned and godless.

"The ground is unstable there. None call it home, not even those who could afford to," Deimos said as they descended the stairs. He gestured to Blix; the bird took to the skies for reconnaissance.

"Why?" Vrana gripped the railing tightly, unready for her adventure to come to an end by way of a misplaced step. "It seems a waste."

"There is little division between the classes in Geharra. The Northern District is used as a reminder of when that is not the case." He cleared his throat hard, adding another tiny crack to his sickening mask. "Serra," he said as they returned to the street level, "you and Vrana will see to the waterworks. If the water has turned bitter, it is there we will find an answer. Lucan and I will check the gathering halls and churches for signs of Penance. If they've come, they will have wasted no time with the conversion."

"Do you think our people are still alive?" Vrana asked, wrapping the faerie silk cloak around her.

Lucan kicked a stone at his feet into the grass. He looked at Deimos and balled his hand into a fist. "Let's not get our hopes up." He shook his head at the Bat and brushed past him. "Penance didn't come here to take prisoners; otherwise, they would've captured the city, and we wouldn't be standing here like a bunch of fucking morons." He stopped in front of Serra and sighed. "Take care of the girl."

Vrana cocked her head. "I don't need anyone taking care of me."

Lucan laughed and shook his head as he waved off her complaint. "I don't want anyone taking you out, because you're too busy taking it all in. We need good warriors. It's a compliment. Come on, Bat, let's go."

The Piranha didn't need a tongue to tell Vrana this wasn't his first time in Geharra. He navigated the streets the same way a beggar would: low to the ground, close to the walls, always choosing some side passage or backyard over the main thoroughfare. He kept his bow near, one arrow in hand, one eye on the rooftops; and by his example, Vrana did the same. Through Serra's grunts and groans, she quickly learned his limited lexicon. She learned when to stop, when to go, and when to shut up, because her incessant chatting was getting on his nerves. Occasionally, he would pause their journey to the Western District to satisfy Vrana's curiosity about the city: He pointed to a carpenter's shop; a babbling fountain; a well that was covered in chalk. He led her to a playground with an overgrown automobile and a satellite dressed in armor to serve as a sparring dummy.

"They know, don't they? About the Old World? I know they know, but the elders have me second guessing everything," Vrana said as they turned down an alley.

Serra nodded.

"We abandoned certain technologies because we know better." She held her breath as she slid through the narrow gap, afraid that, if she were to exhale, she would become stuck. "What's... stopping... them?"

Without looking back, Serra lifted his arm and pointed to her and himself.

"What happens when we aren't here to keep the balance?"

He shrugged and grunted: *Maybe nothing.*

"Do you ever regret killing the Corrupted?"

Serra shook his head and slipped out into an open street. He turned around and took Vrana's hand and helped her through, her right arm turning red as it scraped against crumbling brick. "Me neither," she quickly added, brushing off her arm. "What if someone were lost on their third trial and wandered into the North? Not necessarily from Caldera, but I mean, if I saw Geharra, Eldrus, or Penance and didn't know they even existed... I understand the elders' reasoning, but the shock of finding out may be just as bad as knowing all along."

Serra nodded and led Vrana to the other side of the street, where a merchant's stall had been overturned. He cleared his throat and grunted: *They're incompetent.*

"You know," Vrana said, sliding around the stall and into another alleyway, "I'm not sure if I can tell what you're saying or if I'm just assuming you're saying what I want to hear."

This time, Serra did look back, and he laughed: *Does it matter?*

"They're manipulators, aren't they?" Vrana could feel heat rising in her chest. "That's why we focus so much on the past: to manipulate the future. But now they're manipulating their own people. Are we a threat, like the Corrupted?"

Serra grunted: *Could be.* He groaned and grunted and outstretched his hand: *Or maybe something is threatening us.*

"I keep rattling on, I'm sorry. Fuck, how did I even get here?" She bit her lip and shook her head. "Are you a homunculus?"

Serra started to laugh, kindly not cruelly, and disappeared into a home where the door had been torn off. Vrana followed after him, taking note of an icon writ in blood above the threshold. "I know I've seen that before," she said, analyzing the shape, which was a circle inside in which strange symbols were held.

Serra nodded, made a cross with his fingers: *Penance.*

They walked the length of the house and exited through the back. Vrana opened her mouth to ask the Piranha another question, but stopped as she began to retch. The wind was sour and slid over her like sludge, as though the air itself had putrefied. They were near the Western Gate, and the booths that once held hundreds fish now only held their bones and the insects that were brave enough to eat from them.

Serra coughed and put his arm in front of his mask to block the stench.

"The smell—I don't think it's the fish." Vrana felt lightheaded, hot spots of nausea dotting her vision. "What happened to Deimos? I mean, could he have really stopped what went wrong here?" She slipped on a streak of blood and caught herself on a chair.

Serra shrugged. He tilted his head and helped Vrana stand up: *No, he couldn't have.*

Vrana listened to the waves of the ocean beyond Geharra's great wall. They were dull and distant, just faint enough for her to consider that she was not hearing them at all. She gripped the chair tighter as the flies buzzing around the pink mounds of fish meat grew louder, until it sounded as though they were inside her skull. Sweat ran down her face, her back. She gritted her teeth and closed her eyes, and it was there she found her, the Witch, against a field of black, the skeleton of a bird at her breast, nursing bloody milk down its throat.

Vrana stumbled backward onto a chair and ripped the mask from her head. She pulled back her hair and wrung it out. She felt a vibration against her leg—or was it a muscle spasm? "I'm sorry," Vrana said, unfastening her cloak and stuffing it into her pouch. "There's something you need to know."

She told Serra about the Witch, more than she had told anybody else besides Aeson and her mother. He nodded and grunted as he did, and although she suspected he somehow already knew all of this, she was glad to have another person she could turn to for support.

"I wanted to see Geharra. I wanted to see everything, really," she said. Her teeth started to chatter in the harsh language of the cold. "But I mostly came to find a way to stop the Witch." She exhaled slowly, and this seemed to help the shaking in her shoulders. "I don't know what I'm doing or looking for. I just hope when I get close enough, she'll get scared, and when she comes for me, I'll be ready."

The Piranha shrugged. When Vrana appeared to have recovered, they moved through a series of archways opposite the fishery and the abattoir into a small building that consisted of a ramp and a desk. They followed the ramp downward, until it opened up to a large room that smelled of mildew and metal. In what little light was left from the outside, Vrana noted several ladders on the perimeter that descended even further into the earth. Serra stepped over a pile of chains that had undoubtedly been used to secure the front door and ripped a lantern from the sweating wall. Leaning in close, he spoke quickly, silently, until a small flame flickered into existence.

Vrana's eyes widened. She held her hand up, baffled. "You can spellweave?"

Serra laughed as he started to wipe away the layers of dirt on the lantern. Light spread across the floor with every pass of his hand until most of the room was illuminated. The snakes and beetles in the wiring and ventilation hissed and clicked and scurried out of sight. Spiders as large as fists climbed their webs to the rafters and crouched low in anticipation. A six-legged lizard with white eyes started to smoke under the light; it slipped behind the paneling of a large control box to hide.

Serra nudged Vrana on the shoulder, pointed to an old service elevator entombed in webs.

"This is the waterworks? There." She pointed to another bloody icon of Penance slathered on the floor. "I doubt very many of the pipes in the city still work."

Serra shook his head: *They don't.*

"Not yet, at least. Until they have the materials again. But there are pumps and wells and baths."

Serra grunted. He attached the lantern to his belt and descended the ladder at the center of the room.

"What if these cities were left here with the intention of helping future societies develop more quickly?" Vrana's voice tapered off as she entertained the notion. "It's all here. It's just a matter of catching up. The last kind thing the Corrupted did for themselves before the Trauma."

She sprinted over to the ladder and peered down into the passage. If there was an end, she couldn't see it. "Thanks for waiting, Serra. It's not like I can't see or anything."

The passage did have a bottom, but it came slowly, leaving Vrana much time to think. She surmised from the station above and the size of the city that this was not the sole entrance to the waterworks; rather, it was one of many maintenance stations that acted as waypoints to the corridors beneath Geharra. Ten thousand people—the city could comfortably accommodate ten times that amount, so why stop there? And Alluvia, why Alluvia? Hundreds of her people taken wherever Geharra went. If it was Penance, they would've surely passed Rime and Traesk before reaching this side of the world. Why not take them instead?

"Serra, what do you think happened?" Vrana gripped the ladder tightly; it was getting wetter with every rung passed.

Serra tapped his thumb against the metal. He rumbled from the deep of his chest: *They're dead.*

"In the Old World, they could kill ten thousand in a day."

Serra hummed: *Yes.*

"It wouldn't take much to finish off everyone else, would it?"

Serra grunted: *Not much at all.*

"We're newborns left to fend for ourselves in a wasteland."

Serra stopped and growled: *Shitty, isn't it?*

A deep puddle was waiting for their feet when they dropped from the ladder.

A mutilated corpse was waiting for their eyes a little farther on.

The man was from Penance, the clothes on his bloodstained back giving away his identity. Two broken bones in each leg told Vrana that the man had fallen from the ladder and the dagger between his shoulder blades revealed that it hadn't been an accident. Through a hole that had been gnawed into his shirt, she saw the same symbol, albeit far less ornate, that she'd seen on the young boy's back during the second trial. It was also the same symbol she'd seen at the checkpoint and in the house they'd passed through. The young boy from the second trial was from Penance. What had he been doing in the South?

"Serra, during my second trial I saved a Corrupted boy. I should've killed him with his father, but I didn't. I took him to the nearest town. I saved him." She felt an immediate relief from her confession.

Serra cocked his head, the Piranha skull staring at her askew. He gave her the thumbs up.

"Was I wrong to do that?" She went to one knee and fingered a chain around the corpse's neck.

Serra shook his head. He searched the man's pockets, producing from the largest a green leaf with sharp edges and crystalline veins: the Gift of Sleep. Vrana kept her surprise to herself; such leaves were very rare. They were said to be left by the Inferi, creatures that climb into the bodies of the restless dead and break their malevolent hold on the world, to prevent them from haunting the place of their death. The leaf, when given to the dying, puts their minds at ease about Death's Nothingness. When given to the healthy, the leaf acts as a strong anesthetic or a hallucinogenic. Her mother would want it and yell at her if she didn't take it.

The Piranha handed the Gift of Sleep to Vrana. Smiling, she returned to the chain and pulled the rest of it from underneath the shirt. "This," she said, fumbling for her satchel, "this is the same as..." She removed the silver necklace and laid it beside the dead man's on his chest. "They're the same!"

Serra coughed and scrutinized Vrana's find. After a few seconds, he shook his head and pointed out the differences: The dead man's was not forged from silver, but some sort of imitation of the metal; there was only one worm, rather than a tangle vying for control of the gem; and the color of the rock was much cloudier than Vrana's. Nevertheless, he ripped the necklace from the man and shoved it into his pocket.

"That means something, doesn't it?" Vrana asked as they rose to their feet.

Serra nodded: *It does.*

The waterworks' tunnel broadened as they proceeded, but the protruding pipes, roots, and crumbling walls made sure that Vrana and her companion earned their progress. Far off, she could hear hundreds of bats flapping their leathery wings, speaking to the darkness in piercing squeaks. As the tunnel twisted and turned, it didn't take long for Vrana to realize that they were going backward, inward, toward the center of the city, where the market Deimos had pointed to stood. She questioned the necessity of their trip to the Western Gate but kept this to herself, as Serra had become agitated since they'd found the corpse.

"The man I took the necklace from," Vrana said, ducking lower to avoid the lantern as Serra turned around, "he didn't look like that man back there or those missionaries near Nora. I didn't see any tattoos either. I think he may have stolen the necklace from somebody."

Serra hummed: *I wouldn't doubt it.*

"But his throat was cut. Whoever killed him had to have seen the necklace. Yet, they left it. Unless—" The sudden sound of surging water drowned out Vrana's words and thoughts. It was moving through the stones above their heads, which meant that they were close to the waterworks. "Unless…" She listened sharply now, hearing the strain of machinery nearby. "He killed himself. When I was attacked at the hospital—" she emphasized the word "hospital," but Serra didn't react, "—the thieves wanted it back. Either they intended on selling it, or someone had sent them to retrieve it."

Serra growled: *We're here. Be quiet.* Again, he attached the lantern to his belt. He moved several barrels in the tunnel to reveal another ladder and then mounted it. He flicked his finger against the iron bars: *Hurry up, girl.*

Vrana did as she was told. She descended the ladder, and when her feet found the floor again, she fell backward, as though all the oxygen had been drained from her blood. A bitter odor burned at her nose, in her nose, eating away the hairs and mucus. She went to take a step forward, but stopped herself, because she could feel the great openness of the space before her. In that humid, sweltering darkness, she could hear the slow turn of waterwheels, the steady streams along the aqueducts, the annoyed cadence of a restless reservoir, and the guttural groans of the sewage channels.

Serra raised the lantern to his face and spoke to the flame it held.

Expecting the fire to grow, Vrana found herself stunned as it leapt from its container and danced about the noisy cavern, setting aglow lamps, lanterns, and torches that had long since died out.

What she heard she now saw, and what she saw she now feared: Wooden platforms and stretches of scaffolding choked with pulsating roots from a massive growth, a plant the size of a tree; at the center, in the water, it reached up and outward, into the pipes, into the channels and aqueducts, its roots secreting a milky substance into the waters with reptilian indifference. Purple sprites, not unlike those in Vrana's basement, worried at the mass' core, but they couldn't break through the blight.

"I knew that couldn't have been right," she said as she took from her pouch the roots of Wormwood. "I found these on the beach. I don't know as much as I should, but I do know Wormwood shouldn't be growing there. The water here must lead into the ocean. That…" She paused, recalling all that her mother had told her about botany. "… Is a Crossbreed. I only remember it because I begged my mother to tell me about the ridiculous things people have tried to create. Wormwood, Death's Mantle, Black Fey, Nausea, Malaise, White Chrism…" She had tried and failed, for lack of ingredients, to recreate the experiment as a young girl. "This is what turned Geharra's waters bitter. It doesn't kill, Serra. They're not dead. The Crossbreed doesn't kill. The Crossbreed controls."

CHAPTER XVI

Vrana lifted herself out of the manhole and onto the street, her hands scrambling for Serra's as the ladder worked itself free of its bolts. Serra pulled her across the cobblestones and then let her go as she took off her mask and curled into a ball, her palms pressed hard against her head. She shut her eyes tight, but they continued to twitch and roll behind their lids. Serra handed her a piece of ka'thar meat; she shoved it in her mouth, but forgot to chew it. The world felt as though it had sped up and spun off its axis. She started to shiver, and with the cold sweat that poured out of her, the effects of the Crossbreed finally began to leave her system.

Able to focus again, Vrana opened her eyes and saw Serra, too, struggling to overcome his exposure to the Crossbreed. Sitting on the street, legs outstretched, arms limp at his side, Serra looked like a doll left behind by its master. With his chin to his chest, Vrana could see that he was constantly swallowing something down his throat. After a moment of this, he looked up, gave one final twitch of the shoulders, and nodded at her to show that he was ready.

They helped each other up and then helped themselves to some more food to silence their growling stomachs. Vrana swallowed the ka'thar meat he'd given her and drank the water from her pouch until it was as dry as her lips. Serra let her have a sip from his own pouch, and then, hand-in-hand, the two went on unsteady legs into the great and ruined market before them.

"It'll stop soon," Vrana said, putting her mask back on.

Serra craned his neck as he scanned the ransacked square, searching for silent thieves with sharp teeth and blunt knives.

"You have to ingest it for it to take hold," she continued, wishing to be out of her armor, which was irritating her already irritated skin. "It weakens your will, makes you more susceptible to influence. Penance put it in the water supply, and then they preached their way into Geharra's brains." She tipped back her mask to let the air run over her face. "With that much of the Crossbreed in their bloodstream, the priests could've made them do anything."

Serra shook his head and continued with her into the desolation of the market. A heavy gloom hung about the area, pouring over the surrounding buildings in stifling waves of gray. The sky sat low against the city, a murky sea of shipwrecked clouds broken down in marbled waters. They stepped over a puddle colored copper from the spilled paint running out of an artist's tent. Prized possessions of the poor and privileged clung to their feet, as though to be prized and possessed once more. Jewelry and expensive clothing rolled and slithered with the wind, now no more valuable than the dirt that scuffed them.

"I don't understand why they didn't fight back," Vrana said. She turned her head and outstretched her arm, receiving Blix as he landed upon it. "Blix!" She bobbed her arm, encouraging Serra to pet the crow, which he did gently, appreciating the life the little annoyance brought to the bazaar of the dead. "I hope you've something good to tell us," she went on, poking Blix's stomach, "because Deimos is going to want a report."

Serra groaned: *The Crossbreed.*

Vrana ran her hands through a pile of beautiful scarves, touching each petal of every floral print done in the darkly colorful Russian aesthetic. Her eyes found an African pot farther down the table, its rich brown coat decorated with diamonds of blue and white. The wind howled for her attention, and when she turned to answer, she noticed the hint of a Roman aqueduct in Geharra's architecture. *Did they extract from the past as we do?* She looked at Serra as though he could read her mind. *It shouldn't matter, the Corrupted's course must always be the same. If it wasn't, then how could we justify killing them?* She looked at Serra and was glad he couldn't read her mind; she wasn't sure she wanted to hear his answer.

Serra nudged Vrana: *What else do you know about the Crossbreed?*

"Sorry," she said as she admired the blade of a katana. "The

Crossbreed is supposed to be a myth. It's something every botanist tries to make but fails, because the components are not meant to work together. It's a game, a trick you play on apprentices. A long time ago, before the Trauma, someone supposedly grew one. There's an illustration of it, and it looked exactly like that thing in the sewers. I don't understand. From everything I've read about it, that's the kind of environment that it shouldn't be able to thrive in."

Serra shrugged one shoulder: *Maybe whoever wrote it all down lied on purpose.*

"Maybe. But how did Penance figure it out? And why not the other myths? The Bloodless would've made more sense. It could've drained the city dry over the span of one night. They chose the Crossbreed for a reason. Maybe everyone is still alive."

Serra grunted: *Controlling someone can be far worse than killing them.*

Vrana nodded and then went stiff. Footsteps. Yes, she had heard footsteps: slow, deliberate footsteps in the rolling fog from someone who didn't wish to be heard. She twisted her body, straining her muscles as she fixed an arrow in the bow and let it fly into the murk. A hiss of pain and a stumbling shape told Vrana she'd met her mark, while Serra's sudden grunt and grip on her wrist told her that she shouldn't have.

"What are you doing?" Vrana cried, ripping free of his grasp and losing some skin in the process.

"That was my fault," the shape or, rather, Lucan said (*Damn him,* Vrana thought), as he stepped into view. He winced as he rubbed at the bloody tear in his forearm. "Can't say I wished your aim was better."

"Didn't want something taking me out while I was taking it all in," she said. "I wouldn't make a habit of sneaking up on people."

"Far too late for that," the Beetle said, chuckling. "After all, that's how I met my wife. A witty remark and a slip into the shadows, and she thought she'd escaped me. Ten years begs to differ, I say." His stomach rumbled with discontent. "Apologies, drinks were drunk that were not meant to be. Am I not cheerier for it, though?" The sarcasm was almost as heavy as the alcohol on his breath.

Vrana stepped aside, and Lucan filled the gap between her and Serra. "I didn't know you were an alcoholic." *Careful,* she quickly thought, *he's not Bjørn.*

"Well, you don't know very much about me at all, do you?" He picked up a smock and shredded it with the pincers of his mask, making it a bandage for his dripping wound.

"Where's Deimos?" Vrana looked behind him, at Serra, who shrugged.

"Waiting impatiently up ahead." Lucan tightened the poor excuse for a bandage. "We found something, and by the looks of it, you two have, too."

Vrana and Serra nodded in unison.

"Are you glad you came?" Lucan asked, his question directed at Vrana.

She nodded. "I keep hoping we'll find Geharra and Alluvia, but if we do, then that means we'll find Penance, too."

"I wouldn't worry about that." The Beetle rubbed his pincers. "If we run into any trouble, I'm sure your Witch will lend us a helping hand."

Twenty minutes later into the mist, Vrana, Serra, and Lucan wandered into the appropriately named Fountain Square. It was a cobblestoned plot and meeting point wedged between the market and the Eastern District. Rising from the fountain's center was an abstract sculpture depicting Corrupted overcoming the amorphous threat to which each figure was connected. Deimos sat on the edge of the construct, peering into the dirty, leaf-choked waters that covered the bottom of its six-foot pool.

"Deimos," Vrana began. She proceeded to tell him and Lucan about the Crossbreed far below the city's streets. Serra grunted and nodded his head to confirm the Raven's tale. "If they were able to get the Crossbreed into enough people's systems, they could've easily taken the city over the course of a week or two. Or days."

"Envoys from Penance arrived in the city months ago. They bore gifts and apologies. They wanted to end the 'petty rivalry' between the cities," Deimos said. He waved the scroll clutched in his filthy hands. "They brought forty men and more food and drink and fineries than even Geharra could refuse. Fortunately for us, the council of Geharra documents everything." Deimos unrolled the scroll, removed a rectangular piece of paper from inside, and held it out for Vrana to take.

"You don't seem surprised by the Crossbreed," Vrana said. She took the piece of paper.

"Not at all," Lucan added.

The Bat rose up from the fountain and looked at his companions. "Very few things surprise me anymore."

Vrana screwed up her face at Deimos as Lucan mumbled, "What the fuck?" beneath his breath. She looked down at the piece of paper and instantly recognized that it had been torn out of a personal journal. It began with a review of the items presented by Penance to the council, as though they intended to return them if need be. Toward the bottom of the note, the scrawl became slanted, less formal, warped by worry and fear:

The Eastern Gate is shut; what little trading was being done has now ceased. No one is willing to answer my questions. Penance is here—the last to jaunt through now milling about outside—and they have brought gifts. Six crates, each an herbalist's boon. My happiness was surpassed only by my trepidation as I discovered amongst the jars curious ingredients— Wormwood, Malaise, Black Fey, Grave Soil— the presence of which was highly questionable among the other, more medicinal materials. I remember a legend brought to fruition in brief moments of madness and dreams. But what I've catalogued would not bring to life this Crossbreed. No, something is missing—a seventh box perhaps.

These people of Penance have taken an interest in our sewers of late, claiming to bring to our systems their refinements. They move in the disguise of good will through our very chambers. The rest of the council balks at my suspicions. Perhaps I shall do the same—move in disguise, that is—tattoos and all, like a proper priest from the Holy Order of Penance.

I am a tolerant man, but I cannot tolerate their preaching any longer. Already, they shout from the street corners, and already do our people gather to graze on their lies. Something foul has found its way into Geharra. I must root it out.

"The corpse in the tunnels," Vrana whispered in realization. "Who wrote this?" She handed the note back to Deimos.

"Geharra's master apothecary Ezra Miller. He sat on the council, too," Lucan grumbled. "We went to the council's chambers and also the chapels. Before Penance arrived, several smaller and already established groups of the Holy Order became very active. They knew they were coming, and so they paved the way." Lucan spat and let the cold wind wash over him. "Schemes upon schemes, made in secret, based on what could be if such and such…" He growled. "If you learn anything from this miscarriage of duty—" he looked at Deimos, "—let it be this: None are more dangerous than the entitled who feel they have nothing to lose."

Vrana thought back to the dying missionary in the bloodstained field. "What is this?" She leaned over the fountain's edge and pointed to clusters of vermillion veins spreading like fractures across the sculpture's base. "That's not the Crossbreed." She stood and threw her hands up in frustration. "Deimos, what the hell is going on? Those veins, they can't be here."

The vermillion veins to which Vrana referred couldn't be there, because the place to which they belonged was weeks away, on the eastern reaches, where it festered and fed on fear and rumor, seemingly sustaining itself on the violence and depravity committed by those it had called to fill its hellish corridors. While its origins varied and were seldom agreed upon, the name of the location itself was unchanging. They called it the Nameless Forest; for, like the Black Hour, it had no definable or constant features. But unlike the Black Hour, the Nameless Forest was not bound to time. It was everything that the Black Hour could be and worse; it was a physical manifestation of madness, a tumorous mass of the natural and unnatural twisted together and left to rot like a corpse upon the land. To the outside world, the Forest was innocuous and inviting—a sea of green leaves swaying in a forever breeze—but to those who'd entered and managed to return, the Forest was a place of infinite space and possibilities.

The vermillion veins, which were known to grow only out of the trees of the Nameless Forest, had once been of great interest to those early settlers who'd happened upon its infernal borders. Curious and careless, the settlers drank from the vermillion veins their vibrant drink, and saw through fevered hallucinations God and Its machinations. Their addiction led to their own destruction, however: The settlers turned on one another, dismembering friend and family until only one remained, a young child just as nameless as the Forest itself. It was said the boy emerged from the border town, gathered up every piece of every body, placed them at the Forest's edge, and to the sound of a bell then sank into the pile of hundreds of severed limbs, never to be seen again.

"The Nameless Forest is near Penance," Vrana said. She could feel her mind overworking itself to make a connection between the two. "Some say the Nameless Forest is ruled by five sons who were born from the rape of their mother, a maiden from the frozen North. What if... what if— is it possible they found a way in? If there's a place the Crossbreed came from, it could be there!"

Deimos shook his head, dismissing her theory. "I've heard stories of this before, Vrana. This isn't the first time the vermillion veins have been recorded outside the Forest. Cultural strain... when something truly awful has happened... they've been known to appear, like chalk marking a crime scene."

"Then they're all dead," Vrana said, lowering her voice and her head. "Then they're all dead," she repeated. Now it seemed the only logical conclusion, but why hadn't she considered it sooner? Geharra and Alluvia had vanished without a trace. Where else do so many go so quickly if not to Death?

"Who else was watching the city?" Lucan sounded heated, as though he meant to strike Deimos down. His hand rested on the hilt of his sword. "The elders were fools to trust you, but they were not foolish enough to trust only you to keep watch."

"There were five," Deimos muttered, his cold composure quickly warming to his companion's anger. "Two from Caldera, myself included, and three from Alluvia." The Bat spoke to Vrana now: He meant to teach her something. "Geharra requires little intervention. They manage themselves well enough and call upon us when they cannot. It's not unreasonable to think the other watchers were gone as well when Penance arrived."

"Then where are they?" Lucan countered.

Deimos stepped towards the Beetle, until both were close enough to kill the other before anyone else could stop them. "Is it not obvious what happened to them, to all of them?"

"We need to talk before I do something to you I'm going to regret." Lucan backed away from the Bat and removed his hand from his sword's hilt. "Vrana, Serra." He held the arm Vrana had nicked.

"We will eat here, in one of these houses. Where we're going—" He paused, swallowing the pain in his voice, and then didn't finish his sentence.

Vrana readied herself, checking her daggers and shifting the weight of her bags. She held out her ax, blocking Lucan's path should he try to move past. "And just where are we going?"

"The Northern Gate," Deimos spoke up, "where Geharra puts all its dead things."

Vrana couldn't taste the food, nor did she feel filled by it, but she ate it all the same. They occupied a crooked house with a black pointed roof, which loomed over the neighborhood like a hooded figure. The air inside the house was stale, as though it had been trapped there for years. It was a place of innumerable hallways and rooms, and each was marked and marred by holes and craters in the floors and framework. The companions searched the place, and convinced there was no one to be found, they separated once more— Deimos with Lucan, Vrana with Serra. The Piranha, apparently not used to the company of others, quickly abandoned the Raven for an empty room at the corner of the house and told her in three grunts to watch her step.

In her lonely wanderings, with fistfuls of food in her hand, Vrana stumbled upon a portrait yet to be completed, pools of dried paint still in the palette. The picture was of a mother and her young daughter, their right arms exposed, uncorrupted. Vrana's thoughts turned to Nora, and she wondered if those in the painting were distant relatives of the mayor. *Of course they're not*, she thought. *It's a mark of shame, of embarrassment. I'd leave it out, too.*

"I've tried, but I can't do it anymore." Vrana heard Lucan's voice nearby, and when she crossed into the room beside the portrait, she found it coming through the gaps in the floorboards.

She took off her mask and brought it to the ground with her. Deimos and Lucan were on the first level of the house and she the second. The material in between the two was incredibly thin and perfect for eavesdropping. Acutely aware of her surroundings, she looked up and scanned the room for evidence of its previous occupant's personality. The room was tilted, sunken in at the center, and clearly had not been cleaned in several years. She stretched across the floor toward one of several towers of journals. Removing one off the top, she found its pages covered in overly detailed accounts and observations of all the goings-on in the house. She saw that the other journals were the same in content, put back the one she held, and then brought her ear and eye to the ground, taking up the previous occupant's favorite pastime.

"Come here," Lucan said. He grabbed Deimos by the neck and threw him across the living room. "I understand why you did what you did, but look what you let happen!" He grabbed the Bat and knocked off his mask.

Deimos shuddered as the skull rolled down his back and hit the ground.

Vrana's eyes widened. She tried to call out and put an end to the conflict, but the sight of Deimos' face stopped her. He was bald, heavily scarred; one eye was bright blue, the other cloudy and white. There was a hint of a beard on his cheeks and chin, but it was too scarred there to grow.

"Get your anger out now, Lucan," Deimos said, picking up his mask and putting it back over his head. "We'll talk when you're done proving to the rest of us how much of a man you are."

Lucan screamed and punched the Bat in the stomach; then he closed in and held him. "I don't give a shit what happened to the Corrupted here, but you let our own people down. I know it's a strange concept to you, but there were ones that I loved in Alluvia!"

After catching his breath, Deimos looked up and wrapped his hands around the Beetle's neck. "You think I don't know about love and loss? You think I don't know?" he asked as he slowly choked the life out of his friend. "I made a mistake but, if it would bring him back to me, I'd gladly let the lot of Geharra and Alluvia die again. Don't act as though you wouldn't do the same for your wife, for your daughter."

Lucan gasped for air as Deimos released him. He held his neck, which looked red and sore, found the nearest chair, and sat in it, a cloud of dust rising over him as he fell into the cushion. "My daughter is in the backyard, no heavier than the stones that mark her grave. Nothing is bringing her back." He sighed, took off his mask, and set it on his lap, revealing his sweaty, splotchy face. "I don't have my medicine."

"I know," Deimos said, sitting beside him but leaving his mask on. "I like to think this would've gone differently if you had."

"The mood swings are getting worse." He shook his head to show he didn't wish to talk about the issue any longer.

Vrana jumped and stifled a scream as Blix sank his claws into her back. She wagged a finger at him, and then returned to the loose floorboards.

"Did you bring Vrana here because you thought she'd do well, or because she was a liability staying in Caldera?" Lucan looked up at the place through which Vrana peered.

Vrana scooted back, her heart pounding in her chest. *What is he talking about?*

"Both," Deimos said. "If I didn't take her, the elders would've found something else for her to do to keep her away from Caldera until it was deemed safe she returned."

"I don't believe Adelyn would agree to any of that," Lucan said.

"Adelyn would agree to anything to keep her daughter safe, even if it meant putting her in harm's way."

"Even if it meant lying about the North and the Corrupted cities."

"She wasn't the only parent. The elders are constantly testing the waters. When we were young, they sent us to live with the Corrupted."

Lucan put his mask on. "The elders don't know what they are doing."

Deimos stood up, outstretched his hand, and helped the Beetle to his feet. "The elders know all too well what they are doing. They just know too much to get anything done. They'll set the map back to as it should be and tell the students the truth."

"I needed someone to blame," Lucan said, still holding his friend's hand. "Everyone else will, too." He sighed. "You have to tell her what happened."

Deimos nodded: He would.

"Is she a liability being here?" Again, Lucan looked to the ceiling.

"What is she putting at risk? There's nothing left." Deimos shook his head. "No, she's not a liability. Her Witch saved us outside Nora that night."

Vrana's eyes darted back and forth as Deimos and Lucan left the room. She went to her knees and saw Serra standing behind her.

He grunted as Blix landed atop his shoulder: *Get up, time to go.*

CHAPTER XVII

Four creatures stood in the shadow of decadence, but only one was moved past the feeling of indifference. The Raven, with her sharp eyes and even sharper mind, put words to the images from the books she'd read and that she now saw before her. Rippled marble, scalloped stone, ornate arches, godly homes; aristocratic hideaways and idiosyncratic retreats modeled after postmodern gothic monstrosities. Here stood a testament to the Corrupted's ingenuity and craft, and yet the council of Geharra had made of its masterpieces mere symbols to be feared and forgotten.

Perhaps the Corrupted and Vrana's people were not so different after all.

"Wipe the stars from your eyes," Lucan said as he nudged Vrana. "All things are rotten on the inside."

They went through three small gates and checkpoints that guarded the Northern District, and once in the grand promenade they kept to the right, following a trail of sea-green paint long dried upon the ground. Large holes in the street marred the magnificence of the scene, while alleyways beside them plummeted into dark chasms. They passed a building brimming with golden flourishes, but through the windows Vrana saw it was bisected, its expensive innards having fallen into a glinting gulf than ran beside it.

The Northern District was the finest graveyard she had ever seen.

"This is where the secrets are kept and those who know them that should not," Deimos whispered. "Prisons sit beneath our feet. You can reach one from the second gate and another where we're headed."

"I thought you said Geharra was better than most of the Corrupt-ed cities." Vrana stopped for a moment, kicking free from the grasp of a tangle of vines. She wanted to continue challenging Deimos, but now didn't seem the time.

"It is," he replied. "It was."

Five minutes into the Northern District and Vrana felt an irritat-ing longing for Aeson which she couldn't explain. Her heart began to beat nervously, and her stomach became a cage for wayward butter-flies. *I should have waited*, she said to herself, as though withholding her feelings for him would have made this moment all the more bearable. *It was reckless and selfish*, she thought, absently kicking a pebble into a crack, *but then again, isn't it always? There wouldn't be so much written on love if it was simple, if it didn't hurt. I hope he's okay.* A smile formed across her face. *My mother is probably driving him crazy. I wish they could see this. Maybe one day.*

Fifteen minutes later and there was a smell so foul and permeating that Vrana's jaw locked shut and her nose closed, and breathing seemed to be something her body was willing to forgo for as long as it took to be clear of the stench. Her nose wrinkled, and she gulped at the air above like a fish, as though there was some pocket untouched by that fetid mixture of shit, filth, and sweat. She looked back at Serra and was comforted by his obvious discomfort. Deimos and Lucan appeared unaffected by the putrid odor, but then again, they were expecting it.

"Can we g-go a d-different way?" Vrana stammered. "I can't fuck-ing breathe."

"This is the way." Lucan coughed and dropped his head low.

Vrana covered her nose and mouth. "I heard you two in the house."

"You can fight," Deimos said, leading them through a park with a bloodstained merry-go-round, "but sneaking is another matter entire-ly."

"I wanted you to hear," Lucan said. "Thought I'd make a big sce-ne."

"This smell, this is Geharra and Alluvia," Vrana said.

Serra grunted: *It has to be.*

"Some may still be alive," Lucan said, hopeful. "I don't think Pen-ance's intentions were to murder the city and town."

Deimos nodded. "That much is obvious from the Crossbreed you two found." He brought them around the back of a mansion, where purple curtains waved liked flags of surrender. "Something went wrong. And if something went wrong, then there may be someone still alive."

"What does this mean?" Vrana watched as Blix flew ahead, high above the field of putrescence through which they trudged. "There's not a lot of our tribe left, and even for the Corrupted, ten thousand is a lot."

"It means the world is getting smaller. It means the Corrupted will come together, while we struggle not to fall apart."

Lucan opened a squeaky gate and let them pass through. "It means we've a lot of work to do."

"The elders wanted to get rid of me because of the Witch!" She felt like an outcast, even though she'd made herself one in her decision to leave.

Deimos raised his hand. "Not now, Vrana. Everyone, quiet."

Vrana tightened her grip around the ax and considered taking off the Bat's head.

Lucan pointed to Serra and then lifted a finger to the mouth of his mask.

Serra nodded happily and raised his middle finger in response.

One does not see the string of pearls among a heap of diamonds, and so Vrana was surprised when they veered into an iron-fenced yard and stopped before the steps of a beautiful church. Its front door was chipped, beaten in by overzealous parishioners too impatient to wait for heaven. From on high, its massive stained-glass windows scrutinized the city like drug-addled eyes. Around the foundation, holy inscriptions had been carved into the stonework, coupled with faded images of religious iconography entirely foreign to Vrana. It was from here and the black bowels of this basilica that the foul smell of lingering death originated.

"There is a doorway in the floor behind the altar," Deimos said as he started up the steps. "It leads to a tunnel."

"We'll follow it," Lucan continued for the Bat, "and see what lies at its end. When we've finished, if we're not finished ourselves, we'll see to destroying your Crossbreed." Lucan looked to Deimos for approval, who nodded in agreement. Through their fight, the men had succumbed to cliché and found forgiveness for one another.

"It's almost night. We'll rest here." Deimos cocked his head as he sensed words of outrage form upon Vrana's lips. "The odor will only worsen as we proceed. It's better to numb ourselves to it."

Blix rested atop the church's pinnacle and cawed: He didn't mind sleeping outside.

Several overturned pews like bulwarks impeded their way as they crossed the threshold of the church. Candlesticks and candelabras lay bent and broken in puddles of hardened wax. Pages ripped from their leathery bindings flapped overhead in the gathering darkness, held afloat by a permanent gust. At the center of the nave, a heatless flame burned in suspension over an altar, weeping ruby ashes onto its white linen cover.

"They filed in one by one," Vrana said as she followed the dusty footprints to the center. "All of Geharra and Alluvia." The smell of death and suffering here was so overbearing that, in some way, it made it all the more bearable. She turned around and, looking at the rows of pews, asked, "Who were they trying to keep out?"

"Those who knew better, those who the Crossbreed had not yet affected," Deimos rumbled.

Serra grunted four times: *Can you be immune?*

"I'm sure," Vrana said. "They probably had to find people who were to transport it."

Deimos nodded and brought his companions around the altar and into the eerie light, showing them the doorway that gaped behind it like a festering wound. It breathed back at them deeply, slowly; rancid air pressing hot against their masks and eyes. Serra was the most affected, the openness of his mask doing little to guard him from it. He stepped back and gathered himself, sighing and shaking his head, until he vomited onto a light blue tapestry.

"Hey," Lucan whispered, taking the Piranha by the shoulders. "Put your mind elsewhere." He waited until Serra nodded. "Different place, different time. Here's your chance to do what someone should have done for you, yes?"

Vrana knew he was referring to the Scavengers' tower and the taking of Serra's tongue. "Is this their church?"

"The Scavengers'?" Deimos shook his head. "No, this was a church of the Holy Order of Penance." He pointed to a large painting on the wall, which was streaked with the orange light of descending dusk. "'The Holy Child, who speaks and acts on his Father's behalf,'" he quoted.

Vrana strained her eyes to make out the child's face. He looked familiar, but the artist had taken some liberties with the boy's shape and features, presenting him as though he was an angelic creature pretending, and failing, to be human. She'd seen the image before but couldn't place it. "There's no Corruption on his arm," she noted, turning to face her friends.

"Why should there be? The god of Penance is beyond error." Lucan laughed. "There are those who have seen the child through open windows, though. They say his arm is no less pink than his peers'."

With night came the cold, and with the cold, the acrid breath of the tunnel was dampened and made more bearable. Using the contents of the church, Vrana and her companions formed a blockade between themselves, the hidden doorway, and any curious beast or body from the streets of the Northern District. Serra moved his mouth until a small fire was born in the middle of a book of psalms. Deimos urged them to eat, and they urged him to be quiet, for the thought alone turned their stomachs.

"Deimos," Vrana said as she held the silver necklace in her hands, the color of its red gem strangely similar to the altar's flame. "Where were you? Why did you leave?" She met his eyes above the Piranha's ghostly fire. "You've kept things from me. I've let it go long enough."

Deimos crossed his legs and placed his hands upon his knees. He exhaled as though he were preparing himself. "Far north of here, if you keep to the shore, you'll find a place before the Frigid Wastes, where the land stretches like an arm across the sea. The soil is thin, would be manageable, if not for the toxic fumes that surround the land bridge. If you breathe them in, they will blister your lungs and burn your throat and kill you before you make it a quarter of the way across."

"What's on the other side?" Vrana leaned forward; she knew there was a terrible thing waiting to be told at the end of this story, but until that point, she was hanging on his every word and loving every moment of it.

"The Dead City. The last remaining modern city of the Old World, untouched by the Trauma. Everything you've ever read about is there, abandoned and unreachable. If the Corrupted had the means, they would go there to take this world over again."

Vrana bit the side of her mouth as the wounds from the Horror of the Lake began to sting. *Not now*, she thought, *please, not now.*

Deimos huffed. He seemed to consider removing his mask, then decided against it. He started to scratch at his knees and shiver. "My husband Johannes and I were miles from Geharra, searching the outposts in the wilderness there. There was a woman, a fur trader we'd seen often in passing." Deimos' hands became claws; and he bent forward, and all at once, in the shadow of fire, his body darkened, his skin tightened, and he became as the Bat, hunched and hungry and hateful. "She told us of a pale green light in the Dead City and something massive moving behind the buildings. I thought nothing of it, but Johannes wanted to know more. There was no reason not to investigate, and I never could say no... say no to him.

"We left the next morning. Geharra was without incident and the elders without orders. As watchers, it was our responsibility to seek out of the truth of the claim, even though we knew we'd find nothing. No one ever does—that's why they call it the Dead City. We reached the land bridge a week later and slept near where the sea boiled. We used binoculars; we went as close as we could; there was no truth to the claims." Deimos stopped and leaned back into the shadows, so that he was no more than a dark shape with a bat skull. "Johannes, when he was younger, had an infection, leaving his right ear deaf. He didn't make for much of a sentry, so I often stood watch while he slept. But the night was quiet and the journey had been long. I lay down beside him, kissed him goodnight, and when I woke the next day, he was gone... and I was lost.

"I searched Mirror Lake and the snowbound forests—Hoarfrost and Gelid. I followed hidden trails to forgotten caves. I went as far as our village, Eld, and Corrupted's Eldrus. I didn't know what I was doing or where I was going. Eventually, I returned to the land bridge of the Dead City and wandered the shore there, thinking I'd find him in the waters, thinking something had taken him. My lungs seized and bled, so I turned back. At that point, I had lost track of time, of everything. But I did find something, finally: a cabin shrouded in icy willows." He began to pick at the skin on the tips of his fingers. "On the porch, I saw the hollowed-out head of a fox upturned, filled to its brim with snow. Johannes had been the Fox. It was Johannes' mask.

It was his." Deimos cleared his throat. "Johannes... he... it had been his.

"I saw him through the windows. His back was to me. He was sitting in a chair. I kicked open the door, but I was too late, months too late. What they had done to him.... I knew it was him, because he was mine, but anyone else—I don't think they could be sure. I waited until nightfall, but I knew his killers weren't coming back. They didn't do it for the coin, I thought. They'd left his mask, the only part of us that's worth anything to them. I waited until nightfall, and then I brought what was left of him to Mirror Lake and buried him where we'd first met. After that—after that, I knew what I was doing, where I was going. I hunted his killers, and I killed them all.

"I found the fur trader, and she told me there had been four, for they'd bragged in passing of what they'd done. I found the first in a small cottage along the White Whispers. I broke him, and then he told me where I could find the others. I let him live long enough to think he would survive, and then I threw his bones into the river. The last three found me midway, where the Spine kisses the edge of the Dires. They were hunting with their sons. They told me the woman, the fur trader, had orchestrated the killing, to rid her territories of Johannes and me. They didn't know why she wanted me left alive. But it didn't matter. It was done. I killed the men. In front of their children, I killed them, and I left the bodies there for the boys to bury.

"When thoughts of Johannes no longer brought me to tears, I returned to Geharra and saw that I had failed them, too. I have failed everyone. I hope that their sons find me one day. I look forward to it. I truly do."

Vrana's voice trembled as she said, "I'm so sorry, Deimos."

Serra grunted his condolences.

"I was wrong," Lucan said. He took off his mask and left it in his lap. "I'm sorry, brother. Not one of us would have done differently. If you had stayed, you would've died."

"If I had stayed," Deimos said, his words heavy with spit, "I might have been able to help. He might... he might still be alive."

I know how he feels, Vrana thought, watching as he wept quietly in the shadows. *Caldera... the Witch... if only I had made it back sooner.*

"No," Lucan urged, almost shouting. "No, you wouldn't have helped. They would've killed you or did whatever they've done down there to you." He looked over at the doorway in the floor behind the altar. "And then what? Where would we be? By the time the elders realized something was wrong, it would've been too late."

Deimos shrugged. "You say this now, but in the morning, when we find them, you'll hate me again, and you'll be right to."

"How do you think I feel?" Vrana spoke up. "I brought the Witch to Caldera. She could be there now, finishing everyone off. No, I know it's not the same, but in a way, it is. I heard you. They let me go to get rid of me. Until I kill her, I don't even know if they'll let me come back. But I didn't ask her to kill our people. You didn't ask Penance to take Alluvia and Geharra. Why should you feel guilty for the choices someone else made? I did, but I don't anymore. That's what the Corrupted do. They wring their hands and beat themselves up and don't do what needs to be done, and once they do, it doesn't matter, because it's too late. I have to kill her. You have to find out why this has happened. If it had been our people who did this to Geharra, would that make it better?"

Deimos mirrored Vrana's surprise as he nodded and said, "You're right."

"I don't know where this is coming from," Vrana said, chuckling. "I don't know if even I believe it, but right now, I think I have to. This is who we are supposed to be. This is what we're supposed to do. I'll cling to that if it helps get us through."

Serra grunted in agreement. He took a bite of some bread he had sitting beside him.

"She's gotten pretty good with her speeches," Lucan said, trying to lighten the mood.

Deimos nodded again. "I'm glad that you're here, Vrana. I wish that… I wish that you could have met Johannes. You would have gotten along well."

"One day," Vrana said with a smile, lowering the raven's head onto the floor.

Deimos laughed and looked away. "Maybe, yes. One day. Anything could happen in this strange world." He stood up and exited the church, but he left with more hope than when he'd entered it.

Sleep came easier than Vrana expected. She had only one dream. At first, she thought it was a memory, but realized when she woke that the moment had never occurred. In the dream, she sat in the warm stream outside Caldera, as she had done many times in the past when faced with a dilemma. Only Aeson had accompanied her to this place; yet, beside her sat her mother, braiding flowers into her hair. The surface of the water was like glass, and it fell slowly through her fingers in thick strands. Along her arm, a beetle crawled, its antennae quivering about its painted head. Atop the bank, she saw Aeson, and he didn't have his mask. He was speaking to her, but the words meant nothing to her. She turned to ask Adelyn what he meant, but where she'd sat, a small bird now floated atop the yellowing water. Vrana reached for the bird without hesitation and then pulled back as the stream bed gave way to gray Void. She tried to stand up, but she fell, and as she fell through the caustic, yellow water, she saw her mother floating beyond, but it was not her mother; yet, it didn't seem to matter, for she went to her all the same; and she took her, in tentacles.

"Vrana," she heard Deimos whisper.

"What?" Vrana said groggily. "What is it?" She felt for the handle of her ax.

"You were whimpering."

Whimpering? Her face flushed with embarrassment. She sat up and rubbed her eyes. Vrana was unmasked, but Deimos, like always, was not. *Does he never sleep?* She took a sip of water and breathed in the sickly air. "Are you okay?" she asked him.

The flames above the altar twisted in a helix, its light coloring the Bat with red violence. The mask, damaged as it was, appeared even more so, and now seemed as thin as paper. Deimos ran his fingers over the white markings on his body, where the nerves were deadened from disease. He nodded to show that he would manage and waited for her to lie back down on the hard floor.

After an hour of struggling to fall back asleep, Vrana turned away from her companions. Through a gap in the barrier they had created, she noticed something near the entrance. She strained her eyes, and then shuddered as she saw it with terrifying clarity: the cursed wolf, its face as pale as bone, watching her party with great interest.

CHAPTER XVIII

They woke early and said little to one another. The doorway behind the altar breathed its noxious fumes as belongings were packed and bodies were stretched. Deimos' and Lucan's swords met in a short sparring session, while Vrana and Serra watched, too tired to participate. They forced down what little food and water was left and then checked their reserves to ensure they hadn't spoiled.

Vrana excused herself from the church. The air outside, despite still reeking of rot, seemed so much clearer in comparison that it was euphoric. When he saw her, Blix came down from his roost and nibbled her fingers. She petted him softly, her hand shaking as it ran across his feathers, until she heard Deimos calling her name and telling her it was time to go.

Vrana headed back inside the church, meeting everyone at the altar. The doorway behind it in the floor opened up to a steep and narrow staircase of rough stone and thick condensation. They descended slowly, one after the other, with their hands pressed firmly against the walls to stop themselves from slipping down the steps. Serra whispered a fire along the top of the staircase to light their way, as Deimos told Vrana in short, agitated sentences that the church was one of many that had been built over sacred sites. Lucan whispered that the older sects of Penance thought these places could be used as conduits to communicate with their god.

"When Geharra found out," Deimos said as Serra's fire slid past him, "they built prisons down here to desecrate the area. The petty rivalry has gone both ways between the cities."

"We are almost there," Lucan said as dust cascaded onto him from above.

"How far did you two go?" Vrana asked.

"Only to the bottom of the stairs," Lucan said, looking back at her. His voice deepened. "You'll see."

And so she did.

The ceiling opened up as they stepped off the staircase and into a wide, unbending tunnel that had been carved directly into the earth. A dirt path lay before them, smoothed over by the thousands of feet that had shuffled down it to their deaths. Across the walls were thick smears of dried blood, sticky clumps of torn hair, and pale strips of hard flesh, all of which came together to form a mural of pain. Out of madness or humiliation, shirts, dresses, and pants had been stuffed into the cracks and crevices. Teeth and fingernails rolled and tumbled past Vrana's feet, as the tunnel continued to push its rancid breath through the hardened throat.

The first room they found was a large, spherical chamber occupied by several long tables, across each of which were stacks of documents, as well as inks and pens. The documents were torn, wrinkled, and waterlogged, and after Deimos pointed the detail out, Vrana saw that they bore the official crest of Geharra. The papers consisted mostly of names and addresses of those who called Geharra home. Vrana surmised that those whose names had been crossed out had been taken over by the Crossbreed and convinced to march into the Northern District. There were those, however, who appeared to have escaped the black line of the inquisitor's quill. If they made it out of the city, then it wouldn't be long until the rest of the Corrupted were aware of what Penance had committed here.

The second room they found was farther down the tunnel and smaller. While the death of ten thousand Corrupted was a calamity, the death of hundreds of her own was far worse. In this second room, stacked high in tall cages, were masks, hundreds of masks, bloodied at the neck, as though they'd been cut off from the heads of those that wore them. Deimos fell against the doorway, and Lucan fell against Serra. Vrana covered her mouth and wept harder for strangers than she ever had for most friends. *This is not just a tomb*, she thought, passing between the rows of iron bars. *This is a vault.* These masks were the spoils of Penance's efforts, to be traded and paraded for coin and regard. The venom of hate flooded her mouth as she spotted a severed foot still in its manacle. She knew she was a hypocrite to feel as she did, where she did, but she didn't care. They all had to die.

In the third room, which branched into several smaller compartments, they found five soldiers hanging from the ceiling, ropes around their necks, and a sixth on the floor whose rope had snapped sometime after he'd shit himself. Out of the pocket of the eldest corpse, Vrana saw a Polaroid photograph, its edges dirty with fingerprints. After they made sure the soldiers were dead, she removed the photograph and saw that it was a picture of a woman in a sundress and a straw hat, sitting with a drink in hand on the hood of a truck. The two had never met, and would never meet, and yet the soldier had fallen in love with this woman from the Old World. She returned the photograph to its place in the man's worn pocket, did one last sweep of what was now clearly a barracks, and left.

The fourth, fifth, and sixth rooms were cramped pockets of hollowed earth that had been dressed in the symbols of the Holy Order of Penance. They were chapels, places where the people of Geharra could kneel before their captors and seek forgiveness for blasphemy. Each room was fitted with an altar covered in white linen. Sacramental food covered the floor—breadcrumbs, leaves, and seed—filling in the places on the ground that had been worn away by the bloodied knees of prisoners. Toward the end of each room, there was a curtain, and when Serra pulled each one back, they found priests, their stomachs split open, bibles—*Helminth's Way*—stuffed inside.

Vrana backed out of the room, into the tunnel. The place was taking its toll on her. "They left everything behind. Anyone who finds this will know what they've done."

Deimos followed after her, drawing his sword at nothing in particular. "As I said, something went wrong."

The breathing grew louder, more forceful as they progressed. Serra's flame began to falter and sputter, as though the dark were water drinking its light. Somewhere, tiny creatures moved unseen, their feet pattering on the dirt, their teeth grinding away on bones. Just when the passage seemed as though it would never end, it split into two corridors, each identical and without any indication of what horrors they held. They chose the passage on the right, for no reason other than that it smelled worse than the one on the left, and disappeared down the panting gullet.

"This is it," Vrana said, the stench worsening as they went. They readied their weapons and did their best not to trip over the articles of clothing strewn about their feet. "What if Penance tells them to attack us?"

Serra breathed new life into his spellwoven flame and grunted: *Then we have no choice.*

They were so close now to the lungs of the labyrinth that there were no breaks between disgusting exhalations. The coppery taste of blood grew even sweeter on Vrana's tongue. The tunnel continued to split and twist, ovoid doorways hovering beside them like cloaked figures. They didn't stop, only peered inside them as they passed, finding large chambers choked with snakes of chains and small quarters with splintered beds. Farther on, fledgling roots from the far-off Crossbreed had burst through the walls of the tunnel; from their pointed tips, the roots dripped their signature milky substance into the bowls placed beneath them.

As another light worked its way through the stifling blackness, Serra pointed his finger and said with a grunt: *There.*

At first there was nothing, and then there was everything. They stepped onto a gently sloping ramp that ran in a spiral the outer edges of the great hollow before them. They steadied themselves as they neared the edge of the ramp, the ground still slick with long ribbons of red, and then, with wide and doubting eyes, looked over the precipice.

A lake of blood lapped against the rocky shore below, the surface choked with hundreds of bodies and thousands of limbs. Teeth and fat formed a chunky film over the sickening mire, only to be broken up moments later by intestines. Men, women, and children, bare and broken, bunched eagerly against one another, as though desperate to show to their onlookers what had been done to them. Heads were bashed in, eyes gouged out, stomachs split open, jaws ripped off; between their legs were bloody holes and stretched flesh, each penis, vagina, and anus torn apart by the pleasures of priests. Breasts had been chewed on and skewered, and mouths filled with sex organs that had fallen off or gotten in the way. Babies were bloated or obliterated—no more than a sum of disparate parts floating aimlessly among the dead. At times, the massive grave would shake, throwing waves of crimson and cruor into the air and onto the ramp. Those bodies that had swollen into veiny sacs of death burst, their guts blowing open and releasing waves of gas into the hollow. Other bodies, the softer bodies slipping into mushy decay, would simply break apart when the vibrations started, unraveling like long strands of pale, wet yarn as their entrails fell out of them in soggy handfuls. And when it seemed all there was to be seen, more corpses pushed their way to the surface; on a bed of shit, piss, bile, blood, and semen, hundreds of corpses, thousands of corpses, mutilated and desecrated, worked their way to the top of the lake, each layer more decayed than the last, until there were only bones.

Vrana pulled herself away, back peddling toward the tunnel as she ripped off her mask and vomited through her fingers. There was no telling between Corrupted and her own: in blood, all looked the same. Questions for which there would be no answers raced through her head. *That's everyone. That's all of them. That can't be. Why would they do this? This can't be right; this can't be all of them. This is the Crossbreed. This is the Crossbreed showing me what it thinks I expect to see.* She continued to puke and then retch. *Are they going to do this somewhere else? So many, so many. I can't, this is… I can't.* She slid down the wall, paying no mind to her companions, who still stood at the edge, stunned. *Maybe it was the Witch, or maybe it was the Skeleton. Fuck. Fuck, fuck, fuck.*

Vrana searched the hollow for a place to rest her eyes, trying to find something untouched by the blight. Looking up, she noticed a corpse in red robes crumpled at the top of the spiraling ramp. *Ten thousand Corrupted. Hundreds of our own. Two more times and there will be nothing left of the world.* Images flooded her mind from the lake of the dead—little boys with no lips, little girls with no hair, fistfuls of veins and arteries—and she started to whine and rock and hit the ground. *Will the elders even care? How many have we killed over the years? Is this so different? It feels different. Oh fuck.* Her eyes fluttered and wandered the hollow once more, stopping at a large gap between two large rocks at the lowest end of the ramp.

Vrana slid the raven's head over her own and gripped her ax tightly. Without a word, she left her shaken companions and traveled down the ramp. Lucan was the first to follow, with Deimos and Serra close behind. Guttural noises echoed off the chiseled walls, sending ripples of flesh across the lake. A bloody mist sprayed across the hollow, streaking their armor in gore. Vrana fought every emotion and biological impetus to keep moving. Her thoughts turned to home, to Aeson, and her mother, and then she pushed the thoughts out of her head, afraid their memories would be somehow sullied here. *No trial could have prepared me for this*, she thought to herself. *No one should have to be prepared for this.*

Vrana found the gap between the large rocks and noticed the makings of a room beyond. Again, as she had in the Western District, she felt vibrations against her leg but ignored them, thinking it to be nothing more than the rumbling of the lake. She gripped the edge of the entryway, her balance wracked by nausea and then pushed herself through, ready to kill whatever stood on the other side.

It was the prison Deimos had told her about, or at least a part of it. There were hundreds of empty cells that had fallen to rust, with bars bent and missing or broken off so as to impale. No stairs seemed to lead into this place, nor were there any discolored bricks to suggest a hidden doorway accessed elsewhere. *This is where they kept Alluvia*, Vrana said to herself, noting the feathers and scales from the masks of her people on the floor. She searched each cell rapidly for survivors, but found nothing.

"Did you know this was here?" Lucan asked as the lake murmured behind him.

Deimos shook his head. "No, I've never seen this before."

Serra groaned: *What do you know?*

"Listen," Deimos whispered. He tilted his head back to the wooden rafters above.

Vrana stopped and followed the Bat's example. Something was moving between the supports. Lucan disappeared into the shadows. Serra took to the walls, probing for outcroppings to hold his weight. The Raven circled the bloodstained hall, stalking her prey with murderous intent.

The beams creaked beneath the observer's weight, snowing wooden shavings onto the masks of Vrana's companions. Deimos undid his bow, nocked an arrow, and pointed it at the vague shape materializing in the dark. From his perch, Serra whispered a flame onto the arrow's end.

"Wait!" a girl's voice cried out.

Vrana's companions looked to her, confused. She shook her head back at them: She hadn't spoken.

Suddenly, a shape fell through the air and then landed nimbly on its feet. Quickly, Deimos trained his bow on the shape, the flames on the arrowhead turning white hot. It stood there for a moment, bent over, face obscured by hair, sweating skin glowing in the spell light.

"Stop," Vrana said, reaching her hand out as though to catch the arrow. "Stop."

The observer stood upright and its hair fell to its shoulders. It took a step forward, closer to the Bat, and revealed itself. "We have to leave," the girl said breathlessly. She showed her arms, which were free of Corruption. "We have to leave right now."

CHAPTER XIX

The girl was no older than fourteen, but her demeanor suggested otherwise. Her dark brown skin was covered in dirt and blood. Her hair was thick, matted; a white scar was traced onto her scalp, running from neck to ear. Vrana knew it had been days since the girl had eaten or drank, for her face was gaunt and lips chapped. She shivered where she stood, eyes like black opals fixed on Deimos' hideous mask, while her fingers twitched at her side.

"You're from Alluvia, are you not?" Deimos asked, staring down at the withered child.

She nodded, looking past him to the hollow as though to escape. "I've seen you before." She turned around to address Vrana, Lucan, and Serra. "Are you from Caldera, too?"

"We are," Vrana said. "How long have you been hiding?"

The girl shook her head. She licked her lips, bit off the dried skin from them. "We have to leave."

She started for the breach between the rocks, but Deimos stepped in front of her. "What happened here?"

The girl rubbed her face in agitation. "You don't understand."

"Help us, then," Lucan pleaded.

"Wait." The girl ran her fingers through her oily hair. "My mask."

Mask? Vrana watched as the girl hobbled on sore, calloused feet across the prison's floor to the farthest cell. *She's too young for a mask… isn't she?* Stone crumbled at the girl's touch as she moved loose bricks from the wall to the ground. A gasp, and then a sigh of relief. The girl returned, but not as she'd been: Over her head, she wore the body of

149

an octopus, the tendrils of which ran down her back and chest. It was slightly transparent, with a warm orange hue that flared when light passed through it.

"What's your name?" Deimos tilted his head as she picked up the dagger she'd dropped earlier.

"R'lyeh…" Her voice trailed off. "It's from a book. We choose our own names in Alluvia."

Serra grunted a tired grunt: *What happened here?*

R'lyeh sighed. After many false starts, she finally found her words. "I still don't know how they took us. It was late, and I remember waking up. There were horses outside. I felt bad all day. I went to bed early, and the soldiers were there when I woke up. I remember walking across the plains with my people. We were shackled. They treated us decently, the soldiers—always feeding us and giving us something to drink. But that didn't make me feel better. Made me sicker. I remember Geharra, all the people lined up in the streets." The girl's body went limp at the memory of defeat. "I knew something was wrong, but I couldn't put it together. Someone said we had been betrayed, but I didn't know what they meant. They led us through that church. Is that how you got here?"

Vrana and the others nodded at her.

"They pushed us past the crowd. No one cared. I thought they would kill us, but they didn't care. They took our names down, took our masks off. You couldn't see the bottom of the pit when they threw us in here." R'lyeh's voice began to increase in pitch, and the fourteen-year-old who had wanted to appear much older was quickly losing her strength. "I don't know how many people lived in Geharra, but I thought it would never stop. They just… walked off that ledge." She pointed to the overlook with the robed figure. "All day, all night. No one said anything, just did what they were told. At first, I couldn't hear them hit the bottom, but after a few days…"

"What were they trying to accomplish?" Lucan asked. "Did you overhear anything?"

"I, uh, there…"

We need to slow down. She's going to faint. Vrana opened the satchels at Serra's side and removed their reserves. She handed her bread and meat and a sealed canister of soup. The girl accepted the food without hesitation, but rather than gorge herself, she ate slowly, methodically, all too aware of the effects of starvation. *She's smart. She had to be to survive this.*

Vrana asked R'lyeh how long she had gone without eating, but the girl didn't hear her. Deimos sat on the floor, and by his example, the girl did the same, with the others quickly following suit.

"T-thank you," the Octopus stuttered as crumbs clung to her tentacles. "Whatever they were trying to do, I think something went wrong. I don't know when, but something was stolen from the leader." Again, she gestured to the corpse on the ledge. "And they sent people to find it. I heard guards talking about how they needed it and that the man—he was a priest, I think—decided to go on anyways. About a week ago, they had... killed most of my village and most of Geharra, and the bottom of the pit was... red. The priest said that their offerings were poor. That's when...

"Some of the guards wouldn't do it, but eventually, everyone gave in. When it started, they only beat them, but then it got worse. I saw everything, heard it in my sleep. The priest told... he told—he forced the men... the women, their husbands... the kids. I don't know why it had to be... When there was no one left, he made the soldiers go in the pit, and that's when the others turned on him and themselves. I—it was—after a while, it's not so bad. It doesn't even... I just pretended they were monsters—everyone—it made it easier not—not to care."

R'lyeh bit into a heel of bread and stayed there for a moment. A trail of tears ran down her hand and off her arm. "They came for what was left of Alluvia. We tried to fight them, but we were too weak. I saw an opening, and I got away; climbed up, up there. Everyone was dead the next day. I got my mask, ate what was left, but I heard voices, footsteps, and whispers, so I came back here, climbed back up, and found a hole in the wall." She started laughing. "I got turned around in there. I thought I was going to die. I was okay with that. I know there's worse ways now. Then I heard you."

"Are they all dead?" Lucan moved closer to R'lyeh. "Did no one survive?"

"I don't know." The girl pulled her knees close to her body, held them tightly. "The soldiers were from Penance, but there weren't many of them; that's why I couldn't figure out how they took over the city. I don't see how they could have done this without Eldrus or Traesk noticing. I wish you had come sooner."

Deimos sat silently as R'lyeh finished her portions. Serra grunted and mumbled a few more wordless questions for the girl, and she answered him with no difficulty. Vrana struggled to fathom the consequences of Penance's actions. *Is this how it starts? Is this how the world ends?* She felt homesick, and she found herself worrying about Caldera.

"What's going to happen now?" R'lyeh asked. The pit hissed as its bloody contents sloshed and spilled over onto the ramp, as though it had its own tide. "Will there be war?"

Deimos contemplated on this, then spoke. "The world is such that one city does not have much favor with the other. Eldrus will not respond unless provoked. People will want revenge and will seek it, but they will do so under their own banners." This was the Bat Vrana had initially met, cold and to the point. "Alluvia will not go unanswered, R'lyeh." He sensed that she didn't believe him. "I swear it."

Serra growled and groaned: *What were they trying to do?*

R'lyeh shook her head. "I don't know. They didn't speak much, the soldiers; only the priest did, and I think he had his own reasons for being here; he said he had to prove himself. I think some of them wanted to stop the killing, but they couldn't."

The lake's fetid waters seemed to have risen while they were away, washing farther up the ramp and leaving behind a stain. As they marched toward the top of the spiral, Vrana found herself staring at the girl, trying to determine if her composure was one fortified by shock. *We'll never be the same,* Vrana thought as she looked into the pit, watching an infant sink below the waters, its belly ripped apart. *Nothing will be the same.* How romantic it had all seemed, discovering the fate of an abandoned city. She wondered if she would have felt differently had the events not been clouded in mystery. Would she have approached Geharra, not with nervous excitement but burning hate and blinding pride? Yet, for all her revulsion and the doubts it instilled, Vrana knew with some sad certainty that this was still the place for her to be. *Maybe I should have been the Vulture; maybe that would have been more appropriate than the Raven.*

"There's nothing," Lucan, who had moved ahead with Serra, shouted from the top of the ramp. "It just ends."

With little else to investigate, they turned their sights to the ledge. The fabric of the corpse's robe was draped over the edge, hanging like hardened candle wax above the pit. The man appeared to be in his late forties. Around his wrist were golden bands with the sacred marks of Penance. In his fist, he held a small wooden block engraved with a circle. There were no marks upon his body to suggest a cause of death. Perhaps Death had been resentful of the man who'd done Its job so well and punished him for it.

Deimos inspected the priest for quite some time before saying, "To whom did this man answer?"

"No one," R'lyeh said. "There had been messages, but he threw them into the pit. He said he was doing the will of god and that no-body questions god." She laughed.

"There's not much to see here, Deimos." Lucan put his hands on his hips and sighed. "I say we gather what we can from the tunnel and be on our way. Blix can carry word of what's happened till we return."

Serra nodded, tapping his fingers on his sword's scabbard.

"My mom and dad! They're still alive. They left for Eld a week be-fore the soldiers took us."

"You're welcome to go where you please, R'lyeh," Lucan said softly. "As far as I'm concerned, you're welcome to do whatever you want."

Deimos agreed to this. "Vrana, take the man's charm, the object in his hand."

"Why do we need this?" she asked as she bent down and pried it from the corpse's clutch. She turned; something had brushed against her leg.

"Because charms are not given; rather, they are earned." He watched as Vrana flipped the object over. "And those who hold them are held as Exemplars of the charm; therefore, there can be only one who's its keeper."

"What does it represent?" She rubbed the smooth face of the charm, feeling something like static bite at her fingers.

"Restraint."

"A new Exemplar is chosen only when the previous one dies," Lucan said. "We can't trust that what we see here will remain here. This will tell the elders who this belongs to, because Deimos and I both know the last to keep it." The Beetle took another glance at the body. "And unless his god has given him the power to turn back time, that man is not Samuel Turov."

Vrana stood up. She felt an urge to kick the corpse into the pit but resisted. Again, something stole past her, and she spun in place, trying to locate it. R'lyeh seemed amused by her behavior, but Vrana was not. As she fixed her ax to her side and reached for the two daggers, she felt movement in one of her satchels. At this point, all of Vrana's companions were captivated by her performance. Eyebrows furrowed, she tossed the charm to Deimos and dug into her belongings for the source of the strange vibrations.

"What is it?" Deimos asked, stepping forward. He slipped the charm into a pocket. "Vrana, mind your footing."

The lake of the dead gurgled like a slit throat as bodies gave way to organs, limbs, and bones, building with themselves a monument of suffering. Vrana ripped the silver necklace from the satchel and held it high, its gem catching the light, and shone it across her companions' masks. The hollow went quiet. She gasped as her arm began to lower, not of her own will but by the will of the necklace, as though it had become heavy with intention. Vrana strengthened her grip on the chain and tried to push herself forward, but a searing pain coursed through her body. It felt as though the scars from the Horror of the Lake had reopened. Clenching her teeth, she doubled over and held herself, waiting for the agony to end. *Stop, please*, she begged, feeling lightheaded and unsteady.

"Vrana!" Lucan cried out, stepping onto the ledge.

She held her breath, looked up at the Beetle, and found that the pain had stopped. He outstretched his hand to guide her onto the ramp. She took it without hesitation. As Vrana's thoughts cleared, she realized that something was amiss. She pulled her hand away from Lucan's. The necklace. She scrambled backward, looked down into the yawning mouth of unending rot, and saw upon a ribcage the glow of the necklace's gem.

"Damn it!" she cried.

"It's okay, Vrana," Lucan said as he helped her to her feet, catching her against his body. "I saw Serra playing with one earlier. Maybe he'll let you borrow it."

"No," Vrana said, stepping onto the ramp. "It was…"

Her words were lost as a deafening drone shook the hollow, splitting stone and sending rocks into the lake of blood. All of the air in the burial chamber was sucked inward, past their feet, through their fingers and hair, into the pit. Vrana, shielding the girl's body with her own, pushed R'lyeh back down the ramp and towards the tunnel.

Deimos and Serra followed after, supporting Lucan, whose shoulder had been struck by debris. A red light flashed through the hollow and drank the rest of what little color was left in the grave.

"What's happening?!" the Octopus yelled into Vrana's ear.

The lake was no longer a lake, but a torrent of flesh and blood and bone spewing upward through the center of the hollow. Swathes of muscle and putrefying organs rained down upon the ramp. Thousands upon thousands of bodies were heaved from the pit; they twisted and tore through the air from the force of the explosion. Blood showered Vrana and her friends in thick sheets, flooding their masks and mouths with the taste and smell of death.

Holding R'lyeh closer now, Vrana felt her way to the tunnel; she could not hear the Octopus among the chaos, but was sure she was screaming. From the corner of her eye, Vrana saw something moving beside her, and thinking it was her companions, she turned to face them.

It was not Deimos, Lucan, or Serra, but a massive beast moving among the murdered, swimming through the river of gore, hurling itself at the earth, through the earth, until it was vomited onto the surface, where it washed in waves the plains with its vile afterbirth.

CHAPTER XX

There was little they could do but stare at the gaping hole above. Blood trickled and streamed down through the layer of roots ruptured by the beast. The sunlight, which seemed so severe, poured through the hole and revealed the grisly scene in all its detail. While there were still remains of Geharra and Alluvia scattered across the chamber, the majority of the dead seemed to have been taken topside by the creature.

Lucan groaned as he yanked pieces of rock from his forearm. "We need to go." His voice shook as he spoke.

"I'm sorry," Vrana said. *It's the attack on the village all over again.* "I didn't know. If I had known, I wouldn't have dropped it, went out there with it…"

Deimos shushed her. "We didn't either, Vrana. We all took a look at it."

"What was that?" R'lyeh asked, trembling; one more trauma and there would be nothing left of the girl.

"Let's get above ground first," Deimos said, trying to remain calm, while Serra moved aside rocks that had fallen in front of the tunnel.

Vrana felt numb. There was nothing she could do but keep going. She wiped the blood off the hilts of her daggers so as to grip them better. She set the bow on the ground; its string had snapped. Bjørn would be mad, but she didn't care. Serra took the remainder of her arrows and consolidated them with his own. She found herself staring at R'lyeh, and R'lyeh at her, as though one was waiting for the other to say something.

"Where are we?" Vrana asked as she heard the beast lumber overhead.

"Near the mountains, the eastern side of the city, I believe." Deimos had one last glance at the area, too wary to brave the blood-slicked ramp for more evidence. "Let's go, before we can't get away from it."

Lucan, sounding dizzy, said, "I think that's it. That's why they captured Alluvia."

R'lyeh turned around, desperate to hear his theory.

"People will come now, and they'll find the masks," the Beetle continued. "If they're convinced we can do something like this, then they'll either worship us or, the more likely of the two, hunt us to extinction."

Silently agreeing and about to leave, they then heard it: nails, scratching frantically at stone, and breathing, fast and hoarse and fevered. Vrana noticed the shine of Serra's eyes as he turned to face the hollow, bow and arrow in hand. Lucan pressed himself against the cobblestone wall and dabbed his fingers at the bloody hole in his mask. He asked Serra what he saw, but there was no reply. R'lyeh tried to leave Vrana's side for the Piranha's, but the Raven took her by the wrist and held on tight. The sounds grew louder, desperate. Serra nocked an arrow and pulled it back as far as his body would allow and waited.

A hand—rather, a claw—reached up and clamped down onto the ramp. Another followed, and then there was a head, a pulpy mass of flesh that housed a dented skull and two sunken eyes. It was covered in blood from its hellish ascent out of the pit. The thing didn't throw itself onto the ramp as one might expect; instead, like an insect, it outstretched one sinewy leg, planted it, and then pulled itself onto the ramp. Human. It appeared human, and had a wilted cock between its legs, but the way in which it carried itself seemed wrong to Vrana.

"A survivor..." R'lyeh whispered.

Deimos shook his head. "No."

Serra's muscles tensed and twitched. He loosed the arrow. It whizzed through the air and burrowed into the center of the man's chest. A thick, brownish fluid spewed from the wound; he pounded his fist on the ground. Skin began to drop from the man's body as he pulled at the arrow's shaft; he twisted it, tried to rip it free. The flesh sloughed off in wet sheets as though it had been grafted onto the beast, and from where it had fallen, pale white skin shone through, veiny and rough.

Vrana's eyes widened. She took a step back, blocking the girl with her body. "It's a... it's a flesh fiend."

At the mention of its name, the creature became still. It sat as a dog would, in a puddle of blood, as its stolen face sagged and swung back and forth across its true visage. Serra grunted and launched another arrow at the flesh fiend. The impact forced the creature to stagger back, off the ramp and into the pit. It didn't scream as it fell into the dredged lake, for it had long since mastered pain and all its forms.

"What the fuck is going on?" Vrana moved backward and encouraged R'lyeh to do the same. She strained her ears for the sound of the fiend's impact, but she only heard its brethren and their sharp claws clicking against stone as they scaled the sides of the pit, all too eager to finally climb out of untold ages of nightmares.

They ran, because that was all they could do.

Vrana kept R'lyeh close as they barreled down the tunnel. Lucan struggled to maintain pace with the group as more blood seeped from the wound in his head. The fiends scrambled after them on all fours, leaving trails of dead flesh in their wake. Serra fired several more arrows, catching one fiend in the throat, another in its eye. They collapsed onto the ground and then were dragged away into one of the rooms to be eaten later by their own.

"Almost there," Vrana whispered into R'lyeh's ear.

Deimos lagged behind the group, urging them forward as he unsheathed his sword. Arrows flew over his head and past his shoulders as he put himself between the creatures and the faltering Beetle. In the dark of the tunnel, it was impossible to tell how many flesh fiends had crawled out of the pit. Deimos braced himself and then started swinging, slicing off outstretched arms, groping hands, and wagging tongues. Limp bodies smacked against the side of the tunnel, clogging the path with their sputtering corpses. The flesh fiends' teeth chattered hungrily as they threw themselves at the Bat, and he knocked their crooked teeth from their white gums with his fist and elbow.

"Deimos!" Lucan cried groggily, having regained his senses and caught up with Vrana, Serra, and R'lyeh.

Vrana looked back; her heart pounded like a drum in her chest as a wave of flesh fiends swelled before the Bat. Deimos had reached his limit, and adhering to his own advice, he turned to flee. But he'd waited too long. He fell hard against the ground as a fiend dug two fingers into his calf. He screamed in agony as more fingers found their way into his skin and peeled it back.

"Take her!" Vrana shouted, leaving R'lyeh to Serra and Lucan's care.

She ran forward, dropped to one knee, and swung upward with her ax, running its blade into the closest fiend's mouth. She pulled down and kicked the writhing thing off and into the others.

"Leave me," Deimos begged, struggling to his feet.

"Shut the fuck up," Vrana cried, cleaving a creature in two, causing it to dump its intestines onto the floor.

"Vrana, please," he appealed, as though he truly wanted to die here.

"I'm returning the favor, now get the fuck up and go."

Deimos screamed as the tender, dripping wounds along his body tore further open with his movement. Vrana ground her back against his as they moved together down the tunnel. The flesh fiends began to throw their grisly costumes at the Raven, obscuring her vision as the flaps of flesh slapped against her mask. Two lunged at her, and she caught one under its arm with a dagger and the other with the ax through its skull. Arrows flew past her, knocking out the rest of the fiends, but at the same time revealing the others that had formed behind them. Their numbers, it seemed, were endless.

"Vrana, the staircase!" Deimos shouted.

Vrana nodded and hurried past the Bat, leaving him to the care of Serra. She found R'lyeh and, simultaneously, they buckled to exhaustion. Like flesh fiends, they climbed each step on hands and knees, but they kept slipping on the condensation that slickened the staircase. Lucan kicked his feet as hungry hands grabbed for his ankles, smashing malformed noses into malformed skulls. Serra grunted and groaned and wheezed as he conjured weak wisps of fire and flung them at the beasts, which did nothing more than singe their skin.

"There!" Vrana shouted, pushing R'lyeh ahead of her. She shielded her eyes from the blinding white light of the midday sun. "We're almost there!"

Don't stop, damn it. Vrana rubbed her leg, muscles burning from strain. *Don't stop.* She heard Lucan scream as four ribbons of flesh

159

peeled away from his side. *Don't stop.* Her hands landed heavily on the steps, the sound lost among the echoing madness. The inside of the church began to take form up ahead. *Don't stop.* She reached for the final steps, and, covered in the substance of hell, lifted herself out of perdition.

She threw herself onto the church floor, gasping. Like an insect caught in the light, R'lyeh crawled ahead and hid beneath a pew. With Serra came Deimos and Lucan; they pulled one another from the secret place. The Beetle and the Piranha stood behind the altar, stabbing and shooting down into the doorway as the flesh fiends hissed and spat, trying to get out.

"Vrana," Deimos grunted as he propped himself against the altar. "Help me."

The Raven did as she was told. The flame, which still burned above the satin cloth, wriggled as Deimos wrapped his hands around it, and as Vrana wrapped hers around his. Together, with what little strength they had left, they pushed the flame down, into the altar, and out of existence. Immediately, the door in the floor slammed shut, taking with it three heads, eight hands, and any hope the flesh fiends had for escaping isolation that day.

They gave themselves a moment to catch their breath and clean their wounds, and then they were gone. As they exited the church, they saw that large portions of the Northern District had collapsed, leaving massive piles of expensive rubble and choking clouds of dust. Looking to the furthest stretch of the northeastern wall, they found huge splotches of blood, a backsplash from the beast's birthing.

"Blix!" Deimos shouted, and from the sky, the crow wheeled toward them, until it was close enough to be touched. Deimos whispered a message into the bird's ear, and then he was off, back the way they'd come, back to Caldera.

They paused again in the market, which appeared as though a great wind had swept through it, leaving everything in a further state of disarray. Though they could not see the creature, they could hear it, feel it as it seemed to pace in debate somewhere outside Geharra's walls. Lucan took a seat at a workbench, removed his mask, and took a deep breath; Serra, without being asked, came over and changed the Beetle's stained dressings. R'lyeh, like the Beetle, was quiet as she picked pebbles and splinters from her feet and palms. Now that they were out and in the light, the girl appeared much smaller, more fragile. Whatever barrier the girl had put between herself and the events around her seemed to be working, but Vrana knew it wouldn't be long until it eventually fell.

"About two hundred and fifty years ago," Deimos started as he teased flesh fiend bone fragments from his calf, "there was a man by the name of Victor Mors. He was a scientist, a philosopher." Deimos lifted the bandages over the places where his flesh was missing. "He studied many subjects, but toward the end of his life, he became fascinated with the religions of the Old World. Six Pillars—now Penance—was a greater power back then, and as a citizen of Elin—now Eldrus—he feared them."

Serra and Lucan looked up at their leader. Vrana could see that they had heard this story once before, but appeared to have forgotten it or filed it away as bullshit. R'lyeh continued to work at her cuts, minding the neighboring bruises as she went. The hurt was a distraction her mind needed to keep from killing itself.

Deimos struggled to speak. "Victor Mors," he said finally, "felt that there was some truth in their tales about the end of the world."

Fresh blood trickled down the Bat's leg. He stood up, knowing that it wouldn't be long until he or the others wouldn't be able to if they kept sitting. He hurried through the market, leaving a trail of his misery for his companions to follow. "He did not believe it was something that was inevitable—rather, that it was something that could be provoked. Victor called this the apocalypse, using the oldest definition of the word."

"What does it mean if…?" R'lyeh asked, wincing as she tried to keep up.

"'To make known that which has been hidden in a world of lies,'" Deimos said. "He felt that this would then bring about the end of all things."

They rounded a corner and slipped into an alleyway. The gore-beast's rumblings grew louder, almost deafening. A hot blast of pungent air stole through the alley, melting their senses.

"According to Victor, it was the supernatural world that has been hidden."

They exited the alleyway into the Eastern District, where its portion of the great wall loomed ahead, with a meandering, lumbering shadow darkening its highest walkway.

"He believed that the end would come not when this was known but when those who were aware of its existence realized it could be manipulated."

"But that doesn't make sense." Vrana stumbled as Lucan fell into her. She lifted him up and handed him off to Serra. "The supernatural isn't a secret. The Corrupted know it and see it every day."

"There are many things still unknown in the fathomless spaces, the Membrane; things that, unlike the merfolk, the world will never be prepared for."

"The Worms of the Earth," Lucan said, almost laughing. "Deimos, not even the elders seemed convinced when they told us this story."

Serra sighed and grunted: *They haven't seen what we have.*

"I didn't think much of it either, Lucan, but now I see no other explanation."

"Worms? What the hell are they?" Vrana asked. "Are you saying that's what came out of the pit?"

Deimos thought on the question Vrana had posed to him and then nodded. "The Worms are not dangerous by themselves. They answer only to those who've birthed them and do only as they will. The Worms must be sustained by the substance of their birthing, or they will die."

R'lyeh batted an insect off of her mask. "How many are there?"

"As many as there needs to be, at least that is what Victor Mors wrote. They are weapons, and when a nation summons one, the next nation will do the same. You see, it's like giving a knife to someone who wants desperately to end their life. It is only when humanity is at its lowest, most depraved point that the Worms have a chance of being awoken, because it is depravity that calls them and in which they thrive. They serve their masters, and their masters alone, but only do so to hasten their masters' destruction."

"Here's the knife, kill yourself, stop talking about it and do it," Vrana said harshly.

"Exactly." Deimos quickened his pace, crossing through yards and doorways, under bridges and over ledges, until they were at the steps that scaled the Eastern District's wall. "Their only purpose is to speed up the inevitable."

"What's the inevitable?" R'lyeh asked as they climbed the stairs, the rotting wind buffeting their shivering bodies.

"Trauma," Lucan answered.

Serra grunted: *Ruin.*

"If that is, in fact, what has happened here, then Penance must decide if they wish to lay claim to what they have done," Deimos said, leaking blood down the stairs from his wounds.

Vrana felt a dizzy R'lyeh cling to her as they climbed the stairs, the city of Geharra shrinking in their haggard ascent. "Can Penance get away with this?"

"When you hold the keys to heaven, you can get away with anything," Lucan said, holding Serra's hand as he spoke.

"Victor may have been wrong. Then again, perhaps Penance knows something we do not." With all his effort, Deimos brought his flayed leg onto the final step and then waited for the others to join him at the top. "It's possible this has nothing to do with Victor's writings. But you do not do as they have done, kill as many as they have, to inadvertently create... that."

Vrana reached the top of the wall and gasped. The Red Worm sat upon the plains, a swollen mass of blood and bone. The ground below it was black and muddy, the grass brittle and bent. Hundreds of flailing tendrils writhed beneath the creature, drumming the ground in a hungry riot. The Red Worm moved like a centipede as it scurried in quick, unpredictable motions across the plains. Atop its body of rot and disease was a bulbous head with not one face but many, thousands, all stretched across the fleshy pillar in various states of untold agonies. It was difficult to determine how large the Worm was from the wall, but it seemed to stand at least twenty or thirty feet high; with one swing of its body, it could smash the whole of Caldera.

"What happened to Victor?" Vrana asked, feeling an out of body experience coming on.

"He was murdered." Deimos slid his hands under his mask and rubbed at his face. "Initially, Six Pillars were divided into six quarters, one for each of the surviving faiths. Assassins from the Lillian Quarter came to his study in Elin and cut out his tongue for his blasphemy. Once he had finally drowned in his own blood, they took his writings and disappeared."

"Luckily, other people had heard his speeches and took note," Lucan added, his voice distant, as though coming from outside his body. "It's been so long. We figured, I figured, the original meaning had been lost." The Beetle trembled. "If he had known, he would have never spoken a word about the things."

Vrana cringed as she watched animals pad across the plains toward the great moving grave. "What can we do?" The animals howled, yelped, and cried as they put their lips to the blighted ground and paid homage to their new lord of death.

"Nothing," Deimos said, turning to her. "We will do nothing."

R'lyeh nodded her head; she'd had enough. She moved her fingers absently through her hair, combing out the blood.

Lucan exhaled so loudly it was as though he had been holding his breath since they first left Caldera. His body went limp, and his armor moaned as it stretched and cracked.

But Vrana knew better, and so did Serra. The Piranha spoke, as he always did, from the deep of his throat: *What can we do?*

The Bat turned his jagged head to the halcyon sky. Vrana sensed the struggle within him to say the words that needed to be said that none wished to hear. "A convoy comes," he said somberly, pointing to the eastern horizon, where Penance soldiers rode on ka'thars, their shining plate mail the only hint of their approach. "Lucan and I will go to them and present ourselves as Corrupted. Serra, you will go back to the waterworks and reduce the Crossbreed to ashes. Vrana, R'lyeh…"

He looked at them with consternation, as though their task would be the most difficult. "You will go back to Caldera. You will tell the elders what has happened here. You will not question me. This is what must be done."

CHAPTER XXI

A red wind ripped across Geharra's plains, spreading crimson omens where it went. From the great wall, Vrana, R'lyeh, and Serra watched as the Beetle and Bat, holy robes slung over their shoulders, waded through the marsh outside the city. The merfolk welcomed the men into their drowned dominion and then stripped them naked. They took Deimos' and Lucan's right arms and weaved a spell into their flesh that left it deeply Corrupted. The men embraced the merfolk as old friends would embrace and then stepped out of the water, to make their way towards the soldiers kicking up dust on the sunburnt horizon.

Serra pulled away from the wall and his companions. Vrana and R'lyeh tried to stop him, by grabbing at his hands and tugging at his heart, but the mute had become deaf to their pleas. They followed him to the Western District, and the Western District welcomed them with salt upon its breath and a rattle in its throat, as thousands of fish bones rolled down its streets. Serra hurried into the water-works and then wreathed the doorway in fire, so that his companions could not follow after him. They said goodbye as smoke swirled around him, like a shade desperate to be touched, and he said nothing in response, for he had no tongue.

This was three days ago.

Vrana didn't allow herself or R'lyeh to stop until the city of Geharra had disappeared into the folds of the land. They had little left to eat and had slept even less; so, hours later, they made camp beside a stream and cased the area. In the belly of a hollowed tree, they waited for animals to pass, with Vrana's ax claiming a rabbit and R'lyeh's daggers—the Cruel Mother's talons—two squirrels, and three and a half frogs. The fire they built was weak, barely rising from its cage of kindling, but it was enough to cook the food and, for a moment, silence their stomachs' rumbling discontent.

The next morning they stripped off all that they wore, found the deepest part of the stream, and cleaned their skin until it was pink and sore. Vrana mixed some of the specimens she had collected for her mother into a soapy wash and scrubbed it into the girl, herself, and their equipment. Despite her best effort, Vrana could still smell the stench of the Red Worm, as though the very memory of it had begun to rot in her mind. She urged R'lyeh out of the stream when they'd finished, but the girl ignored her as she stared silently into the waters that had turned red with the blood of ten thousand.

"I can't sleep," R'lyeh said, turning where she lay beside the crackling fire they'd built. "It's all I see."

Vrana watched as the girl fiddled with the tentacles of her mask and then threw it. Just a few days ago, she had been like R'lyeh, removing the raven's head whenever she had the chance. Now, like Deimos, she kept it on, even when she wanted desperately to take it off, for without it she was weak, powerless—no better than the remnants of Corrupted that still stained its feathers.

"Were they your friends?" Vrana could tell it hurt R'lyeh to speak, but she was glad she made the effort.

"I think so," Vrana said. She took off the raven's head; the girl needed Vrana's strength, but she also needed the kind of warmth neither a mask nor a fire could provide. "I didn't know them as well as I would've liked. I think Deimos and Lucan will manage, but I'm not sure about Serra."

"Because of the Crossbreed? That's what it's called, right?"

"Yeah." Vrana pressed herself against the side of a tree and rubbed her back on the bark to snuff out an itch.

R'lyeh sat up, one hand holding her tired head. "Can someone be immune? To the Crossbreed?"

Vrana nodded and said, "I think so. Maybe that's how you got away."

R'lyeh lay back down and looked into the deadlights of the starry sky. "I just did what they told me because there were so many of them." Without asking, she took the faerie silk cloak at Vrana's feet and threw it over her body. "I tried to help. When we started fighting back, I tried to help. I didn't just run away."

"R'lyeh," Vrana said softly. "The only things we can control are the things we do. Could you have really done things differently?"

"No," R'lyeh said, shaking her head. "If I didn't run, the guards would've killed me, too." She stretched out her leg, slid her toe under her mask, and brought it back to hold. "I'm not old enough to have this," R'lyeh admitted, having already had enough on the subject of Geharra.

Vrana smirked. "Fooled me. And just how old are you?"

"Fourteen," R'lyeh said, as though she herself were uncertain. "I wanted a mask, so I made one." She held the shell of the octopus up and scrutinized it. "I think I did a pretty good job." Her eyes shone with welling tears. "I think I earned it."

She'll talk when she's ready, Vrana thought to herself, *but will I?* "You know, it's just supposed to be the head. Not the whole thing."

"It's an octopus!" R'lyeh exclaimed. "The whole thing is a head. I think it's pretty unique. I'm not sure if I can say the same for yours, though."

Vrana playfully kicked a pile a leaves at R'lyeh. "It's not like we have a choice. Besides, this raven was something else. I didn't just fire an arrow into the sky and take the first thing that hit the ground."

R'lyeh set down her mask. She picked at the dirt with her fingers. "You don't have a choice? In Alluvia we choose our own aspect—names, too."

"Not in Caldera," Vrana said, surprised. "My mother is of the Raven, so… yeah."

Again, R'lyeh sat up, elbow to the ground, hand to her chin. "What would you have picked? If you could've?"

Vrana began to braid her own hair, stopping periodically to inhale its fragrance. "A bee: No man can resist my honey."

R'lyeh's mouth dropped open. She tried to speak, but her big grin kept getting in the way. And then she was laughing, loud and hard; the kind of laugh that's mostly forced, but it doesn't matter much, because it feels good all the same. She wiped the tears from her eyes, but they came right back as she giggled and snorted uncontrollably.

"If things don't work out as a watcher, I suppose I could always be a comedian." Now Vrana was laughing, but only because R'lyeh's laughter was so contagious. *There's still some innocence left in there,* she thought as she shook her head at the girl.

"I'm sorry." R'lyeh composed herself. "I thought you were the really serious type."

"Well, I wish we could've met under different circumstances." Vrana grabbed R'lyeh's wiggling toe and tickled her foot. "But I'm glad we did all the same."

R'lyeh pulled back, annoyed but not offended, with the hint of a smile showing beneath her frown.

"What are your elders like?" Vrana asked, changing the subject, not wanting to let the girl in too close, too quickly.

"Smarter than the rest of us, or at least that's what they say," R'lyeh joked. "I don't know. They weren't around. But they were nice. They... they're the ones who sent my mom and dad to Eld... before Penance came." She lowered her head; she sounded sad, but there was something else behind the sadness, something like a lie. "What about the elders in your village?"

"Anguis, Nuctea, and Faolan... I haven't decided how I feel about them yet." *She looks up to me,* Vrana thought, *and what she sees she may become.* "They've done a lot of good for Caldera, but for some reason, they, along with everyone else, neglected to mention just how many Corrupted and their cities are in the North."

R'lyeh looked at Vrana, dumbfounded. A log snapped in the campfire, and a hundred burning ashes flew upward, threatening to singe the fabric of the sky. "That's really fucking stupid." R'lyeh covered her mouth and snorted: She was already more Vrana than Vrana had realized. "I mean, why?"

"Our keeper, Aeson—" She paused and felt that terrible happiness his name brought to her. "He told me once the elders hold back information so that we aren't biased, so that we can figure some things out for ourselves. But he wasn't talking about Geharra, Eldrus, or Penance."

"They tell us we have to kill Corrupted to keep the balance. That's not biased?" R'lyeh bit her lip. "Is Aeson your boyfriend?"

Vrana cocked her head and chuckled. "Yeah, he is." Had this been the first time she'd confirmed their relationship? Both to herself and to someone else?

"You sure about that?" R'lyeh bore her teeth as though ready to feast upon the details.

"Yeah, I am." Vrana turned her head towards the sound of a snapping twig, but there was nothing in the darkness, save for darkness. "Yeah, he's my boyfriend. I've just never said it aloud before. He's more than that, really. But yeah, boyfriend."

"My parents went to Eld to find out why there's so few births every year," R'lyeh said, abruptly changing the subject, which suggested to Vrana the girl once had a crush of her own. "I bet that's why they didn't tell you. Caldera is where the warriors come from."

"That's what they say?"

"That's what they say." R'lyeh nodded. "I guess the elders have to be more careful now."

"When we get back, I'll help you find them," Vrana offered.

R'lyeh shrugged and lay down, turning her back to Vrana.

The Black Hour came and went without incident. Vrana watched R'lyeh closely as she tossed and turned in her sleep, mumbling incoherent pleas to nonexistent threats. She wasn't entirely certain as to their whereabouts, but she was certain they'd at least crossed into the Elys. In the morning the fog would return and, with it, hours of endless wanderings through ghostly fields and untouched marshes. The sooner they found the cliff, the better; with the ocean at their side, it would give them a way by which to measure their progress. In regard to geography, the interiors of the Elys bore some similarities to the incomprehensible qualities of the Nameless Forest—paths appearing and disappearing, hills rising and falling, craters widening and consuming. Vrana and her companions had ridden through so quickly and confidently that she hadn't even considered the issue, but now that R'lyeh was in her care, that confidence was compromised.

Vrana took a sip of water and turned her gaze to the heart of the fire, letting the warmth wash over her in tiring waves, and then slept.

When she awoke, she found that she was in the Elys and that she was alone. When she stirred, the rust-colored grass beneath her feet broke off into small pieces, stabbing the dirt that flowed like sand. Heavy, fat drops of rain fell down around her, thudding against her mask. Her hands itched, and when she went to rub them, she found upon each palm a black semicircle. Shivering, she placed her hands beside one another and completed the dark shape. A peal of bells thundered across the corroded sky. From her palms and the circle upon them, millions of tiny, blue figures writhed like maggots. Vrana screamed and shook her hands, but the figures clung to the cracks in her skin. She stood up and bent over as her stomach split open, and something came through.

"Everything all right?" R'lyeh asked.

Vrana opened her eyes and then closed them to keep the storm out. She nodded and put on her mask. The campfire had all but died, and what little was left of it hissed in annoyance at the downpour. She had been wrong: There would be no fog, only rain, which, in Vrana's opinion, was much worse. Unsteadily, she wobbled to her feet and balanced herself with the ax. She felt like an old woman standing there: muscles sore and bones cold, body creaking like the floorboards of the Archive. If this was what it meant to be a watcher, then perhaps she would become a comedian after all.

"Take this," Vrana said, bending over and rummaging through her pouch. "It'll help." She pulled out the cloak of faerie silk and handed it to R'lyeh, who struggled to keep it from slipping through her fingers. "Now you won't have to steal it when I'm not looking."

"Thank you," R'lyeh said. She threw the cloak over her shoulders and pulled it shut. "I looked around while you were sleeping. Going south shouldn't be hard, but it's easy to get lost in these fields."

"If we follow the coast, we should eventually reach Nora," Vrana said, her words puffs of fog on the air.

"Easier said than done." R'lyeh laughed. She centered the octopus over her head and fastened the Cruel Mother's talons to her hips. "My dad and I were lost out here for a whole day once, and we weren't that far from the village."

"We can go to Alluvia, if that's what you want," Vrana said. "Blix will beat us to Caldera, anyways. Your mom and dad might be there, waiting for you."

The Octopus shook her head. "No, we don't have time." She took the satchel, which held the leftovers of their frog and squirrel. She dropped a large rock onto the campfire; a cloud of smoke enveloped her as she said, "I'm ready to go."

The storm brought misery to the Elys, and pain. The rain lashed like a thousand whips at once, until their skin was swollen and numb. The wind hurried them along and then pushed them back, tugging them in every direction but the one in which they needed to go. It wasn't long until Vrana's work in the stream was undone and their clothes and armor were covered in layers of mud.

But despite these deplorable conditions, the Elys was more alive than it had ever been. Mudwallowers, rockjaws, waterdancers, and bloaters scurried, slithered, spiraled, and slinked through the spectral stretches of grass, each one eating the other or their leftovers.

"I hate these," R'lyeh said with disgust as a waterdancer tried to scale the cloak with its twelve jittery legs. "We had a nest of them under our house. Every time it rained, they'd raid the kitchen for sweets."

"We don't have them in the South," Vrana said, laughing. "Are they edible?"

R'lyeh shook her head. "Poisonous, but if we find some puddle spawn, we could eat those."

Vrana stopped. "Puddle spawn?"

"Mm. They fall from the sky and live in pools and puddles, until the pools and puddles dry up. They look like grubs. They're kind of like food for the earth?"

Vrana wrung the water from her hair and turned them further west. "Have you ever eaten one before, R'lyeh?"

The girl hesitated. "No, but I've heard good things!"

Vrana sighed. "There have to be horses in these fields." She spied the outline of what appeared to be the weathered top of a cliff.

"To eat or to ride?" R'lyeh asked.

The Raven looked back and tilted her head.

"Y-yes," the Octopus stammered. "But not this far out, I think." Her voice tapered off. "What if," she exclaimed, "what if we followed the Spine?"

The plains rumbled as thunder bludgeoned the heavens. "Getting there is the problem," Vrana shouted as the rain started to fall harder. "Deimos rode through this place with no issue. No one said anything. In and out. Why do I feel I'm going the wrong way with every step I take?"

"It's silly," R'lyeh started.

Vrana reached the edge of the Elys and, leaning over it, found on the other side a steep drop and the churning sea. "What do you mean?"

"Some people think the Elys is cursed."

The ground beneath Vrana's feet crumbled and fell away. She

stepped back, heart somewhere in the neighborhood of her throat. "Cursed? What do you mean?"

"I guess no one tells the story in the South. They say there is a woman who lives at the center of the Elys, and that's why it is the way it is. She's never satisfied, so she changes her surroundings all the time. People get lost in the Elys because of it; she finds the lost and draws them in, to her home. We've found bodies before. She bites off their faces, fingers, toes… down there." R'lyeh paused and shook her head. "I don't know how they know, but the story goes she makes whoever she finds part of her family. Men are husbands, women wives, kids… kids. More were missing than were ever found. I guess some must make her happy."

Hiding her alarm, Vrana asked very calmly, "Do you believe the story?" and, more importantly, "What do you call her?"

"Something's killing people here." And then R'lyeh laughed. "The Woman in White Satin. I know, right?"

Vrana squinted with her mind's eyes and looked beyond the girl to a small house, its windows wreathed in candles and smoke rising from the chimney, with a swarm of flies darkening the sky above it. She looked farther still, through the window and into the house, where shadows slinked across the wall, wailing like infants, laughing like madmen. And then she found herself not in the field but the house itself, by a crackling fire that gnawed on wood like a dog would bone; and again, she was looking through the windows but this time into the field, where a strange creature with the head of a raven spoke to an octopus with twelve limbs, each oblivious to Red Worm that loomed in the distance, a mountain of flesh defiling all that it touched.

"I think if we forget about it, we'll be okay," R'lyeh said, nudging Vrana from her thoughts. "They say the Woman does it because her heart was broken by a king a long, long time ago. She eats the hearts, too, of course."

There's no forgetting, Vrana said to herself. *She's taunting me. Woman in White Satin… Maiden of Pain. If R'lyeh wasn't with me, I'd go straight to the center. But maybe it isn't you, Witch. Is there another? A sister? A copycat?*

It was an hour until the Black Hour, and Vrana and R'lyeh were so drenched that, if they were to wring out their belongings, they could've had a small lake all to themselves. By the time their jaws started chattering like gossipy skeletons around gravestones, Vrana knew it was time to make camp. She turned to the cliff for shelter, for the Elys had few trees, none of which could provide much of a reprieve from the storm. After an hour of searching, they found a small trail that ran along the side of the cliff, the path itself reinforced by planks of wood that appeared to have been placed there recently.

"Take your time," Vrana said as they followed the trail to the place where it narrowed. Ahead, sneering out of the cliff side, a cave promised stony comforts. Vrana went first, her back to the cliff; she shimmied across slowly, as the weathered path was not wide enough to do otherwise.

R'lyeh cried as the vicious wind buffeted their position. "Go faster," she begged. White roots of lightning spread across the sky. Her knees began to shake as the wooden reinforcements moaned and shed shavings into the sea. "I'm going back. I can't do this."

"No, you're not. Come here." Vrana shimmied faster and then stepped onto the lip of the cave, where the trail widened, ended. She held out her hand and waited for R'lyeh to draw near enough to take it.

"Vrana, please!" R'lyeh shouted, one leg giving out, sliding out, so that she dipped down, cracking her right knee against the rugged path. She screamed and swore as her left leg dangled over the edge. Fat drops of rain smacked against the cliff side, against her, drenching her. "I can't. I can't. I can't."

"Get up!" Vrana yelled. "After all you've been through, this is what does you in? Get up, R'lyeh."

The Octopus said, "You're mean," but then proceeded to stand up, her busted, blood-speckled knee giving her some trouble. She stopped, hunched over, and then crossed the rest of the path, falling into Vrana as she stepped off and into the cave.

"Sit," Vrana commanded, and R'lyeh sat. The Raven scoured the cave, which didn't take long, as it was only a little larger than her cramped room back home. Scuttle crabs snapped at her as she sliced through the shadows, but the crustaceans knew their place. "Trap the crabs with the cloak," Vrana told the girl, and R'lyeh trapped the scurrying crabs with the cloak, holding a handful of them down beneath the slippery material. "Crack 'em." The Octopus took out her dagger and slammed the pommel into each one, until the cloak was stilled. "These, too," Vrana said, pointing to another grouping of the creatures; she wanted to keep R'lyeh busy, until her mind was settled.

At the back of the cave, Vrana found scorched stone and a large pile of dry kindling and firewood. "Someone's been here," she told R'lyeh as the girl gathered up the crabs into a large pile of the dead. "But if they come back," she looked toward the entrance and the trail they'd followed, "I think we'll know."

"No need to worry about that," a scratchy voiced taunted, echoing throughout the cave. Pebbles showered down around Vrana as a face pushed through the shadows above, its eyes bloodshot and mouth bloodstained. "No need to worry about that at all. I'm already here."

CHAPTER XXII

Vrana took the man by his neck and pulled him out of the crevice. He hit the ground headfirst, squealing with delight as blood poured down his face. A banshee wind ripped through the cave, flattening Vrana against the wall, where the name "Gemma" had been carved. The Corrupted jumped to his feet, but R'lyeh sent him to his knees, with a quick cut that threw a line of blood across the rocks.

"Argh," he cried, squeezing his forearm where the girl had wounded him.

Vrana stood up and kicked the Corrupted in the stomach.

"Fitting it should be the Night Terrors who've come to claim my soul!" he sputtered, giggling as he spoke. "Here it is!" He curled into a ball. "Take it! I've no need for it. It's brought me nothing but despair." He wiped the blood from his forehead and made the icon of Penance on the cave's floor. "Make me soulless, like you."

R'lyeh's fingers tapped against the hilts of the daggers. She looked to Vrana for approval to kill the man, but Vrana knew it was more than that; she didn't need to see past the mask to know where the girl's mind had gone. R'lyeh was asking for permission, irrevocable permission to murder not only this Corrupted but all Corrupted to come.

"No, not yet," Vrana said, shaking her head. She eyed the Octopus until the daggers were lowered. "Who are you?" she asked the man, noticing his swollen ankles.

The man squinted and yelled, "You have a face—and a voice!" He uncurled and scurried back against a large boulder. "You're no Night

Terror."

Vrana went to one knee and ground the ax head against his throat. She felt his eyes looking up and down her right arm, in search of hidden Corruption. "Your name."

"J-Jakob," he gasped. He grabbed for the ax to move it away, but Vrana pushed it in tighter, so that he was choked by it. "Trader, I'm … I'm a trader."

Jakob? A trader? Vrana's thoughts returned to that night she'd spent in the shadow-swarmed, seaside library. "Where are you from?"

"Nora," he confessed. Vrana removed the ax from his neck. "Do you like to get to know your prey before you eat it?"

Vrana tensed. She had shown Corrupted mercy before: What would become of her if it developed into a habit? Thunder drummed the world, like two great fists pummeling the skin of the earth. The ocean crashed against the cliff in heavy, hateful waves, as though it meant to bring the whole thing down. She had shown Corrupted mercy before: What would R'lyeh think of her if she showed it now?

"You're safe," Vrana said in a decided tone. "Your mayor asked me to bring you home."

Jakob's eyes widened. He rubbed his reddening throat and pressed himself harder against the boulder, as though he'd meant to slip into another crevice to be away from his captors. "What do you mean?"

R'lyeh, throwing up her arms, said, "Vrana, what the hell?"

"Vrana…" Jakob repeated in a whisper.

"Where's Richard? It's Richard, right?" Vrana pointed to the dead scuttle crabs, and R'lyeh gave her a handful. "You went to Geharra. Share your story, and we'll share our food."

R'lyeh's gaze lingered on Vrana for a moment. "He's Corrupted."

"I see that," she croaked. "Should I kill him for that reason alone?"

The Octopus shook her head and slipped into the shadows, where she could nurse her anger unseen. "I'm sorry," she said, clinking the Cruel Mother's talons against one another. "You know."

"I know," Vrana said; she gestured for the girl to eat, and the girl ate. "Where's Richard? Should we be expecting him?"

Jakob shook his head. His eyes grew large, and his words came out all wrong and covered in spit. "He didn't make it."

"Tell me what happened, or you won't either."

The Corrupted raised an eyebrow at the threat, as though it were a promise he could hold her to. "That wouldn't be such a bad thing."

"Jakob." Vrana opened a satchel and tossed him a heel of stale bread. "On with it."

"Night Terrors…" His cheek twitched, and then he bit down into the bread and moaned. "My final meal. You promise to kill me, even after I tell you everything?"

"We'll see," R'lyeh answered from the shadows, having caught onto the man's madness.

"Mm," he said, taking another bite and then another, until the bread was gone, and he was chewing on his dirty fingernails. He wiped the fresh and dried blood off his face, picked a piece of black meat out from in between his teeth and smeared it on his pant leg. "You been there. I know you have. Did you escape, too?" He shook his head so violently it was as though he were having a seizure. "No, no, no. You went but you weren't there. Wouldn't be asking questions if you had. What's happened? When Richard and I gave Penance the slip, they were rounding them up, bringing them in. What were you doing there? Your people, I mean. How'd they find you?" He laughed and then cringed as he held his side where something was broken or strained. "Faces, voices, villages? I should like to see your face, but I'm afraid it'll look like ours. I thought about killing myself, but I can't seem to do it; not for lack of trying, mind you. I just can't seem to die." He pointed to his ankle, to his side; he showed his wrists, and there were deep cuts running horizontally from them. "That must make me god, and you my minions." He laughed some more, and then he started to weep.

"How long have you been here? And how long were you in Geharra?"

"I don't know, and two weeks." Jakob leaned forward and closed his eyes.

"Start from the beginning."

"My mother's womb was cramped, but it was comfortable. My twin must've tasted good, because I ate him up early on."

Vrana looked over her shoulder at R'lyeh, who flashed the daggers.

"Ha!" he said; a long trail of yellow vomit dripped from his pursed lips. "We'd traveled the Elys before. Most of us from Nora have. It wasn't a problem, never is a problem. We got to Geharra and set up in the market, between Myrtle's Emporium and Myra's Meat Store.

We let them know how much we missed them, which only took a moment—don't judge—and then we went to work.

"We were doing well for ourselves, selling our wares as we'd done—toys for children, tonics for their parents. It's not the kind of business that'll make you rich, but like you, Night Terror, coin isn't my greatest concern in this world. What do you barter with, creature?" Jakob pointed one crooked finger at Vrana. "Is blood the only currency you know? It's the most enduring, that's for sure."

"What happened next?" Vrana asked, sitting down beside R'lyeh.

"Penance." Jakob tipped his head at the holy icon he'd written in his own blood. "They were there when they weren't. You know? It was like they were hidden under all the beds, in all the closets. I see you're having a hard time following my phrasings: They came out of nowhere. There weren't many of them, but it was one hell of a fucking surprise. You don't see that every day in Geharra. We're not smart men, Richard and I, but when the holy come to a city full of sinners, you needn't be very smart to know it's time to go."

R'lyeh shifted in the shadows. "Sinners?"

"Geharra's no worse than anywhere else, but every hero needs its nemesis, and Geharra is Penance's. I reckon we saw forty or fifty or sixty soldiers come through the Eastern Gates. Not many, but enough. We started our packing, and when we were about to be on our way, the council and Geharran guard sealed the city up. No one was getting out. 'Struck a deal they must've,' Richard said, and that made sense. Made a lot of sense. I don't know if you sons of bitches have time to keep up on current events between all your senseless murderings, but some say—said—who the hell knows now?—that the Holy Child is—was—who the hell cares?—is—was missing."

"Penance came to Geharra because they thought the Holy Child was there?" Vrana shared the scuttle crabs between herself and R'lyeh. She could see Jakob's saliva glinting in the storm light.

The Corrupted shrugged, his eyes fixed on the pieces of meat passing between the two killers. "I don't know. I didn't keep that sort of company in Geharra to find out. Give me a bite, would you?"

"Thought you wanted to die," R'lyeh said as she chewed her food.

"By blade or beating but not starvation!" He leaned forward, gripping the bulge that was his groaning stomach. "Please."

"How did you escape?" Vrana tossed the last of the crabs to the man, who quickly swallowed them whole.

"Traders go to a brothel in between the Eastern and Western District. Doesn't have a name. Doesn't need one. Richard and I and some of the others were hiding out there, drunk off our asses. The water, there was something wrong with it. Some contaminate from the Dead City or some lie like that. The soldiers started preaching, started rounding people up in the streets. They kept talking about 'her plant.' We thought they were talking about the Hydra or the Demagogue, but they weren't. It was someone else."

"Demagogue? Hydra?" Vrana didn't mind sounding foolish to the fool.

"All your kind this slow? Or are you two particularly uninformed?" Jakob laughed, farted, and then raised a fist in the air, as though to strike. "Don't ask me how the Holy Order is put together. There's the six Exemplars, the Demagogue, and the Holy Child. The Hydra, she controls them all. Come on, cut my throat. Halfway, at least."

"How did you escape?" Vrana repeated, her tone as dead as the man wished to be.

"Brothel has its tunnels. It's how the royals keep their reputation out of the gutter they seem so fond of fucking in. Everyone lost their minds and let the soldiers march them off to the Northern District. Richard and I and twenty others made a run for it. We got separated from the rest, came out on the coast. I hope the others made it. They were good people."

R'lyeh sounded desperate as she asked, "Who was their leader?"

Lightning broke across the black sky, revealing sinister shapes in the clouds. "Didn't get a good look at him. He was young. No one called him by anything other than 'priest.'"

"They came over the Divide, didn't they?" R'lyeh was gripping the tops of her knees hard enough to draw blood. "They took our people, too, didn't they?"

"I saw some Night Terrors on the last day, like I said. Couldn't figure that part of it out. Thought you all had come together, made a truce, but then I saw the chains." Jakob stood up slowly and went to the spot where a fire had once burned. "Just throw me in it when it's roaring hot. I don't want to die cold and wet. Been cold and wet long enough."

"How did they get over the Divide and into the Heartland?" R'lyeh started to shake, but not because she was freezing.

"King Edgar of Eldrus gave them safe passage." Jakob bunched the kindling together and pulled a flint from his pocket. "I don't like the way world has become. I'd be gone from it."

Soon, the Corrupted had a small fire blazing in the corner of the cave. He sat closest to it, his face inches from the flames, eyes staring intensely at its hissing heart. At first, Vrana and R'lyeh kept their distance from the man, but his convulsions became more frequent, so they moved closer. Vrana knew the girl wouldn't mind if Jakob lost control of himself and fell into the fire—in fact, she appeared to be looking forward to it—but Nora had asked for the man personally.

"What happened to Richard?" Vrana said, waking Jakob as he began to nod off.

"He, uh, didn't make it." The rain outside slowed, lessened— reduced from a pounding to a patter. "He didn't make it through the Elys. I told you everything. You like to kill, don't you? I would like to die now."

R'lyeh said, "What did you do to him?"

"Did you know I have two daughters?" Jakob raved. "Aela and Michael. We thought Michael was going to be a boy, but boy were we wrong!" He smiled and then frowned and went stiff. "I didn't do nothing to Richard! She did! Don't make me talk about it. It's best you don't know. She hasn't seen you yet. You can still move freely amongst the living."

"Jakob, calm down—" Vrana's voice was deep, and her shadow seemed to lengthen from where she sat, "—and tell us what happened."

"If you take me home, I won't tell the others what you're like. I won't tell them about the masks. I can see they're masks. I won't tell them about your kindness." Jakob rubbed at his crimson arm nervously, as R'lyeh drew her dagger and pointed its tip at him. "We came back by way of Elys. It's the only way back without a boat or having to cross the Dires. We crossed closer to the center than we used to, heard there were some plants we could eat there, and we found them and ate them. We were all fucked up and turned around, but we made it, made it to the Spine, or a part of it. You, you assholes need to leave it alone and let us fix it. And anyways, uh, he fell in a ditch, hit his head, and died. We were almost out, too."

"No," Vrana scooted closer to the man, the beak of her mask grazing against his chapped lips, "you said 'she,' and if that's all that happened, then why are you all the way back here?"

"God damn it!" Jakob's face contorted. He closed his eyes hard and pulled his cheeks down with his fingers. "We thought it was one of you, a fucking Night Terror. There was a ditch, there was, and that's where we'd sleep, every time we came home. It was night, and up on the hill a few feet away, we saw something. We thought it was one of you, but it wasn't. 'Maybe it's the man,' Richard said, and I said, 'What man?' and he said, 'You know, from the center. We ate some of the roots there, the red ones.' He was right. We did. But no one believes that shit, the stories."

"The Woman in White Satin," Vrana said, while she thought: *the Witch*.

"Is that what you believe? No, in Nora it's a man. The Boogie-man. He wears a green coat and carries around a sack over his shoulder. He gathers up all the kids in the Elys who're lost, and when his sack is full enough, he sets it down, crawls inside, and tears them to pieces. Then, he makes another sack from what's left of the kids and buries the old one. But that's not who we saw on the hill. It was a woman, but the only thing white about her was her skin. She wore a dress, a rag, really, but that's it. We thought she was hurt, that she needed help."

I found her, Vrana said to herself. *This is the way into the Void.*

"Richard went to her. It was when he'd climbed to the top of the hill that I realized I'd seen the woman before."

"The one who came to Nora," Vrana confirmed.

"The one who drowned all my people. Yeah, it was her. You know about that?" Jakob leaned away from the fire. "Richard screamed because she put her arm down his throat. I tried to stop her, but something held me back. I could feel its body pressing into mine, saw its gray arms across my chest, but I couldn't look back, or look away, and it wouldn't let me go. Don't make me tell this, Night Terror," the Corrupted pleaded. "I've been over it enough."

"One more time," Vrana insisted. *The Witch left him alive for a reason. Did she know I'd find him?*

"She… she… pulled parts of him out of his mouth, wrapped it around his neck. She…" Jakob began to punch the floor, leaving bloody prints from his knuckles. "She waved her hand and he… he hit the ground. Richard, he, Richard… he ripped off his jaw. Fuck. Don't make me. Fuck." Jakob stopped hitting the ground; he started to pull out his hair. "He took rocks and scraped out his eyes. He tore off his... off his... he tore off his fucking cock and threw it at me. His stomach... it went into him, like a starved dog. He should've been dead, but he kept going, Night Terror. Fingernails, lips... ugh, Holy Child, he ripped them off, too.

"Whatever was holding me let me go, and I ran. I fucking ran. Not to the woman but back into the Elys. We were so close. Richard chased me. I could hear him bounding after me. Snorting and snarling and begging to die. I ended up here, stayed here until I thought he'd died or gone. But he's not dead, he's not gone. Every time I leave, he finds me, just when I'm about out. I see her sometimes, standing beside him, petting him, laughing at me.

"I tried to kill myself; cut my wrists, made a noose. I was going to throw myself into the sea before you showed up, but I kept putting it off. She won't let me leave, the cunt; she won't let me die. You have to kill me. I miss my wife. I miss my girls. But I don't deserve them. They don't deserve me, not like this, not anymore. Please, kill me. I know she will do it." Jakob gestured to R'lyeh. "So let her. Quick or slow, it doesn't matter. Just get it done."

"No," Vrana said, running her fingers down the shaft of her ax. "Tomorrow, we leave this place. I will kill your friend, and I will take you home. You will not question me. This is what must be done."

Jakob looked to R'lyeh, giving her one final plea for death, but the girl only shook her head. He considered Vrana for a moment; clumps of hair still stuck to his fingertips. "Okay," he said disappointedly. He lay next to the fire and then slept.

CHAPTER XXIII

When the Spine was broken, its pieces, like bones, were scattered. Corrupted, using the remnants of the highway, then grafted their own roads onto the continental column, but these were destroyed as well. It was down one of those unintended Ribs that Jakob now walked, his shuffling feet picking up cement scabs. To his left and to his right, the Elys shivered and swayed, moved by those things that had once haunted his nightmares and now haunted his days.

Vrana crouched and went quietly across the sodden ground, using her ax to part the ghostly grass ahead. She looked across the road for R'lyeh but could only see where she had been. She had warned the girl and the man about the Witch and her Horrors and had shared her own experiences with the two.

"She attacked one of your villages, too?" Jakob asked; he had calmed when he learned Vrana would escort him home.

"I think she resides in the Elys," Vrana revealed. "I think she takes different forms, but I think it's here she enters our world."

"Are we sharing the world now? Because it seems your kind would have us out of it." Jakob spat into the spitting fire and put his head between his knees. "Maybe she's just following you, Night Terror."

R'lyeh cocked her head.

"No, I don't think so," Vrana lied. "Just don't touch it; Richard, I mean," she said, changing the subject. "The wounds won't heal the way they should." She showed her own scars and added, "Trust me."

Vrana watched as Jakob ambled down the Rib, swaying like the tree at the road's end he seemed so adamant to reach. He hadn't slept the night prior. Vrana knew this because she hadn't either. The Corrupted had sat at the cave's mouth, legs dangling over the edge. As he stared into the obsidian ocean, he would sometimes point, laugh, or sigh, as though images only for him were reflected in the black waters.

"My father killed a Night Terror once," he said, his back to Vrana. "He'd gotten drunk and fallen asleep on the beach down near Calhan's Point. He said he woke up to piss and found a Goat standing over him with a sickle. Father said he caught the sickle with his bare hands—had the scars to prove it, he did—and kicked the goat's legs out from under him. He drowned the Night Terror, because they thought at the time that was the way to do it. He took the mask and showed it off to all of Nora, but I never saw it; someone had stolen it when I was just a baby. Kids in Nora used to tease each other about your kind, make up the worst stories imaginable, but I knew if my father could kill a Night Terror, so could I."

"What's stopping you?" Vrana asked as smoke from the rekindled fire swirled around her.

"Fear," he'd said, turning his head. "I've only seen a Night Terror this close in my dreams, and if I should move against you, the dream will be over."

"You seem more collected than earlier," Vrana remarked.

Jakob laughed at her. "It comes and goes. It's this place, and the Witch. But the waves calm me."

"You don't believe this is really happening, do you?" she asked as R'lyeh turned in her sleep.

"No," he said as he looked at Vrana and then his Corrupted arm, "because these kinds of things don't happen."

Twenty paces ahead, the Rib of the Spine had snapped off, and whereas passage for carts had once been manageable, now it was not, for massive boulders blocked the way. Pieces of the road had been torn up; in the soft soil, the seeds of Petra's Pest had been planted and allowed to flourish. Across the Rib, massive orange weeds were stretched, fat on the life they had choked out from the surrounding land.

"Your people did this," Jakob said nervously. He looked at the hints of wagons in the distance, overgrown and sunken into the mud. "Nora would be a better place if not for you."

Vrana was trying to listen to the man, but her heart was beating hard in her ears as she spied several birds lying dead in the grass and on the side of the road. She picked up speed and brushed the molted feathers from their stiff bodies, making sure not to give away her position. *Crows*, she thought, moving from bird to bird, each one's skull cracked open. *Blix*, she shouted in her mind, scooping up a large bird into her palm. The body was emaciated, nearly naked; the talons chipped, still clinging to flesh; the beak eroded, eaten by acids.

"This isn't good," Jakob stammered, becoming flustered. "Do you hear that?"

It's not him, she said to herself, turning the bird over. *Too skinny. He was never remarkable, but this isn't him. If Deimos sent him to Caldera, he would have never flown so far off-course.* She set the bird down, quickly dug a hole, and put it to rest. *It's not Blix. She just wants me to think it's him.*

"Vrana!" R'lyeh shouted, emerging from the grass and onto the Rib. "Vrana! It's here!"

The Horror of the Field bounded up the road, its distant shape growing larger with every passing second. Vrana cursed the girl and then joined her and Jakob, to watch as death vaulted toward them on twisted limbs.

"Don't let it touch you," Vrana reminded. She hadn't told them the extent of her connection to the Witch or how it had been established. Ignorance, she hoped, would be enough to shield them through the encounter.

The Raven ran forward and met the Horror midway—sideways, ax out, catching the creature in its torn open gut. The Horror of the Field stopped and turned, a rope of intestines slapping against the infected crater where its genitals had been. It was hunched over like a dog, like a flesh fiend; its head was caved in, with large, black patches of dried blood encrusting its eye sockets. Its arms and legs were warped so that the skin was pulled so tightly the creature appeared impossibly thin. From the Horror's jawless mouth, a gift from the Witch rested against the scar tissue: a proboscis, translucent and covered in veins, clogged with flesh and shit.

There was no sign of humanity left in Richard: The Witch had taken it all.

The Horror of the Field looked at Vrana for a moment, and then turned and leapt toward R'lyeh and Jakob. Vrana shouted at the creature and brought the ax down into its back. The Horror whipped around, ripping the weapon from her hands. R'lyeh unsheathed her daggers and went underneath the Horror. With a shout, she rammed the blades into its chest, where its lungs, if it still had lungs, would've been. The abomination swiped its mangled hand, just missing the girl's throat as it passed.

Vrana slammed her fist into the creature's side; the skin there broke and sucked her hand into the muscle beyond. The Horror of the Field shook her off and lumbered toward Jakob. He screamed, but he didn't welcome the death being offered to him. He hurried backward, picking up pieces of the Rib and hurling them at the creature.

"R'lyeh, Jakob, get back!" Vrana commanded; she kicked behind the Horror's knee, and when it went down, she yanked the ax from its back. The Horror reared up and hit Vrana's legs, knocking her off her feet. "Fuck!" she cried as the balls of bone that were its hands pounded her breasts.

"Get off!" R'lyeh drove the daggers into the Horror's neck and twisted. This time it screamed, and as it screamed, the Horror pushed R'lyeh away, sending her crashing into Jakob.

Exploiting its distraction, Vrana kicked the Horror of the Field off her. She jumped unsteadily to her feet and, with both hands, swung the ax through the creature's neck, severing its rotted head from its wretched body.

Vrana, R'lyeh, and Jakob stood there a moment, shaking, as the last of Richard's soupy lifeblood poured out of its neck.

"How do we stop the Witch?" Jakob was panting and crying silently.

"Find a way into the Void and drag her out. R'lyeh, are you hurt?"

After a moment, the girl shook her head and said, "I'm okay, Vrana."

"Are you sure?"

Before the Octopus could respond, Jakob interrupted with, "She lives in the Elys?"

Vrana nodded. "I think so."

"And the more who know about her, the weaker she becomes?"

"Maybe," Vrana said, herself unconvinced. "If anything, it makes her more active, which makes her more vulnerable."

Jakob went to the mutilated corpse of his once-friend and knelt down beside it. He waved off Vrana's insistence for him to move away. He dug into Richard's pockets, the last bits of clothing still clinging to his body. "We are merchants, traders, and to be a good one, you must be registered; otherwise, no city is going to open its gates to you." He removed his hand and revealed a set of identification tags on a chain. "His woman will be wanting this. It's all that's left of him." He rubbed what little tears he had left out of his eyes. "I won't bury this thing. Let it rot. I'll remember him the way he was."

"Jakob," R'lyeh said slowly, "I'm sorry."

"Do you fault me for wanting to die?"

She shook her head. "I get it."

Nora took shape in the murky light of the following evening. Jakob led them to the deadfall on the outskirts, the place where the Witch had sometimes stayed when she first came to his town. The pile of twigs, branches, and trunks stood three times as high as the Vrana and was longer and wider than Nora itself. From the lattices formed by the curving branches, it looked like a gigantic ribcage. The deadfall rattled when the wind passed through it, moaned even, somehow reminding Vrana of a book she had once read and not finished.

"Jakob," R'lyeh had said as he guided them toward the deadfall, "what happened here?"

"This was a small wood that the children used to play in. I played here when I was a boy. When that Witch came to Nora, she left by way of here. We surrounded the woods. We could still hear her inside, but we couldn't find her, so we cut it down, all of it. The next morning we knew she'd escaped. Trees don't grow here anymore."

"Do you want to know what happened in Geharra?" Vrana asked as she and R'lyeh found a place to sit.

"If you have to ask me, then you know that I don't." Jakob started toward Nora. "When I tell the others about the Witch, they'll want to help, especially the women. Anything to hurt the bitch who took their men."

"You still don't believe we are who we say we are?" Vrana asked.

Jakob shook his head and, as he disappeared into the dark, said,

"Not at all."

Vrana threw her cloak around herself and R'lyeh to hold at bay the frigid breath of the sea. "What's the matter?"

R'lyeh shook her head, the preserved tentacles sliding across her chest. "I don't like being this close to Nora. What if they come for us?"

"They won't. Not after what happened last time we were here."

R'lyeh pulled the cloak closer, struggling to keep her grip on its silky exterior. "Because of the flies," she said. "Why would she save you if she knows you mean to kill her?"

Vrana shrugged. "Maybe she enjoys watching me. She took to that man in the hotel. Maybe I'm the first since then. I don't know, R'lyeh." *When I've figured it all out*, she wondered, *is that when the Maiden will be done with me?*

"We haven't talked about the Red Worm much," R'lyeh said, her voice sounding distant, like a whisper daring to be heard.

"We can, if you'd like."

"No," R'lyeh said resolutely. She coughed out the signs of a cold. "Thinking about it is enough. For now."

"Are you sure the Horror didn't hurt you?"

Then: A black shape tore through the night, moving fast down the hill upon which Nora sat. It darted back and forth, sweeping its long shadow across the land. It was a horse, Vrana realized, and it and the hooded figure in its saddle were heading directly for the deadfall. She turned to R'lyeh to tell her to hide, but the Octopus was far ahead of her, having already found a niche inside the wooden ribcage. For a moment, she thought the girl's bloodlust had been extinguished, but then she saw the daggers in her hands and thought otherwise.

"Two?" the hooded rider questioned as it stopped inches away from Vrana. A second horse appeared from behind the rider, having followed without the need of restraints.

"Nora," Vrana said as the figure pulled back its hood and dropped from the horse. Vrana gripped her ax. She still could see in her mind's eye the mayor commanding the crowd that night outside the town. "Allinora."

Nora scoffed at the Raven. "Don't be a bitch. Where's the Bat?"

Vrana shook her head.

"I know what happened," Nora said. The right side of her face twitched where her cheek was bruised. "I've my watchers just as you do. And if backwoods Nora knows what's happened, so does most everywhere else."

"What happened to your face?" Vrana tilted her head toward the mark.

Nora peeked over Vrana's shoulder; R'lyeh was coughing and cursing as she brushed against a coil of thorns. "After you set the flies on us, we had ourselves a talk. It seemed some thought I was in league with your kind. I expect they saw us in the library. A woman got uppity and put her fist to my face. So I put mine in hers, but unfortunately for the woman, the cow forgot to take her tongue off her teeth. Who's that in there?"

Vrana ignored her. "There was nothing we could do for Richard."

Nora licked her lips. She shoved her hand into a pocket and left it there. "So Jakob said. It seems we are both in your debt." She ran her other hand down the side of the horse and called the second one forward. "Two horses for two men. But I know how you Night Terrors are, always wanting more. So what will it be?"

"I've asked Jakob to spread word of the Witch and learn more about her if he should travel again."

"And the abortion of Geharra?" Nora cocked her head. "I suppose that's more of a group effort than anything else." She removed her hand from her pocket, a small square of paper between her fingers. "Put this in your elders' hands, and I'll put my men to work. I'll send an excursion to the Elys and root out the cunt.

"There will be war now, or something of the sort. There is much to learn in times such as these. You'd be surprised what finds it ways into a transaction on an empty stomach."

"What is this?" Vrana took the note, which was not sealed, and slid it into one of her satchels.

"None of your concern, little bird." She relinquished the horses to Vrana's care and turned away. "It was nice meeting your friend."

Vrana couldn't be sure, but it seemed the horses given to them by Nora were the same as those they had left behind at the gates of Geharra. The beasts needed little guidance, as though the destination had already been whispered into their ears. Vrana was grateful for the horses, her legs even more so, but it was R'lyeh who appeared most affected. She didn't say much as they rode through the borders of the forest, but when she did, she spoke warmly, her body close to the horse, its heart calming her own.

"Did you have a horse back home?" Vrana asked, watching as R'lyeh seemed to soothe the creature with her touch.

"I liked to think I did." R'lyeh sat upright. "He was nobody's. I don't know why he came around. I was the only one he let touch him." R'lyeh yawned. "I thought this one was him. They look just the same."

They stopped when the moon was at its highest in the sky, and their eyelids refused to stay open. They weren't fully in the South, but they were close enough that Vrana could allow herself to relax. Camp was set hastily, poorly, and if there was anything lurking nearby, it had gone unnoticed and would now have the opportunity to claim a free meal. R'lyeh was reluctant to be parted from her horse, but eventually complied—pouting like the child she was until sleep silenced her.

Vrana knew that she would dream, knew that she would never be without dreams, for her hand bore the Witch's mark and her mind the Worm's; and yet, she dreamt of neither. In her dreams, she was without a mask, weapons, or armor. She was very aware of many things of which were of little consequence to her. She was hardly nude, but felt as though she was beneath the dress she wore, which was soft and blue like a piece of the sky. Vrana was in a home that was not her home, running her hands under the faucet of a sink, acutely aware of the floor beneath her feet, which was cold and rumbled as though something had awakened below.

She turned and found before her a kitchen fitted with a table, refrigerator, pantry, and cupboard. Farther on, she saw a hallway lined with photographs in thin frames of men and women, young and old, smiling and without Corruption. Sighing, Vrana twisted her neck to the windows beside her and saw with watering eyes a stretch of grass greener than she had ever known, with fences like fangs clamping on tightly to the plot of land.

"Mom?" she heard a voice call from somewhere inside the house.

Vrana said nothing in response. She waited a moment for the speaker to make their appearance, following with her eyes the sounds emanating from the ceiling above, where feet plodded on weakened wood. No one came, though, so she took a seat at the table that hadn't been there a second ago and listened to the birds that were singing outside. Content, she folded her hands in her lap and watched as shadows lengthened across the tabletop, off the tabletop, and onto the floor, up the walls and down the hall. *Clouds*, she thought naively, looking once more out the window, where swarms of helicopters cut through the sky. *Clouds covering up the sun.*

"What do you know about the Old World, Vrana?"

One eye opened, with the other following close behind. Vrana coughed herself awake. "Huh?"

"We never got to it. I found a part of a railroad track a few years ago—a television, too, or at least I think that's what they called them. I don't know." R'lyeh pushed her hair behind her ears. "I thought it was interesting, but nobody else seemed to want to talk about it."

"Well, you would have loved growing up in Caldera." Vrana sat up. Her back was wet, covered in sweat. "So I bet you know all about this world, don't you?"

"Maybe, not everything," R'lyeh said. Branches fell from the canopy above, a predator of the night looking for a place to rest. "I'll make you a deal," she said with an impish grin.

"Will you now?" Vrana laughed. "I want fifty compliments… about my hair, my armor, about how good I kill stuff. And that's every morning I'm talking about."

R'lyeh snorted. "Are you always this cocky?"

"Only when I'm trying to be funny. You first, R'lyeh."

The Octopus stretched out her tentacles, all four of them. The talons of the Cruel Mother glinted in the moonlight as she moved them from the patch of grass where she'd hidden them. "There are a whole bunch of towns and villages and settlements between Eldrus and Penance. They trade between one another. I heard they think they are separate from the city-states, but the teachers always told us they fall under Eldrus' rule. That's the Heartland."

"In the Old World, there were many nations, and they were all connected to one another. You could speak with someone thousands of miles away. It only took a second. Telephones, that's what they called them. And they had the Internet, too, which was like a telephone, except you could talk to millions of people and read millions of things, like a huge, never-ending library."

"Why don't we have those things?" R'lyeh asked, amazed.

"I don't know. Maybe we shouldn't have those things. Maybe

that's why our people keep the Corrupted the way that they are now."

"Hmm. Did you know the royal family in Eldrus was murdered three years ago?"

"I did know that," Vrana said. "All but one was killed, right?"

"The youngest, Edgar, but everyone thought he'd died. When they found the bodies in the keep, Ghostgrave, his was missing. The council thought he had been taken for some sort of ransom or blackmail or something. Edgar was the good one, the one everyone hoped would take over; even the elders, I think, felt that way."

Vrana could sense R'lyeh enjoyed educating her. "But that's not what happened, is it?"

R'lyeh shook her head. "He came back a year later with a child. People said he was different, changed. People said they saw him riding out of the Nameless Forest before he made his way back to Eldrus; that's where he got the boy from."

"Is that so?" Vrana said in disbelief. "Nobody leaves the Nameless Forest. Then again, if nobody leaves, then how do we know what we know about it, eh?"

R'lyeh bit her lip. "That's true. Tell me more about the Old World."

Vrana laughed. "It's hard to find a place to begin, R'lyeh; it existed for millions of years. Before the Trauma, humans could cross the air and sea and see into space; all they needed was money and power."

"And we didn't exist then?"

"No, we didn't."

"I liked killing the Horror," R'lyeh revealed.

"Me too. What did you like about it?"

"Everything," R'lyeh whispered. She paused and then said, "You called them humans. Were they not Corrupted in the Old World?"

"I guess not. Their arms weren't red, if that's what you're asking."

"And our purpose is to keep their numbers low, like ours," R'lyeh said to herself. "If we didn't exist in the Old World, then where did we come from?"

Vrana tapped her finger on her lips. "Constantly, the humans asked themselves the very same thing. Maybe if they knew the answer, none of this would have happened. Our keeper told me to think of the earth as a body, an organism, and that its response to the Trauma was us, our people, so that it could heal."

"Do you believe that?"

Vrana shrugged. "It sounds nice, doesn't it?"

R'lyeh looked at the ground, sighed, and lay down, her back to Vrana. "I don't believe it. Everyone would be alive if that were true."

Vrana didn't disagree with the girl. She watched R'lyeh until she stopped whimpering in her sleep, when the waking sun set fire to the night sky.

CHAPTER XXIV

They were a half a day's journey from Caldera when the horses refused to go any farther. R'lyeh tried to convince hers to stay with them and see them through the last of their journey, but when its companion took off, the horse was quick to follow.

"Do you think they will make it back?" she asked, taking a few steps forward to see the beasts once more before they were swallowed up by the horizon.

"Absolutely," Vrana said, taking R'lyeh by the shoulders and turning her around. They went forward. "We're going straight across. You can swim, right?"

Ahead, a swamp shifted restlessly in its mossy cradle. Vrana had passed through this area on her third trial, but she had been much deeper south, where the water was shallower. She'd considered going that way again, but with their horses gone and their patience gone, the more dangerous route somehow became the more appealing. If there were any reward to be gained from the decision, it was Vrana's sudden realization that she could not see Kistvaen's peak from where they now stood. The spellweaver had made it and, with the others, had caused the mountain to disappear once again.

"Um, Vrana," R'lyeh said as she teetered along a half-submerged log, a red wisp circling her head.

"Ignore it." Vrana hopped and landed on all fours onto a fallen tree, sending ripples across the swamp. "It'll try to take you somewhere you don't want to go."

"Where's that?" R'lyeh said, following behind Vrana. She jumped onto the fallen tree as Vrana leapt off it and onto two trunks.

Vrana stopped to catch her breath. They were crossing the deepest part of the swamp, and with a keen eye and a bit of balance, doing so would be easy enough. Felled trees, thick vines, and large rocks littered the place, ensuring that they would always have a bridge to the other side. No, it wasn't the path, crude as it was, that worried Vrana; rather, it was the shadows she saw in the water, following them as they went, waiting with open mouths for a hand or a foot to break the surface.

"A small grotto," Vrana finally answered. The wisps were no mystery to her. "They'll lead you down a darkened path, where the trees close in so you can't escape." Vrana pushed herself off the stump, grabbed a vine midway, and flung herself onto a bed of debris. "They'll take you to the grotto and sing to you until you're too tired to fight them off."

"Then what?" R'lyeh called, one leg dipping into the water as she lost her footing on a stump. She pulled it out before something could pull her in.

"Then they enter all the cavities of your body and eat you from the inside," Vrana said, almost laughing. "But wait! There's more!" Vrana smacked a wisp that floated too close to her, and it fell apart like a dandelion. "Afterwards, they take over your body and make you walk around. They try to get you to convince others to follow you back to the grotto."

"That seems awfully complicated." R'lyeh bent down and impaled a fat beetle with her dagger; it writhed on the end as she slid it under her mask and into her mouth.

"Everything has its rules."

Out of nowhere, R'lyeh asked, "What's the point of hiding the mountain?"

Vrana stopped in a patch of roots that looked like dead snakes. "When I first met Nora, she said her town was in a panic after Kistvaen reappeared. I think the point is to do just that: If our people can make something that large vanish, then it's probably in the Corrupted's best interests to leave us the hell alone."

R'lyeh spat out the remaining legs of the beetle. "We used to talk about all the villages." She jumped onto a vine; it spun her in circles as she swung over to a bed of rot. "They said the people of Caldera burn hot, like the inside of the mountain."

"It's been hundreds of years since Kistvaen was active. I think most people think it's not even a volcano. They think the old elders just made that shit up to scare the Corrupted away." Vrana paused for a moment. "So, what else did they say about Caldera?"

R'lyeh laughed and joined Vrana in the patch of roots. "That you were a bunch of bloodthirsty warriors, and that if you wanted something done right, you find a Calderan to do it. Did they say anything about Alluvia?"

"Only that they give the best compliments," Vrana said with a laugh. "'Alluvians are resilient, and they are the most open-minded amongst our people,'" she quoted.

"I like that," R'lyeh chirped, nodding her head. "I'd like to go to Rime one day, to see the snow."

"Well, I wouldn't mind stopping by Traesk to see if Serra had any relatives. Maybe we'll make a journey of it one day."

They continued on in silence, having decided that they were making too much noise. After several more logs, trunks, and vines, their feet finally found purchase on sodden land. Ahead, through the crooked, black trees, where the swamp thinned away, Vrana glimpsed the southern expanse, its golden grass and hardened earth just as she remembered it.

"What's that?" R'lyeh whispered.

Vrana turned her head and found beside them an inlet hidden behind a curtain of Weeping Willows. "A boat," she said, cocking her head as the wind pulled the hair-like leaves aside. "A person," she added.

Towards the middle of the inlet, where the water bubbled and hissed, a small, wooden boat sat. On the shore, holding the boat's tether, a woman stood. She wore a sheer, white dress that covered her from head to toe. It hung loosely over her body, and although they could almost see through the dress, the woman's body was only visible in the places where the material touched her.

The Ferry Woman tilted her head; Vrana looked down and saw that the woman was holding a dead bird by its legs.

"Is that... the Witch?" R'lyeh moved closer to Vrana.

"No," the Raven said, turning away, feeling nauseous, "it's not her."

Vrana couldn't help but cry as they came upon the fields of Caldera. *It's still here*, she thought to herself, laughing happily. *Everything is still here.* The crops of the field appeared plentiful and unspoiled, and they gave themselves to the harvesters with ease. The crack of wooden swords could be heard from the practice yard, followed by the triumphant, prepubescent cries of their wielders. Vrana looked to the walls for the watchers and found them there; she looked to the hideaways in the trees and found them there, too. Through the ground, she could feel the vibrations of lives unfettered by disease, despair, and destruction.

The Witch had not returned.

The Worm had not yet found them.

"Your village is beautiful," R'lyeh said quietly. She stepped back as she looked up, following Kistvaen to its top.

"It's just as much mine as it is yours."

R'lyeh's breathing became shallow, and her voice quivered when she spoke. "You must be so happy to see your mom and dad."

"It's just my mother and I," Vrana said, realizing she hadn't told R'lyeh about her father's disappearance, about his probable death.

"Oh." R'lyeh sighed. Beads of sweat formed on her skin. "I'm sorry. I don't feel very well." She began to tremble, and then she fell.

Vrana caught her and held her close. "My mother is a healer. She'll take care of you. I promise."

Behind R'lyeh's mask another had been placed, and the cracks that had gone without mending were spreading fast.

As they stumbled through the village gates, two things became quite clear to Vrana: Blix had arrived, and all had heard his message. Like peasants prostrating before royalty, the people of Caldera parted as she passed, the masks of the Fox, Rabbit, Eagle, and Cat, the Toad, Deer, Boar, and Bull downcast. Even though she knew he would not be there, Vrana found herself looking for Aeson, scanning the open doorway of the Archive for his skull, the elders' house for his figure.

She could feel R'lyeh's fingers wrapping around the straps of her armor. She worried what would become of the girl when they were separated so she could heal. The talons of the Cruel Mother, which as far as Vrana was concerned were now R'lyeh's, would need to be removed, hidden away, until the Octopus could be trusted with them again. *What else could I have done?* Vrana closed her eyes as she felt the girl's sickly warmth against her. *I should have seen this coming. I should have told her about my father. It may have made a difference.*

Vrana saw her mother before she saw her. She was backing out of their house, arms filled with baskets, the baskets filled with tinctures. Vrana didn't need to say anything, for when her shadow fell upon Adelyn's, her mother immediately turned around, set the baskets aside, and went to her daughter. At first, Adelyn seemed confused as to where to put her hands, unsure if she should embrace the Raven or see to the Octopus at her side. Either choice would feel a betrayal.

"Who is she?" Adelyn asked, making her decision.

"R'lyeh, of Alluvia," Vrana said, allowing her mother to share some of the girl's weight as they brought her inside. "Does everyone know?"

Her mother nodded. "After Blix arrived with Deimos' message, the elders called the village together and told us what had happened." She gestured toward the dinner table, and they lowered R'lyeh onto it. "She needs the open air. Your room is too stuffy."

"She saw everything," Vrana said loudly as Adelyn left the room and then returned with the baskets she'd been carrying. "She was in the pit when it happened."

"Poor thing." Adelyn's voice trembled as she spoke. She set the baskets on the bench beside the table and started to search them. "She has no one left?"

Vrana shook her head. "She said that her mother and father left for Eld before the soldiers came, for a meeting." Vrana slowly slid the mask off R'lyeh. "She's dehydrated."

"You both are," her mother said, disappearing and then reappearing with two flasks of water. "Drink," she commanded, handing one flask to Vrana and pressing the other to R'lyeh's lips. "What did you say her name was again?"

"R'lyeh."

"R'lyeh," her mother repeated softly, "I need you to sit up a little so that you can drink this water."

"Who... who are you?" R'lyeh asked shyly, her eyes half open.

"I'm Vrana's mom, sweetie. If you like her, then you'll love me. I'm much nicer and much funnier. There you go." She placed her hand on R'lyeh's back and helped her up. "Drink this, you'll like it, I promise."

Vrana watched as her little companion guzzled the contents of the flask, spilling some of it down her chest. The heat seemed to be leaving her body, the red of her flesh giving way to a soft brown. The girl looked starved, was starved; the bones behind her skin were like fossils pushing through rock. She put her palm to R'lyeh's forehead and wiped away the sweat that had formed there. She reminded Vrana of the young boy, but this one, she decided, this one she would not abandon.

"Your mom and dad are in Eld, is that right, sweetie?" Vrana's mother asked, helping R'lyeh to lie back down.

"No…. Yeah… I… I think so." R'lyeh twisted her head, trying to find her mask. "They had to go to… no babies?" She coughed.

Vrana's mother shushed R'lyeh as she unfastened a stopper from a vial. "I know about that, and I know something else. Guess what that is?"

R'lyeh shook her head pathetically.

"I know a couple of birds who love flying up to Eld this time of the year. Vrana's going to go send them on a trip to tell your mom and dad that you're safe here with us. Vrana's going to tell them to go somewhere else for a while so they are safe, too. Does that sound good?"

"That sounds good," R'lyeh said dryly. Her eyes finally closed, and she went to sleep.

Fifteen minutes later, winded and ready to fall over, Vrana reached the other side of the village, task completed. Svaya of the Eagle took the note Vrana had quickly written out and whispered its meaning to one of his winged messengers. A peck on the hand and a clutch of meat for the journey, and the bird was gone.

"You look well, considering," Svaya said as he took a seat in the sunlight outside his hovel. "Did no one else return?"

"No," she said, trying to determine if he meant to blame her for her companions' absence, "just the girl."

Svaya tightened the wrap that ran from heart to knees across his body. To Vrana, the man looked like a half-dressed mummy too long away from its sarcophagus. Adelyn had told her once that Svaya wore the wrap out of medical necessity, but when Vrana asked for specifics, she refused to elaborate any further.

"After you left, word spread of your involvement with the Witch," Svaya said, fastening the last bit of fabric to his body. "Most, myself included, do not blame you, but there are those who have suffered loss and have become Corrupted in mind. More parties were dispatched, but nothing was found. A few still need someone to blame. I would tread carefully until their grieving has ceased."

Alarmed, Vrana lowered her voice and herself to Svaya's place on the ground. "Where did these rumors come from?"

Svaya shrugged. "It is not a large village; much can be heard in the quiet of night. The Jackal, who lost all but one of her pups, is especially worried by your return."

"My initiation feast afterwards certainly didn't help, did it?"

"For some, smiles were faked as salt was rubbed into open wounds." Svaya stood up, held out his hand for Vrana to take. "Nevertheless, you have done well and have endured more than most. I need not see your face to know that what we have been told by the elders is a poor summarization; your voice reveals all."

"You're too kind," Vrana said, baffled by the man's reception, for up until this moment they had rarely exchanged words with one another. "Now that I think about it, I haven't seen Blix."

"Faolan has him. Much can be learned from animals if one knows how to listen."

The elders were expecting Vrana, but stubbornness steered her toward the Archive instead. She greeted the archivists as she passed, and they responded as they always did: not at all. It would take her forty-five seconds to reach the book on grave digging and thirty more to place it between the grooves in Psychology. But she didn't go to the book on grave digging, the aisle on Psychology; instead, she found herself gravitating towards the Theater of the World, a small, rotund room at the back of the Archive where all known maps were kept.

"You fucking assholes," Vrana murmured, leaning over the large table upon which the world atlas sat, its parchment too pristine to be anything but a copy. "Just like that, you made it all disappear."

She started in Caldera. With her finger, she followed the land to Nora, to Geharra, and then returned home. She revisited the emaciated Den of the Unkindness, tapped her finger against the blighted lands where a name, Marcus Proust, had been written. *That's it*, she thought. *That was the name of the zealot who tried to take over Caldera years ago.* She laughed—Aeson would be proud—and then went eastward to Cadence, the village where she'd left the young boy. *I don't remember it having a name last time.* She traced over each letter in the village's name. *Why does it now?*

Vrana shrugged and worked her way up the coast and then moved inward to avoid the Nameless Forest, just in case. She followed the turbulent waters of the Divide, past their village of Traesk. She scaled the Quiet Mountains, braved their wintry storms, and went to Penance behind them. Miles from the holy city, hamlets and colonies sat along the icy shore, their names upon the parchment too small to read without a magnifying glass. With little left to be seen in that snowy part of the world, Vrana braved the hinterlands and frozen timberlands and passed over the mountains once more. She flew as a raven might through the white sky, over their village of Rime, and turned toward the Heartland of the great, traumatized continent.

Here, the towns reluctant to be under Eldrus' rule stood, keeping watch over the river lands, farmlands, and Spine. There were five towns in all, and Vrana traveled between each. There was Nyxis nearest Eldrus, with Hrothas to its east and Islaos to its west. Furthest south of the city-state, there was Cathedra, and furthest east, with the Nameless Forest only a few days away, Gallows.

Vrana went to Eld next and conjured in her mind an image of R'lyeh's mother and father. She proceeded northward, to the Black Tundra and the glaciers like white towers in the solid sea. She veered south to Mirror Lake where Deimos' beloved rested below its reflecting waters. She shivered sadness and then, trudging through brambles and weeds, made it to the map's edge, where a small part of the Dead City sat, which was nothing more than a splash of black across the tawny parchment. She sailed the sea to the continent's southernmost point, where, hundreds of miles below Caldera, the desert of the Ossuary began.

"I didn't believe them when they told me."

Vrana pulled away from the map and saw standing behind her Korr, a former classmate. He had always been the largest in her class, strongest, too; although, when it came to asking Vrana out, he had been as weak as they come. She would have said yes, and now as she stared at him, covered in dirt rather than blood, a harvester's mask over his face, she was glad she had not. Once unrivaled in melee and archery, he had now given himself to the field. Vrana didn't have to be top of the class, not that she had been, to know why. He was scared. He had given up.

"I thought the elders were testing me, my resolve. When did they tell you?"

It was Deimos who told me first, not the elders. "After the initiation, but I never saw this," she said, looking back at the map.

"They changed it after you left, put it back the way it was when we were too young to notice." Korr leaned against a wall. "They called our class together and told us. You should've seen us. We were ready to tear the elders apart."

"Did they tell you why they did it?" Vrana asked. She stared at the mass of roots that made up his mask, trying to determine where one mask began and the other ended.

Korr laughed and shook his head. "It makes sense. I don't know why I didn't think about it before. Since we've been born, Vrana, all these years, between Alluvia, Caldera, Eld, Rime, Traesk... there's been one hundred and fifty births."

"That's eighteen years," Vrana said in disbelief. "That doesn't seem right."

"That's why they lied to us." Korr pushed away from the wall of the Archive and slid his hands into his pockets. "They can't waste us. Do you remember how everyone wanted to leave Caldera? To kill Corrupted and bring back pieces of the Old World and all that?"

"I remember you wanted that."

Korr laughed again and nodded at the map. "Not anymore. We are outnumbered. It's suicide to go into the North. Job well done, elders. I'm staying here."

"I don't think that was their intention, Korr. I've been there, and I'm a tenth the warrior you are. Well, maybe like half the warrior you are. Not to toot my horn, but I think I could give you a run for your money."

"It doesn't matter." He bowed his head and backed away. "That's how most of us feel now. Eighteen years is a long time to lie to someone, especially when everyone else is doing it, too." He sighed. "It was good seeing you. I'm glad you made it back."

"Don't be like that!" Vrana shouted as Korr backed out of the Theater.

He looked over his shoulder, laughed, and said, "Don't be a stranger, Vrana. You're braver than most of us now. They're going to want to use that as much as they can."

CHAPTER XXV

Aeson stood in the doorway of the Inner Sanctum, skull lit by the blazing torch he held. His body seemed more muscular, more defined—less like that of someone whose sole form of exercise was moving one book atop another. Behind him, his hollowed-out home glowed cerulean, and the air itself had a fibrous texture that refused to stay still.

"What took you so long?" Aeson said, his voice echoing around them.

"What do you think you're doing down here?" Vrana replied, stopping before him. A feather fell from her mask into the flame of Aeson's torch. "We had a deal."

Aeson clicked his tongue against his teeth. "A couple thousand to go and you'll have gone to bone. And I'll have you know," he said, stepping closer to Vrana, "I did what you asked, and I think you might regret it later, because your mom told me a whole lot of things you'd rather I not know."

"You're lying," Vrana said, trying not to smile.

"Terrible and terribly embarrassing things," Aeson continued. He pretended to cringe. "You do know where pee comes from now, right?"

Vrana slapped the torch out of his hands, sending it with a crack and spew of flames to the tunnel's floor. "Whatever happened to that pillow you used to fu—"

"Vrana!" Aeson said, pulling her close but, in her opinion, not close enough. "I'm so glad you're back." He ran his hands gently up her neck, under her mask, and lifted it off slowly. "That's better."

"Not quite," she said as she did the same to Aeson, taking off his mask and lingering for a moment on his lips. "Almost there," she said, leaning in and pressing her mouth hard against his. "Ah," she said stepping back, skull in hand; a feeling of warmth rushed through her body, across her shoulders, down her arms and legs. "Much better, indeed."

Aeson led Vrana, with many short, passionate stops along the way, to the small hot spring nearby. Carefully, he helped her out of her armor and clothes and then admired her when he'd finished. Aware of her bruises, wounds, and scars, she moved to cover them, but he took her arms and wrapped them around him instead. Vrana closed her eyes, pressed her head against his chest, and wondered how she'd managed to go so long being anywhere else.

"I always forget this is here," Vrana said as she floated through the cloudy waters. She pushed her hair behind her ears and exhaled all the tension that had built up inside of her. "Do you think R'lyeh will be okay?"

Aeson waded towards Vrana and held her hand. "No," he said, "but what about you?"

"It's not the same." She looked up at him and kissed his neck. "She saw it happen. For days, she watched as her people and all of Geharra were butchered, raped; I only saw what was left."

"Your mother and the elders will do everything they can for her, you know that." Aeson kissed her on the top of her head. "But you're older than her and initiated. No one's going to stop you from holding it all in, burying it. I know you, so come on."

She squeezed his hand tightly and then nodded. "It was the worst thing I've ever seen. I can't get it out of my head. Not for long, at least. The Crossbreed, they made one. And there were flesh fiends, too. But the pit... fuck, Aeson. The Corrupted deserve everything we've done to them. But if you add up everything we've done to them, it probably looks the same. So what the fuck is the point of it all?"

"The good outweighs the bad," Aeson whispered.

"No it doesn't. It just leads to more bad." Vrana laughed and shook her head. "I'm not saying kill everyone and everything." She exhaled loudly. "I don't know what I'm saying, actually."

"You didn't talk to R'lyeh about this, did you?"

"Didn't seem right for me to." Vrana made small waves in the steaming water. "She'd been through enough. The last thing she needed was a pessimistic rant confirming all the terrible and hateful things she was feeling."

"Keep her away from the elders. They'll put that hate to good use."

"In some ways, I'm glad I saw what I saw. I mean, I'm not glad that it happened, but…"

"Nothing will ever be as awful as that day in Geharra."

"No," she said, and sighed. "And if it is, if it is worse than that day in Geharra, then I'd say this world is on its way out."

"It may already be."

Vrana cocked her head. "Then why are we holding it back?"

"Selfish, I suppose." Aeson grinned and said, "Living can be a very selfish thing."

"Do you want to know how it happened?" Vrana volunteered.

Aeson nodded, a strand of hair falling in front of his eyes. He reached over the edge of the spring and groped in the darkness. "Did you run through a swamp?" he remarked jokingly, curling his nose as his hand returned with a chunk of soap.

"What the hell do you think I am? Some kind of princess?"

"A swamp princess, maybe."

Vrana punched Aeson's arm. "Do you remember that necklace I showed you? The one with the red gem that I found near the Spine?"

"I do." Aeson slid the soap down Vrana's back, rubbing it against her glowing skin. "While you were gone, a watcher found one of our own near the Spine: his throat had been cut, and his mask was missing. He was supposed to be monitoring Geharra, like Deimos. His name was Ghis."

"He must have stolen it! He was going to bring it back to us!" she shouted; a part of the fog surrounding the events had finally lifted. She tried to turn around, but Aeson stopped her and continued to scrub at the dirt on her side. "The priest who was giving orders must have sent those thieves from the hospital after it… but how did Ghis die?" She bit her lip and searched her thoughts. "The necklace was the key. When I dropped it… fucking idiot… I know, I know… but when I dropped it, that's when it happened."

"The priest had to have known that without it nothing would happen," Aeson mused, his hands moving lower, past her waist. "I read once that insanity is doing the same thing over and over again and expecting different results."

"I don't think there's any doubt he was insane, Aeson." This time, Vrana did turn around. She put one arm around his neck and the other on the small of his back. "How long have we been doing this with the Corrupted, expecting things will be better?"

Aeson smiled, kissed her forehead. "Most, I think, just hope that things won't be as bad as they were before. I don't know what's going to happen. I don't know if the elders do, either. It's kind of out of our hands."

"I don't believe that." Vrana searched Aeson's eyes for the truth; they looked down, away, burdened by the lie he'd spoken. "And neither do you."

"I wish I could tell you more, but I can't." He ran the soap across her breasts, stomach, and thighs.

"I know," she said. She caught his hand, took the soap, and dropped it to the bottom of the spring. She guided his hand back up her thigh. "But there is something you can do for me."

Though they tried as best they could, neither Vrana nor Aeson would allow the other to sleep; therefore, when morning made its unwelcome arrival, both parties were less than enthused to go about the errands of the day. They parted from one another awkwardly—Vrana found the wall of the tunnel gave more support than her shaking legs—and promised to meet again, above ground, to break bread with the recovering R'lyeh. There was more Vrana needed to ask and tell Aeson concerning the Worms of the Earth and the Witch, but he would hear none of it, for the elders were anticipating her, and he had kept her too long (but, in her opinion, not long enough).

She checked in on R'lyeh, who told her in between yawns that she was fine and just needed a few more minutes of sleep. Adelyn, however, didn't stir when called, and Vrana found her snoring loudly in the basement garden, head against the back of the chair she sat in. Vrana covered her mother with a blanket, kissed her on the forehead, and made for her bedroom where her belongings waited.

"No," she said to herself, moving the books on the Witch to one pile.

"Not this either," she said, placing the components she'd collected for her mother on top of them. "Here we go." She removed the

THE BONES OF THE EARTH

priest's charm of restraint and turned it in her hands. "Oh yeah…"
She tipped her bags over until Nora's note fluttered onto the floor.
"Don't read it, Vrana," she told herself as she unfolded the letter.

It goes without saying that nothing will be the same. We will do as we must to survive, but as far as we are from the rest of the world, for us that may not be enough. Be discreet about it—rumors breed faster than my people here do (blessing and a curse, I say)—but more than anything else, be quick.

Your carrier pigeon, which I'm sure has read this over by now, did me a great favor (two favors if you include the delivery of this letter). It's come to my attention that we share a common enemy, her and me; so I will do what I can and forward what I find.

Vrana proceeded to the house of the elders with purpose. The ground was damp, and her feet pounded so hard against it they left tracks of fury through the village's center. At this hour of the morning, only the watchers and harvesters were willfully awake, and by their movements it seemed to Vrana they were still possessed by the specter of sleep. She made every effort to acknowledge them as they passed so to study their reactions, to determine who continued to harbor ill feelings towards her for the Witch's attack and if she should expect to see them leaning over her bedside one lonely night.

Paranoia begets paranoia, she quickly concluded as each welcomed her with congratulations, a pat on the back, or an unexpected and incredibly strong hug ("Thank you," she choked out to Egla, who was known to have something of a histrionic personality). Vrana explained to them in short, succinct sentences what had happened, and they ate up each word as though they'd missed their morning meal. She found it strange how they seemed to look up to her, these ideals of their craft, these surveyors of worlds old and new, and liked it very much. *Then again,* Vrana thought to herself as she spoke to the last watcher, *what exactly did the elders tell them? What did they leave out? Lie about?*

Past the center of the village, the bakery, and the barracks, Vrana found the house of the elders. It was hardly the largest building in Caldera, and it was far from the most aesthetically pleasing; if not for the lush garden behind it where she had feasted so many weeks ago, no ine would suspect the importance the house held. She approached the front door, the creaky boards of the porch announcing her arrival, and found it locked.

Vrana searched the windows for shadows of life and found only dead darkness. "Why would they be awake at this hour?" she grumbled. "If I were an elder, I'd sleep all day."

"Perhaps it's good that you're not."

Vrana spun around and saw before her Faolan, the Wolf elder, in a white robe that did little to hide her nude body beneath it. "I didn't see you standing there," she sputtered.

Faolan chuckled. "That's because I wasn't." She held out her hand for Vrana and waited until she took it. "Come. We have been waiting."

For the children of the village, the garden of the elders held within it an intrigue that could not be resisted. As a young girl, before discovering the maps of the Archive and the joys of swinging a sword, Vrana spent most of her time here. At supper, she would return home with a pocket full of flowers, petals, roots, and soil, and give them to her mother to replenish her stock ("My sneaky little bird," Adelyn used to say). Afterward, Vrana would reflect on all that she had done and devise plans which would lead to the discovery of new paths the following day, for each visit to the garden was as though it were the first.

Today was no different. With one hand holding tightly onto Faolan's, she was pulled through rows of roses and aisles of ivy; under overgrown arches and over understated bridges. They passed blooms of Murk, Mire, and Moore and coils of Callous, Solace, and Snare. They waded by ochre stalks of Reprieve and crimson reeds of Hunger; stepped over thorny Veracity, while grazing bristled Bite; moved through green corridors of Null, Void, and Nicety; and pricked their fingers willingly on blue Calm and bluer Content. So quickly were they moving that Vrana felt as though the garden itself was expanding before their very eyes, creating a place for their feet to fall where there was once nothing. *One could be lost in worse places*, she thought, deciding that, if she were to resign from this world, it would be the garden to which she turned to live out her final days.

Minutes, or what may have been hours later, Vrana found herself on the edge of a small clearing around which a tall wall of roots had formed. In the middle of the clearing there was a trellis wreathed in vines, and within it an obsidian boulder sat, catching the morning light and keeping it greedily for itself. Vrana looked over shoulder to sneak a glimpse of the path that had brought her here but found that it was no more.

"You have done so well," Nuctea stated, bringing Vrana's attention back to the clearing, where the Owl stood a few feet away.

"Forgive us for not being longwinded," Anguis added, stepping up and standing beside the startled Raven. "We have much to discuss."

The elders allowed Vrana to speak without interruption, so that when she finally finished, her jaw was sore and her tongue numb. She told them everything, leaving nothing to interpretation. As she removed the priest's charm and Nora's note, Vrana realized that the elders seemed unsurprised by her tale. She could not help but wonder how much Blix had told them, how much the fat little bird had taken in and understood about the events that'd transpired in Geharra. *There's something else*, she decided, staring into the chunk of obsidian, where the world was reflected darkly. *Did they know before they sent us?*

"And the Corrupted who held this charm was young, is that correct?" Anguis said, running his thumb over its surface.

Vrana nodded. "Lucan said it belonged to someone much older."

"Yes," Anguis said, holding the charm close to his face, scrutinizing its craftsmanship, "its keeper, Samuel Turov, Exemplar of Restraint, was the last to hold it. There are six Exemplars altogether, and each has two apprentices who assist them."

"Turov's apprentices were Mishra Dis and Alexander Blodworth," Faolan interjected. "Those who are sworn to an Exemplar are in the Exemplar's custody till exile or death. Until this happens, they are groomed and given audience with those who may elect them to their masters' position one day."

"Then..." Vrana's thoughts turned to the pit once more, her stomach twisting at its memory, "was the priest Blodworth?"

"What do you know of the Holy Child?" Nuctea asked Vrana.

"I, uh," she mumbled, biding her time as she tried to remember what she knew of the boy. "We saw his portrait in Geharra. Jakob said he went missing. The Holy Child, he's a figurehead."

Anguis rested his hands on his knees; a snake slithered up his leg and wrapped itself around his neck like a collar. "It is not unheard of for religions to elect a speaker of their faith: a pope, prophet, or messiah."

"A Christ," Vrana said.

Anguis nodded. "But what is unheard of is for someone so important and well-guarded to disappear, leaving no hint of their whereabouts—especially someone who is to be the embodiment of god and therefore impervious to all earthly perils."

Vrana's voice rose as she said, "Jakob told me Penance may have come to Geharra because they thought he was there."

"It is no coincidence that, when the Holy Child went missing, so, too, did Samuel Turov." Nuctea whistled at a passing bird. "There are no places the Exemplars cannot tread in Penance: even the Holy Child's bedchambers are open to them."

"But they found him!" Vrana cried with uncertainty, the words of the missionaries outside of Nora finally given meaning ("He has returned to us. Your sins will go unanswered no longer."). "Right? Was he in Geharra?"

"Yes, they did," Anguis said, surprised. "But not in Geharra."

Vrana cocked her head. Her throat felt dry, and she began to shiver, despite the southern heat. There was a tightness in her face as though her skin had been pulled hard across her bones. She smelled the air, and it smelled of blood.

"Cadence, a small village, east of here, belonging to a pagan faith. They found the Holy Child there," Anguis said.

The young boy, his father, Vrana said to herself, a warm sweat forming on her neck. *No, I would have known when I laid eyes on them.* "Cadence?" she asked meekly. *Is that why they put its name back on the map?*

"We expect Turov brought him into the southern cradle because of the Corrupted's ambivalence to venture here." The snake unwrapped itself from Anguis and broke apart into a cloud of vibrant dust. "It worked well enough, for a time."

Vrana slid her hands underneath her to stop them from fidgeting. "How did they find the boy?"

"Someone in Cadence must have recognized him, told someone." Faolan paused, staring at Vrana as though she expected a response. "The soldiers came quickly, put the village to the sword."

"Did... did they find Turov?"

Faolan shook her head. "No, not yet, for returning the Holy Child has been of the highest priority to Penance. Too long had he gone without an appearance. The people were beginning to doubt, to whisper of revolt."

"Why would the Exemplar take him?" Vrana asked, her voice shaking under the burden of the secret she was keeping.

Anguis cleared his throat. "There are those in Penance who feel the boy is no different than any other Corrupted. They feel he is being manipulated, abused. Turov may have believed this as well, or perhaps he had his own reasons for taking the boy."

And they will never be known. Vrana looked at each of the elders, their eyes piercing the bones of her mask. *Because I killed him.* "What about Alexander Blodworth, then? If he was just an apprentice, what was he doing in Geharra?" *Keep talking,* she told herself, *harbinger of death, agent of entropy. They know. I know they know. So keep talking.*

"When there is no answer, a distraction can be just as effective at silencing a rumor," Anguis said. "What better a distraction than one that concerns the city you've been taught to despise?"

"They did this to Geharra because the Holy Child had disappeared?" Vrana shook her head. "They had to have other reasons."

"Perhaps." Faolan leaned towards Vrana. "But it seems to us the Red Worm was not part of the plan. With Mishra dead and Turov gone, an Exemplar was needed."

"We think that Blodworth was sent to Geharra to prove himself worthy of the role," Nuctea added. "The effects of the Crossbreed would be attributed to the Holy Child, which would restore the people of Penance's faith. It would have bought the Order favor and time."

"Smug would be those who saw their enemy learn the error of their ways," Faolan said; it sounded like a quote.

Why would he fire on me if he was harboring the boy? "They couldn't have expected to keep the city under their control like that forever," Vrana sputtered. *The young boy did have strange markings on his shoulder. It was him. Fuck, it was him.*

Anguis grunted in agreement. "I do not think they intended to. If they never found the Holy Child, or if the Crossbreed had become known, they could have reported he'd been killed in Geharra and a war would have been fought in his honor."

"But it seemed Alexander Blodworth had his own intentions," Faolan said. "The apprentices are almost as well-read as their masters;

it is not inconceivable that they would learn of the Worms of the Earth. After all, it was assassins from Six Pillars, pre-Penance, that had killed Victor Mors and most likely took his journals on the creatures."

Vrana felt her throat constrict. She dared not close her eyes, for she knew of the terrible images waiting in the dark there. "What about the Red Worm?" she managed to say, trying to think of anything but the pit.

Anguis rubbed his face in contemplation. "As of right now, there is little we can do. Penance must lay claim to the Worm, sustain it with bloodshed, or it will die. If they do wish to accept responsibility—not blame; that's something else entirely—then Eldrus will be forced to respond, if they haven't already."

"'The Red Worm stood high above the ground, raining gore upon the land, and the creatures of the land ate its bounty and were thankful for it,'" Faolan quoted, which was most certainly a passage from Victor Mors' writings.

Vrana slid her hands under her mask and rubbed her temples. "Where is Eldrus in all this? Jakob, he said that King Edgar hated Penance, that it was strange for him to let Penance's convoy pass over the Divide to get to Geharra."

"That is strange," Nuctea remarked. "Perhaps you have heard so little of Eldrus because King Edgar has had little to do with the affairs of the land of late."

Faolan yawned, resting her chin on her hand. "Two years ago, there was a rebellion, a group led by a man whose family was butchered by the King's men. The man was said to have been killed, too; yet, he returned from the grave and marched upon the city with a group of the oppressed from the Heartland towns and villages."

"We did not intervene," Anguis continued for the Wolf. "We were curious to see how the events would unfold. In the end, however, the group was put down, and the man vanished, likely into the Keep's deepest cell. The rebellion made the King and his advisor wary. But there have been whispers of a secret alliance between Eldrus and Penance."

Nuctea nodded. "Yes, there have."

"King Edgar may be more involved than we thought," Faolon added.

"This note," Anguis said, opening it and reading it quickly, "you have read it, yes?"

Vrana didn't respond.

"What do you make of it?" Anguis handed the note to Faolan, who read it and passed it to Nuctea.

"You… help the Corrupted," Vrana said, her tone accusatory.

"We help Nora," Nuctea corrected, sliding the note into a small pocket. "It seems she's willing to help you as well."

Vrana looked at the obsidian boulder, its surface shifting like that of an ocean. "It seems I'll need it."

"She'll make good on her word, Vrana," Faolan said. "If you still wish to destroy the Witch, we know of a place that may interest you."

"Where?" she asked as she covered the scars on her arm from the Horror of the Lake. "The Elys, isn't it? She's been in that area multiple times, and the stories they tell… it sounds like her. I would've stopped, I would've gone to the center, but I had R'lyeh."

Anguis stretched his legs and said, "The center of the Elys is home to the Inferi; it's covered in fields of the Gift of Sleep. I do not doubt what has happened to you, but there are many stories of the Elys; and oftentimes, it's because someone has wandered too close to the center."

"For the living, the Gift of Sleep is a hallucinogenic," Vrana said. "She was there, though. I think it's worth investigating."

"It is," Anguis agreed. "We'll be sending a team to the remnants of Alluvia. Several will be assigned the task of investigating the center of the Elys."

"Okay," Vrana said, nodding. "Then, what are you guys talking about?"

"It was Mara who first informed us of the Witch, and it was Mara who reminded your mother about the books she'd found. She met one of the Witch's creations on a bridge outside the small town of Nachtla." Faolan held the side of her white robe to keep it from the wind. "There is a house at the center of Nachtla the Witch was said to haunt. Mara had already lost interest in the tale when she learned this, and at the time, we hadn't a reason to pursue the truth of the claim."

"Where is Nachtla?" Vrana asked, having never seen it on the village map, which didn't mean much of anything as the elders, up until this point, had been constantly changing it.

"South of the Nameless Forest, east of Cathedra, near the sea. Its people abandoned the town for Cathedra and Gallows fifteen years ago. The yield was poor, and the air oppressive."

They want me to leave, to be rid of me should the Witch return, Vrana thought, *but I can't leave Aeson or my mother, not yet. And R'lyeh? She'll need me.*

Anguis stood up, and Faolan and Nuctea followed his example. "We have not heard from Deimos, Lucan, or Serra, but we do not worry about their wellbeing. If any flesh fiends found their way into the sewers, Serra will make short work of them. As for Deimos and Lucan, posing as soldiers of Penance will be amongst the easiest of their accomplishments."

Vrana nodded, standing up. She had not expected news of her companions, but it comforted her to hear that the elders were confident in their abilities. She scratched her legs, which were irritated from the grass, and picked away the little black ants that were scurrying across her chest. She didn't feel as though she had contributed to the meeting in a meaningful manner, and the purpose of it was lost on her. Until…

Anguis stepped forward, took Vrana by the shoulders, and leaned in close enough so that she could see his pale face beyond the skull of his mask. "We have not heard from Deimos, Lucan, or Serra, but we must continue on without them. We encourage you to seek out Nachtla but painfully implore you to go much farther."

"What do you mean?" Vrana tried to pull away but was unable. She looked to Nuctea and Faolan, but they were gone. She looked beyond Anguis and saw that the wall of roots around them was unraveling fast.

"There is an island two miles off the coast of Nacthla," he hissed, "in the center of the Widening Gyre, the Sailor's Bane. On this island, our people have a village unknown to but a few, for the waters allow no trespassers."

"There's no village…" Vrana began to say, stopping herself, as she was all too aware of the elders' talent for making things disappear. "Why are you telling me this?" she said, her hands scrambling to grab onto Anguis as she felt the ground below her feet give way.

"Because you are invested, persistent, and trustworthy," he appealed. "Because the only other person in this village who truly knows of the horrors of Geharra is a traumatized thirteen-year-old girl."

Vrana cried out as the garden melted around her, like a painting left out in the rain. She felt Anguis release her, and, afraid that she may fall into fathomless space beneath them, she held onto him tighter, hugging him as a scared child would a father. "I can't do that again. I can't see that again," she lied.

"You won't have to," he said as he eased her onto the ground. Once again, she was at the entrance of the garden of the elders, the back of their house a few feet away. "It is our village, yes, but if another Worm will be born to this earth, it will be from there. No one will force you should you choose not to go, but this will not be like Geharra." He released her. "The chamber below the village must be sealed in the event Eldrus or Penance learns of its location."

Vrana gasped as her lungs burned for air. "And if I say no?" she managed to ask.

"Then, regretfully, another will be recruited. You've always a choice Vrana," he said, bowing slightly, "even if it is the illusion of one." He deliberated for a moment, scratched his neck. "You now know more than most in our tribe. If you go to the island and do this for us, you will know even more."

Vrana swallowed words of insult so that she could take the bait. "Like what?"

Anguis leaned in and whispered this into Vrana's ear: "Why we aid Nora, and why her arm is free of Corruption. Why so few of our people are born each year, and what we've decided to do about it." He pushed his mask against hers, to be sure no one else could hear. "You will know where we've come from and where we've been. You will know why the flesh fiends have become myth, and why it is best for them to stay that way."

CHAPTER XXVI

"Who the fuck does he think he is?" Vrana shouted, her voice, muffled by her mask, carrying through the tunnel beneath the Archive. "What am I supposed to say to that? Oh, no, I'm sorry. Not interested. That sounds neat and all, but it's not really my kind of thing. What the fuck?"

Aeson lifted up his mask and held it at his side. A bat fluttered by, chirping frantically in pursuit of a meal too small to be seen. "They're very good at getting people to do things for them, but in general, they don't lie."

"Oh," Vrana said, throwing her hands into the air, "well, that makes all the difference. 'You will know where we've come from and where we've been.'" She shook her head, disgusted. "You can't say no to something like that."

Aeson nodded, biting his fingernail. He looked at her for a moment and then said, "Why are you so angry? You've always wanted to leave Caldera."

Vrana clenched her teeth. "I'm more offended than anything else."

"The island exists, Vrana," Aeson said. He ran his fingers through his hair, slapped his neck; a cave spider crawled along his knuckles before leaping into the shadows. "I hate these damn things," he said, massaging the reddening mark it left.

"Thanks for telling me about it, the island," Vrana retorted. "Also, it would have been nice to have been prepared for the Worms."

"Vrana, that's not fair. How did I know it would be a Worm? And the island? I just found out about it while you were gone," he said softly. "I wish that I could tell you more, but I can't. You know I can't. And as much as I would love to ask you to stay, to never go back out there, to never leave the village again…" He raised the skull and lowered it onto his head. "I would never do that to you. You'd hate me for it. And you'd be right to."

Vrana bit her lip. For all her ire, she could not help but admit to herself that the thought of returning to the field excited her. "Just as it would be wrong of me to ask you to leave this place, to do something else—to tell me everything," she grumbled.

"How you'll reach the island is beyond me: Hundreds of boats have tried to sail those waters in the past, and they all failed." Aeson laughed. "I couldn't even say what the island is called or where it falls exactly on a map; that's how little I know about the place."

"They mentioned a chamber, some area where they believe there's another Worm. They said I could seal it. Is that possible?"

Aeson exhaled, bewildered. "It must be."

"One person, though," Vrana said as she became fixated on the glowing, yellow rocks embedded in the wall, as they dimmed and brightened and dimmed once more, "doesn't seem enough."

"They sent four to Geharra, and that's a massive city. The village on the island must be much smaller. By the elders' logic, the mathematics makes sense." Aeson waited for Vrana to laugh.

She didn't. "You don't seem all that worried about me. Does that make me a bitch for wishing that you were?"

"If I thought falling apart would make you stay, I would be in a million pieces right now."

"Fair enough," Vrana said, carefully resting her head against Aeson's chest, minding the beak of her mask so as to not gore him. "You would stop me if you didn't think I could do this, right?"

"I'd try," Aeson said shakily.

At nightfall, Vrana returned home, where she found Bjørn exiting through the front door, her armor thrown over his shoulders. When she asked him what he was doing, he wrapped his massive arms around her, squeezed until she felt deflated, and told her he was not surprised she'd survived the ordeal. She thanked him, said that she had missed him, but only a little, and asked the Bear what he was doing putting his paws all over her armor.

"Everything, everything is a mess. This will take weeks to clean," he complained, though she knew he had been secretly looking forward to this moment ever since she left.

"I have a few days, at best."

"Going on a vacation, eh? You've just come back."

"There's more to be done."

Bjørn nodded and belched, the sound sending what appeared to be of one of Anguis' snakes slithering into a nearby bush. "That's wrong of them; you've just initiated. Don't let them wear you down like those masks of theirs."

Vrana kicked a stone and sent it soaring toward the center of Caldera. "I want to," she said. "I want to go."

"Aye, you're so convincing, girl. Will you be fighting flesh fiends this time, too? Or will it be one of those Worm things I keep hearing about?"

It was the elders with whom he was aggravated, not her. "It won't be like Geharra."

"And Geharra wasn't supposed to be like Geharra," Bjørn said, spitting in the direction of the house of the elders.

Trying to lighten the mood, Vrana said, "And this is coming from the same man who stared Death in the face?"

The Bear barely laughed. "Stepped aside, didn't It? You don't have to prove anything to these people." He held out his arm, gesturing to the village. "Not after what I heard them say about you because of the Witch."

I'd almost forgotten, she said to herself, finding that, once again, she had too many things to take into consideration and not enough time or willpower to process them. "I'm not trying to prove anything," she snapped. "I won't be able to sleep knowing that someone else is doing what I started."

"Penance started this, girl."

"You know what I mean, damn it," she said, feeling herself go red in the face. "I don't... I don't want to see what I saw in Geharra ever again. But that doesn't mean I'm going to avoid it."

"How did it happen? How was the Red Worm woken?" Bjørn shifted his weight to one leg and stared at her accusingly. "I don't mean the sacrifices either."

"The necklace," Vrana began, "there was a necklace; it was a key of sorts. I found it during my third trial, carried it with me. I just wanted to figure out what it was. I had it in my hand, and it fell into the pit. That's... how it happened."

"So you dropped it?" he said, the muscles in his neck tensing.

"I did," Vrana said, trailing off. *Is he blaming me? Why?* Her eyes felt large, heavy with the tears that only surface when one disappoints those whose opinions truly matter. *But it wasn't me, was it? The necklace wanted me to let go.*

"Do you blame yourself?"

Do I? "No, I don't."

"I hope you're telling me the truth, girl," Bjørn said, eying her suspiciously. "Guilt will guide you to the grave, if you let it."

"I gave you my reasons, old man," Vrana said, stepping up to him, the mountain of muscle and scars.

"So you did." He knocked her back playfully. "Where's my bow?"

"What bow?"

"The one you absconded with, the one you just had to have."

By the time the cloud of dust cleared around Bjørn, Vrana had already disappeared inside the house, locking the door behind her. Her timing was impeccable, for just as her stomach had finished growling, Adelyn emerged from another room with several plates filled to their edges with food. The smell of the rice, cooked meat, and vegetables made her salivate like a dog, and like a dog, she hurried after her mother to the table, begging for scraps.

"Hey," R'lyeh said weakly, waving at Vrana.

"Hey, how are you feeling?" She closed the gap between them and took the girl's hand. "You look a little better than before."

"I do?" she said, grateful for the compliment. "Thanks."

"What kind of nasty potions is she making you drink?" Vrana asked as her mother set the table quietly.

"Oh, I don't mind them," R'lyeh claimed, though her pained face suggested otherwise.

"That's right," Adelyn chimed. "She doesn't mind them because they are good, and good for her. Don't pay this one any attention, R'lyeh," she said, taking off her mask and sitting down beside the Octopus. "She was the pickiest child when she was little."

"She doesn't seem that way now," R'lyeh said, snickering as Vrana ripped off the raven's head and began to shamelessly shovel food into her mouth.

Vrana looked up at her mother, food pasted to her face and on the tips of her hair, swallowed what she was chewing, and smiled grotesquely. Once she began to feel the consequences of her gluttony take form inside of her, she leaned away from the table, wiped her face with her arm, and apologized to R'lyeh for her lack of manners. R'lyeh accepted her apology and set upon her portions ravenously. Vrana's mother could not help but laugh as she sipped on a cup of wine, pleased with her patient's progress and her daughter's presence.

"They, the elders, they want me to leave again," Vrana murmured from her food-induced coma. Her eyes shifted lazily to R'lyeh, who was struggling to stay awake.

"I know," her mother said, finger dancing around the rim of her cup.

Vrana pursed her lips and said, "What don't you know?"

Her mother looked back at her, confused.

"Do they tell you everything? Why'd you let me go north when you were so willing to let me believe that it more or less didn't even exist?"

"That was a selfish mistake; the elders were very convincing." Adelyn crossed her legs, leaned forward on both elbows. "Our numbers are low, and preservation of our young is more important than ever." She thought for a moment, took a drink, and said, "Did you want me to stop you? Slap your hand like a child and say no?"

Vrana shook her head. "Of course not."

"Where are they sending you?"

Vrana hesitated, and then, after realizing she told the same sensitive information to Aeson, said, "Nachtla, and an island off the coast of the Nameless Forest, in the Widening Gyre."

Adelyn choked on her drink. "Why Nachtla?"

"The Witch had an extended stay in the town. I guess the elders think she may have left something behind."

Her mother stared off in the distance. She nodded and reached across the table for the snoring R'lyeh's plate. "Does she still come to you?"

"Sometimes," Vrana said, "but it's mostly these scars." She ran her fingers over the raised flesh that scaled her arms. "I can't tell if they hurt because they are healing, or if it's because she's trying to reach me."

"Healing, I'd say," her mother said hopefully, taking her daughter's arm and rubbing it. "I've seen the Sailor's Bane. It's very misleading. The current is strong, but sometimes the water hardly moves."

"Because of the Nameless Forest close by," Vrana said, her guess more of a question hoping for an answer.

"Most likely," her mother said with a sigh as she gathered up the remnants of their meal.

"Have... have you ever been there?"

Vrana's mother smiled. "Before I met your father..." she paused in search of words suddenly lost. "Before I met your father, I'd made it a goal of mine to go everywhere, see everything. I saved the Nameless Forest for last—you know, just in case the stories turned out to be true and the trees ate me."

Vrana smirked.

"Being the impulsive girl that I was, I took one look at that horrible stretch of land and said 'Why not?' Of course, if someone had been with me, they would have given a day's worth of reasons to turn away, but I was alone. I did everything alone. I thought I was smarter than everybody else."

"You probably were," Vrana said, remembering the state of awe that she would be in when she used to watch her mother mix and brew potions from the unlikeliest of ingredients.

"Probably," Adelyn said, laughing loud enough to make R'lyeh groan in her sleep. "I'll never forget it, that Forest; the way the tops of the trees moved in slow waves. And the smell, so thick and rich— a blend of hundreds of species that even I couldn't name. I remember feeling the wind rushing past me, as though the Forest meant to pull me in, take me in."

Vrana felt another hunger growing within her. "Did you go in?"

Adelyn shook her head. Her eyes dimmed: The memory had reached its end. "No," she said, "no, I didn't. I came close, but I got scared. I saw through the trees and in the grass debris—pieces of wood and stone and tools—and I stopped where I stood. A long time ago, there had been three villages built beside the Nameless Forest, each one meant to harvest what they could from it. The Corrupted were especially interested in the vermillion veins growing on some of the trees. I was, too, for a while.

"The length of time changes depending upon who you ask, but shortly after those towns were built, each one was abandoned." Adelyn stood up and balanced herself.

"That sounds like Geharra," Vrana mused. She thought about the veins she'd seen in the city's fountain and Deimos' indifference to them.

"A few days later, they found the Corrupted that'd gone missing from those towns. They were strewn across the trees, half-disintegrated, miles of webbing pouring out of each of their mouths. The Corrupted abandoned the project, abandoned the towns; left the fate of the forest to the stories that—" Vrana's mother yawned, paused, and yawned again. "—that you always hear about."

"That sounds like Geharra," Vrana repeated as she, too, yawned.

"That sounds like we need to go to bed," Adelyn said. "Help me wake the little one up."

"Okay."

Adelyn chewed on her lip. "There's something I…"

Vrana turned around. "Huh?"

"Nothing." She smiled. "I was going to say there was something I wanted to tell you. But I forgot."

"Just like that?"

"Just like that."

Because it was the very thing she wanted to do more than anything else, Vrana found that she could not fall asleep. The food, drink, and her mother's anecdote had stirred her thoughts. She lay in her bed, one hand on her nervous stomach, watching the images in her mind on the lids of her eyes. Again, she saw Deimos and Lucan trudging through the waters outside Geharra, giving to the merfolk their masks and the nearing Corrupted a lie. Once more, she watched as Serra retreated underground, tasked to kill what should not have been given a chance to exist. She wondered if the Bat and the Beetle had fallen on the swords of Penance's soldiers, if the Piranha had become lost to himself in the Crossbreed's haze.

Vrana turned on her side, opened her eyes, and stared at her mask, the raven's head. The beak was scuffed, faded, and a few feathers had fallen from the skull. *Maybe I am a raven after all*, she said to herself. *A raven follows Death and revels in its works and keeps the company of violence. A raven gathers secrets like a magpie gathers trinkets. A raven is a shadow, a shade—all those things we tell ourselves we could not ever do and then do anyway.*

"At least I'm not a crow," Vrana said. She stretched out her limbs and then went stiff. "Oh no," she said, sitting up, "Son of a bitch! I forgot about Blix."

Without ceremony, she awoke the next day and proceeded to the house of the elders to deliver her decision. She would do what was asked of her; and in her opinion, the sooner the sealing was done, the better it would be for everyone. There was no doubt in her mind that word of the Red Worm had spread across the continent. It would only be a matter of time until armies assembled and politicians postured to make threats and promises they couldn't see through. The last thing that she needed to worry about were roadblocks and encampments impeding her progress, especially if the story of the Worms was true, and the birth of one would provoke the birth of another.

Of course, Aeson would not take the news lightly, though he would try to appear indifferent. While she would never will it, Vrana often wondered what it would be like for her to take his place, to be the one to watch him walk away under the thought that he may never return.

"He'll forgive me," she said to herself as she walked in the alley between two houses. "R'lyeh will, too."

At that moment, Vrana stopped where she stood, ankle-deep in a fresh puddle of mud. Mag of the Jackal stepped in front of her, a small blade in hand. She looked disheveled, defeated. Her mask, halfway to bone, was dirty, riddled with holes through which her long, dark hair ran. Svaya had warned Vrana about her, and here she was, having tracked her prey at last.

"Running off again?" Mag asked, her torn garments revealing the scar on her chest where her left breast had been.

I should have brought my ax, Vrana thought as she eyed the weapon the Jackal held. "I'm so very sorry for what happened to your children."

"Are you?" Mag moved to prevent passage. "You didn't seem to be that night in the Archive. You looked right past us as we suffered."

"I didn't know what had happened," Vrana said, remembering the scene: the children atop the tables, wailing and gripping at their skin as it threatened to fall to the floor.

Mag's breathing became shallow. "Did you know that she would come?"

Vrana shook her head and gave the woman a sympathetic look, even though she knew Mag could not see it.

"Why did she do it?"

"I don't know," Vrana said. "To prove a point, maybe," she followed-up. "Put that knife away."

Mag was taken aback by the command. She took a step forward, raised the blade to challenge Vrana. Vrana contemplated and then grabbed the Jackal by the wrist and twisted her hand until the knife fell into the mud. Mag wrenched free of Vrana's grasp and hissed. She watched as the knife sank into the muck, as surprised as Mag by what she had just done.

Mag rubbed at what was likely a sprain. "Is she still with you?" Just like that, her anger was gone.

"Yes," Vrana said, "but hopefully not for much longer."

"Little Shagha keeps asking me where her brothers are." Mag pulled her clothes tight against her body. "I tell her what happened, but then she asks again the next day."

"I just need to find a way to the Witch," Vrana said. "Spread word of her so that others can be prepared. It's fear that feeds her."

"Isn't it always?" Mag sighed and started to turn away. "I never saw her."

Vrana cocked her head. "What do you mean?"

"I thought I did, but I didn't."

Doubting her, Vrana said, "You probably don't want to remember. My mother described her to me. She was definitely the woman from my dreams."

Mag shrugged, said something under her breath, and walked away. Vrana stayed in the alley for a moment, the point of the knife pricking her toe. She tried to understand what the Jackal had been getting at in regards to the Witch, but found she could not make sense of the woman. Not only had her mother seen the Maiden of Pain but so, too, had Aeson. Vrana stepped out of the mud and wiped her feet on the foundation of the nearest house. *Is that what will become of R'lyeh and me? Hollow women haunting alleyways, looking for someone to hurt with all our hate?*

Anguis was exiting the garden when Vrana arrived at the house of the elders. Three black vipers were slithering behind him, baring their hollow fangs at nothing in particular. He nodded at her as he tightened his grip on the stone cupped in his hand.

"It is lively today," he said, drawing Vrana's attention to Kistvaen, where rocks and boulders were falling from the cliffs into the morning fog.

"What's happening?"

"Hmmm." He knelt down on one knee, allowing a viper to slither up his leg and onto his arm. The stone he carried glinted in the sun; by its texture and color, Vrana could see that it was obsidian. "Have you decided?"

"Is that from the garden?" Vrana pointed at the stone, which seemed to have been chipped away from the much larger boulder at the maze's center.

"Yes," the Snake said, "a piece of the mountain."

Vrana leaned forward, catching in the stone's surface a reflection that was not of their surroundings. "What's it for?" Her eyes followed the stone as Anguis stuffed into his pocket, the images of fire she'd seen seared into her mind.

"Have you decided?"

Vrana cleared her throat. "Yes."

Anguis put his hands on Vrana's shoulders. "The island is known as Lacuna."

"How will I get there?" She shrugged off the Snake.

"From Nacthla's highest tower, go east. Where the land meets the sea, there will be a small dock and your guide." Anguis stopped speaking as a group of children dashed by. "You will go alone."

"No," Vrana said boldly, "give me Blix."

"Of course," he said. He whistled a sharp melody that made Vrana's ears ring.

Her eyes widened as she caught sight of black wings beating against the blue sky. "What did you do to him?"

Like the masks of those accomplished figures in Caldera, bits of bone shone through Blix's feathers. The crow was thinner than she remembered. Vrana noted how his beak was weathered, chipped away, not unlike the beaks of the birds she'd seen in the Elys. Did the Horror of the Field do this? Or was this the work of the elders?

"What happened to you?" Vrana asked the bird as it landed carefully on her outstretched arm. "What did they do to you?" She ran her fingers across Blix's neck, down his back.

"Deimos gave him a message, and he delivered it to us. But somewhere in his journey, Blix was delayed." Anguis clicked his tongue at the vipers coiling around his feet, and they slithered away with purpose.

"What do you mean?" Vrana stepped back with Blix, into the shade cast by the house of the elders. The village was beginning to take notice of the conversation. "Where did he go?"

"Most of the images were lost, but Nuctea was able to retrieve a few from his mind," Anguis said, joining Vrana. "There were flashes of Alluvia and the Heartland and the Elys. And then there was darkness, and pillars, and curtains over glistening pits."

"You too?" Vrana cried as Blix nipped at her finger lovingly. "The Witch took him into the Void."

"She took Blix into the Void," Anguis lowered his voice, "but when he came out, he came out in Nachtla."

"That's why you're sending me there?" Vrana shook her head. "This isn't a coincidence. She knew you would find the images and tell me."

Blix screeched in agreement as he clawed his way up to her shoulder.

"It would be wrong of us to expect you to go to Nachtla after seeing to Lacuna. The choice is yours to make. No one will fault you if you do not."

There is nothing dishonorable in knowing your limits. "Sure," Vrana said, nodding. "Maybe Deimos and the others will be back by then."

Anguis gave no response. He tilted his head and dismissed himself into the house of the elders.

CHAPTER XXVII

"I'm leaving tomorrow morning," Vrana said to Aeson, pulling his arm tighter around her body. They were back at the hot springs.

Nuctea had come to Vrana's home shortly after her meeting with Anguis and delivered the deadline. She was sure R'lyeh had overheard: the girl had locked herself in her room and refused to leave it for the rest of the day.

"It'll be months until I see you again." Aeson took her fingers and kissed their tips.

"I'll be quick." She reached over with her other hand and flicked his lip. "I promise."

Aeson sat up, stretched out his legs, and dipped them into the hot spring. "I should come with you. I should know about Lacuna. I should come."

Vrana bit her lip and also sat up. "You should!"

Aeson stared at Vrana's rippling reflection in the steaming water. "If only they could be so easily swayed."

"I'm sorry, Aeson." She rested her head on his shoulder, her hair sticking to his skin.

"Vrana," he said and kissed her above the ear, "let's not have our relationship turn into one of those tortured tales lining the shelves of the Archive. You'll be back, and I'll be here, waiting."

Vrana smiled, touched his chest. "Don't you dare think of me, boy."

Aeson laughed. "Hurry up and leave already. My other girlfriends will be here soon."

"Girlfriends? Not bad, not bad." She looked into his lying eyes and saw within them her own. "Give me my clothes, sir. I've had my fill."

Aeson shook his head and tossed her belongings across the cave.

In need of her armor and his charming personality, Vrana scoured the village for Bjørn. Eventually, she found him towering over the ten-year-olds in the training yard, orchestrating mock battles with wooden swords and battered shields. He celebrated their yelps of pain and darkening bruises with a squeeze of their shoulders, and then nudged them back into the fray. For those who preferred the bow and its companion, the arrow, the Bear would sneak up on them mid-draw and howl into their ears. Vrana remembered Bjørn had attempted this once when she was younger; and as a result, she turned the bow on the Bear and fired an arrow directly into his chest. Fortunately for him, and her, she'd been a rather weak child; the arrowhead only went in a few centimeters before calling it quits.

Vrana liked to think that this was how they became friends.

"Leaving again?" Bjørn said with his back to Vrana.

"Feel free to go in my place, if you'd like." Vrana clapped her hand on the Bear's shoulder. "What are we learning today?"

Bjørn shook his head at a young boy who appeared as though he was going to turn on his grass-stained heels and flee from his partner. "They're soft," he remarked as the young boy cowered beneath his shield, like a turtle in its shell. "Knowing about the North has made them soft."

Vrana bit her lip. "You don't think the fact that they are ten has anything to do with it?"

"You would've cut a man's throat at their age if need be," Bjørn said, still refusing to make eye contact with her.

"I'm not and wasn't a normal girl," Vrana admitted. "No child, not even a Corrupted, should be asked to do that."

"No one is going to ask them." He shouted at a small girl to watch her footing.

"It's not as though my class was particularly fierce." Vrana took her hand off the Bear, punched him in the arm. "Korr became a harvester of all things."

Bjørn laughed and looked at the ground. "And look what you've become."

"If not for the Witch," Vrana started, considering her words, "I wouldn't mind being the elders' errand girl."

"Are you sure? I can't imagine the sight of ten thousand dead sits well with anyone."

Vrana sighed. "I'm sure you've seen your fair share of shit. I'm not going to break. I know when I need help."

Bjørn cleared his throat. Finally, he looked at Vrana, the hint of his face deep in his mask, and said, "Anguis is a snake for a reason." He threw his hands up into the air as a small, brown-eyed girl tripped over her feet and landed teeth first. "See me later for your armor."

Vrana did as Bjørn commanded. She had sex with Aeson again, and both parties pretended afterwards they were okay.

Later, she promised her mother she'd be safe, and apologized to R'lyeh for leaving her so soon.

"Don't worry about it," Adelyn said as the Octopus retreated into her room, leaving Vrana feeling like a selfish asshole.

"Please, take good care of her."

Vrana's mother put her finger under her daughter's chin. "Don't worry. If you don't take care of yourself, it won't matter what I do for her."

"I mean that much to her, don't I?"

Adelyn nodded as R'lyeh slammed her door. "More than you'll ever know."

The elders met her midday on the outskirts of Caldera. They handed her a light blue stone the size of her palm, and they told her it would seal the Worm's chamber. Then they conjured another horse from the fields, and she mounted it. She sat there a moment, Blix treading on her scalp, and waved to those who'd gathered to see her off (Adelyn, Bjørn, and Aeson, and that was it). Not saying a word to them, she tightened her armor, fastened her weapons, and kicked her horse into a sprint.

And just like that, she was gone again. It was as though she had never returned. Ceremony could wait. Sometimes, to protect something, you have to make it unremarkable.

Summer was waning, and soon autumn would fall upon the heated land and cool its temper. A day out of Caldera, Vrana decided she wanted to see Cadence, the village where she'd unknowingly led the Holy Child of Penance.

It had been music and the maddened flames of a bonfire that led Vrana there first. Now, she had the tornados of smoke twisting on the horizon to guide her way.

Cadence had collapsed under the weight of its declared blasphemy. Houses were gutted, smoldering altars to the god of ruin. The bonfire, which had once stood before a score of dancing bodies, had fallen over, revealing the burned corpses of the village trapped inside. Vrana considered for a moment that these corpses could have been wayward travelers offered up in human sacrifice, that the people of Cadence were cruel and had deserved their fate, but she knew better. Penance had come to this village upon receiving word of the Holy Child's location and murdered it for daring to look upon him and seeing, with unworthy eyes, their lord's vessel as he was: Corrupted.

Blix cawed and clutched the roof of one of the few houses still standing. He scanned the devastation carefully, as though taking notes. Vrana nodded at the bird, which he took as a sign to move further into Cadence, and dismounted from her horse. The conjured beast's flesh swirled and coalesced with the substance of its making— soil and rock, root and bone—as it stood diligently beside a dry trough.

Vrana felt partially responsible for Cadence's outcome, if only for giving the boy into their custody. Ax in hand, nose wrinkling at the smell of burnt flesh and rain, she rummaged through the rubble of misery, finding more dead among the debris. Bodies clogged her path as she went deeper into the village, their arms rigid, outstretched, forever posed in a plea for mercy. Had the welfare of the Holy Child truly been Samuel Turov's reason for stealing him away from Penance? Or had his act of kindness been premeditated, preapproved by those who shared his station? She wished Alexander Blodworth had still been alive the moment they happened upon the pit, so that she could have taken him by the throat and bled from him his secrets.

Vrana let out a sharp whistle that brought the horse to her. She mounted it, had one last look at the last of Cadence, and then kicked the beast into a gallop. The village became a gray blur of squandered potential, and before she knew it, Vrana was in the countryside once more.

Days later, at dusk, when the conjured horse had finally returned to the earth, Vrana found herself a niche in the land, a shallow cave wreathed in weeds, and rested. The carcasses inside told her that something had recently been there, but her hunger countered the prospect that this thing may make a very nice meal itself. She consulted the map from the elders to verify what she already knew, that she was still days away from her destination, and removed the sealing stone for closer inspection. It was the color of a robin's egg, with streaks of white, as though the image of lightning had been seared into its surface. The stone was heavy to hold, and the notion of what was inside intrigued Vrana. The elders provided no information as to where they'd procured the object or how it functioned. They told Vrana to simply find the chamber, drop the stone into the Worm's hole, and swiftly leave the scene.

"Don't wait around to see if it works," her mother had whispered to her the night she left. "Come back to us. Don't wait around there. Be smart about what you see and hear. Please."

At midnight, Vrana camped at the entrance of the cave, ears pricked and eyes set on the field before her. Moon cats padded through the brittle grass, the limbs of their prey flailing through the gaps in their fangs. Black boars meandered with snouts to the ground, tusks signing the soil with their red signatures. An alligator in a distant lake clamped its jaws shut and rolled its meal into an early grave. Nearer the cave, where the trees grew out of one another, a skyswallower ambled forward on two legs, planted itself, and extended its jaw. Vrana could not help but smile as the creature's skin became camouflaged with the colors of its surroundings.

"Awesome," she whispered. Then: "What's that?" She gripped the ax and leaned forward.

She strained her ears, lifted up her mask to hear more clearly. Someone, or something, was crawling in the underbrush. Her mind immediately went to the last place she wanted it to: Geharra's pit, and the flesh fiends inside. *It's dark, and I'm alone,* she thought, *so why wouldn't it be one? Now that I know they're out there, I'll see them everywhere.*

Vrana waited with bated breath, a stilled sentinel of the forgotten cave. While she watched the strange shape crawl through the shadows, she searched her thoughts for all she knew about the flesh fiends. They were said to move through the fissures in the deep earth, their fear of, or vulnerability to, sunlight having driven them there. Some claimed that Vrana's people had locked them away underground so as to prevent them from surfacing for new flesh. Others, however, stated that the flesh fiends had merely become lost in the catacombs of the world. Their origin was often a point of contention among self-proclaimed scholars as well. Were they newborns that had clawed their way out of the Old World's cadaver? Or had they existed before the Trauma, under a different name, fulfilling a different role?

Vrana was tired—and tired of waiting. Carefully, she backed into the cave and found a place where she could rest. She lifted with the handle of her ax a loop of razor nettle and laid it out a few feet before her. She rummaged through her satchel for a vial she had taken from her mother's supplies prior to leaving. Finding it, she removed the stopper and made a circle around her with the cloudy contents. Extracted from a grumbler's gut, the liquid smelled like soured milk, burnt hair, and rotted teeth. She would not sleep well, but when she did, she could do so without worrying about waking to something gnawing on her neck.

The next morning Vrana awoke to find the circle unbroken and the razor nettle undisturbed. She was certain she'd dreamt while she slept, but the moment she tried to grasp it, the dream was gone. She gathered up her belongings and shambled towards the sun. At the mouth of the cave, she yawned loudly, stretched and squealed, and then stumbled backward, in shock, as her eyes finally adjusted to the light,.

All around her and throughout the field were strips of fur and muscle, chunks of skin and shards of bone, souvenirs for her viewing from the unseen hunter. Vrana stepped over a stiffened skyswallower; its mouth had been torn apart, its tongue crammed into its throat. *That could be me*, she thought, staring at a patch of blood-striped grass, where flies fought for property on a pair of lungs. *Why didn't it come for me?*

The days that followed were uneventful and the nights equally so. Vrana slept without harassment and traveled freely the untended roadways of the eastern expanse. There was little to find beyond Cadence, and it seemed strange to Vrana that the Corrupted had neglected to colonize this side of the continent. As the days wore on, her mind began to turn on itself. She began to see in every distant forest and ragged mountain the spires and steeples of civilization. *Is that a town? Is this the Heartland?* It never was and never would be—she was still weeks away from the Northern kingdoms—but unfortunately for Vrana, common sense had a tendency to flee when it was most needed.

"I could always wander amongst the Corrupted, like Mara," Vrana mumbled to herself days later as she consulted the map under the shade of an old oak. Voices lifted her eyes from the parchment to a hill crowned with orange grass. "The hell?"

Two young Corrupted males were walking down the hillside, each bearing a bucket, one filled with water, the other fruit. They were shirtless, and the Corruptions on their right arms glowed like hot coals. They spoke loudly, went about their business carelessly. If they'd seen Vrana, then they weren't intimidated by her presence, which made it all the more imperative she move from her position.

"David, David, David—it doesn't matter what you think," one Corrupted said. He stumbled over a rock, sloshing a bit of water on the parched earth.

David laughed at his friend and said, "Martin, Martin, Martin—you're too gullible. You'd swim in the Black Reef if someone said you'd find gold there."

Martin shook his head and spat. "I'll take my cock over gold any day."

Vrana moved carefully around the tree, pressing her back hard into the crumbling bark. From where she sat, she noticed embedded into the soil the stump of a wooden pole. Running her fingers through dirt, she found the remains of a telephone cable, once vocal chords of a now-muted nation.

"What are you going to do then, eh?" David asked as they stopped, dropped their buckets, and rested.

A shadow glided over Vrana. She looked up and saw Blix circling against the clouds. *Stay there.*

"I'll see what he's about."

"You know what he's about." David picked up his bucket, snatched an apple from inside, and bit into it. "How can you put your trust in a man who ran when things stopped going his way, yeah?"

"Well, he's not really man is he?" Martin grinned as he said this.

"He got captured, anyway."

Vrana cocked her head, confused.

"That's bullshit, and you know it! Who're we meeting if he's locked up?" David laughed. "When's the meet? Maybe I'll come with."

"Blue-haired woman. Hex. That's her name. Or something like that."

"That does sound…"

Vrana felt a surge of adrenaline within her body as David paused and looked toward the old oak. Had he seen her? Heard her? Left with no choice, she stood up, forced to do that which she should've done a few minutes earlier. It hadn't been since the crowd outside Nora that Vrana had fought a Corrupted. *Maybe I'll just take a limb from each to keep the balance and then let them hobble on their way. I don't have time for this shit.*

But before Vrana could step out from behind the tree, the Corrupted were already panicking, dropping their belongings in favor of the knives they kept in their pockets.

"Just… just leave us alone. We'll go!" David cried.

"David, David," Martin said. "Over there, there's another! There's two." He tapped his friend and pointed to Vrana as she came out from behind the tree. "It's a goddamn ambush."

CHAPTER XXVIII

R'lyeh had followed her, and she'd brought all the hate and pain she was saving for Penance. She was crouched low, brandishing the talons of the Cruel Mother in each hand. She was drenched in sweat and sunburned and almost as dirty as she'd been when they found her in the pit. Dried blood covered her arms and mask, and dangling from her hair were strands of a cobweb, its eight-legged architect still attached.

"Please," Martin begged, swinging his knife back and forth between R'lyeh and Vrana. "Please, let us go."

R'lyeh launched at the Corrupted, leaving Vrana no time to think. The girl tackled Martin to the ground; a yelp escaped her mask as his knife glanced across her side. R'lyeh put her elbow into his throat, and as his eyes bulged from their sockets, she stabbed him repeatedly in the stomach. He tried to push her off, but he was dying too fast; all his strength was running out with the blood now pooling beneath him.

Vrana screamed at R'lyeh for her to stop, but the girl ignored her; she continued to twist the talons, and her fist, deeper into Martin. David tried to bring his blade down onto the girl, but Vrana intervened, catching him by the wrist and shoving him away. Quickly, he came to his feet, lip bloodied from where he'd bitten into it, and moved to save his friend.

"No!" Vrana cried, ducking as David slashed at her. She spun around; hit him in the back of the legs with the head of her ax. As he tried to get up, she slammed her fist into his face, cutting her knuckles on his teeth.

"R'lyeh!" Vrana kicked the girl off Martin, and as R'lyeh fell backward, her hand slipped out of his stomach gash, dragging with it a chunk of liver. "What are you doing?!"

"What I'm supposed to!" she sulked. She wiped her hands on the ground, giving the grass a new color to wear.

"Why are you here? How are you here?" Vrana said breathlessly, watching as Martin writhed—and then died.

David groaned as he sat up; winced as he yanked free a tooth dangling from his gum. "Get it over with, Night Terrors," he said, spitting out mouthfuls of blood.

"He's Corrupted, Vrana," R'lyeh said, as though challenging Vrana.

"Get up," Vrana said. She looked at Martin's torso: Insects were already crawling inside it, biting and chewing their way to the best parts. "Get up," she repeated, gripping her ax tightly.

"I thought you'd be happy to see me." R'lyeh stood, the daggers dripping gore onto her feet.

They were too far from Caldera to turn back, and the Octopus was too far gone to make the trip on her own. Vrana shook her head. Would she hold it against herself if she were to slap the girl? Her mother had done all that she could for R'lyeh—she'd tended her cuts and bruises and filled her stomach to its brim—but it hadn't been enough.

David started to laugh nervously. His hand searched the grass for his knife, and when he found it, he stood up on shaking legs. "What is this? Who are you?" He swatted at Blix as the crow flew past his head. "You're not Night Terrors."

He thinks we're human, Vrana thought. *This isn't how Night Terrors are supposed to act.*

"What do you want? I've nothing!" David snarled.

I got no reason to kill him, but we can't just walk away. Vrana approached the Corrupted and outstretched her ax, so that it rested beneath his chin. "Who were you talking about?" she asked, biding her time.

"What?" Strands of bloody saliva clung to his lips.

Vrana tensed her arm; she could hear the edge of the ax scrapping against his stubble. "The man you were going on about with your friend."

"He wasn't my friend." David's cheeks twitched, and his eyes became glassy. "You're with him, aren't you? He's disguising himself as a Night Terror now, isn't he?"

R'lyeh joined Vrana. The man took a step back, his attention held by her daggers. He was terrified of her, the thirteen-year-old. "Answer us," R'lyeh growled.

"Go fuck yourselves," he snapped. "I know better."

"Are you going to kill him?" R'lyeh cocked her head and sheathed her weapons.

As soon as the daggers were out of her reach, David pulled himself away from Vrana and threw R'lyeh to the ground. He slashed her palms and forearms as she tried to block her chest and neck.

Pissed, and rolling her eyes, Vrana buried the ax into David's skull. Instead of moving his body, she left the man to die on R'lyeh, so that she would know the weight of her actions.

After one day and twelve hours of silence between the two, Vrana and R'lyeh had finally reached Nacthla. Vrana hadn't really considered what she'd expected the town to look like, but she was certain that, if she had, it wouldn't have been what now stood before them. Nachtla sat in the center of a shallow valley beset on all sides by craterous earth. To Vrana, it seemed as though there had once been a mountain formation in the area, but she figured time must've done away with it. Grass grew here, the yellowed and parched variety, but only in patches. Trees, too, decorated the dusty, color-streaked epidermis, but they were without leaves and seemed as though they would crumble like ash at the slightest touch. Vrana didn't need to know much about agriculture to know this was no place to live, but then again, had it always been this way?

Moving closer, they saw that the town was much like Geharra—a combination of Old and New World aesthetics. A paved road split the town in two, and where the ignorant tenets required cement, they'd laid cobblestone instead. Many buildings were dilapidated, while others merely looked that way due to poor craftsmanship. But then there were those places that stood out among the squalor: great houses of power; a long, blood-red hotel; and a tower with stained glass. The Corrupted had clearly treated these remnants of the past with great reverence, for they'd been quarantined behind high walls and pointed fences.

R'lyeh cleared her throat and asked, "What now?"

Vrana didn't respond immediately, and when she did, she said bluntly, "We're going to Lacuna."

"That's not here?" R'lyeh stammered.

Vrana, still angry with the girl, ignored her question. She followed Blix as he led them down the valley's slope.

"I was only doing what the elders asked me," R'lyeh said under her breath.

Vrana gritted her teeth. "R'lyeh, please don't lie to me."

"I'm not," she said, shaking her head.

Vrana stopped and turned around. "Then why are you telling me this now?"

R'lyeh shrugged and nudged a rock with her foot. "I didn't think you'd listen before."

"Who sent you? Anguis?"

R'lyeh nodded. "It was my idea."

Vrana whistled to Blix, and hearing her call, he went to her. "To follow me?"

R'lyeh hummed. The sun passed through her mask, and the veins inside glowed. "Before you left, that day you tried to tell me you were going, I went to the elders. I didn't know what to say, but they let me in anyways. They said that my mom and dad were okay; they'd sent word they were safe in Eld." R'lyeh mumbled something, patted the side of her leg nervously as she searched for her voice. "I told the elders I had to be with you."

"R'lyeh, no. You need to be in Caldera with my mother." Vrana considered reaching out to embrace the girl but decided against it.

"That's what they said. But Anguis came to me the night you left; he said that I could follow you if I did what he asked."

Blix hopped off Vrana and landed on R'lyeh's shoulders. He nuzzled his head against her neck. "What did he ask?"

"That I go to Keldon's Hill and kill the Corrupted there. He said that if I was quick enough, I would find you. He didn't tell me why they had to die, but that didn't matter. He gave me a map—" she produced from a pocket the same map given to Vrana, "—and food, and told me he was s-sorry for everything that'd happened to me."

"How did you reach me? I was on horseback."

"So was I, but Anguis made mine in secret, without the other elders. It was too weak. When it died, I ran the rest of the way."

"R'lyeh, this is not what you need, not after what you've been through." Vrana clenched the fist that she'd used to hit David and imagined it colliding with Anguis' face instead. "This is fucked up. They're fucked up."

The girl shook her head. She started to pace. "I don't understand. They were Corrupted. It's what our people do."

"You're thirteen, R'lyeh, and you butchered that man. If they were meant to die, then so be it. But you're…" She sounded like her mother.

"I watched… I watched my village be tortured, raped… killed. I'm not a child, Vrana. They took that. I'm not stupid enough to think I can get that back. And I know you're not either." She paused and then asked, "Why aren't we staying in Nachtla?"

"Because…" Vrana continued down the slope where a dirt path awaited. "Because if this is where I will find the Witch, then I'm sure she will try to kill me. We need to reach Lacuna, an island off the coast, first. And then we'll deal with the Maiden."

At the bottom of the valley, the path split: To the left, Nachtla, and to the right, a bridge spanning a stream. If this was the place Mara had first happened upon the myth of the Maiden of Pain, then that meant the bridge before them was the very same the Twinned Horror had haunted. Following Anguis' instructions, Vrana aligned herself with the tower that rose out of Nachtla and made for the bridge—and the ocean beyond.

"This is where Mara killed those kids the Witch mutated," Vrana said, nodding her head at the covered bridge. "Do we cross it?"

R'lyeh grunted what must have been a "yes" and said curiously, "What do you think made all those craters?"

Thoughtlessly, Vrana looked to the nearest one, which was wide and several feet deep and also the place from which the stream had once originated. "Bombs," she guessed, "from the Old World."

"Maybe," R'lyeh said, sounding unconvinced. "There's so many of them, though. I don't know. They remind me of little lakes."

"Little lakes?" Vrana laughed and then, mid-grin, began to realize there was more to Nachtla than a house through which they'd gain access to the Void.

"What?" R'lyeh asked as Vrana stopped a few feet from the bridge, half-turned toward the town.

Vrana waved off R'lyeh, afraid that, if she were to respond, the

239

thought would be lost. With her eyes, she followed faint lines of purple and green that were streaked across the earth. *I've arrived at ---, a small town in the foothills of the --- mountains.* She closed her eyes, felt her heart in her throat. *There seems to be no less than one hundred lakes and ponds in the surrounding area, which I find bewildering, as it does not appear this part of the world has seen rain in quite some time.*

"This is the place," Vrana said, shoving her hands into her bags for the books on the Witch, which now sat on her bedroom floor. "This is the place where she took him!"

R'lyeh tilted her head.

"Do you remember the books that I showed you and Jakob in the Elys?"

"Yes," R'lyeh said, "there was the one that was kind of like a warning and then the other about the man, the investigator, or whatever he was, that fell in love with the Witch. Wait." R'lyeh absently rubbed the tentacles of her mask. "You're saying this is the town from his journal?"

"The Ashen Man covered in flies—I saw him in my dream the first time I visited the Witch and again outside Nora when the townspeople had us surrounded. This is the place." Vrana licked her lips with satisfaction. "This is the place where she opened a door to the Void to take him through."

"And it never closed," R'lyeh added excitedly.

"Or she left it open on purpose." Vrana looked past R'lyeh, to Nachtla, the facades of which shone harshly under the beaming sun.

"Do you think you'd be here if she left Caldera alone?"

Vrana shook her head. "I doubt it, but she keeps coming to me. Maybe she wants this." She sighed. "But the bitch is going to have to wait."

"Why Lacuna?" R'lyeh broke into a sprint as Vrana hurried toward the covered bridge. "I've never even heard…"

Vrana held up her hand, and R'lyeh stopped where she stood. From the rafters of the bridge, up in the darkness and past motes of dust, something swung in and out of sight. Wood shavings fell through the air, shaken from their rest on the rickety supports. The wind howled as it funneled through the bridge, carrying with it the smell of decay. Bubbles and steam began to rise from the milling water below, hissing as it ate away at the supports.

Vrana turned to R'lyeh, put her hand on the girl's shoulder, and said, "How about we go around for once?"

Vrana didn't find herself as taken by the sight of the ocean as she'd been by the misty cliffs of the Elys. They stood upon the hood of a yawning cove, feet struggling for purchase on the algae-slickened rocks. A turbulent sea lay before them, spiraling and crashing into itself, spewing its salty breath in stinging waves at the mainland. Islands like fangs ruptured through the swirling gray—uninhabitable places under constant abuse. Driftwood, debris, and dead fish tumbled onto the beach, rejected offerings from the black deep.

"Is that the Nameless Forest?" R'lyeh shouted over the churning waters, the spray of the sea soaking her mask.

Vrana looked to the north and saw growing on a twisted peninsula the cancerous, wooded nightmare. She felt a sense of vertigo as her eyes tried to penetrate the haze that shielded it. She felt warm and then felt a desire to explore the Forest's unknown corridors, to follow the fabled vermillion veins from bark to source. Death would be waiting there, she knew, should reason give way to curiosity; and she wondered, being Its dutiful servant, if Death would show her mercy when It came to collect her limp body from the Forest's floor. She—

"Vrana," R'lyeh continued, touching her, waking her, "where's Lacuna?"

"Out there," she said dreamily. She cleared her throat and said, "We're looking for a dock. It must be inside the cove."

"Why are we going to Lacuna?"

Anguis never told her. An immense sadness washed over Vrana as the girl shifted where she stood, wrapping her arms around herself in a feeble attempt to combat the breeze. As a friend, she wanted nothing more than to lie to R'lyeh, to spare her the pain that would inevitably follow once she learned their reason for visiting the secret island. A Worm had taken everything from the girl: For what reason short of madness would R'lyeh wish to stand in the presence of another?

"I think there might be a village there, one of our own." Vrana opened her bag and removed the sealing stone from it. "There is another Worm on the island. It's not awake yet. This—" she held up the stone, water drops from the ocean dotting the surface, "—will make sure the Worm stays that way."

"Oh," R'lyeh said. She turned from Vrana and eased her way

down the side of the cove.

CHAPTER XXIX

How the dock was able to withstand the onslaught of the ocean was beyond Vrana. It was small and swayed with the tug of the current, and more often than not, it stood submerged beneath the foamy waters. The gaps between the planks of wood were large enough to see a foot caught, and ragged enough to see the same foot riddled with splinters.

"Are we supposed to take a boat?" R'lyeh pointed to a rope, a tether snaking through the water. "I'm not getting on a boat."

"Of course not," said a woman's voice from behind them.

Vrana and R'lyeh spun around; weapons readied, they searched the shadows of the cove for the voice's owner. Silt slugs and salt bats slithered and scampered up the sweating walls, while ghost crabs and rock wraiths scuttled and glided into tiny alcoves. For a place so close to Death, life seemed to prosper.

"Over here," the woman continued, emerging from the gloom of the cove. "You don't got to worry."

The woman was thin and her body well-defined. She was a Night Terror, and she wore upon her head a mask comprised of the carapaces of entwined centipedes. The woman was unarmed, and practically unarmored. Vrana's eyes widened when she noticed the crimson pigmentation along the woman's right arm—*Is this one of the imposters David spoke of?*—but quickly realized it was nothing more than paint.

"You've me to thank for your witch hunt," the woman said, putting her hand on her hip. "It's nice to finally meet you, Vrana. The last time I saw you, you were chewing on one of those crystals in your basement."

"I'm sorry," Vrana said, lowering her ax, "but I have no idea who you are."

The woman laughed as she dug her feet into the white sand. "Mara."

Vrana's voice rose in pitch as she said, "It's... it's nice to finally meet you."

Mara nodded and, pointing to R'lyeh, said, "Who's your friend?"

There was something about the woman that reminded Vrana of Nora. "R'lyeh," she said, looking at the girl as she uttered her name, "of Alluvia."

"I see," Mara said, bowing her head at R'lyeh. "I won't waste time trying to comfort you by saying I know how you must feel. I couldn't possibly know, and I hope that I never do."

"Thanks?" R'lyeh murmured.

"What are you doing here?" Vrana looked over her shoulder as a large wave slammed into the dock.

Mara laughed and passed between the two. Her bare feet padded against the dock as she climbed its creaking stairs. "Waiting for you, of course," she said, beckoning them to come to her.

After a moment of hesitation, Vrana and R'lyeh joined Mara on the dock, and together, all three creatures looked upon the Widening Gyre, the Sailor's Bane. The sea had calmed considerably since they'd arrived, and had retreated significantly as well. Causeways of rock and sand were now visible, whereas once they had been hidden, and it was on these unstable bridges to oblivion that Mara was fixed.

"No," R'lyeh said, backing away.

"Then stay here," Mara said, coldly. "But after what you've both endured, this will seem like nothing at all."

"How far is Lacuna?" Vrana asked, lifting her head to Blix, who was circling high above, waiting for orders.

"So they told you the island's name?" Mara laughed. "That's better than what I got." She dropped off the end of dock and sank up to her ankles in the wet sand. "It's far, but the journey is quicker than you might think. The laws of things don't really apply here."

"What about the Nameless Forest?" R'lyeh asked, her voice high and girly, the demon that had possessed her to kill asleep once more.

Mara nodded at Vrana, who also stepped off the docks. "Pay it no mind. If the Nameless Forest wants you, it'll have you. Come on. We need to get across before the water returns."

One by one, they navigated the sandbars and rock walls. The ocean eddied beside them, lapping against the makeshift paths; intimidating them, encircling them, the ocean was a predator of infinite form and endless hunger. The wind, cold and sharp, stung their skin and burned their lungs and seemed adamant in seeing them thrown to the greedy current. Mara, of course, went fearlessly, for she had likely walked this watery trail more times than she could count.

"Lacuna, like Caldera, has its own spellweavers who see it shrouded from prying eyes," Mara said. "You won't know it's there until it is."

Vrana looked back: In a moment, they'd cleared a mile. Impossible. "Have the Corrupted ever found the island?" she asked, steadying herself on the wobbling rocks. Blix landed on her shoulder and outstretched his wings, as though he thought it would help balance her.

"Of course," Mara said. She reached the end of the rock wall and planted her feet on a small plot of land already an inch submerged beneath the returning tide. "We took it from them."

"What?" R'lyeh blurted out as she followed Vrana off the wall and onto the plot.

"Many years ago, our people from Traesk followed a group of Corrupted, the Forlorn, here," Mara said, the ocean, which was up to her knees now, pulling at her like a persistent child. "The sea wasn't so restless then; boats could travel it if their captains were smart enough. In those days, 'keeping the balance' was a phrase too often taken advantage of by some of our more bloodthirsty kin. They spotted a group of Corrupted carting off captives to this island, and they followed, though it wasn't to set anyone free."

Mara waved them over to the edge of the plot, where a series of smoothed boulders protruded from the water. Following Mara, Vrana pulled herself up onto one of the massive rocks, growling as her fingers ran through bird shit.

"Give me your hands," Vrana said, lifting R'lyeh up onto the boulder. She ripped a piece of seaweed from the girl's goose-pimpled leg. "Are you okay?" R'lyeh was wavering, and looking like something the sea had spat out in disgust.

Mara continued onwards to the next boulder, unaware or uncaring that her companions were lagging behind. "The Corrupted had formed a colony on the island," she shouted as a wave crashed into the rock, drenching her. "It seemed as though they'd been living there ever since the end of the Trauma."

"Did the watchers kill them?" R'lyeh asked as she, again, accepted Vrana's help onto the second boulder.

"Yep," Mara said as she hopped onto the third and final boulder. "The Corrupted living on Lacuna were entirely self-sufficient, but what they could not cultivate quickly enough was life. They kept coming to the mainland for offerings, sacrifices to be given up to their lord. Why is that? Why is it that humans always seem to think the best way to get on their god's good side is to rub his nose in the corpses of all his children they've killed?"

R'lyeh coughed and went ahead of Vrana. "Very strange," she said without emotion. She jumped across the misty gap and landed beside Mara.

"And so our people stayed?" Vrana put her hands on her hips and leaned over the edge of the boulder, feeling her stomach sink as portions of the sea began to spiral inwards.

"It was an outpost, for a time." Mara put her hand against the side of R'lyeh's mask, as though she could feel her face through it. "But the ocean turned against us, so we used its anger to our advantage. We hid in its fury."

"Did any of the Corrupted escape?" R'lyeh asked, stepping away from Mara. She rejoined Vrana as she leapt onto the third boulder.

Mara nodded and went to the edge of the rock. "A few, yes. They scattered to escape the ire of their god. The Forlorn was a splinter group of the Lillians, which is now known as the Holy Order of Penance. Some returned to Penance while others rejoined their brethren, the Scavengers, another Lillian splinter group, at the black tower south of Elys."

Vrana looked to R'lyeh. Addressing Mara, she said, "I've seen it. When we went to Geharra…"

"Come," Mara interrupted as she put one foot over the edge of the boulder, "we're running out of time."

The tide had all but returned when their feet found the last path by which they would reach Lacuna. It was a thin strip of rock and coral that could've easily destroyed the hull of a ship if given the opportunity. Looking back once more, Vrana saw that the mainland was a small sliver of browns and greens much farther back than the distance they'd traveled.

"Is that the island?" R'lyeh asked.

"Yes," Vrana said, answering for Mara as she hurried her steps, each one bringing into the world another detail of the island so few even knew existed.

Lacuna was a small island guarded by a withered atoll. The trees that covered its every mile were beyond count and seemed to have prospered under the heavy rains that undoubtedly passed through there. There was no sign of civilization beyond the beach; in fact, there didn't appear to be any wildlife either. Vrana tried to imagine a sailor's reaction upon reaching this place but found it difficult to determine whether it would be one of excitement or despair. *At least the ocean is calmer*, she remarked to herself, noticing the waves gently lapping against the shore.

"What do you think, R'lyeh?"

"Ask me when we get there," R'lyeh said. She laughed and looked over her shoulder and then stopped where she stood, the stutter of a word trapped in her mask.

"What?" Because Vrana could not see the girl's eyes, it took her a moment to realize that R'lyeh was not staring at her but beyond her. "What's behind me?" she asked, noticing that Mara, too, was looking back the way they'd come.

Vrana turned around slowly as the waters continued to rise and wash over her feet. What she found standing behind her was something she was certain could not be. On the narrow ledge, out of isolation and nightmare, a flesh fiend stood. The skin that it wore was pale and wet, held in place by stones that it had been stabbed through the flesh and into its body. The fiend was female, or wanted to be—two sagging breasts and a hole between its legs suggested so—and had long, stringy hair that was matted down with kelp. In its right hand, the flesh fiend held the spinal cord of some poor creature as though it were a dagger.

A sour odor rolled off the flesh fiend and entered Vrana's mask; she took a step backward. The creature sprinted toward her, its rubbery appendages oozing a thick, black liquid, like sweat, as it went. With no room for proper footing, trying desperately to resist the call of the strengthening current, Vrana found herself teetering on the thin strip of land. The flesh fiend swung at her with the spinal cord, digging its teeth into its own lips with every pass of the bone. Vrana stumbled away, one foot after the other, waiting for an opening to strike.

"We're out of time!" she heard Mara shout. "You have to keep moving."

It was true: the narrow path was disappearing with every passing second. Reasoning they only had half a minute before the ocean would claim what it'd been denied, Vrana pushed the fiend back with the head of her ax, turned, and fled. She could feel the hairs stand on her neck as the hot breath of the creature fell upon her. But she didn't look back; she kept her eyes on her feet as the waters rose past her ankles, her shins.

"Vrana!" R'lyeh cried.

She lifted her gaze from the ground. Her neck snapped forward as the flesh fiend threw itself against her. In an instant, all their cautious efforts were undone. Vrana plummeted into the sea, her lungs pleading for the air that had been pushed out of them. She felt the ax leave her grasp, felt the mask leave her head. She felt the flesh fiend climbing up her body, marveling with its fingers the contours of her figure. As the fiend's mouth found her hipbone, she grasped its hair, closed her legs around its neck, and twisted. The creature dug its nails into her back, gnawed at her stomach. She howled with pain as the water warmed with her blood.

Vrana could feel the pull of the current as their bodies brushed against the ocean floor. She shoved her thumbs into the flesh fiend's eyes and felt them burst; they leaked like jelly from the dented skull. The creature released its grip, and Vrana saw in that moment she could easily reach the beach. But before she started swimming, the flesh fiend was on her again, unimpeded by its lack of sight. It ripped off a piece of flesh that had been attached to its chest and draped it over Vrana's face.

A new mask, she thought, feeling lightheaded, *better suited for us all*. The flesh fiend drew back the flap of skin, bending Vrana's neck until it seemed as though it would snap. She bit at the skin, which was unusually thick, and spat out bits of it, until it tore in half in the fiend's hands.

She pushed the flesh fiend off her. Struggling against the tide, she thrust herself forward, using the floor of the ocean for momentum. Sensing the creature behind her, she grabbed a large piece of coral and, as she turned, swung it, catching the fiend in the head and knocking it away. Vrana tried to take hold of the ground once more but found that her arms would not do as she willed and that the sunlight, bright as it was, could not stop the darkening of the world.

CHAPTER XXX

Vrana smoothed out the wrinkles in her soft, blue dress and stared at her soft, white hands as though they were not her own—and they weren't. She turned in her seat, which creaked and tipped slightly to the left, and rested her elbows on the wooden table beside her. Her nose twitched as she caught the scent of something baking nearby; though when she looked at the stove, she saw that there was nothing inside. She noticed the long, dark shadows retreating across the kitchen floor and was glad that the helicopters had gone.

"Mom?" Vrana heard a voice call from somewhere in the house.

She stood up, putting her feet to the humming floor, and moved hastily out of the kitchen, down a dim hallway, and into an empty living room. On the furthest wall, just beyond the sun-faded couch, a television buzzed loudly, the screen covered in white noise. Picture frames along the mantle were face down, knocked over by a great tremor or an angry hand.

"Mom?" she heard a voice shout out once more.

Panicked, though she didn't know why, Vrana rushed up the stairs, holding on tightly to the crayon covered bannister as she climbed. Again, the voice asked for its mother. Vrana came to the second floor, rounded the corner, ignored the door farther down the hall, which was hanging off its hinges, and stepped into a child's room.

"What's the matter?" She looked down upon the boy whose voice she'd heard.

The small child was surrounded by toys that had fallen in battle to the spikey, armor-clad figure he held in his hand. His golden hair was uncombed and glowed ever so slightly in the sunlight. There didn't appear to be anything wrong with the boy, other than that he was not getting the amount of attention he felt he deserved.

"Is everything okay?" Vrana heard herself say, the voice coming out of her throat choked, the concern in it feigned.

The boy looked up at her and said, "I saw something outside."

"What did you see, sweetheart?" Vrana put one knee to the ground, one hand through the child's unkempt hair. Vrana had felt motherly before, in her encounters with the Holy Child and R'lyeh, but what she felt now as this body of hers comforted the boy was anything but motherly.

The boy made a bubble with his spit and set the action figure down. "A big monster," he mumbled, looking over his shoulder to the octagon-shaped window beside his bed. He turned his head towards Vrana and said, "When's my real mommy coming home?"

Vrana's body launched forward, her hands in search of the child's neck so as to break it. Before she could reach him, though, the house started to shake violently. She stumbled backward, into the hallway, where the bloodied body of an old man had rolled out.

"Get away from her, Alexei!" the old man croaked, a waterfall of blood pouring over his lips. "She's dangerous! She's a monster!"

Vrana felt a hateful panic swell in her chest. She looked back into the boy's room and saw long, dark shadows pouring through the window. They stretched across the floor, like black limbs aching to be cracked, and slithered toward Alexei. Vrana felt herself rise off the ground, the tips of her toes barely touching the carpet beneath her. She felt the need to say something, yell something, but before she could, the boy's room collapsed upon itself, crushing Alexei where he sat.

"No!" Vrana heard herself shout. She stumbled back in the hall as pieces of the ceiling were torn away above her. She looked up, floated up through the falling debris; pushed through the attic, through the buckled supports and cracked shingles. She pushed through the roof, into the air, where she stood there suspended, horrified, as a god moved across the land, undeterred by the humans that were desperately trying to kill it.

Vrana blinked, and then she was no longer in the house. She was somewhere else, somewhere terrible and gray, where black spires twisted out of the rocky soil, rising high as though to puncture the weeping sky. *This is the Void,* she realized as she moved formlessly through the wasteland, *so am I alive? Did they save me?* With no landmark in sight, she floated aimlessly from craters to quarries, over unearthed catacombs and endless chasms, until a bright, blinking light drew her attention to an isolated valley.

"What is this?" Vrana whispered, rippling the air with her words.

She descended into the valley carefully, for it was infested with roaming swarms of countless black flies. Though she didn't have a body to call her own, that didn't mean they couldn't see her; so she waited for an opening between the black waves. When one appeared, she hurried through, using the glow of the beacon she'd seen as her guide through the buzzing sea.

"What is this?" Vrana whispered as she found the floor of the valley, and the source of the light.

Anguis, Faolan, Nuctea; Deimos, Lucan, Serra; Nora, Jakob, Mag; Mara, the Holy Child, the Skeleton; Aeson, R'lyeh, Adelyn; and hundreds of others Vrana could not identify stood at the center of the beacon. With every blink of the light, another joined the ghostly congregation, stepping out of nothingness to stare blankly at those before and beside them. Vrana called out to those whom she recognized and those that bore the skulls of her tribe, and but except for a shift in the flies above, there was no response.

I know they're not real, Vrana thought, wanting to touch Aeson to be sure, *but why are they here?* Drawing closer, Vrana could see running from each individual a cord. Spotted and thick, it hung in the air like an umbilicus, connecting heads to hearts and hearts to hands. Every time the beacon pulsated and another was added to the gathering, the cord would slither out from under the tongue of someone nearby and force itself into the newly indoctrinated. *I know they're not real,* the Raven thought again, cringing as the cord slipped into the penis of a newcomer.

As she turned away from the sickening spectacle, she realized that the valley had gone silent. The hungry swarm had vanished and left behind in its wake a clear view of the tattered sky. "Somebody wake me up, somebody wake me up," she repeated to herself, the sides of the valley shedding pebbles and rocks as it trembled. "Somebody wake me up if I'm not already dead. Somebody wake me up..."

Vrana paused in her ascent as she heard these words pour over the sharp precipice: "Without a tongue, one can speak freely, I imagine."

The Ashen Man stood above her, millions of black flies rushing out of every orifice of his body. He held his arms at his sides, a guard tasked to keep watch over his terrible Maiden's domain.

He's here to help, she thought, *like he helped that night in Nora.*

"Better to die here," the Ashen Man said, his voice rumbling like thunder throughout the Void, "so that she may not reap what you've sown."

All at once, the flies massed and threw themselves at Vrana. Though she knew she had no hands, she tried to protect herself with them all the same. And then there they were, forming before her, followed by arms and shoulders and then her stomach, which was wrapped tight with bloody bandages. And with the appendages came a hot, nauseating pain she could've done without.

The flies set upon her like vultures to meaty bone, spitting on her new skin to melt it. Vrana swatted at the insects, took large handfuls of them and crushed them in her fists; they continued unabated, fighting for a place in the dark of her screaming mouth. The Ashen Man reached his hand through the black cloud, the hint of his form among his million minions, and with all the hate he had for her...

"Vrana!"

She sat upright, and then lay back down, the burning pain in her abdomen too great to withstand. She could still taste the sea, which was comforting, as it meant she'd not been asleep for too long. Her hands felt at the bed upon which she lay and the sheets soaked with her sweat. Figures moved around her in the dimly lit room, talking in whispers. Certain she'd spotted R'lyeh, she called out to the girl but received no response. More creatures passed through Vrana's field of vision—a Fish and a Bird; an Eagle, Eel, and an Ape—but they, too, seemed deaf to her pleas.

"Somebody answer me," Vrana said groggily, "or I'm going to fucking kill all of you." She turned her head as she heard someone approaching the bed. "Speak up, right now."

"How are you feeling?" Mara said, her image wavering as Vrana's eyes struggled to adjust to the light.

"You need a better way to get to the island." She tried to sit up again but couldn't.

Mara laughed. "We have our ways." The bed sank as she took a seat. "But everyone has to cross the Gyre their first time. You did well."

"Did I?" Vrana rubbed her face hard and wished for the comfort and privacy of her mask. "Why was there a flesh fiend in the ocean?"

"The better question is why are there so many in the ocean?" Mara's mask of centipede carapaces shuddered with undead life. "Rest, and when you've rested, we'll see to your task."

Vrana's hand shot out and found Mara's. "Where's R'lyeh?"

"Sleeping, and eating, and nervously pacing around the village, waiting for you to get better." Mara patted the top of Vrana's hand and said to someone, "Give her the Dreameater potion. This one's dreamed enough."

When Vrana awoke again, she found that the curtains in the room had been pulled back, allowing the warm sunlight and coastal sounds to fill the space. She couldn't determine how long she'd been asleep, but saw from the healing of her stomach wound that it must have been at least a few days. Putting her feet to the floor, she stood up without need of support and made her way to the glowing outline of a door.

Vrana sighed, wiped away the dried drool at the edge of her mouth, and pushed the door open. Beyond, she found the small, arboreal village of Lacuna, its people too distracted with their daily tasks to take notice of her. Many of the homes had been built into the trees or the ground itself—a precautionary measure taken to avoid giving sailors a reason to brave the Bane. Wild animals, which were curiously absent during their initial arrival, roamed the village freely, the pigs, monkeys, and goats oblivious or uncaring of their eventual fate.

"Where are you, R'lyeh?" Vrana squinted, catching a glimpse of a field of crops beyond. She put one foot over the threshold, but before going further, she saw at the corner of her eye a familiar shape. "Ah," she said, following the wall away from the door to a chair bearing her mask, "my old friend."

Vrana donned her mask, which smelled and felt as though it had been thoroughly washed. After searching the room and finding the rest of her belongings missing, she emerged from the house filled with purpose. She hurried down the hill upon which the house sat, a cloud of dirt trailing behind her. She studied the masks of the people as she went, none of which appeared as though they were indigenous to the area. *This is an ark*, she thought to herself, passing a Hound, a Bear, and an Ice Dweller. *Nobody truly lives here.*

Vrana took another look at her surroundings, trying to determine where the leaders of Lacuna would reside, for that was where she would find Mara, R'lyeh, and Blix. There were several tree houses, each of which were impressive and naturally hidden from prying eyes, but they seemed too unstable to hold people of importance. She considered that the elders may have established themselves underground but saw by the traffic moving in and out of the tunnels with supplies and tools that this was unlikely as well. So she turned her attention to the homes that circled the yard where she stood, which were neither large nor remarkable.

"Hiding in plain sight," Vrana mumbled, moving from porch to porch, window to window, "just like this village. Just like Kistvaen. Just like we ought to do."

"What's that?"

Vrana turned around, heart racing, and saw Mara standing behind her. "Where's R'lyeh? And Blix?"

"Resting," Mara said, picking dried blood out from under her fingernails. "I don't remember your bird being so thin."

"The Witch had her hold on him," Vrana said, her words slow and slurred. She looked up at the blazing sun and found herself sagging beneath it. "I don't know what's wrong with him."

Mara, sensing Vrana's discomfort, took her hand and said, "We'll see to him. There are medicines here that cannot be found on the mainland." Mara tightened her grip on Vrana, dabbed at a spot of sweat on the Raven's chest with a piece of her shirt. "Walk with me, because I know if I ask you to get back into bed, I'll just be wasting my breath."

Mara led Vrana around the village proper, which extended no further than the circle of houses she'd stood in earlier. At the outskirts of Lacuna, there were fields of crops that shouldn't have been: The conditions were hardly agreeable to the corn, wheat, rice, tomatoes, potatoes, and berries that not only grew in the fields, but among each other as well. At first, Vrana thought this was the work of a spell-weaver, but the fact that there was a Worm asleep on the island suggested otherwise.

"The storms must be terrible," Vrana said as they left the field for a clearing and then a cliff, where the blue ocean yawned beyond.

"Not at all." Mara finally released Vrana's hand, which had grown clammy and dependent on the woman. She brought her to the cliff and invited her to sit on its edge. "It rains just enough and never more."

Vrana bit her lip as she sat down and threw her legs over the rocky edge, the cool breeze enveloping her. "Where is the Worm?" she asked bluntly.

"Deep down, in the mining tunnels." Mara nudged Vrana. "Don't worry, the Corrupted didn't get very far. The chamber is easy enough to find."

"How long..." Vrana covered her mouth as a wave of nausea crashed against the shore of her stomach. "How long did you live with the Corrupted?"

"Small talk?" Mara laughed.

"Everything has been moving so fast since my second trial." She shrugged, ripped a root from the cliff, and flung it. "I don't know. I just want this to be over."

"Well, I hate to break it to you, Vrana, but this isn't going to be over anytime soon." Mara poked at an emerald ant that had crawled onto her leg. "If it makes you feel any better, it doesn't have to be you."

"But it does," Vrana insisted. "Deimos, Lucan, Serra... they are somewhere else. And the Witch... it has to be me."

"Anybody with half a brain and an empty pack could've brought the sealing stone here," Mara contested.

"What are you trying to say?" Vrana asked, her voice cracking.

"Only that your decisions should be your own." Mara picked up the ant, slid it under her mask, and ate it.

"Nobody forced me to come to this damn island."

"Not even the elders?"

"No." Vrana took a breath and refrained from calling Mara a bitch. "I made the choice. I brought the Witch to Caldera. I saw the Red Worm beneath Geharra. I made the decision to be here. I could die doing this..." Thoughts of Aeson pushed tears from her eyes. "I'm not going to risk my life just because somebody asked me to."

Mara hummed and stood up, red imprints from the ground drawn onto her legs. "You're good, but not that good. The world will go on without you. I don't think you of all people should be here."

Vrana looked up at the Centipede, whom she was now certain had never known affection, and nodded. These were words of encouragement and advice disfigured by years of callousness and disappointment. "You didn't answer my question," Vrana said, once again taking Mara's hand as she came to her feet.

"Ten years," Mara said. "That's how long I lived with the Corrupted. I left the day after I was initiated. Thought I could do better talking to the humans rather than killing them. I wasn't the first to do it, but no one had done it as well and as long as I had."

"You're a talented woman but not that talented," Vrana murmured, following Mara back into the fields.

"Exactly." Mara stopped at a crossroads at the center of the field and took the path that led away from Lacuna. "I met a lot of people, made a lot of friends in high places. Put to the test the belief that our kind and the Corrupted could not bear children together."

Vrana came to a halt and cocked her head. "What?"

"Do you know what we do on this island?" Mara ignored her. She stepped off the path and into a thick copse.

"No," she shouted, following after her.

The copse was densely packed, lit only by the shafts of light that had worked their way through the canopy. A small pond sat at the northernmost point, its waters constantly circling inwards, much like its larger cousin the Gyre. Around the pond, long blades of rust-colored grass protruded from the ground like wild hairs.

"What did they tell you?" Mara crossed the copse toward a rock formation only a foot taller than herself.

"That I'd find a way to reach the Witch in Nachtla." Vrana watched with intrigue as Mara began to manipulate the stones on the rock formation. "That I'd..." She laughed and shook her head. "That I'd 'find out where we came from and where we've been' and why the flesh fiends became a myth."

The Centipede looked over her shoulder and nodded. "Not even I could resist that temptation." She pushed her palm against a smoothed piece of sandstone and something clicked into place within the formation. "Do you still steal away to Aeson every chance you get?"

Vrana kept quiet.

"This mechanism works the same as those that guard the three tunnels to the Inner Sanctum. Where do you think we learned it from?" Mara said as she bent down and twisted a small key between two fused rocks.

"No sudden movements." She backpedaled to the pond and beckoned Vrana to stand beside her. "They are quite skittish."

Ancient gears within the formation turned and groaned, and at the structure's center, the rocks pulled away and slid into the ground. A gust of hot air trapped within blew through the copse. The sound of feet in ascent came shortly thereafter, followed by the sniffling of noses and clearing of throats. Vrana strained her ears as she heard raspy whispers and what seemed to be the din of a bell.

"Does this lead to the mines?" Vrana asked, standing on the tips of her toes to have a better look inside the formation.

"That, and much more," Mara said, amused. "Save your questions. You'll have plenty more in just a moment."

Vrana scratched at her stomach. "I don't like you."

"Very few do," Mara said indifferently. "There they are."

Fifteen adolescents with children at their sides emerged from the structure, wide-eyed and hesitant. Half of the children and half of the adolescents were Corrupted, bearing the crimson defect on their right arms. Those that didn't wear the mark of humanity stood among them unassumingly, picking their noses or biting their lips.

Vrana turned to Mara. "Why are there Corrupted on the island?" Her eyes darted back and forth between the faces of the children. "How are there so many children? What are they doing in the mines? Mara?"

Mara turned her head slightly and lifted her mask just enough to show her that she was smiling. "They are gifts from the Blue Worm."

"What the hell are you talking about?" Vrana stepped away, into a tuft of the rust-colored grass, which pricked her feet. "What the hell are you saying?"

"The elders of Eld mean well, but if we had waited for them to solve our fertility problems, we'd have all died out by now."

"The Blue Worm?" Vrana shouted. "I brought the sealing stone to keep it asleep, and you've woken it up?"

Mara shook her head. "Vrana, dear, it's always been awake."

258

CHAPTER XXXI

Grim thunderheads loomed over the deepening gloom of the island.

Inky waves spilled across the bone-white shore, grabbing with thieving fists idle tributes from the sands.

Twenty blazing eyes blinked in the coves below Lacuna as small ships were loaded with unlabeled stock.

"Why not seal it sooner?" Vrana backed away from the balcony carved out of the bluff and faced Mara.

Mara shuffled past R'lyeh, who was sitting on a small chair beneath a guttering sconce; Blix ruffled his feathers as she passed. "That would've been a waste."

Vrana's head throbbed from a migraine born from her anger with the woman. Mara had refused to answer the her questions until the party had been reunited. "The children are a gift from the Blue Worm?" Her eyes followed a line of girls moving about the docks, which the balcony overlooked. "How? Why?"

Mara took a seat on a couch not much larger than R'lyeh's chair and crossed her legs. "It was half awake when we took the island from the Scavengers," she said, scratching at the stubble on her legs. "The Trauma and the Corrupted's sacrifices had roused it from its slumber. With some coaxing, we woke it up, and in its fitful waking, it turned the ocean violent."

"Didn't you know what you were doing?" R'lyeh said loudly. She shook her head. "I don't understand. What the hell is wrong with you?"

"Make no mistake, little Octopus," Mara said, pointing at the girl.

"I'd little to do with Lacuna's beginnings. I only took over operations six years ago."

"Why is the Blue Worm helping our people?" Vrana interjected, stepping between R'lyeh and Mara, as though to physically block their conversation. "It has to have a reason."

"Of course it does. No one and nothing does anything unless there is a benefit to be had." Mara turned her head at the sound of a crate falling onto the dock.

"Half of those children are Corrupted," R'lyeh said in disbelief. Having not been witness to those that had emerged from the copse, she added, "Are you using them?"

"As slaves?" Mara threw back her head and laughed. "Look how well that worked out for the humans. Aren't we supposed to have learned from their mistakes?" She cleared her throat. "There is some misinformation regarding our kind and the Corrupted and what happens when we fuck."

R'lyeh looked at Vrana, confused.

Vrana nodded at the girl. Tired of Mara's smugness, she cried, "Will you just fucking say it? We didn't come all this way for stupid fucking games."

"Didn't you just initiate?" Mara said, as though Vrana didn't have the credentials to be outraged.

Vrana fell back against the cavern wall. "I'm sorry."

"No you're not," Mara quipped, "but that's okay."

"Please," R'lyeh begged, pulling her legs up and under her.

"The Corrupted earned their name for a reason," Mara started, "though what truly colored their right arms red is still a mystery." She paused for a moment. "The elders tell us that our kind and the Corrupted cannot bear children together, that we are of two different species, but that is not entirely true. Impregnation is difficult, seldom successful, but it is certainly possible."

"I don't..." R'lyeh began to tug on the tentacles of her mask. "What?"

"The elders of Eld look inward, using what little tools are left from the Old World to try and make our bodies better for breeding," Mara continued, "and one day they may have their answer, but it will be too late. Under the right circumstances, the Corrupted and our people can reproduce, with fifty percent of the offspring bearing the Corrupted gene."

Vrana pushed herself away from the cavern wall. "The right circumstances?" she stammered.

"When our people and the Corrupted fuck, and that's really the best word for it—there's too much anger and cultural confusion to make the act enjoyable—it's not long after that the woman will learn if she is with child. The gestation period for human offspring is nine months; for our kind, it is four."

R'lyeh leaned forward. "What about…"

"One," Mara said, holding up her pointer finger. "It takes one month for a child from a member of our tribe and a Corrupted to gestate."

"You said it takes the right circumstances," Vrana reminded.

"It does, because in most cases, the offspring is deformed, deranged; not fit to live more than a few hours outside its mother, and if it does, it's quickly killed because it cannot be tamed or reasoned with. The Corrupted called them demons once, but we all know them best by their true names: flesh fiends."

"That can't be," R'lyeh said, ducking as Blix cawed loudly and began to circle the room.

"I've no reason to lie to either of you," Mara retorted. She looked at the docks and said, "We have been preparing to leave since we got word from Anguis that you were coming."

Flesh fiends? Vrana scratched at the top of her hand until the skin was red and speckled with hints of blood. *Is it possible?* She turned away from R'lyeh and Mara and looked over the balcony, into the spiraling pools of the Widening Gyre. *How far removed are we? Is the balance just a means to satisfy our inherent bloodlust?*

"Vrana?" R'lyeh called.

"Why do you need the Blue Worm?" Vrana continued to stare into the ocean, mesmerized by its constant aggression.

"To ensure an egg is fertilized after every encounter." Mara sounded cold, detached.

"And why does the Blue Worm need you?"

"To be used, and to be fed." Mara cocked her head as Vrana turned to face her. "The Worm gives us our future, and we to it the fiends that are born."

"But she was attacked by one," R'lyeh said, her voice soft and doubting.

"Some escape; some, it lets live. A hundred or so have taken up

261

residence in the reefs and the atoll; a few in the woods, even. They feed on and fuck each other, and at the end of the day, really, they are no different than the Corrupted or us. The only difference is that they know who they are."

"If you've been at this for years—" Vrana crossed the room, crossed her arms; stood over Mara, tall and imposing, "—where are all the children?"

"Like I said, we have safer ways of leaving the island." Mara stood up, forcing Vrana to back away. "Once they are old enough, and a suitable placement has been found, they leave for the mainland."

"To our villages?" R'lyeh started to rub the side of her leg, a nervous tic developed at the slaughter of Alluvia.

"Sometimes—most go to Traesk—but there are those untouched by Corruption that are set aside for more important duties."

Vrana received Blix onto her arm. "Like what?"

"Oh, what did they call them in the Old World?" Mara moved past her, to the steps that led down to the docks. She shouted an order to a Hound carrying several baskets. "Sleeper agents, that's the word. The humans are superstitious, but if you concoct a convincing enough backstory, they'll take in a child without Corruption and elevate them to a higher status than they deserve." She shouted another order. "If you've been to Geharra, then you surely stopped by Nora."

Vrana gritted her teeth. "I have."

"Well, if you'd had the pleasure of meeting their eponymously named mayor, then you would've met a child of Lacuna."

Vrana's mind returned to that night in the library when she first came upon Nora. *What did she say?* Vrana searched her thoughts for the exchange. *I said that her arm wasn't red, and she said neither was mine. When I tried to tell her I wasn't human, she said that maybe she wasn't either.* Vrana's thoughts hurried along to the night weeks after their meeting, when the Red Worm had ripped itself free of Geharra's womb. *The letter to the elders asking for help—it wasn't an alliance. She's part of the tribe.*

"How many agents are there?" Vrana said finally.

Mara shook her head. "I couldn't tell you. We lose contact with some."

"How do you keep in contact, then?" R'lyeh interjected.

"Depends on the distance," Mara said, starting down the steps that would lead to the boats. "For those that are difficult to reach, we have our ways. In fact, most of what the spellweavers know was taught to us by the Blue Worm." Mara craned her neck toward the two, as though she enjoyed blowing their minds. "It is, after all, no easy feat to make a mountain disappear, to make an island vanish."

Vrana gestured to R'lyeh to come to her feet, as Mara was headed away from the balcony to somewhere else. "In Caldera, the spellweavers were kept a secret," Vrana said, "until the Witch gutted one."

"Of course they were," Mara said, descending the creaking steps. "They are rare and in short supply."

Vrana twitched as Blix's talons clamped down onto her skin. Together, with R'lyeh, all three followed as Mara went across the boardwalk, drawing from the busy workers quick glances and short whispers. Vrana counted four small boats, each large enough to carry a crew of no more than ten. It didn't seem enough to evacuate the island entirely, but what did she know? And of what she did know, how much of it was true?

"I don't... this is too much," R'lyeh said as they turned at an intersection and made their way toward the tunnel that led topside. "How do you determine who's a spellweaver?"

"We don't," Mara said, ducking beneath a low-hanging rock that arched over the boardwalk. "As I said, they are rare and in short supply. They are artifacts from the Old World. Vrana..." Mara pulled back the two wooden doors that divided the tunnel from the docks, letting in a gust of hot air. "Your mother told me that your third trial took you to the hospital near the ravines."

"The homunculi?" Vrana crouched beneath the rock. "The homunculi?" she repeated. "Those are spellweavers? They're us?"

"Mm," Mara said, waiting for the girls to pass before locking the door behind them. "Makes you wonder, then, where we came from."

"Huh?" R'lyeh said, her mask glowing in the torchlight. "What do you mean?"

Vrana laughed and shook her head.

"She's got it." Mara chuckled. She pointed to the ramp they'd descended earlier, the mouth of which was housed in a hollowed tree. "Here."

"What does she mean?" R'lyeh persisted. "What do you mean?"

"Well, if the homunculi are of our tribe, and if half of every birth between Corrupted and our people results in a flesh fiend, what does that make us?" Mara ripped a torch from the wall to keep the shadows away. "It's not so much about where we came from but why we can't seem to shake the notion that we are so much better than everything else."

In a matter of hours, Lacuna had become a ghost town. The trees, and the homes they held, swayed eerily in the moonlight, stripped of personal belongings. The small houses that circled the village howled emptiness, the bitter wind that passed through them giving voice to their discontent. No longer did animals, masked or unmasked, roam the sandy soil, nor would they ever again. Soon, the island would be reduced to an oddity, a tale told around fires to frighten the young and enliven the old; and eventually, the lie would become more believable than the truth.

Vrana stepped back into the house that sat upon the hill overlooking Lacuna. "When are you leaving?" she asked Mara, who was placing the girls' possessions on the bed.

"Tired of me already?" Mara joked. "I'll leave when the deed is done."

"And how are we going to get out of here?" R'lyeh lifted the octopus mask off of her head.

"After you've sealed the Worm's chamber, you'll come topside, and together we'll go by boat to the mainland." Mara stepped away from the bed.

"The Blue Worm is going to let us do this?" Vrana asked, making no attempt to hide her doubt.

"It will, because it has no reason to stop you." Mara slid past Vrana, pushed open the door that she stood beside.

"Wait." She reached out to catch Mara with her claws, but the woman was quick and pulled away. "Deimos said that these things bring about the apocalypse."

Mara shrugged. "Maybe," she said, grasping the door handle and pulling it shut as she exited, "but the philosopher Victor Mors has been dead for a long time and was considered a madman when he was alive. Apocalypses come in all shapes and sizes. Sleep tight."

It seemed Vrana's body had no intention of taking Mara's advice. In the dead of night, after lying still and trying desperately to get some rest, she turned over and found on the other side of the bed an equally awake R'lyeh.

"I'm glad you're up," she said, turning on her side as she kicked the blankets onto Vrana.

"So am I," Vrana said, smiling.

R'lyeh blew a loose strand of hair away from her face. "I can't believe I'm doing this again."

"You don't have to." Vrana took the strand and brushed it under R'lyeh's nose. "You can stay with Mara until it's over."

"I'd rather not," R'lyeh said, cringing as the hair tickled her skin. "Besides, this seems different."

"It does, doesn't it?"

"Do you really believe her?"

"About what?"

"The flesh fiends," R'lyeh said, the words rolling off her tongue slowly, as though she was afraid to remind Vrana of the encounter.

Vrana's hands moved to her stomach, which was almost healed. "I guess so. At this point, I feel like she has no reason to mislead us."

"But that means we're related to them."

"I know." Vrana yawned. "Now, I'm wondering if that has something to do with our people and the low birth rate. If it's this hard to procreate, maybe we weren't mean to."

R'lyeh bit her lip. "Does that mean Serra is a homunculus?"

"I—" Vrana shook her head. "I don't know. The homunculus in the hospital was like a statue, a mold of something. Deimos did say they found him there, though. Honestly, R'lyeh," she said as she laughed and rolled onto her back, "I'm not sure what the hell's going on anymore."

"How many people do you think know what we know?"

"Not many. I'm not sure what that means for us, though."

R'lyeh punched her pillow into a more comfortable shape. "What did you want to do after you were initiated?"

"Explore the land, which is exactly what I'm doing now, so I shouldn't complain, but, shit, I didn't think it'd be like this. What do you want to be when you grow up, R'lyeh?"

R'lyeh hesitated to answer, as though she hadn't considered Vrana would ask her the same question. "It's stupid."

"I doubt it."

"I want to know more. I don't want to be a keeper, screw that, but at the same time, I want to be really good at kicking ass, like you, you know." She grinned as Vrana grinned. "Something like a really badass librarian."

"Badass," Vrana repeated, remembering that it was Aeson's favorite word, a word which he had once used to describe her. "We're bound at the hip now, aren't we?"

"I'd say so," R'lyeh agreed.

"You have to take care of yourself first, though."

"I'm trying."

Vrana smiled, and she nudged the girl.

"Why," R'lyeh began, her voice suddenly sounding quite serious, "why do you think it's okay that they... feed the Worm here?"

Vrana furrowed her eyebrows. "What do you mean?"

"Geharra... Alluvia..." R'lyeh's breathing became shallow. "I guess I'm saying it seems... I guess I'm saying it seems... okay... since they are doing something for the good of—of us."

"They're two entirely different circumstances, R'lyeh," Vrana said, tracing with her finger a trail left by a tear on the girl's cheek. *I'm sure Alexander Blodworth thought he was doing good, too*, Vrana thought but didn't say aloud.

"I guess," she said, sounding thoroughly unconvinced. "I mean, I don't feel bad for the flesh fiends. I guess I just don't see how we're all that different from the Corrupted. I know we're not."

"I wish you'd stayed in Caldera," Vrana said, moving closer to the Octopus.

R'lyeh wiped her eyes as she shook her head. "I can't sit in some classroom."

"You could've gone to your parents. You could've had them brought to you."

R'lyeh started to chew on her nails, and then she closed her eyes. "I don't want to risk it. Knowing they are alive is enough until everything gets better. I don't want to risk... something happening. They're—well, you and your mom—you're... you four are all I have."

"R'lyeh." Vrana stared into the girl's eyes. "Did Anguis really send you to kill those two Corrupted at Keldon's Hill?"

She nodded.

Vrana paused for a moment, remembering the carnage she'd awoken to outside the cave days before R'lyeh had attacked the men. *If I asked her if it'd been her hand that had slaughtered those animals, would she even tell me the truth?* Deciding that she would not, Vrana pulled away from the girl and told her goodnight.

"Vrana?" R'lyeh called out later, one final question in need of a response.

Vrana pretended not to hear here.

CHAPTER XXXII

At sunrise, they rose. R'lyeh sharpened her daggers—the Cruel Mother's talons—while Vrana turned the sealing stone over in her hands. The white streaks etched into the rock's surface glowed warmly, and shocked her fingers when touched. She tried to understand why creatures as powerful as the Worms would allow an object such as this to exist, and then realized the futility of trying to understanding creatures as powerful as the Worms.

Maybe they have no ulterior motives, Vrana said to herself, smiling at R'lyeh as she slid the stone into her satchel and picked up her ax. *Maybe they prosper because we expect them to.*

Mara came to fetch them from their quarters shortly thereafter. When they were finished here, there would be little Vrana and R'lyeh could say about Lacuna, for they'd only known it by its exodus. Whatever great deeds and horrible atrocities had been committed would be carried away by those waiting to depart below. It was easy enough to imagine the process by which the great, writhing engine was fed, but the imagined said little of reality, and it said even less of the machine the engine gave life to.

"What was it like to live here?" Vrana asked as they passed through the field of crops at the back of the village, which had already begun to die.

Mara brought a long sword with her and used it to clear a path. This was the first time Vrana had seen the woman with a weapon, and it worried her. "Lovely," she said, "but all things end."

"How did you get to be in charge?" R'lyeh shouted, having lagged behind. She sounded distracted and kept looking back the way they'd come.

"I've fooled many Corrupted over the years into letting me into their beds and halls. The elders of Traesk were looking to make better use of this island, and since I knew the Corrupted better than most, I was assigned as overseer of operations."

Vrana slowed as she waited for R'lyeh to catch up. They were at the fork in the tall grass, where waited the path that would lead them to the copse. "Are you okay, R'lyeh?"

She nodded feebly.

Vrana guided the girl to the breach in the dense foliage. "Are the Corrupted still in the chamber?"

"No, they gave themselves to the Worm."

Vrana stumbled sideways as R'lyeh fell into her. The girl's breathing was shallow, her body dripping with perspiration. She tried to catch her balance, but her legs gave out and she collapsed in the grass. She was panicking, and the anxiety that was gripping her head and heart was guiding her hands to the daggers at her side.

Vrana, knowing all too well what the girl was capable of, went to her knees and took her by the arms so that she could not draw her weapons. Mara, having seen all that she had seen, unclasped a bag at her side, produced a tiny vial, took out the stopper, tipped back the girl's mask, and forced its contents into her screaming mouth. R'lyeh flailed as the Centipede held her mouth shut until it was clear she had swallowed the liquid.

"No, I can't! I won't!" R'lyeh shouted, digging her heels into the dirt.

"She should've stayed in Caldera," Vrana said, shaking her head. "She shouldn't be here."

The beating of Blix's wings preceded him as he descended upon the scene and clamped down onto Vrana. She needed only to glance at the crow to know that Mara had failed to heal him. The bird was still gaunt, his beak still weathered, and now his feathers appeared oily, clinging to his speckled flesh.

"There she goes," Mara whispered as R'lyeh relaxed, eyelids half open. "She'll be calm until we're done here."

Vrana released R'lyeh's arms and stood up. She cringed as she caught the foul scent of Blix. "What do I do?"

"I tried to help him," Mara said, nodding at Blix, "but the Witch weaved a spell too tight to be unwoven."

Vrana looked at the crow, rubbed his head, and told herself that he would be fine. Despite often forgetting about Blix, she could not bear to lose him.

Mara propped the girl's body up and wiped away a bit of drool seeping from her mouth. "Just follow the tunnel, and you'll find the Worm's Chamber. Give it the stone and get back here as quickly as you can."

"Why? What's going to happen?"

"I'm not sure." Mara bent down, picked up R'lyeh, and held her like an infant against her body. "The Widening Gyre, the Sailor's Bane—it's going to disappear. And I know for a fact there is a group that has been watching this area very carefully, trying to find a way in."

"Who?" Vrana stepped aside as Mara marched past towards Lacuna.

"I have an idea. Old friends, I suspect." Mara looked back, already a small figure in the distance. "When it's finished, come to the docks, and I'll get you home."

Vrana tore through the copse, and the copse tore through her, cutting, pricking, and stinging her skin as she went. She approached the rock formation, and without hesitation, she went through its doorway. On the other side, she found a tunnel lit by the same glowing rocks that lined the passage to the Inner Archive. The path before her, which led downward into the heart of the island, was wide and sat at a slight angle to the entrance. Vrana tried to imagine how many children had made the journey from the Worm's chamber but found that all she could think of were the thousands of doomed prisoners that had marched willingly to their deaths beneath the streets of Geharra.

Apprehension saw that Vrana proceeded slowly, her back stiff, waiting for a bludgeoning from clichéd betrayal. The air in the tunnel was surprisingly fresh, calming even. Knowing this would be her first true encounter with a Worm of the Earth, she had to consider that all anomalies, however agreeable, were likely of the creature's design.

Though it pained her to see R'lyeh in such a state, Vrana was glad the girl had remained topside; she didn't trust the Blue Worm to leave such a tarnished mind untouched. *Will it leave mine alone?* she wondered, drawing a breath as she reached two wooden doors at the tunnel's end. She looked at Blix, who was still perched upon her shoulder, and wished that he could speak to give her a word of support.

The wooden doors were not locked, so Vrana pushed them open with the head of her ax. A gasp escaped her dry lips as her eyes fell upon the great space beyond. A blue light befitting the name of the beast said to live here drenched the hollow. Small hovels and large pools filled with crystalline water sat upon and within the expanse of soft, red grass. It was difficult to determine how far the chamber stretched across the belly of the island, but it seemed to Vrana she could walk forever in any direction and never reach its end.

She was hesitant to send Blix forward, but she needed his eyes to see what she could not. Vrana removed the sealing stone, which was absolutely radiant in her hands, and held it high so as to guide her across the subterranean plains.

There appeared to be five hovels in her partition of the chamber, and she expected to find more beyond the natural wall that divided the area. Glancing through the glassless windows as she passed, she found that each hovel was roofless, with nothing more than a bed, pillow, and blanket to comfort its once-inhabitants. These homes, if they could truly be called homes, had not housed love, pleasure, or ecstasy—but the dull groans of duty and desperation.

Blix's cawing echoed around Vrana. She followed the sound to its feathery source. Rounding the natural rock wall, she not only found the blue light to be much brighter here, but that there seemed to be more pressure in this part of the chamber. With every step she took, she felt an invisible vise closing in on her head, pushing both her skull and the Cruel Mother's into her brain. Blood began to leak from her nose and her ears, with the pressure worsening the closer she came to the light's origin.

"It's there, isn't it, Blix?" Vrana said, gritting her teeth, blood running down her throat. She expected the bird to fall to the ground at any moment, but he seemed indifferent to the pain. "What did the Witch do to you?" she rambled on, trying to distract herself from the discomfort of feeling crushed. "Maybe I should have had her weave a spell onto me. Another one, at least."

Vrana dragged her ax through the rust-colored grass as she walked beside several pools. She felt her stomach drop as she heard something splash in the waters a foot away. With all her strength, of which there was little left to use, Vrana lifted her ax and leaned over one of the pools, using the glow of the sealing stone to probe its depths.

Another splash, but this time it was behind her. Vrana whipped around, blood flinging from her nose into the crevices of her mask. A wave of crystalline water from the disturbed pool washed over her feet. She could feel the sealing stone sparking, the electric current running along its surface adhering the rock to her hand. Would the Blue Worm be as large as the Red? The almost blinding light of the sealing stone suggested that it was near, but where?

Through the ripples and refractions, Vrana could see that something was alive at the bottom of the pool, moving wildly, hypnotically.

"Is that you?" Vrana asked the Blue Worm.

It was, but not all of it. Before Vrana could react, something blew out of the pool behind her and wrapped itself around her ankle. A yelp escaped her lips as it yanked her to the ground; her chest and head slammed into the ruddy soil. She twisted around as she was pulled backwards and saw that a long, bruised tentacle had attached itself to her leg. The ax was useless, too large and imprecise to cut the appendage from hers, and the daggers at her side were too difficult to reach.

"Blix!" she cried out, unable to hear her own voice over the pressure in her ears. "Blix!" she yelled again, her leg numbing in the beast's grip.

The tentacle wrenched Vrana into the pool from which it had emerged. Frantically, she swung her ax at the sides of what was now obviously a tunnel, hoping to gain purchase. The walls, however, were coated in a thin membrane, and the ax passed right through.

She kicked her feet, dug her toes into the tentacle to no avail. It whipped her through the tunnel, smashed her against the membrane and rocks. Just when it seemed they could go no further, the tentacle pulled her upward, through another watery passage. If the end was in sight, Vrana could not see it, for the light of the sealing stone was blinding.

Her stomach dropped as the tentacle flung her up out of the water and into the air. She felt the pressure leave her body as she fell through a flashing, blue mist. For a brief moment, she was calm, at ease; serene as a landscape dusted with snow, untouched by wind, unbroken by noise. And then her body crashed into the ground, into a stretch of muscle covered in arteries, veins, and tiny skulls, cracked and deformed.

"Give me the stone and I will cease to be," a voice whispered.

Vrana lifted her head and saw with unworthy eyes the gruesome glory of the Blue Worm. It sat upon a bed of children's bones, a hundred slithering tentacles encircling its midnight form. The mist that Vrana had fallen through and that filled the chamber emanated from the creature, rolling out from under its mass in dampening waves. How large it was Vrana could not tell, but even in its constricted state, it dwarfed the Raven and could destroy her with ease.

"Having second thoughts?" A hurricane of tentacles spun around the Blue Worm, dull lights like eyes blinking in the abyssal body they guarded.

Vrana scurried rearward on all fours, hands sliding over the greasy texture of the sinewy floor. A sharp pain shot through her abdomen as she backed unknowingly into two large, wooden doors—the very same she'd passed through to reach the Worm's lair. It was then that she realized there were no walls in the chamber, only a seamless expanse of roiling murk.

Vrana slid up the doors, using them for support as she came to her feet. She could somehow hear Blix clawing at the wood, even though she could see there was nothing on the other side. She held the sealing stone as far as she could from her body while she readied the ax, should the Blue Worm launch a tentacle her way.

"Give me the stone, and go back the way you came," the Blue Worm uttered.

Vrana swallowed her fear and took a step towards the creature.

The Blue Worm unraveled a tentacle, slipped it into the pool that had brought Vrana to the chamber, and stirred the water. "What do you want to know?"

Vrana shook her head.

Out of the water, a hand rose and clamped down on a bundle of veins. Moments later, the pale flesh fell from the bones, and the skeletal remains sank back into the pool.

Vrana took another step forward, her feet slipping into the folds of muscle. "Why did you help them?" she asked finally.

"Help?" The Blue Worm retracted its tentacle; from its tip, secretions like semen fell into the water.

"What will happen if you take the stone?"

"Sleep will come."

Vrana took another step. "Why do you want this?"

The Blue Worm's tentacles splayed out across the bones, revealing for a moment the black figure that stood at the center. "Would you rather I kill you?"

Vrana watched as the dripping tentacle reared back. "They're your children, not ours."

The Blue Worm rumbled and tightened itself, so that it was no wider or taller than Vrana. "You hesitate, and the womb is no place for the born."

The Worm is right, Vrana thought. *What am I doing?* She was terrified, yes, but intrigued. She didn't feel as she had in the presence of the Red Worm—that is, weak and minute, a pile of limbs to be added to its macabre figure. Was it because she knew more of the Blue Worm's actions and their contributions to her tribe? Or was it something else, something more manipulative? Given her surroundings, she knew she should flee, and yet she stayed, anchored by curiosity in the bloody cradle of Lacuna.

The Raven took another step. The Blue Worm emitted a low growl; the sealing stone was beginning to have an effect. "How many of you are left?"

"The Green and the White, for now."

"Where?"

The Blue Worm sent several tentacles slithering across the ground toward Vrana. "The Centipede has too many questions, and so you are here to do what she could not."

Vrana felt her heart pound as the tentacles snaked around her feet. *Is that why she didn't come? The elders knew she couldn't do it.* Vrana directed the light of the sealing stone at a nearby tentacle, and it began to shrivel as it retracted. *Did she give something to R'lyeh to make her panic?*

"What is it you wish to know?" the Blue Worm persisted. A thick layer of mist rose over the creature as it pulled back and downward into the bones upon which it sat, disappearing. Skulls, jaws, ribs, and feet all moved like discarded treasures as the Worm shook the pile from within.

It's not worth it, Vrana told herself. *Give it the stone and leave.*

"Much has been forgotten since the Trauma," the Blue Worm said, pale lights flashing through the gaps between the bones. "Why use an ax when a gun would serve you better?"

Ignore it and give it the stone. Vrana plodded toward the shifting pile of broken skeletons and held out the sealing stone, which was becoming unbearably hot. "Take it."

"You've seen my brood? My legacy?" the Blue Worm remarked with pride, still refusing to surface.

"Take the stone and sleep," Vrana insisted.

"Why not ask of Caldera's mountain?" the creature whispered. The chamber tensed, the veins and arteries tightened. "That is mine, too, after all. Why not ask of the black rock? Surely, you've seen it."

"Take the stone."

The Blue Worm rose out of the bed of bones, the remnants of the dead clinging to its bruised flesh. It encircled Vrana, walling her in with one hundred dripping tentacles. The milky light of the chamber faded as the Worm covered her completely, leaving only the sealing stone to illuminate the darkness of the creature's hold. She could hear and smell the Worm's organs hissing and popping, but it didn't seem to care.

"You will do much for us." The Blue Worm leaned in close, and through the burning light of the stone, Vrana could see a human shape to which all the tentacles were bound. "Why not ask of your father? I'm sure he's around here somewhere. He'd like to say he's sorry."

Vrana screamed as she shoved the sealing stone into the Blue Worm's body. Immediately, it began to wither, its appendages becoming hard and brittle, like the branches of a smoldering tree. She cut her way through the carcass as the tortured cries of dead children rang out across the chamber. The ground began to spasm, and the veins, arteries, and sacs that crossed it ruptured and burst, spewing blood and amniotic fluid into the swirling air.

"Blix!" Vrana shouted, for she could still hear the crow clawing at the door. "Don't come in!" she warned, reaching for the handles.

A cold sweat broke out across Vrana's body as she felt a hand close on her side.

"Yours to have," the Blue Worm whispered in her ear.

Vrana looked to the hand at her side, which was the color of coal, and saw dangling from its thin fingers a silver necklace with a blue gem inside a tangle of worms.

"A necklace for a stone, a stone for a necklace," the Blue Worm offered.

"Keep it," Vrana said, mind returning to the red-gemmed necklace falling into the flesh pit of Geharra. "I don't want it."

"You say that now," the Blue Worm said, laughing. It lifted the necklace to Vrana's eyelevel. "Take it, do what you will with it; the door will not open otherwise."

Vrana swallowed her words of protest, snuffed her want to sever the Worm's head from its body. Without looking at the Worm in full—it was naked and unguarded—she ripped the silver necklace from its hand, pulled open the wooden doors, and threw herself into the long tunnel that would lead her out of hell.

CHAPTER XXXIII

It had been morning when the Raven descended into the island and midnight when she climbed out of it. A violent tempest awaited her as she staggered out of the rock formation. She forced Blix into a satchel to protect him from the storm, and he nipped at her hand to show he appreciated the thought.

"What happened?" Vrana shouted to herself, shivering as sheets of rain fell across the area. "Where is it?"

The trees of the island creaked and moaned as the mad wind twisted their backs and brought them to the muddy ground. Vrana stood on the tips of her toes and saw across the parted land the ruins of Lacuna, the buildings jagged shapes like debris across a war-torn field. She shoved the blue-gemmed necklace into the satchel opposite Blix's and made for the passage that would lead her to the docks.

Halfway to the village, Vrana stopped and watched as torches moved like fireflies across the western shore. Though the moonlight was weak, it was enough to see that there were three small boats on the beach. Mara had warned Vrana that a group had taken interest in the island, and now they were here, having arrived far too quickly to suggest that their interest was nothing less than an obsession.

As she came to the outskirts of Lacuna, Vrana found the door to the dockyard torn off, lost somewhere in the glistening glade. She entered the passage through the hollowed-out tree, the sconces inside having been robbed of their flames. Blades of grass and wet leaves clung to her feet as she hurried into the depths of the island once more.

"Vrana!" R'lyeh called out from the passage's end. "Vrana, you're okay!"

R'lyeh? She could hear the girl's voice, but the passage was too dark to make out what was in front of her.

"Mara, she made it!" she heard her say.

Am I hallucinating? Vrana quickened her pace, rubbing the top of Blix's head as she went. *What did the Worm do to me?*

Just as she was about to doubt her own sanity, Vrana collided with R'lyeh, sending both the girl and herself to the ground.

"Are you okay?" Vrana cried, scrambling to her feet to embrace R'lyeh. "Sorry Blix," she whispered, squishing the crow as they hugged.

"I'm so sorry." R'lyeh began to weep. "I really wanted to be there."

"It's better that you weren't," Vrana said, her eyes beginning to adjust to the dark. She slid her hands under R'lyeh's mask and stroked the girl's hair to calm her. "Where's Mara?"

R'lyeh took Vrana by the wrist and led her to the docks, which had been torn in half during the calming of the Bane. Wood shavings coated the surface of the cove's black waters, bunching up against the supports that had yet to be toppled. At the farthest end of the inlet, a small boat without paddles or a sail waited, with Mara standing at its bow and an emerald orb of light hovering over its stern.

"She said that she can spellweave a little," R'lyeh muttered as they navigated the remains of the dock. "She said the Worm taught her how."

"I wonder what else she's learned," Vrana retorted, steadying herself on the rickety walkway as the waves pounded against it.

"I was so scared you wouldn't come back," R'lyeh admitted, not taking her eyes off Mara.

"How do you think I felt seeing you like that?"

R'lyeh sighed. "I don't know what happened." She batted a moth away. "It's not the first time."

"Later, then."

One by one they descended a ladder off the side of the walkaway and boarded the boat. Mara nodded at Vrana and tapped the emerald sphere with the tip of her sword. The conjuration began to melt, dripping onto the stern and spreading at an alarming rate over the entirety of the boat and its passengers.

"What did you do?" Vrana lurched forward as the boat propelled itself into the night.

"The waters are too turbulent to sail any other way," Mara said. "It'll be slow going, but we'll reach Nachtla soon enough."

"Then how did they get across?" Vrana took a seat, her back to the dock, and laid her ax the across her lap.

"Who?"

"Vrana..." R'lyeh started, touching her damp side.

Vrana ignored the girl and said, "The Worm told me you should have been the one to seal it away."

"Not everyone can be as dedicated as you," Mara said, sounding defensive. "We all have our shortcomings."

"Are you a homunculus?" Vrana ran her fingers through the fine layer of emerald light that surrounded the boat, which hummed with every pass.

Mara laughed. "You know that I'm not."

"How is it you can spellweave?" Vrana shrugged off R'lyeh's attempt to get her attention.

"Practice. And promises." The centipedes on Mara's mask started to shift, changing the shape of the headpiece to something more pointed and severe. "I swear, Vrana, that I would never betray you."

"Mara," R'lyeh said, "I thought you said everyone left."

Vrana swung her legs over the seat and turned toward the docks. Twelve torches burned brightly in the hands of twelve cloaked figures standing on the structure's edge. Their robes, tattered and torn, fluttered in the changing wind, with the hints of weapons glinting behind the dark fabrics.

"Who are they?" Vrana said, lowering her voice, even though she knew the spell had made the boat anything but invisible.

Mara crouched, closed her hand around a portion of the emerald light, and ripped it free. "It's time to find out," she said as she molded the light into a ball, whispered a word, and threw it across the cove at the shuffling figures.

Like fireworks from the underworld, the eerie emerald orb exploded in the cove, showering the docks in nightmarish green light. The twelve figures pulled back the hoods of their robes, as though they were eager to make their identities known. There were six men and six women, and although Vrana could not see their arms, she was somehow certain they were Corrupted. They appeared ordinary enough by their faces alone, which were unmarked by madness or ritualistic scarification.

"Who are they?" Vrana repeated.

Before Mara could answer, a thirteenth figure emerged onto the docks, the group parting as it passed. The figure moved gracelessly, its legs wracked with infections or fractures. The cowl hung like a curtain over its body—neither fitting it nor forming to it—and a dented breastplate protected its chest. Like the others, the thirteenth figure looked up at the gems of light falling through the cove and then pulled back its black hood.

Vrana gasped as the thirteenth figure let the hood fall to its shoulders. Where there should have been a face, there was only bone: a skull with hardened eyes, veined and glassy, bulging from their sockets. *The Skeleton*, Vrana said to herself. *The Skeleton from the Black Hour.* Her hands went to the bags at her side for the key from the keep—which was back in Caldera.

"The Marrow Cabal," Mara whispered. She became frantic and began to murmur incantations that seemed to make the boat increase in speed.

"I've seen him, the Skeleton," Vrana confessed.

Mara shook her head. "You're wrong, Vrana."

"No, I'm not." She looked to the docks to confirm her statement. "I've seen him."

"That's who led a rebel group to Eldrus to kill King Edgar," Mara said, still not believing the Raven. "How could you know him?"

"The Black Hour." Vrana's neck burned under R'lyeh's scrutiny. "After my second trial, I was lost, and I stumbled into the Black Hour." She could hear R'lyeh draw a deep breath. "It was raining, and I took shelter in a keep. I fell asleep, and when I woke, I found him, torturing a man. There were bodies everywhere, and I could hear what sounded like a mob closing in. When I went to escape, everything vanished—the keep, the mob, the Skeleton."

"Does that mean he knows who you are?" R'lyeh asked, a shiver coursing through her body.

Mara chanted one last hymn and said at its end, "The Black Hour is a perversion of what has been and could be. There's not enough known about it to come to any conclusion other than it is real to those experiencing it."

"When I met him, he seemed obsessed with finding a way to reverse death."

"He certainly came to the right place," Mara said. She exhaled loudly. "But the Worm is gone, and so are we. There is nothing they can learn from Lacuna."

R'lyeh hummed. "What is he doing?"

Squinting, Vrana saw in the last of the light the Skeleton's bony hand moving back and forth. "He's waving us off."

Vrana kept to herself for the following twenty minutes. Her mind felt sick, dizzied, and fevered. Her hands busied themselves in the bag at her side, petting a sleeping Blix, as her thoughts oscillated between the Blue Worm and the Skeleton. Could she leave it to mere coincidence to explain these two encounters with the King's would-be assassin? If Mara was correct, then their meeting in the Black Hour was known only to Vrana; it was nothing more than a secret dream. Yet, she didn't believe that, not entirely. Was she bound to the Skeleton as she was to the Witch? Would they be forever entwined, the three of them, each twisting around the other, until the threads of their being frayed and snapped?

Vrana sighed, took off the raven's skull, and told herself she was simply not that important.

R'lyeh had been the first to break the silence aboard the boat, with a snore like an old man's.

But it was Mara who was the first to say anything of importance. "We've been out here for too long."

Vrana surveyed the sea, watching the black waves carry debris long held under by the tow of the Bane. "Did we drift off course?"

"No," Mara retorted, shaking her head. She drew her sword at nothing in particular and said, "The spell wouldn't allow that to happen." She ran her hand through the emerald glow coating the boat. "It's still strong. Something is wrong."

"Mara," Vrana started, "what did you give the Worm to spell-weave?"

Mara seemed to hesitate for a moment. "My eggs," she said finally. "It was a fair trade."

R'lyeh yawned. As she sat up, her mask rolled over the top of her head and fell behind her. "Are we there yet?" she asked, hands fumbling for the dried octopus body.

The boat came to a grinding halt. Vrana's initial thought was that they had reached the mainland, but this was not the case. In a matter of seconds, the ocean had frozen over. Jagged waves encased in ice loomed like the claws of a beast reaching from its prison deep within the solid sea. They had sailed into the Black Hour, Vrana realized, and this time she could not chalk it up to mere coincidence.

"Vrana," R'lyeh said, her voice quivering. "Vrana!" she yelled, losing the nerve she had so recently recovered.

Vrana removed her mask, took R'lyeh's hand, and pressed it to her cheek, so that the girl could feel something that was alive. "Breathe." She dried her tears the best that she could. "If I give you the daggers, will that help?"

"I know I'm weak," R'lyeh said, nodding and taking the Cruel Mother's talons, "but they help me be strong."

"You are strong," Vrana insisted. She could tell Mara was trying to get her attention.

"Not like you." R'lyeh wiped her nose.

"It takes its toll." Vrana turned to face Mara. "I just don't let it show."

The ocean began to shake, sending white fractures across the dusted icescape. Lights the color of Corruption winked from the waters below their feet. The sea became a window as shadows slithered behind its glassy surface, making the tiniest of cracks dreadful gateways.

"Get out of the boat," Mara ordered, stepping onto the ice.

Vrana nodded, put R'lyeh's mask on the girl, and then put on her own. She asked Blix if he was doing all right, and he responded by pulling the flap of the satchel shut with his beak.

"What do we do?" R'lyeh asked between the chattering of her teeth.

Vrana opened another one of her bags, removed the faerie silk cloak, and threw it around the girl. "We wait it out. That's all we can—"

The ocean heaved high into the air a cloud of ice and freezing water. A colossal tower bored the Bane's breast, twisting like a screw as it worked its way toward the sky. Vrana, R'lyeh, and Mara tried to flee, but the force of its emergence put them on hands and knees, face to face with the shadowy beings on the other side of the sea.

"What's happening?" R'lyeh shouted.

Blix, unable to endure the abuse any longer, burst out of the satchel and took flight. Vrana's eyes followed as he soared across the starless heavens toward the tower that seemed to hold them there. It was a skyscraper, a stolen bone from the Old World's body. Angular, starved, and stripped of color, it swayed where it stood like the wakened dead, charged to frighten one last soul before collapsing into dust.

R'lyeh pulled the faerie cloak as tight as she could around her body, fresh snowflakes from above now dotting the fabric. "Where did they all go? The buildings, I mean, from the Old World." She sounded awestruck.

"Now's not the time," Vrana said gently, her attention taken by the fissures and the shadows collected within.

"We have to keep moving." Mara's sword arm tensed as a chunk of ice fell from the sky and burst at her feet.

Mara turned to lead them into the frigid darkness, but the lights beneath their feet began to flare and burn red again. Vibrations, and then tremors. More shadows spread across the frosted glass. The ground cracked, snapped. They moved away from the boat as it twitched and sank into the softening ice. The noises grew louder, the vibrations harder, as they rattled the sea. The ice buckled, screamed; a geyser of metal blew through the surface, sending the boat high into the night.

They picked a direction and ran as the second skyscraper wound out of the hole it made. The shadows were swarming beneath their feet towards what Vrana could only assume was an escape. She could hear more buildings tunneling through the ocean. Ice and snow rained down upon them as the hidden architects of the Black Hour built their tribute to insanity.

"Not much longer," Mara assured. "Always an hour and never more."

Vrana shivered at the sounds of madness that rode in on the wintry wind. Laughter; the wailing of an infant. The shadows had broken out of their cells and were now closing in around them with murderous intent, pouring through the alleyways and streets of the growing city.

"What are they?" R'lyeh said, scrambling as the layer of ice beneath her cracked in half.

Vrana grabbed the girl, caught a glimpse of the black swell of death behind them. Blix cawed overhead until he was sure he had

SCOTT HALE

their attention and then flew on. They followed after.

"I don't know," Mara responded finally. "They may be new to this world."

New to this world? The merfolk in the rivers outside Geharra—Deimos had said the same of them. They're not new. We are. And they hate us for it.

Mara hopped backward, curses passing through her lips as the ground rumbled and shook. She held out her arm to bar Vrana and R'lyeh from nearing. The ground fell inward, and a power line like a crucifix rose out of the crimson haze trapped within the ice, wires rising with it, ripping through the ocean's shell.

Mara looked back as though to tell them it was safe to move forward but sighed instead. "Go, follow Blix," she said, sounding defeated. She dropped her arm, raised her sword, and walked past Vrana and R'lyeh to meet the wailing shadows.

"What are you doing?" Vrana grabbed Mara's arm.

Mara tugged away and laughed. "I'm not sacrificing myself, if that's what you think."

Mara uttered words that Vrana had never heard before, eldritch invocations that seemed to bloody the very throat through which they passed. Her body thinned, and flesh tightened around bone. She pulled her stomach in and released a primal cry that echoed across the temporary landscape.

Her mask began to shift as it had done in the past, but this time it didn't remain atop her head; rather, it expanded and broke apart, each centipede crawling off in opposite directions, some down her spine, others across her arms, chest, and legs, where they dug into her skin, their carapaces now hers.

"What's going on?" R'lyeh asked breathlessly as they ran after Blix, Mara growing smaller and smaller behind them.

Vrana ignored the girl, because she didn't know how to answer her. More laughter; more wailing: The ocean sounded like a nursery overseen by a madman. Vrana craned her neck as she wiped away the snow that had formed in the sockets of her mask. An emerald mist swirled around Mara, its wispy fingers pushing into her mouth, eyes, and nose. The shadows were near enough to kill the woman; and with their bared fangs, silver and dripping, it seemed they had every intention to.

If Mara was going to die, it would be when she said so. She lifted her sword, the blade dripping with black oil, and stabbed it into the ground. But what happened next could not have been what she'd intended. Or perhaps it was.

Her body lifted off the ground and exploded.

Before Vrana and R'lyeh could comprehend what had happened, the Black Hour ended, and they were plunged into the warm and restless waters of the Sailor's Bane.

CHAPTER XXXIV

Vrana was not going to lose the girl, not after everything they'd been through. She grabbed R'lyeh by the wrist and held on tightly as the ocean's current pulled them under. She drew R'lyeh close to her body, so that she could wrap her arms and legs around Vrana, and once she had, she made for the surface.

Somewhere, something seemed to have thought they'd suffered enough, for when Vrana's head broke through the waves, she saw that they were in the shallows of the sea. She dug her feet into the sand and plodded forward, too afraid to release R'lyeh should a cheated Death rise out of the waters to take her.

Images of Mara flashed through her head as she trudged toward the cove, the woman's body tearing apart, giving to the shadows her blood and bones. Had Vrana ever witnessed someone die before, Corrupted notwithstanding? It had always been the aftermath, the grisly remains of a crime. She felt strange, empty; half expecting to find the woman still standing beside her, cold and calloused but alive.

Vrana dropped her ax on the beach and lowered R'lyeh to her feet. The girl took off her mask, slicked her hair back, and spat up the salt water sitting in her throat. Blix flew past them, leaving a trail of feathers to flutter in the moonlight, and landed on a fresh deadfall. Vrana tore limbs from the trees gathered on the shore, coveting the driest branches like gold. It would not be a frigid night, but they were drenched, and the Black Hour had taken all the warmth from their bodies.

"You were right." R'lyeh sat on a dune, brought her knees to her chest, and held herself. "I should have stayed in Caldera."

"Me too." Vrana marched past R'lyeh, arms filled with the makings of a fire, to the inside of the cove. "Grab my ax."

The girl did as she was told, tucking her weapons behind her belt and picking up Vrana's. "Why did she do that?"

"I don't know." Vrana dropped the firewood at the center of the cove, scaring off several rock wraiths. "I don't think it was intentional."

"Me neither." R'lyeh offered the ax to Vrana, but the Raven told her to set it down instead. "I don't—" she swallowed her words, but they came back up, "—I don't want to watch anyone else die."

Would I be as composed as her if I'd seen all that she had? Vrana stole some stones from nearby and made a circle around the wood and kindling. "I'm sorry, R'lyeh."

"It's too much." She was holding her mask by a tentacle, like a child would a stuffed animal by its arm. "Is it because you're older?"

"What do you mean?" Vrana started to assemble the framework of a fire.

"It doesn't seem to bother you."

"It does." Vrana shuddered as she still heard the sound of Mara being ripped apart. "But not much. I guess that's good. I don't know." She sighed and fell back on her palms. "My mother said my father dying made me resilient."

R'lyeh's voice became a dry whisper as she said, "I didn't know your dad…"

Vrana stood up quickly and looked upon her creation with disdain. "Disappeared into the Black Hour. That's what some say."

"And now you've been in it twice," R'lyeh said, hand over her mouth. She cast her eyes to the ground, dug her feet into the sand. "I'm afraid that, if we go home, everything will get worse."

Vrana gave no response as she wandered to the back of the cove, feeling her way along the rocks.

"Your mom was so nice to me, but lying there all day was unbearable. I only felt better when Anguis let me leave." R'lyeh cleared her throat. "What are you doing, Vrana?"

"Listening. And looking," she said, hands probing the darkness for the place Mara had emerged from when she and R'lyeh first happened upon the area. "She'd said there were other ways off the island and…"

Vrana slipped into a nook and found within earthenware and the beginnings of a tunnel now sealed. She hauled the pots and vases out one at a time, so that she could have a better look at their contents in the ghostly light of the moon. "This must run beneath the ocean, to Lacuna. I guess this is how some got off the island."

"Do you think they made it?" R'lyeh treaded toward the Raven, Blix following close behind. "Do you think the Black Hour got them, too?"

Vrana patted the slab of stone that sat in front of the tunnel for secret switches, of which there were apparently none. She exited the nook and said, "Lacuna was kept hidden by the same spell that shrouds Caldera's mountain. I bet you each boat had a spellweaver. I'm sure they made it out."

"I hope so," R'lyeh said, plopping down beside the pilfered goods. She removed the seals that held the contents inside the pots and vases and said with a grin, "Food."

R'lyeh warned Vrana that, although the meat was clearly cured and coated in additional preservatives, it may have been tainted. Vrana, thinking with her stomach rather than her mind, told R'lyeh that they should then take very small bites. After having their fill, they moved onto the other containers and found within three vials of fluid that would burst into flames when mixed. Wasting no time and holding the concoctions as far away from her body as possible, Vrana doused the wood she'd gathered and watched with immense satisfaction as they burned.

"This is nice," R'lyeh said without emotion, chewing on the meat like a cow would grass. "Do you think Mara left this for us?"

Vrana shook her head and scooted closer to the fire.

"Did you hate her?" R'lyeh grunted as Blix flew past and plucked the meat from her mouth.

"I didn't hate her, but I didn't care for her either," Vrana said. She smiled as Blix landed beside her to savor his catch: It was the first time she'd see him act like himself in a while. "I do wish she was here with us."

R'lyeh sniffled. She tried to cover her eyes, but her tears fell too quickly to be hidden. "I'm sorry."

"What is it?" Vrana leaned close to the girl.

"I need to tell you something, but I can't."

Vrana nodded. She knew by the girl's statement that she was hoping Vrana would force the information out of her, but instead she said, "When you're ready."

R'lyeh shook her head, dropped her hands, and let the fire dry her tears.

"I was going to keep this to myself, but I need your help." Vrana noted R'lyeh's change in posture as she dug into her bags. "From the Worm," she said, taking the silver necklace out and holding it by its chain, the blue gem glowing in the firelight.

"Why… why did it give that to you?" R'lyeh stammered. "I thought you sealed it."

"A necklace for a stone, a stone for a necklace." Vrana dropped the piece of jewelry back into the bag and pulled it closed, for she feared having it out in the open for too long. "The necklace brought the Red Worm to life, and the stone sent the Blue Worm away. It wouldn't let me leave unless I took it."

"Does that mean the Red Worm's stone is still somewhere in Geharra?"

"It must be," Vrana said, not having considered this. "I wonder if that's why Deimos sent Serra back: not only to kill the Crossbreed but to get the rock."

"What are you going to do?" The girl's eyes lingered on the bag where the necklace was stored.

Vrana shrugged as Blix cuddled up against her leg. "What should I do?"

Taken aback, R'lyeh murmured, "Oh, uh, I don't know. You could toss it into the sea."

"Considered it. But these things have a way of finding themselves in the wrong hands."

R'lyeh agreed. "Could you give it to the elders?"

"I'd rather not." Vrana took off her mask and put it in front of her. "That's better."

"If it's with you, you'll know it's safe." R'lyeh's mouth hung open as she considered her next sentence. "At least, that's what has worked for me," she said, flashing an awkward smile.

Vrana closed her eyes, the dizzying warmth of the fire relaxing her body, causing her to nod off where she sat. She shook herself awake, wanting to return R'lyeh's kind words, and found that the night had fled, chased away by the burning light of day. She sat up, having lain down at some point in the hours before, and wiped away the sand that had dried on her skin. She felt groggy, and then she felt numb as she heard the cries of a young girl ride in on the wind. She looked to where R'lyeh had been sitting and saw across the beach footprints leading out the cove, with hundreds of tiny black dots following them.

Dead flies.

Vrana put on her mask, grabbed her ax, and followed R'lyeh's trail. She rounded the outside of the cove and headed up the slope that would give her a clear view of Nachtla. Screaming. She heard screaming now. Vrana's heart pounded as her mind turned on her, flooding her with images of the girl's lifeless corpse. *It's not her*, she told herself, reaching the hilltop. *It can't be her.*

But it was.

Across the dusty landscape, the R'lyeh sat, her legs crossed, and her hands in her lap, one bruised eye swollen shut, the other red and wide with fear. She was breathing hard, and when she saw Vrana, she started to shake her head weakly. Thin streaks of blood fell down her face from the hairless patch of tender flesh on her scalp.

"R'lyeh!" she yelled.

The girl's head tipped back as her throat stretched and swelled. A cry of pain escaped her lips, and hundreds of black flies followed. R'lyeh fell over as the last of the insects cleared her lungs, the cloud surrounding her too dense to determine whether she was still breathing.

"I didn't want it to come to this," said a man's cold voice.

Vrana gripped her ax so tightly that the tendons in her forearm threatened to snap. Hatred would have her murder anything and everything that stood before her. She turned around slowly, only because she feared that, if she took her eyes off the cloud, R'lyeh would be stolen away to the Void.

The Ashen Man waited behind her, tensed and shivering, as though he was struggling to keep his place in this world. His hands were curled into fists, and they were bloodied up to the wrist. Close enough to touch him, Vrana saw that his body was rough, textured; he was covered in endless scars from countless years of mutilation. He had no smell about him, nor did it seem that his eyes, which were the color of smoke, granted him sight. The man didn't appear to breathe at all, having likely lost the need for the function long ago.

Vrana readied her ax. "I'm going to kill you."

The Ashen Man nodded. "Either way, something good will come of this."

Words would not avenge R'lyeh, so Vrana swallowed her confusion and swung with all her might at the Ashen Man. He threw his arms in front of himself, absorbed the blow with flesh and bone, and pushed her away. He groaned, held out his hands; dripping sores opened on his palms and sides and wept into the air hundreds of buzzing, black flies. Vrana went to throw her mask from her head, for she knew the insects would try to drown her in their bodies, but before she could, the Ashen Man took her by the right arm and broke it.

Vrana screamed as the terrible aching pain brought her to her knees, ax falling beside her. She bit down into her lip as the need to vomit became almost too great to bear. Images flashed through her mind, but they were not images she'd ever seen: images of the Ashen Man suspended above a boiling mire, before his skin had lost its earthly warmth to the cold gray of the Void.

"Why help us at Nora?" Vrana said through her teeth.

"Because she willed it." The Ashen Man took a step towards her.

"Why kill us now?" Vrana leaned on her left side, hand inching towards the ax.

The Ashen Man went to one knee, flexing his bloodstained fingers. "Because I will it."

Vrana fell to her side, grabbed the ax, and buried it deeply into the Ashen Man's neck. The blade worked itself free as he stood up, thick tongues of brown blood spewing from the gash. Vrana pulled back, swung once more; the ax cut through the man's ankle, sent his foot across the chapped earth. His ragged stump slammed into the ground, and he went to his knee again.

"Is she dead?" Vrana yelled, raising the ax into the air. The black cloud covering R'lyeh had yet to relent.

He didn't answer.

Vrana brought the ax down upon the man. His arms shot out in front of him, and he caught the weapon by its handle and ripped it free from her grasp. The Ashen Man threw the ax away, sending it over the hill towards the beach. He tackled Vrana, crushing her broken arm under his weight. She punched him in the face, clawed at his milky eyes, but it was her weak arm. He put his hand over her mask and engulfed it in flies. Vrana closed her eyes, her mouth, and moaned as the insects' wings and appendages worked at her lids and lips.

"You cannot kill her." The Ashen Man moved his hands to Vrana's neck and squeezed hard. "This way is better."

Vrana's throat constricted. She flailed wildly, kicking at the man's stomach and digging her fingers into his wounds, pulling away chunks of flesh and muscle to no avail. She could feel her mind being ripped open, images that didn't belong there cutting themselves into memory. She saw the Witch atop the Ashen Man in an Old World room, his hands bound to the posts of a bed, a smirk upon his face. She watched as the Witch pulled back the fabric of the Void, as the Ashen Man reached through and dragged back twin boys on a bridge too paralyzed by fear to flee.

"Fuck you," Vrana spat with the last of her breath. She would not beg.

The Ashen Man put his knee into her stomach and then reeled backwards. Vrana gasped as the flies left her mask to tend to their master. She struggled to breathe, her throat almost too tight to let air through. She propped herself up on one arm and saw with thankful eyes her salvation.

R'lyeh stood behind the Ashen Man, the Cruel Mother's talons dug deep into his shoulders. She pulled them downward, splitting his back open. He didn't cry, nor did he flinch as she kicked him forward onto his face. She straddled him as he tried to turn over and hacked away at the back of his head.

"R'lyeh," Vrana rasped.

The Ashen Man threw R'lyeh off him, the white of his skull showing through the back of his head. "I'm sorry," he said, brown blood dripping from his mouth. His blind eyes searched the sky, and as the sound of beating wings fell upon him, the Horror of the Void said once more, "I'm sorry."

CHAPTER XXXV

A black shape streaked across the mottled firmament and descended on the Ashen Man. Blix—it was Blix, and although he looked like a skeleton, it seemed his need to defend them had given him strength. The man screamed and howled as the crow's claws and beak tore at his flesh, causing him to experience pain for the first time since the battle began. He continued to apologize to Blix as the bird pecked out his eyes and dug out his ocular cavities; his words slurred and eventually stopped as the crow pulled away parts of his brain.

"Blix." Vrana whispered, still lying down; Nachtla in the distance sitting like a black crown atop her head.

The crow pushed away from the Ashen Man's ruined body. He wavered for a moment, the matter of his brain dangling from his sockets, and then collapsed onto the ground.

"I'm so glad you're okay," R'lyeh said, panting. She was covered in the man's strange blood, and her swollen eye seemed to have worsened. She hobbled over to Vrana, wincing from the wound on her head. "I'm so glad to see you."

"I thought you were dead." Vrana took R'lyeh's outstretched hand and came to her feet. Her broken arm hung limply at her side, throbbing excruciatingly. "What happened?"

"I'm an idiot," she said, cringing. Without consideration, she embraced Vrana and put her head to the leather chest piece. "I woke up before you, heard something. I should have—but you were so tired. I don't think he could reach us in the cove. We were too far from Nachtla." She exhaled. "Are you okay?"

Vrana shook her head. She lifted her mask—the inside of which was covered in dead flies—and dropped it carelessly to the ground. "What did he say?" She touched her throat; she could still feel his hands wrapped around her neck.

"Not much," R'lyeh backed away, bent down, and held her head. "Oh god." She picked out the tiny corpses of flies from the sides of her mouth. "I'm sorry." She shoved her fingers down her throat and threw up the rest of the bugs left inside her. "Ugh, god."

"What did he say?" Vrana persisted. She could a feel a migraine scratching at her skull.

R'lyeh wretched. She wiped her lips and said, "That he was sorry, and that you had to die."

"What about the Witch?" Vrana turned her head to Blix who was beak-deep in the Ashen Man's neck. "Blix! Get the hell away from him." She grabbed a loose rock and chucked it at the bird.

"I don't think... I don't think she sent..." R'lyeh pointed to the crow. "Blix? Is he all right?"

Blix let out a harsh caw, fiercely flapping his wings as he lifted into the air. *Oh no*, Vrana thought, watching the Ashen Man's blood dribble out of his mouth. *Was it poisoned?* Blix flew in circles around the scene, feathers falling in handfuls from his speckled skin. Vrana and R'lyeh tried to catch the bird, but it slipped through their hands, leaving behind an oily residue on their fingers.

"Stop!" Vrana shouted as the crow rose into the air, fell, and rose once more. "R'lyeh..." she held out her arms, stunned. "I don't know what to do." She looked at the girl, not as an adult but as a child watching the last of her youth dissolve away. "R'lyeh, I don't know what..."

Blix slammed into the ground with a sickening thud. Vrana and R'lyeh started for him and then stopped as he shook, purple fumes pouring from his pores. The crow's back split open, spine jutting into the air. Two white hands moved through the folds of Blix's flesh, larger than the tiny body they were rising out of, and clamped down on opposite sides of the bird's torso.

"Vrana..." R'lyeh took a step back.

The white hands curled, seized the soil, and pushed the rest of their owner through. Pale arms followed by white hair: The Witch, the Maiden of Pain, rose through the entrails nude and grinning, the world about her twisting, spinning. She stood suspended in the air, the tips of her toes hovering above Blix's ravaged carcass. Her bones creaked and cracked as she contorted her body and looked upon its gaunt exterior with amusement. She ran a finger across her breast, shivering at the forgotten sensation.

"You fucking bitch," Vrana spat out, so blinded by rage she could hardly see.

The Witch's lip quivered. Her wild eyes rolled over to R'lyeh, who was sliding her mask over her head like a soldier would a helmet in preparation for combat.

Vrana made an effort to reach the hill where she knew the ax waited on the other side. The Witch moved her dried lips, and Vrana's legs went numb. She laughed silently as Vrana fought against the paralysis.

"Little girl," the Witch said at last, her voice breathy and soft, "tell Vrana goodbye."

The Octopus went for the daggers, but before her hands could find their hilts, she was picked up by an invisible force and thrown to the ground, the impact knocking her unconscious.

"Get it over with," Vrana barked.

"That's not like you at all." The Witch cocked her head at the Ashen Man. "I never sent him to kill you."

"Then what was he doing here?" Vrana inched her leg forward, the numbness already waning.

"'No, it is from awareness that the Maiden recoils, spitting and biting from the Void as the collective conscious becomes increasingly aware and anticipates her violent arrival,'" the Witch quoted, sounding pleased.

I know that, but from where?

"From the book you read before your initiation feast," the Witch said as though replying to her thought. "It's not true, you know."

I'm going to die. Vrana looked at her mask, bent down, and slid it over the top of her head. It seemed so bulky now, so unwieldy, but it was an escape, if only a little one. "What do you mean?" she managed to say.

The Witch floated toward her, her semi-translucent skin catching the sun and showing her icy veins. "It's the opposite, actually. The less who know of me, the farther my Void is from your world. I whispered lies to the author, and she took them for truths. Simple and obvious, and yet it worked."

"Aren't you proud of yourself," Vrana hissed, limping away as she regained full movement of her legs.

"It's been so long since I've had someone new to talk to, Vrana," the Witch said, her gaze stabbing at Vrana's back. "Don't bother with the ax. I won't let you have it."

Vrana straightened up, looked over her shoulder. "He came to kill me to stop you," she said, spotting the ax at the bottom of the hill, slightly covered in sand.

The Witch stared back, smug, one emaciated hand rubbing at a red spot on her thigh. "You've done so much for me. When the world changed, I was almost forgotten."

"And then Mara stumbled across your creation."

"There was no more fear to be had in Nachtla. Most had left, and I'd put all that I had into those little boys. But then she came, this Mara of yours, and killed them. I watched from my Void as curiosity consumed her. Seth made sure she found the books." The Witch glided over to the Ashen Man and landed onto his back. "And she did the rest."

"Then why me?" Vrana caught a glimpse of R'lyeh stirring out of the corner of her eye.

"You?" The Witch stepped off the man she called Seth and padded toward Vrana. "There's nothing special about you," she said with a sneer. "That creature in the lake was meant for Mara, but you happened upon it first. It all worked out, though. I've seen so much and been to so many places thanks to you."

The Void, Vrana recalled, *the people gathered in the Void*. She had seen the elders there, her mother, and Aeson, too. R'lyeh and Deimos, Serra and Lucan—they, among tribesmen and Corrupted, had been present as well. *She's spreading like a disease; attacked the village just to make sure I wouldn't let her go.*

"I kept a close eye on you thanks to Blix. Instead of chasing Worms, perhaps you should've kept a closer eye on me, too."

"I should have let your lover kill me." Vrana noticed another welt form on the Witch's skin. *Keep her talking. She can't stay here for long. This world is rejecting her.*

"Lover?" The Witch laughed and stopped a few inches before Vrana. "He meant well, but this way is better." She turned to address the Ashen Man. "So thank you, Seth, for your betrayal."

With the Witch's attention off her, Vrana's unbroken arm reached out and grabbed the Maiden by her gray hair. She pulled the woman's head down and drove the beak of her mask deep into the Witch's ear.

"R'lyeh!" Vrana screamed as she released the Witch and ran for the girl. "R'lyeh, wake up!" She scooped up one of the Cruel Mother's talons. "R'lyeh, get up!"

Vrana dropped the dagger as she felt the bones of the raven's head dig into her own. Agonizing, unbearable pain unlike any she had never known overwhelmed her as her skull seemed to shrink and fracture. Her eyes widened and watered as they bulged into the sockets of the mask. Vrana's tongue stretched forward, the blood vessels that lined it popping and bleeding out. The ends of the mask's feathers pricked her skin as they worked their way into her neck and collar, and hung on tightly as she tried to rip them free.

"Your people think humans to be animals, and yet you run around dressed as animals," the Witch said. "Your people think humans to be Corrupted by violence, and yet violence is all that you know."

Vrana shrieked as her jaw jutted forward into the beak of her mask. Her teeth pulled free of her gums and fell out of her mouth, down the inside of the beak, and out onto her feet.

"You have always been the raven and it you," the Witch whispered, lifting Vrana's head by her chin. "Accept who you are, so that you may live a fuller life."

Vrana dropped to her knees, buried her hands in the feathers that covered her neck. Frantically, she searched for the edges of her mask and found, where they should have been, only rough flesh and hard bone.

"My pet," the Witch said, stroking the Raven as she wept, "I'm going to tell you something now." The Maiden of Pain unlatched the Raven's satchel and removed the Blue Worm's necklace. "I'm going to take this, and you, and when she wakes—" the Witch held out one crooked finger at the unconscious R'lyeh, "—she's going to follow. And after she's given everything to find you, and trust me, she will, there won't be a soul on this earth that does not know my name."

CHAPTER XXXVI

R'lyeh missed her mom and dad. They told her they would be back soon, and she had no reason to doubt them, because she knew they hated leaving her just as much as she hated seeing them go. She didn't have many friends in Alluvia, and the elders certainly weren't going to let her wander into the Elys, so she decided to do what she did best: annoy others until they sent her away.

She didn't need to ask a spellweaver to know this was one of the hottest days of the year. She only had to put her hand to her forehead to see that if she went an hour without water she'd look just as withered as Granny Rags. It seemed, then, being an annoying pest would have to be put on hold until she'd sampled the cool waters of the village's well.

"Hot day, isn't it?"

R'lyeh looked up from her feet, which were surprisingly dirty given that she'd been outside for no more than ten minutes. Derleth the Eel was leaning against the well, the sight of his muscles just as pleasing as they had always been to R'lyeh. He was a watcher and seldom came home.

"It is," R'lyeh said.

She lifted the octopus mask off her head to give the impression it was too hot to wear. In actuality, she wanted to show him that she had cut her hair the day prior and see his reaction to its length. Derleth was ten years older than her, but she didn't care. She wasn't looking for a boyfriend; she just wanted someone to notice.

"Are you trying to show off your haircut?" he asked, seeing

through her ruse.

"No," R'lyeh said, looking every-which-way but his. "But now that you've brought it up…"

"Will you do me a favor?" Derleth stepped away from the well and stood over R'lyeh.

"I'm kind of busy," she said, knowing all too well she'd ride on the back of a moon cat if he asked her to.

"Well, someone else then."

"Hold on," R'lyeh said as he moved to abandon her. "I think I can accommodate you."

"I thought you'd come around," Derleth said. He took another step towards her. He gloved his hand and shoved it into his pocket, looked around as though to make sure they were alone, and removed a strange root. "Do you know what this is?"

All of a sudden, R'lyeh felt slightly faint. She took the root, pressed it to her nose, which seemed to come as some surprise to Derleth. It smelled odd and made her quite relaxed, but other than that, it seemed harmless. "No," she said, handing the root back, "I've never seen it before." It left a milky residue on her fingers.

Derleth quickly placed the root back into his pocket and exhaled, as though he'd been holding his breath the entire time. "How do you feel?"

"Like taking a nap," R'lyeh said, rubbing her temples.

"What if I told you to jump down the well?" Derleth asked, his eyes following her from within the eel head.

"I'd tell you to go to hell," R'lyeh remarked. She laughed and then wondered if she'd been too blunt.

Derleth hummed with interest, though at what R'lyeh could not be sure. "The elders asked me to drop these in the well, to purify the water. The problem is I might be allergic; a lot of people are, I think. I've the rest at home. Come by later and help me? I'd appreciate the company."

R'lyeh found Derleth's behavior to be strange of him, but she was feeling more agreeable than usual. "Sure," she said, and because the operation sounded rather covert, she added, "I'll see you at the Black Hour."

"Perfect."

The soldiers of Penance arrived a few days later and took them by surprise in the middle of the night. R'lyeh had fallen asleep early in the evening, so when they grabbed her, she was still wearing her mask. This, she thought, must have been why they didn't kill her as they dragged her across the center of Alluvia, for they had killed the rest of those her age and younger. She kicked at the ground and cried into her hands as she was manacled with the rest of her village and forced to watch as those who didn't go quietly were split in two and piled high.

"We've been betrayed," she heard someone whisper as they were marched into the night.

"They mean the best," another voice said drowsily.

"It is a nice night for a walk," the woman beside R'lyeh stated, as though the chains about her ankles were not rubbing them bloody and raw.

Geharra rose out of the land with the morning sun, and when they passed through its massive gates, they found more soldiers waiting just beyond. R'lyeh was starving and dehydrated, and she had never been more afraid in her entire life. Her people, however, didn't seem to share the same sentiment, for they did as they were told, and took the beatings given to them as though they were precious lessons not to be squandered.

"Please," R'lyeh whispered at the Corrupted as they moved through the cobblestone streets of Geharra, "please, help us."

The Corrupted only stared back, with glassy eyes and warm smiles.

R'lyeh hated her people for doing nothing to stop the soldiers as they forced them through a church to a tunnel in its floor. R'lyeh hated the portrait of the Holy Child on the wall, his hollow eyes staring down on her as the breasts she'd been so eager to develop were fondled in passing. R'lyeh hated herself for not dying sooner as they ripped off her mask and threw her into a cage, surrounded by those she once annoyed and now pitied.

R'lyeh woke up to a headache so severe she considered suicide. It wasn't the first time she'd considered it. Vrana was gone, and she was alone. She couldn't see out of one of her eyes, the swelling having worsened over the course of the night. She remembered everything that had happened and found that the memories were without emotions to accompany them. She was alive, yes, but all things considered, she was as dead as dead could be.

R'lyeh secured the Cruel Mother's talons, slid down the slope away from Nachtla, and took Vrana's ax. She went to the sea with blood on her hands and lips, and offered what little remained of her body to it for cleansing. The salt and the sand in the water cleaned her wounds and cleared her mind. She scanned the horizon for the ships from Lacuna, and left when she didn't find them.

R'lyeh didn't return to Nachtla, because although it seemed the logical thing to do, she was, in fact, not suicidal. Instead, she traveled northward toward the Divide and the Heartland. She was not certain what she would find there, but she found enough food along the way to see that she reached her journey's end. The Witch had taken her best friend, her only friend, and when she was finished, there would not be a soul across the continent wouldn't know about the Maiden of Pain.

Outside Gallows, R'lyeh found a small shack belonging to a fur trader. The woman seemed to have been expecting the girl, and it took her a moment to realize the woman was in hiding. The fur trader begged for her life and apologized about a Fox; though, for what she apologized R'lyeh didn't know, as the woman was gurgling blood too loudly to be understood.

After moving the body to the woods outside the shack, R'lyeh stripped naked, hid her mask, and fitted the woman's clothes to her body. She'd never understood why her people had insisted on wearing masks to differentiate themselves from the Corrupted; it seemed so much easier to dress as them instead and eat away at their society from the inside. She had gathered some of the fur trader's blood into a cup after killing her, so as to paint her right arm red to avoid suspicion from townsfolk.

When she decided that she was ready to infiltrate Gallows, she swung open the shack's door, daggers hidden in her pants, and proceeded through the trees with Vrana's ax in hand. She would tell the Corrupted that she was a woodsman's daughter, and they would believe her, because she believed it herself. Lying came easily to R'lyeh now; after all, she'd lied to everyone about her mother and father ever since Geharra. Her mother, her father, they never went to Eld;

they had returned to the village that night Penance came.

The only nice thing about watching your parents die, R'lyeh reflected to herself once, *is that you get to see their faces every night.*

The woodsman story, however, turned out to be of no use to R'lyeh. When she crossed into Gallows, she found the people stricken with fear by the mountain of flesh in the distance.

The Red Worm was on the move.

And so was she.

YOU HAVE BEEN READING

"THE BONES OF THE EARTH."

ABOUT THE AUTHOR

SCOTT HALE is the author of *The Bones of the Earth* series and screen-writer of *Entropy, Free to a Bad Home, and Effigies.* He is the co-owner of Halehouse Productions. He is a graduate from Northern Kentucky University with a Bachelors in Psychology and Masters in Social Work. He has completed *The Bones of the Earth* series and his standalone horror novel, *In Sheep's Skin.* Scott Hale currently resides in Norwood, Ohio with his wife and frequent collaborator, Hannah Graff, and their three cats, Oona, Bashik, and Bellatrix.

Printed in Great Britain
by Amazon